AS LONG AS WE BOTH SHALL LIVE

JoAnn Chaney is a graduate of UC Riverside's Palm Desert MFA program. She lives in Colorado with her family. Her debut novel, *What You Don't Know*, was longlisted for the Crime Writers' Association's New Blood Dagger Award and was one of BookRiot's Best Mysteries of the Year. *As Long As We Both Shall Live* is her second novel.

ALSO BY JOANN CHANEY

What You Don't Know

AS LONG AS WE BOTH SHALL LIVE

JOANN CHANEY

PAN BOOKS

First published in the United States 2019 by Flatiron Books

First published in the UK 2019 by Mantle

This paperback edition first published 2020 by Pan Books
an imprint of Pan Macmillan
The Smithson, 6 Briset Street, London EC1M 5NR
Associated companies throughout the world
www.panmacmillan.com

ISBN 978-1-5098-2426-7

9 8 7 6 5 4 3 2 1

A CIP catalogue record for this book is available from the British Library.

Typeset in Minion by Jouve (UK), Milton Keynes
Printed and bound by CPI Group (UK) Ltd, Croydon, CR0 4YY

Visit **www.panmacmillan.com** to read more about all our books
and to buy them. You will also find features, author interviews and
news of any author events, and you can sign up for e-newsletters
so that you're always first to hear about our new releases.

A thief he will rob you, and take all you have
But a false-hearted lover will send you to your grave
They'll hug and they'll kiss you and tell you more lies
Than the crossties on the railroad or the stars in the skies

—"On Top of Old Smokey," traditional
American folk song

I hate you so much that I'd destroy myself to take you down with me.

—Rita Hayworth, Gilda

There are two dilemmas . . . that rattle the human soul. How do you hold on to someone who won't stay? And how do you get rid of someone who won't go?

—Danny DeVito, The War of the Roses

YOU CAN'T
ALWAYS GET
WHAT YOU WANT

If you try to kill your wife without a plan, you will fail.

There are plenty of assholes who do just that, men who decide to murder their significant other on the spur of the moment because they're angry or drunk or jealous or just plain tired of the nagging or they don't want to go through the hassle of a divorce, and they get caught. They always get caught. There are plenty of wife killers moldering in prison, spending their days staring at the cement walls and playing basketball and doing a whole lotta nothing, wishing they hadn't done that Google search on *how to kill someone and git away with it* on their home computer so all the cops had to do was look at their browser history and then—BAM!—dead man walking.

Or these men will wish they hadn't done it in their home, right in the bedroom so there was blood left all over the mattress and walls, and the cops were able to swab it right up, trace evidence left every which way, no matter how much bleach these guys splashed around or how many times they ran the Shop-Vac. These men end up wishing they would've left their wives instead, strapped on their sneaks and vanished, disappeared into another city, changed their name and found some other woman to shack up with. There's not a better place in the world to start a new life than good old *'murica*, any fifth grader with a history book can tell you that.

But these guys still think they can get away with it. But they'll also tell anyone who'll listen that they love their wives. We're soul mates, it was love at first sight, I couldn't possibly have done it because *how would I live without her?* But these men manage to live, oh yes they do, they dab their tears at first, they promise there will be vengeance, they lock themselves away from curious eyes. But then, after a while, they start showing up at Red Lobster on Friday nights with a new woman. They sell their wife's car, they jam her clothes in black lawn bags and take them down to Goodwill. They move on too fast, and if it wasn't a witness that tripped up their scheme, or the bloodstains left on the carpet, or their suspicious internet searches, this will get them caught. They'll paint themselves right into a corner, so when the cops come knocking, grinning and twirling the handcuffs, it's not all that much of a surprise—except to them, maybe. Most criminals don't have much in the way of gray matter in their upstairs, and that's likely why they ended up as criminals to begin with.

And let's be honest here. When a woman is murdered, it's probably the husband. It's almost always the husband. Hell, anyone with basic cable and the slightest interest in the melodrama of true crime knows it. A woman is killed, her husband is the first suspect. And with good reason. Men kill their wives, women kill their husbands—you can't be tied to someone for any significant amount of time without at least considering knocking them over the skull with a baseball bat. And it's nothing new. The same thing's been happening since the beginning of time, and it'll keep on until the very end.

So here's the thing: if you want to kill your wife, *don't*. Don't kill her, don't touch her. Ditch the bitch if you have to, get on with your life. Or make it work. But kill her? Nope. You want the opposite of Nike's advice: Just *don't* do it. Because sooner or later, no matter how careful you think you've been, you'll get caught.

MAMA, JUST KILLED A MAN

CHAPTER ONE

September 3, 1995
Madison, Wisconsin

Her life would be so much easier if she'd never gotten married.

It was a terrible thing to think, but the truth is never nice. That's something her mother always said, that there are pretty lies and ugly truths. And the truth is that her life *would* be easier without Matt. Oh, she loved him, she couldn't deny that. And that was the problem, wasn't it? Love's got teeth, it's got claws, and once it hitches you to a person it's so tough to rip yourself free. Marriage, she thought, might just be a crock of shit.

And while she might complain about her husband, and sometimes she actively *hated* him, he was still better than every other man she'd ever dated. And maybe that was love. The body's chemical reaction to finding a person who irritates you less than everyone else.

Janice thought all these things even though it had only been a year since she walked down the long linoleum-floored hallway of the Windsor Creek Community Rec Center, clutching a thin handful of wilted roses as she entered the small, windowless activity room they'd rented for two hours. Janice's mother was the only one who took pictures of the wedding, even though she'd had her reservations about the whole thing, said she didn't trust Matt, he didn't seem like a *good guy*, but she'd still snapped pics on one of those disposable cameras you could buy at the drugstore and drop off to be developed once they're all used up. Only one picture came out good enough to frame. In it, Matt and Janice are standing together, holding hands, and there are a few signs taped up on the wall behind them—notices about kids at the pool needing to be accompanied by an adult and wiping down the exercise equipment after use—and a cheap office clock, the hands stuck at 12:05 for the rest of eternity. Janice is looking at Matt in the photo, her veil puffing out around her shoulders like a cloud, and she's smiling. Happy. Matt's smiling, too, but he's not looking at his bride. His face is turned away from her, his eyes are almost closed, as if she isn't there at all.

A handful of people had attended the ceremony, and it didn't last long since the pastor had a funeral booked right after and had to leave, and when Janice had heard that she'd almost canceled the whole thing. She thought it was a bad omen to have the pastor marry them and then rush off to bury someone else, but they'd already put a nonrefundable deposit down on the room and had paid for the sheet cake from Aldi, and she couldn't walk away from that kind of money. And a year after her wedding, when her mouth is full of blood and her eyes are burning from the gasoline fumes and she can't stop shaking from the pain, Janice will remember the old saying—*money makes the world go round*—and she'll think that if she'd only been able to wash her hands of that lousy two hundred dollars her whole life would've been so much different.

You see, just about one year into her marriage to Matthew Evans and less than twelve hours from this moment, Janice will be dead.

CHAPTER TWO

It was almost two in the morning and she should be at work, the graveyard shift at the old folks' home where she worked the front desk, answering incoming calls and helping out with any resident emergencies. Her boss had asked her not to call it the graveyard shift. *Morbid*, Jesse called it. Most of these people have one foot in the grave already, we don't need to remind them of it. Jesse wouldn't look at her when he spoke, but only down at his hands. He was a strange guy, retired army, in his thirties and still living with his Irish mother, walked everywhere because he didn't own a car. But he was a nice guy, too. Shy, quiet. *I should've married a man like you*, she said once, jokingly, and Jesse hadn't said anything, just went outside to smoke one of his filterless cigarettes. She watched him through a window, saw him take a few puffs and then grind the butt out on the trunk of an oak.

"I'll be a little late today," she'd told Jesse earlier when she called the home. He'd answered on the second ring, although there'd been a long pause between him picking up the receiver and the sound of his voice, as if the movement had happened in slow motion. But that was Jesse for you. He moved like he was wading through a vat of warm molasses.

Some people thought he was a few eggs short of a dozen, but he was just thoughtful. "I have some personal business to deal with."

"Is this about that husband of yours?"

"Maybe."

"Who's going to cover for you?"

"Can't you do it?" Janice had asked. "Jesse, this is important. I just need an hour. Maybe two."

He sighed, and she'd known then he would cover for her.

"Ms. Ruby's already been asking for you," he said. "I know you're sneaking her food in the middle of the night. She's not supposed to eat outside of mealtimes."

"It's toast," Janice said. "And it's not so much that she's hungry. She's lonely, needs someone to talk to."

And now a part of her wished she'd just gone to work, strolled in right on time and punched the clock. She'd probably be in the home's kitchen right now, dropping white bread into the toaster and fishing a small plate out of the cabinets to take to Ms. Ruby of room 217, who called the front desk nearly every night complaining that she was hungry and couldn't she just have a slice of toast, sourdough bread, light on the butter?

"Is there some sort of trouble?" Jesse had asked. "Anything I can help with?"

"It's no big deal," she'd said lightly. But it *was* a big deal, it was always a big deal if the man you've been married to for only a year was sleeping with another woman behind your back. Woman? Maybe it was *women*, she didn't know. What she did know, or at least suspect: he did it while she was at work, earning money to support his ass while he was in school, because he'd said it was too much for him to hold a job *and* go to college, so she was the one who worked twelve-hour shifts at the Magnolia Senior Citizen Home so Matt could stay home and spend his free time studying, even though she was trying to finish her degree, too. She had a job, she went to class, she cooked and cleaned and kept their lives in order while her husband spent most of his time sleeping and flipping through books and *complaining* about his life. That was one thing she'd come to learn about marriage with Matt—she got the short end of the stick, if she got any of the stick at all. "I'll see you later tonight."

And now here she was, crouched on a curb across the street from their rental house, half-hidden behind the bumper of some neighbor's car. Two hours she'd been there, her ass mostly asleep from the sidewalk and the muscles in her legs prickly and stiff, watching. Waiting for something to happen. And there'd been nothing except the steady glow of lights in the window. No signs of movement. She'd kissed Matt good-bye, laid her hand on the back of his neck and pulled him close, lightly touched her lips to his, and then let him go like not a damn thing was wrong—she should've majored in theater, she thought—and left, got behind the wheel of the old Chevette they shared—the *shit*-vette is what Janice liked to call it when it would crap out, usually at the most inconvenient times and only when she was behind the wheel—and drove away like she was heading into work, but instead she'd just parked on the next block over and walked back to a spot she'd already picked out. And for the last two hours there'd been nothing but the chirp of crickets from a nearby bush and the hum of the streetlights and the irritating rub of the moist, sweaty waistband of her pants against the small of her back, and Janice had started to think that maybe she was just crazy, that Matt wasn't cheating after all, that she'd imagined the smell of unfamiliar perfume on her pillow and the tangle of blond hairs she'd hooked out of the shower drain. And the strange phone calls, let's not forget *those*, the sound of light breathing coming through the receiver and then the vicious click in her ear—but maybe it was nothing, people dialed the wrong number all the time—

A car pulled to a stop in front of their house, idling for a moment before the headlights flickered out and the puttering engine shut off. It was red and small, cute, and it was a woman who climbed out from behind the wheel, just as cute and small as her car. She was wearing a *romper*, for god's sake, thin blue cotton with white flowers scattered over the fabric. It was something a toddler would wear. And this woman, whoever she was, took a few steps toward the house—she'd parked so she was blocking the driveway, Janice noticed, and *that*, maybe even more than the fact that this woman was here to have sex with her husband while wearing a child's clothes, infuriated her—and Matt flung open the front door, came down the steps in that light, quick way he had, his arms hanging loosely at his sides so his hands flopped around his hips, like he was in midconvulsion. She'd always thought it was a ridiculous way for anyone to come down stairs, especially a man like Matt, who normally moved with such ease, but she'd always felt guilty for thinking it, because she loved him, and when you love a person you make all the excuses for them. You see past everything that's wrong and foolish and stupid and make it work.

But now, watching Matt pull the girl close and kiss her, right on the mouth, one of his hands snaking around her back and roughly squeezing one of her ass cheeks before leading her inside the house, Janice realized she was done making it work.

Once they went inside the house, she walked to the shit-vette and sat behind the wheel for a few minutes, trying to catch her breath. She felt sick to her stomach, and actually opened the car door and leaned out, retching weakly onto the pavement, although nothing would come up except a bit of yellow, foul fluid and saliva.

"You knew what he was doing," she said. The sound of her own voice startled her, and she jerked away, rapping her knuckles against the steering wheel hard enough that she gasped out loud from the pain and clutched her hand to her chest. "Quit acting surprised, you knew what was going on this whole time."

Yes, but it was one thing to *suspect* what Matt had been doing, and another to actually *know*. And now that she knew for sure—no denying it, Matt was a douchebag supreme, an unfaithful POS—what was she going to do? Because she couldn't ignore this now. If she didn't do anything, if she kept on pretending things were normal and let Matt do whatever he wanted, didn't that make her guilty, too? Couldn't you even say she was aiding and abetting Matt's cheating, that she was just as much a part of his indiscretions as he was?

Or maybe that was just stupid, because women ignored

this sort of crap all the time. They looked the other way. Turned the other cheek. Pretended like nothing was happening. And maybe in five or ten years this would all be normal, Matt with other women would just be another *thing*—not unlike the way he got his socks stuck in moist little balls when he peeled them off his feet, or the spiky hairs he left all over the bathroom sink after he'd shaved. Just one more thing about him she'd have to accept.

But here was the question: *Could* she accept this?

Or, the better question: Was she *willing* to accept it?

The image of the gun Matt kept hidden in the table near their front door swam to the surface of her mind. She hadn't given it much thought, but she was thinking about it now, wasn't she? You'd better believe it. Matt had called it a Saturday night special, as if giving it some cutesy name made it easier to accept, because he'd seen the fear on her face when he brought it home and the way she didn't want to hold it. We don't have a dog, so we need a gun. That'd been Matt's argument, and she'd gone along with it. Easier just to let him keep it than to argue, even though she was against guns. Guns hurt people, she argued. They *killed* people. She'd always been against gun violence, but he wouldn't listen. Better to be safe, he said, and it'd sat in that drawer in the months since then, until she'd practically forgotten the snub nose and the dull, metallic gleam of it.

But now. Now she couldn't get the image of it out of her head.

So here's the thing: she *could* accept his cheating, just like she'd accepted so many other things, but a year would become five years and that would turn to ten which would turn to twenty, and then she'd be middle-aged. At forty-five would she be willing to accept she'd spent so long with a man who was a cheater? But it wouldn't just be the cheating at that point, she thought. In twenty-some years she'd have a laundry list of reasons to hate Matt, and him sticking his dick wherever he wanted would just be the cherry on the top of it all, and how would she feel then?

She'd probably want to kill him.

She imagined getting out of the car and driving over to their house now and going inside—it wouldn't take long—pulling open the drawer in that table and picking up the gun. She'd never actually held it, but she could imagine the weight of it in her palm, the oily, smooth metal under her fingers.

She imagined pulling the trigger.

"So what are you going to do?" she said. She caught a look at herself in the rearview mirror and found she couldn't look away. Her face was ashen and drawn, her eyes sunken into her skull. It was the way she looked when she was sick. A man had once told her she had eyes that were amber colored in a certain light, beautiful, nearly gold—but there was nothing beautiful about them now, she thought. They were the eyes of a crazy person. A lunatic.

"What are we going to do?" she said, looking right into the mirror. Square into her troubled gaze. She'd always talked to her reflection like this, as if it was a friend in the mirror instead of herself, as if she were two instead of only one. "Right now. What are we going to do, right now?"

CHAPTER THREE

August 28, 2018
Rocky Mountain National Park, Colorado

There were patches of dappled shade along the trail, pools of dark cast by the overhanging pine branches and arms of jagged rock, spots where the temperature seemed to drop ten degrees. Marie was stopped in one of them now, shifting the straps of her backpack to ease the weight digging into her shoulders. It wasn't hot out—not that it was ever really *hot* at this elevation, at least not compared to most anywhere else. But it was late summer now, they'd been hiking the entire day, the sky was clear and blue, the air was damp and muggy since there'd been so much rain over the last few weeks—the most the state had seen in recorded history, in fact—and Marie had been slick with sweat for the last five miles or so. The sweat was bad enough by itself, dripping out of her scalp and running down her face and the back of her neck, but to make it worse her knees were aching, especially the left one. It felt like a tiny, throbbing sun had replaced the cartilage behind her left kneecap, radiating awful pain when the bones ground together. The doctor had said cortisone injections would help, but the thought of a long needle sliding into her knee was enough to set her teeth on edge and she'd decided to pass. For now. If the pain kept getting worse, she might give it a shot, no pun intended.

So she'd been forced to make frequent stops to rest her knee, despite Matt's obvious impatience. He'd sigh and walk ahead, tap his foot and make little mouselike noises in the back of his throat so she'd know how irritated he was, how he wished she'd get the lead outta her ass, as he so elegantly put it, but she ignored him.

She'd gotten good at ignoring her husband over the years.

"Are we in a hurry?" she asked as she stooped over, massaging her kneecap and grimacing. Matt was farther up the trail, his back to her. "Matt? Did you hear me? We got an appointment or something?"

He turned. His cell phone was in his hand. It seemed like phones had gotten smaller and thinner over the years, but Matt insisted on getting the biggest, the one that made it look like he had a book pressed to the side of his head when he made a call. *Go big or go home,* that's what Matt liked to say. He'd built up an arsenal of those kinds of phrases over the years, he used them with his sales team and at home, too. She hated them all. *Step up to the plate. Reach for the low-hanging fruit. Consider your biggest opportunity.*

"No service out here," he said.

"Do you need to call someone?"

"No." He shot her a look she wasn't sure how to decipher. "I was just checking."

This trip had been *his* idea to begin with, although she'd been the one to make all the arrangements. She'd chosen the location and decided the details, but he'd been the one to first bring it up. A spur-of-the-moment trip into the mountains, sleeping in a romantic cabin at night, hiking through the gorgeous park during the day—she'd jumped all over it, because when was the last time Matt had suggested *anything* like this? Never. Family vacations had been one thing—he'd always found the time for those, especially when the girls were little—but when was the last time they'd gone anywhere alone, as husband and wife? She couldn't remember. They'd driven up late on Sunday, avoiding the weekend tourist rush, and had rented a private home that backed up to the forest and had one hell of a view. There wasn't all that much to do in the town itself—you couldn't exactly call Estes Park a hub of exciting goings-on, not unless little ice cream shops and antiques got your motor running—but Marie had enjoyed it so far, she always did like coming up here. Matt had never been, although over the years she'd come plenty of times with the girls and for overnights with friends, and sometimes even for a day trip alone, plenty of water and sunscreen in her pack, to hike one of the trails or take a rock climbing lesson. There was something about the outdoors, something about the tall, scraggy trees and the impossibly blue sky. And there was the quiet. Not that it was exactly quiet, with the sound of birds and humming insects and the whoosh of the river, but it was different. Out here, quiet was *good*, the silence wasn't something that could drive a person crazy the way it did at home, when she always had the TV on or her phone blasting music. At home, silence was something to be afraid of and she tried to get rid of it. She'd tried to explain it to Matt, who just seemed confused. Silence, noise, chaos—it was all the same to him. It was always all the same to him.

Like this: there'd been a half-dozen elk outside their front door this morning, taking slow, deliberate bites from a shrub and watching Marie take photos with unimpressed eyes.

They're just deer, he'd said.

Elk, they're elk, she'd said. *Isn't it neat? It's not as if we see elk every morning at home.*

But Matt hadn't been interested. He'd spent the night before in the cabin's kitchen, carefully organizing their gear, stuffing the packs full of the granola bars and water and sunscreen they'd bought in town the day before. He'd been full of nervous energy yesterday, and he'd made her nervous, too—enough that she'd hardly enjoyed the tour they'd taken through the Stanley Hotel or their leisurely walk down Main Street. During dinner Matt confessed he was excited to go out hiking the next morning, he was looking forward to getting outside and stretching his legs.

They'd started early and had spent the entire day on the move. Around lakes and up steep trails and down hills, only stopping to take photos of wildlife and to eat a quick lunch of tuna dug out of foil pouches with plastic spoons. They'd planned this to be their last hike of the day, even though they'd had to get back in the car and drive to the other side of the park to get to the trailhead, but the view from the cliff at the top was incredible. Not to be missed. Once they'd parked, Matt had spread the map out the car's hood, looking it over and tracing the jagged, zigzag path with his finger as hikers went by, shooting them curious looks as they passed.

He hadn't always been like this. When they were first married he'd been different. Easier. Almost . . . laid back. They'd flown to Las Vegas to get married, a little over an hour from the tarmac at Denver International, and then they were on the Strip, standing in front of an Elvis impersonator and repeating their vows. And years later, when they'd gone on vacation with the girls, camping and fishing and to theme parks, Matt had been the spontaneous one while she'd been the planner, the one who budgeted the money and prepared meals and made sure the gas tank was full and the plane tickets had been purchased. Back in those days Matt had been—fun? That didn't seem the right word for it, but it was also the perfect word. He'd been fun and she'd been the stick in the mud, and now it seemed their roles had reversed. But they were both getting old, maybe that was it. And when people got older they changed, didn't they? Years ago she'd been the one wound tight as a drum, but she'd come to accept how things were, and that put her at peace. Part of that was having the girls—Hannah and Maddie, both of them away at college now, starting their own lives—because there was nothing like kids to help you realize how unimportant everything else was. The other part of it was age. She'd matured over the years, she'd grown up. Tried to think before she acted. Plan things out. That's how getting older worked. You got patient. You got wise.

"All right, I'm ready," Marie said, slowly straightening up. They should've slept in, she thought. Taken it slow. Woke up late and had omelets and mimosas and then come out, but it was another case of them not seeing eye-to-eye on things.

She wanted some time to relax, Matt wanted to get out. And as usual, Matt had gotten his way.

"Good, let's go," Matt said. He was already on the move, fifteen feet ahead, his boots planting confidently on the loose gravel. They'd always been an outdoorsy family—hell, you couldn't live in Colorado and *not* be outdoorsy—but she suddenly wished she were back in the cabin, parked in front of the television with her feet propped up on the coffee table, sipping a glass of red wine. She was tired, she was hungry, and she didn't want to do this. Not anymore. "We still have a ways to go before it gets dark, don't we?"

"All right," she said. She took a small, shuffling step, and then another. It didn't seem right that her knee hurt *this* damn bad, not when she exercised every day—she ran at least four miles every morning, did yoga three or four times a week. She was in the best shape of her life, her body as tight and taut as it'd ever been, but that didn't keep her stupid knee from acting up, especially on days like today, when there was sure to be rain. Her knee always ached when there was moisture in the air, she'd said that to Matt during the drive into the park. "I'm coming."

Matt didn't answer, and he might not have heard her at all. He was too far ahead, walking, his hands flopping loosely at his sides. Marie grimaced again and rubbed her knee. It felt like it was full of sand, or broken shards of glass.

A couple went by in the opposite direction, on their way down to the trailhead, and one of the women gave Marie a sympathetic smile as she passed, then looked back at Matt, the ghost of a frown creasing her forehead. There was something about that man, the woman thought—but she shook it off. It's nothing, she told her girlfriend when she asked what was wrong. A chill, that's all. A goose walking over my grave.

But less than two hours from now she'll see that man again, coming down the trail, huffing for breath and shouting for help. My wife, he'll say. I think she might be dead.

CHAPTER FOUR

It was so *green* up here in the mountains, not like Denver, where the color palette always reminded her of Thanksgiving. Browns and yellows, that was Denver all year long. Parched, except this past summer, when it'd stormed almost every afternoon. The news had said rivers were full to overflowing, that several people had gotten too close to the rushing waters and been swept away, their bodies never recovered. No one was used to all that moisture, especially in the city, or how often the sky was a dismal gray. It was because of climate change, people said. Or maybe it was El Niño. Or maybe it was just a stretch of unusual weather that everyone would forget by the next year.

Marie remembered when she first moved to Colorado from back east, and it'd taken her a few weeks to get adjusted. The air was thin and cold, and it was so dry her lips wouldn't stop cracking open and bleeding until she started slathering petroleum jelly all over her mouth, carrying a small tub of it tucked in her purse. She'd gotten used to Colorado after a while, but wasn't it true that a person can get used to just about anything, given enough time? She thought so.

"It's starting to rain," she said. Matt was still ahead of her, but not as far as he'd been before. In the last twenty minutes he'd slowed to a creep, one small step in front of the next, until she'd caught up and was staring at the back of his old hiking boots. He was getting tired. It'd been a long day and it was finally catching up with him.

"Should we take cover and wait it out?" he asked.

"It's okay, we're almost there," she said. Ahead of her, Matt ducked under a dead tree that'd fallen across the trail. He paused, waiting for her to do the same, held out a hand to help her straighten back up again. "Once we get to the top we'll find a spot and camp out until it stops."

"Okay," he said. His hand was strong and lean, the fingers long, the knuckles sharp and bony. At one time she would've recognized her husband's hands anywhere, the look and feel of them, even the scent of his skin—but would she now? She wasn't so sure, and that hurt a little.

"I love you," she said.

His eyebrows went up.

"Do you?"

She nodded and squeezed his hand before letting it go. She did love him, although she hated him, too, sometimes. He gave her a small smile. She couldn't remember the last time he'd actually smiled at her. Mostly, he ignored her. And when he wasn't ignoring her, they were fighting. About the way he'd put the empty carton of ice cream into the sink instead of the trash can; the way she wouldn't wind up the vacuum's cord when she was done but would just toss it over the handle. Little things, usually, but they weren't always little. Sometimes they argued about big things, parts of their past that kept rising back up to the surface. It was like flossing your teeth and unsticking a chunk of food from a meal you'd had a week ago. It was gray and smelled awful, and you'd never be able to figure out how you'd lived with it so long without even knowing.

She'd thought maybe things had been tense between them because the girls were both grown now, and the only time either of them ever called home was for their bimonthly duty check-ins or if they wanted money. They'd both stayed at school over the last few months instead of coming home, busy with summer classes and jobs and internships and boyfriends, involved in their own lives. The girls had needed her for so long, and now they didn't. She'd once known both of them better than she knew herself, and now they were strangers. And where did that leave her? She'd been a housewife for twenty years, her days had been busy with making meals and shopping and cleaning and the PTA, and now there was a lot of empty space and she couldn't figure out how to fill it. Oh, she kept herself busy at the gym and with books and she still volunteered at the high school, although it'd been two years since their youngest graduated. Marie had tried to tell Matt all this, to talk about her feelings like the marriage counselor had told them to do. She'd tried to tell him how awful it was to not be needed, that she'd always thought the girls would grow up and she'd be free, but the *freedom* had just ended up being *loneliness*. And it wasn't as if *Matt* needed her, either, and she'd known it for a long time. He'd put her neatly aside for a younger woman—younger *women*—slipped around behind her back and she pretended not to notice what was going on, but she wasn't stupid. She knew, and she'd accepted it all, turned her head and looked the other way. Let it go. Like the time a few years back when she'd been digging through her underwear drawer and fished out a pair of panties that didn't belong to her. She was *sure* of it. They were the wrong size—far too small—and they were sexy white silk, something she'd never buy in a million years. They didn't belong to either of the girls, either; they were both too young for anything so flashy. But when she'd dangled them on one finger in front of Matt's face and asked if he'd seen them before, she would've sworn there was a flash of panic in his eyes.

At least, she'd thought she'd seen panic. But in the days afterward, she'd started to second-guess herself. Because it was gone *that* fast. So fast that she'd begun to wonder if she'd imagined it altogether, and if it'd only been Matt's bland, confused face staring back at her the whole time.

"Those are yours," Matt had said. "Don't you remember? You bought those over at Park Meadows that time we had lunch at the Cheesecake Factory right before Christmas . . ."

And Matt told her about how they'd been shopping for the girls, how he'd had to run bags out to the car *twice*, even what they'd eaten for lunch. It made her think that maybe she *had* bought those panties for herself and had just forgotten—not that she *ever* forgot many things, but stranger things have happened, haven't they? So she'd tossed those panties back in her drawer, thinking that Matt must be right; she'd forgotten that she'd bought the little scrap of silk, and then she'd *forgotten* she'd forgotten.

But still. Something about the whole thing seemed *wrong*.

Because she *knew*, deep down, she would've never forgotten buying those panties; she would've never bought herself the wrong size and even if she had she would've taken them right back to the store; but mostly it was Matt. He'd become quite the salesman over the years, and he made his living with the words that came out of his mouth. He sold businesses, he sold products, he sold the American Dream, and he sold her the story of how those panties had ended up in her drawer.

Maybe he was telling the truth.

Maybe he was lying.

She wasn't sure, and after a while it seemed silly to bring it up, because what if she was wrong? Besides, it was easier to accept it and move on rather than argue. It always was. She knew everything, and she had to accept it and *deal,* because what other choice did she have? When you were a woman who'd been taken care of for the last twenty years, when you had no education, no job experience, hardly any *life* experience, this is how you ended up. Dealing with your husband's crap. You could be a feminist, you could rally and hold up homemade placards and march through the streets shouting for equal rights while wearing your knitted pink pussy hat, but in the end you'd still go home and pop the meat loaf in the oven and run a load of clothes through the wash and be trapped like a desperate animal in a cage. You could call it Stockholm Syndrome, or you could call it marriage.

To*may*to, to*mah*to.

"Is this it?" Matt said, swerving off the trail and into a clump of pine trees. He wiped the rain from his eyes and peered up the hill. There was green moss growing on one of the trunks, thick and soft as carpet. She'd done a lot of hiking over the last two years and had told him about this particular trail she'd found the year before, one that didn't appear on any map. It was a steep climb up to a cliff, though, maybe not the best idea if they were tired. But he'd insisted on going up after she'd told him about it. *We can watch the sunset from the top*, he'd said.

"Yeah, just a bit more up that way," she said.

She almost fell once, because the rocks and weeds and dirt under their feet had become slippery in the rain, but caught hold of a branch at the last minute and steadied herself. It'd be a bad thing to get hurt here, out this far in the middle of nowhere, off the established trail. The main path looped down to a parking lot about a mile downhill, but it was a hard hike, and if she fell and hurt herself she'd be in for a wait before anyone could make it out this far into the park, even if Matt could call someone on his cell phone. They were breathing hard as they dug the toes of their boots into the earth and straggled up, using trees and shrubs to keep their balance, the rain pattering softly on the backs of their heads and running down onto their faces. The last time Marie had hiked this she'd had to come back down sitting on her ass—it was steep. Pine needles had drilled into her thighs and a rock managed to snag her pants and gouge her leg as she came down, and that night in the hotel room she'd stood on top of the closed toilet lid and examined herself in the bathroom mirror, laughed at the bruises and cuts and divots left in her thighs.

"We're here," Matt said, gasping when they finally made it to the top and the ground leveled out. He wasn't in the best shape anymore—Matt went to the gym every morning, but he also liked a bowl of ice cream every night, and he liked to drink. Forty minutes at a slow walk on the treadmill wasn't doing him much good, no matter what he thought. She watched him bent over, hands on his knees, greedily sucking down air, but from the corner of her eye. If he suddenly straightened up she didn't want him to catch her watching. He'd be embarrassed and angry, like the time not too long before when she'd come into the bathroom and found him flexing in front of the mirror, turning and twisting to look at himself from every possible angle, pinching the extra fat that'd landed around his middle. She'd stood in silence, watching as he'd preened and frowned over his body, insecure and unhappy, and while a part of her was amused by it, she also felt a sort of mean satisfaction. She'd spent her entire life worrying over her looks—but that's how women were trained to be, weren't they? Concerned about their weight and wrinkles and the state of their hair, while men got off scot-free. Or maybe they didn't, not completely.

She turned her back on Matt, let him catch his breath without her watching. She'd give him that much, at least. Took a dozen steps ahead, toward the edge of the cliff, and looked out. Her bum knee was giving her hell and her skin was beaded with sweat and rain, but the view was worth it. There were miles and miles of evergreens and mountains spread in every direction below them, and much farther on, so far and misty and blurred that you couldn't be sure it was even real or if it was only imagination, was the rest of the world. That was what this climb was like—they'd scaled the entire world. The air was thin and clear up this high, and while everything in the distance seemed to be wrapped in gauze, everything up close was strangely sharp. Marie held up her hand, examined the skin stretched over her knuckles. She could see every freckle and sun spot, every pore and line, in minute detail. It was as if she were looking at herself through a microscope on maximum magnification. Maybe she was giddy—lack of oxygen and water, one or the other, maybe both—or maybe things were just coming into focus.

"Come back from the edge," Matt said sharply. She looked at him over her shoulder. Did he want her back because he was worried about her safety, or was it because he liked to give orders? It was impossible to tell. He'd always been afraid of heights, but he also hated her to be ahead of him—both literally and figuratively. He'd taken enough of those personality tests for work over the years that he'd taken to classifying himself. He was bold, he was competitive, he was a leader. He liked to keep a step or two ahead of her both in life and when they walked, just the same as he did with everyone else. That's how he'd always been.

"I'm fine," she said, turning away. She crept up to the cliff's lip, careful to keep the toes of her boots back from the crumbling rock edge. It was a sharp drop past there, 120 feet or so of open air, straight down to the river running below. A precipice, that was the right word for a narrow ledge like this. A word that somehow managed to sound sharp and dangerous. Over the last few years she'd started doing the crossword puzzle in the newspaper every day, and she'd gotten good at it.

Precipice: *Noun*.
1. A very steep or overhanging place.
2. A hazardous situation.

Behind her were the trees they'd pushed through, and ahead was the rock that jutted out like a pointing, accusing finger, and then air. She closed her eyes and leaned back, took a deep breath. Filled her lungs up with as much oxygen as they'd hold, until they felt ready to burst, then pursed her lips and exhaled through her mouth.

From this cliff it seemed like anything was possible.

"It's like heaven up here," Marie breathed. Matt heard her and pulled a face, looked away. He was still back in the safety of the trees. He couldn't understand what she meant about heaven, of course—Hannah had been six when she'd said that same thing, and Matt had always been at work in those days, leaving her home with the girls. Hannah had said it about the play set they had installed in the backyard. She'd always climbed to the tower at the very top and sat alone, looking out over the neighborhood.

What do you do up here? Marie had asked once, finally climbing up there herself to see what was going on. It was so cramped she'd had to pull her legs up under her chin, but Hannah had been perfectly content. She'd smiled, Marie remembered, and closed her eyes against the cool evening breeze.

It's like heaven up here, Mommy. Heaven.

CHAPTER FIVE

1995

Three sixteen in the morning.

She'd gotten to work, although she couldn't remember how. It was like the drive hadn't happened at all, as if the ten minutes had been completely wiped from her memory. It reminded her of the time she'd gotten drunk at a party and had woken up curled up on one of the old lawn chairs on her mother's front porch—confused and cold and more than a little scared, not at all sure how she'd ended up at home. That's exactly how she felt. Like she'd just woken up from a nightmare.

She couldn't stop thinking about Matt coming down the steps out of the house, his hands flailing, and the way his fingers gripped the woman's butt when he pulled her close. That one image, on constant replay in her head, over and over. Matt coming down the stairs and then his hand on that ass, sinking into the flesh like it was bread dough. Again and again. Hand and ass. Ass and hand.

"You okay?" Jesse asked as he slung his backpack over his shoulder, but she'd waved him away, told him she was fine, he should go home and go to bed. He had lines on the side of his face and she thought he'd probably fallen asleep on a stack of paperwork. He didn't normally work this late. "You don't look okay."

"I'm just tired, that's all."

And she *was* tired, maybe more tired than she'd ever been. Anger has a way of draining a person's energy, that's something else her mother always said. Dieting and exercise were a waste of time, she claimed. It was anger that would drop the pounds, pure rage that would keep your thighs lean and your waist trim. And her mother said this from experience— she was thin as a whip and had spent her entire life in either a nonstop state of pissed-off or a drunken stupor. Sometimes both at the same time.

"Has Ms. Ruby called?" she asked, pushing away the textbook she'd brought in. Normally the night shift was a perfect time to study the diagrams and photos, and she had the first quiz of the semester coming up, but there was no way she'd be able to concentrate. Not tonight.

"Yeah, a little bit ago. Asked for you." Jesse paused. "You sure you're okay?"

"Yeah, I'm sure."

Jesse didn't look convinced, and if he'd been a different sort of man he might've stayed and tried to get Janice to talk, to tell him what was wrong. But Jesse never quite seemed to have gotten the hang of talking to women—to *anyone,* really, even when they worked for him and he was giving out orders—so he just gave her a long look and left.

She sat at the desk after Jesse had left, tracing her finger along the front cover of her biology textbook. There was a sketch of the Vitruvian Man on the front, his arms and legs spread wide. According to Leonardo da Vinci, the ideal man was eight heads tall, but what about the not-so-ideal man? Wasn't there some other way to sort men without whipping out a measuring tape, a reliable way to recognize a bad guy before you rented out a room at the rec center and promised to be strapped to them for the rest of your life, for-better-or-worse?

The water cooler in the corner burbled, startling her. Normally she liked this time of night, when the lights had been dimmed and the residents were all in bed and the TVs were off and the place smelled clean and the carpets still had vacuum lines in them, but tonight she just felt antsy and full of nerves. Like she was waiting for something to happen, but she didn't know what.

Matt and that woman are probably done by now, she thought dismally. He'd climbed on top and done his business and now they were in bed together, naked, watching the ceiling fan spin lazily above their heads. There was a photo of Janice on Matt's nightstand, smiling and looking straight into the camera, and she wondered if he turned it around when he was with this woman. She didn't think so. Not very many things bothered Matt, and she doubted that her photo would get under his skin. He might even find it funny, that his wife was right there while he slipped it to that girl. She wouldn't be surprised—Matt's sense of humor had always been strange, nothing she ever understood. You just don't get *it*, he'd always said, but he could never explain exactly what *it* was.

What are we going to do?

Routine, that'd get her mind off things. She stood up, went

to the kitchen. The stainless steel counters were shining; the bulbs mounted on the ceiling threw down cold light. She took a plastic-wrapped loaf of white bread from the walk-in fridge, slipped two soft slices into the toaster although there were eight slots, then considered and put in two more. After two minutes the bread popped up again, toast now, golden brown on each side, and Janice scraped each piece with butter and sprinkled on cinnamon sugar.

Ass and hand, she thought. Couldn't stop thinking it. It was like a chant in her head, a million voices all coming together to sing. Ass and hand! Hand and *ass*!

It wasn't much of a walk to Ms. Ruby's room with a dinner tray carrying plates of toast and two mugs of milk, to door number 217, up a short flight of stairs and down a hall, and when Janice got there she knocked softly. She had a key, of course, even though most of the residents kept their doors unlocked—she had a master key that would open up every room in the place, just in case there was an emergency, but she still knocked. Just because these people were living in a home was no reason not to be polite.

There was no answer.

"Ms. Ruby?" she called, leaning her forehead into the door and putting her mouth close to the jamb, careful not to let the plates and cups slide off the tray. "Are you awake? I have something for you."

Nothing.

Janice started back toward the stairs. She was later than normal, Ms. Ruby had probably gone back to sleep, and it'd be best not to wake her this late. Or this early, if you preferred.

But that was unlikely, because Ruby had suffered from insomnia since her husband died ten years before, she'd tell Janice that a dozen times some nights. She always slept during the day, when everyone else was up and about, and she'd spend her nights up. *Like a vampire*, she'd said once, with some disgust. Of course, if I were a vampire, I'd hopefully be in bed with Tom Cruise right now. Then she'd laughed, hard enough that she'd ended up coughing and gasping for air.

After a moment Janice went back to Ruby's door and tried the knob. It was unlocked, just as she'd expected. She went inside. This was one of the smaller apartments, just a living room and a separate bedroom, and it was stuffed full of furniture. Big, squashy chairs and doilies—like a hobbit hole, she'd always thought.

"Ruby?" Janice said, nudging the door shut behind her. "I have toast, if you'd like a piece."

The old woman was in the living room, sitting in one of the armchairs in front of the television like she always did when she was waiting for Janice to show up, watching an infomercial about a folding ladder.

"There you are," Janice said, setting the tray down on the coffee table and sitting down in the other armchair. The cushion wheezed beneath her. "I thought your heartburn might be acting up again, so I brought . . ."

She trailed off, at first not sure what was wrong, until she realized Ms. Ruby's head was canted at a strange angle on her neck, that her eyes were glassy and gazing toward nothing. She'd died sitting in front of the TV, waiting for her toast and conversation.

Janice leaned forward, smoothed down one of Ruby's white curls that'd become mussed. The old woman was cool to the touch, but her hair felt just as it always had. She'd never considered it, that the hair of the living and the hair of the dead would feel exactly the same.

Death was a natural part of life, that's what the guy who'd interviewed her for the job had said. Not Jesse but someone else, a man she'd met once and never saw again. She'd heard the same thing in the biology classes she'd taken. If you were alive, you'd die. It was inevitable.

She finished smoothing the stray hair and sat back, taking one of Ruby's hands into her own. The hand was small and thin, covered in age spots. Her palm and fingers were smooth as silk; the skin felt paper thin. Like the pages of a Bible. If she would've come into work on time Ruby wouldn't have been alone during her final moments. Of course, if she'd come in, she wouldn't have had the pleasure of watching her husband sink his hands roughly into another woman's ass, and she wouldn't now still be thinking of the gun in that drawer.

CHAPTER SIX

2018

"Are you ready?" Matt asked. They'd been waiting out the rain under the long arms of an evergreen, snacking on beef jerky and peanut butter crackers, passing a bottle of water back and forth between them. It had stormed hard for less than three minutes and then quickly petered out, and the clouds had rolled away, peeling back to reveal a soft blue sky that seemed to have been scrubbed clean by the moisture.

"Yes," she said, holding open her pack so Matt could drop in his trash. It was an old habit from when the girls were little and she was constantly picking up after them, but old habits die hard. Matt had been ready to stuff the empty wrappers in his own pocket, but shrugged when he saw her offer the pack and tossed in the bits of plastic and paper.

"Take a picture first?" Matt asked, fishing his phone out of his pocket and holding it up.

"Sure." Marie stood up and brushed her hands against her thighs. "Where do you want me to stand?"

Matt blinked, considered.

"Why not out there?" he asked. "With your back to the view?"

"Out by the edge?"

"Yeah." He shrugged. "It'll make a good picture."

"Okay."

She came from under the trees, stopping near the edge and peering out over the cliff. Plenty of open air and trees and rock down there. And the river, of course—Three Forks, that's what it was called—splashing and hissing as it churned its way under the cliff, moving faster and rougher than she'd ever seen before. But it was difficult to see *just* below where she was standing, because the cliff was formed like a tabletop—it stuck way out and then sloped back in, so it was impossible to see straight down. If you got on your hands and knees and stuck your head way over the side, you could see—but why would you want to do that?

"You okay?" Matt asked, and she turned slowly and looked at him. The ground was uneven under her shoes.

"It's a long way to the top," she said.

Matt smiled again.

"You mean to the bottom?" he asked, missing her reference to the AC/DC lyrics. And if that didn't sum up their marriage, she guessed that nothing else would—the two of them had never spent much time on the same page. If any time at all.

"Yeah," she said. "It's a long way down."

"Yes," he said. "It is."

CHAPTER SEVEN

1995

Her shift was supposed to end at eight, when the sun was up and residents would be heading in to breakfast and their first doses of medication and vitamins, but she begged off as soon as the next girl came in, said her stomach was bothering her. She didn't mention Ruby—if she had, she never would've been able to cut out early. The paperwork they had to submit after a resident's death was thick as a phone book and would've kept her tied up for hours. So she left Ruby in her chair, her head stuck at that uncomfortable angle. Not that Ruby was as uncomfortable anymore. Nope, those days were past for her. No more late nights in front of the TV, no more toast and tea. In a way, Janice envied her.

It was only four in the morning when she turned onto their street, and everything was still dark and quiet except her own home, where nearly every window was lit up, although the blinds had all been pulled. She parked on the farthest end, near the corner, and walked the rest of the way, because she didn't want anyone to know she was there. *Anyone?* No, it was a particular *someone* she didn't want to alarm, and that was her husband. She wanted him to think she was still at work, that it was business as usual, he had nothing to worry about.

But *did* Matt have anything to worry about? That was the real question. Oh, she couldn't stop thinking about that gun, and about her husband's hand on that woman's ass, but thinking about it didn't mean anything was going to happen. She didn't want to hurt Matt, but she sure as hell wanted to scare him and the little tart he'd let into their home. And then she'd leave, file for divorce. Start over.

But maybe that was all easier said than done.

Janice walked past the cute little red car and climbed lightly up the steps to the house, paused when her hand was on the battered brass knob. She could turn around, go back down the steps and climb into her car and *drive*. It didn't matter where, as long as it was away from here. West, maybe, to her mom's place. She had some cash in her purse, a full tank of gas, and the credit card she had for emergencies—she could make it. She could be halfway across the country before Matt ever realized a thing, and it would be done. All of this would be behind her, a part of her past. She could look back on this moment in twenty years and laugh. Well, maybe not *laugh*, the thought of a cheating husband would never be funny, but maybe she wouldn't think about it at all.

And Janice would've gone, turned around and walked—her hand had actually let go of the doorknob and she'd started to pivot away on the balls of her feet—but for one thing. A giggle. The window beside the door had been propped open, as it usually was on a balmy night like this, and that's how it floated to her ears—a high-pitched, tinkling woman's sound of delight. And then, a moment later, came Matt's answering chuckle, low and throaty.

It was their laughter that made her decision, that brought her hand back up to the doorknob and twisted it, that lifted her foot and brought her home.

CHAPTER EIGHT

2018

"Please, stop! Don't!"

The woman's scream echoed off the sheer rock face, and birds lifted from the trees, startled into flight.

CHAPTER NINE

1995

A single gunshot rang out. A few people woke, but then went back to sleep. They all thought it was a dream.

CHAPTER TEN

2018

There were five or six people standing in the parking lot at the bottom of the trail, gathered in a small group, discussing their dinner plans in the creeping twilight. They'd have to drive into Estes Park, but there were some good places right on the edge of town, an Italian place and a barbecue joint that had an amazing buffalo—

"Help!" a man shouted, and they all turned toward the voice. He was coming down the trail, stumbling along on the loose gravel, something in his hand. A small rectangle of light. His phone. Something moved in the woods behind him, startled and then dashed away, shaking up the undergrowth. A rabbit, or a small deer.

"My wife, she fell," the man said. He was sweating lightly, gasping for air as if the hike down had been a rough one. "My wife, I think she might be dead."

CHAPTER ELEVEN

1995

You'd think that over ten years, a man would become accustomed to waking up at six in the morning to take the dog out, but Frank Jessup could tell you otherwise. He'd been doing the same thing every damn day of the year for the last decade, and it wasn't even his dog. Sweetie belonged to his wife, but he was the one who had to take the little idiot out when it started yapping in the morning while Sandra snored. And it'd been just the same this morning—five fifty-seven on the dot, Sweetie was jumping up and down on her fat little legs and scratching at the door with nails that weren't trimmed often enough, her eyes about ready to pop out of her head.

So Frank got up, went to the bathroom, and pissed, grimacing at the burning sensation he'd been having in his groin over the last few years, and slipped on his shoes. Sweetie had been barking the whole time, but Sandra was still fast asleep. Sometimes he was sure his wife was faking, just so she didn't have to get up and lap the neighborhood with a plastic bag in one hand just in case Sweetie decided to take a shit, which she sometimes did, which seemed like some sort of punishment to Frank, fumbling around with a bag in the dark, trying to scoop up a warm pile of waste.

And of course, this morning Sweetie decided to take a squat right on the edge of ol' man Vandercamp's lawn, and she turned and stared right at Frank while she did her thing, as if the only way she could perform was through eye contact, and Frank was wondering, as he always did, how one little dog could produce so much shit without exploding. It was business as usual, until Sweetie suddenly straightened out, pinching it off, and started barking.

"Why don't you shut up?" Frank hissed, yanking on her leash. "People are still sleeping, stupid."

But Sweetie kept on barking, really working herself up into a frenzy, the way all small pea-brained dogs are apt to do, until Frank looked around to try to figure out what was driving her nuts. The only people ever out this early were trashmen and the lady who drove around in her station wagon, pitching newspapers out the window, and Sweetie ignored them. And then he saw the man in the street, walking toward him—no, not walking. The man was moving at more of a slow stumble, like he was drunk. Or injured.

"My wife," Matt Evans said. This was once he'd come close enough, stepping into a circle of yellow light thrown down by a streetlamp. He nearly fell when his foot caught the curb but managed to save himself at the last moment. He reached a bloody hand out toward Frank, who shrank away from that reach. Frank recognized him—the young man lived two blocks down with his woman. They were a good-looking couple, kept to themselves. "My wife. I think she might be dead."

And Sweetie barked on.

CHAPTER TWELVE

2018

"You saw her fall?" the ranger asked.

"No."

"What were you doing, then?"

"I was—I was taking a leak, okay? I was back in the trees, and I couldn't see her."

"What was she doing so close to the edge?"

"I don't know. I took her picture, then went to piss. And I heard her scream."

"And after she fell, you looked over the side?"

"Yeah. I crawled out and looked down."

"Crawled?"

"I'm scared of heights," Matt said. He closed his eyes. "But I didn't see her. It was too dark, and there was the water—"

"Yeah, the Three Forks River runs right under that cliff," the ranger said. "Water level's pretty high right now, so she was most likely swept off in the current."

"Where would it have taken her?"

"River's moving quick, so if she survived the fall it would've taken her south." The park ranger pushed his hat back and wiped his forehead. It was completely dark but still warm, and he was sweating just standing in the parking lot. "It's not going to be any use scouting the river while the sun's down—it's a dangerous hike down in the dark, and you can't see anything that might float by. A rescue team would run the risk of injury or getting lost. It's not worth it."

"But if Marie swam out of the river and made it to shore—"

The ranger sighed. He'd worked at the park for almost fifteen years, he'd seen plenty of city folk come out to spend a day in the wild, to hike and take pictures, and it never failed to surprise him how stupid they could be. He'd heard it all: a woman had once suggested that the steeper trails be outfitted with escalators so people could enjoy the views from the top without a hard hike; or one time he'd been asked what they did with all the animals during the winter. And this situation was stupid, too, but it was also sad.

"Let me be completely honest, Mr. Evans," he said. "I'm familiar with the cliff your wife fell from, and there's no way she could've survived. Not from that high, and not with the river moving that fast. We'll have to start searching for her body first thing in the morning."

CHAPTER THIRTEEN

1995

"This Janice Evans?" the detective asked, looking down at the unzipped body bag at their feet. ABRAHAM REID, that's what it said on the badge he flashed at the crew picking through the wet, smoldering remains of the house. Two of the four main walls were completely gone, and the walkway leading down from the front door was scorched black, but the first responders had managed to contain the fire before it spread to the neighbors. The team was still in yellow rubber coveralls and boots, but Reid was dressed in a nice gray suit that hung loosely from his scrawny frame. The old man didn't seem worried about the ash that would ruin his clothes, so no one mentioned it.

"Looks like it," one of the guys said. "Not that you can really tell."

"She was in the bed," another one said. He pulled off his rubber gloves and wearily rubbed the back of his hand across his forehead, leaving a clean streak through the soot that had blanketed his skin. "Skull's cracked in a couple places, teeth are all knocked out. Whoever did this really put a beating down on her, then doused her and the mattress in gasoline and lit it up. It burned fast and hot."

Reid pulled a ballpoint pen out of his pocket and squatted beside the bones the men had collected from the rubble, carefully stirred around the pieces with one end.

"Got at least one tooth in here," he said, standing up again with a painful grunt. "The coroner'll need it to ID her."

"We'll sweep through again, see if we can find anything else."

Reid grunted and pulled something out of his pocket. A candy, the fireman thought at first. A wrapped peppermint. Reid gently pulled both of the twisted ends, the same way you'd pull on the two ends of a Chinese finger trap, and the candy flew out, twisting end over end. Reid snatched it out of the air with surprising speed, closed one gnarled hand over it, and popped it into his mouth.

"Good trick," one of the firemen said.

"Old dogs like me have our ways," Reid said, smiling faintly. It wasn't a candy, but a cough drop—the menthol was wafting from his mouth in a thick cloud. "Soaked in gasoline, eh?"

They all glanced down at those words. It was nothing more than a collection of blackened, hardened bones piled into a body bag—more like the leftovers from a campfire pit than a human being. The skull was the one thing that gave the appearance of a person—you could still make out the graceful curve of the head, the sharp stretch of jaw. Reid looked toward the street, where a crowd of neighbors and police had gathered.

"Let me know if you boys find anything else interesting," he said.

CHAPTER FOURTEEN

Matt's shoulder hurt.

That's where the bullet went through. A clean shot, the doctors said. In one side, out the other. Like a hot knife through butter. It'll heal right up, might not even scar. Be like it never happened at all. The docs here said all kinds of things like that. Friendly, comforting words—but Matt got a good look at their eyes while they looked him over, when they poked and prodded and made notes on their charts, and he might as well have been a pig heading to the slaughterhouse. Cold, that's how the docs looked. Unfeeling. But what could he expect? He was just another patient in a long line waiting to be treated, and they moved on to the next. Maybe doctors have a quota they have to meet and that's why they hurry from one room to the next, asking questions and not really listening to the answers. Janice had been premed and she'd told him it wasn't true, that doctors cared about every person they saw. But he wasn't so sure. Maybe it was the truth, or maybe it was a lie doctors told to keep themselves from going crazy.

Or maybe, he thought, they looked at him that way because they thought he was a killer.

He'd asked for something stronger than the pills that got

delivered to his room in a tiny paper cup every few hours, but the nurse only smiled blandly when he spoke and had backed quickly out of the room. They'd mostly left him alone for the last day, with only the television to keep him company. The TV, and the muted sounds of conversation from the nurse's station down the hall. But it was nothing but garbled, muffled voices that made it through the walls—unless a nurse accidentally left the door open, which had only happened once.

"—poured gasoline all over the body and lit a match. I've got a buddy who works for the fire station, said the whole house came down in less than five minutes—"

"Jesus—"

"What a sick bastard."

His nurse stuck her head into the room then, looking startled and more than a little guilty, and pulled the door shut. She even gave it an extra tug to make sure the latch clicked and it wouldn't ease back open, so all the hospital staff could safely gossip without him eavesdropping. He was on trial out there, the jury was a bunch of medical staff in their squeaky white shoes and wrinkled scrubs, and they'd found him guilty of murdering his wife, without a shadow of a doubt. They'd have him strung up if they got the chance. Guilty until proven innocent.

He'd fucked up this time. Bad.

"Did you kill your wife, Mr. Evans?" Detective Reid asked. The cop had come in not long after the nurse had shut the door, wordlessly dragged a chair out of the corner and pulled it up to the side of the bed. He was sucking on a menthol cough drop, the smell of it surrounding him like a cloud. He was ancient, old enough that he might've started his career with law enforcement back when booze was illegal and women couldn't vote.

"No."

"Then maybe you'd like to explain how your wife ended up in her current—*situation*?" Reid asked. He was sitting with his legs crossed, in the graceful way only young women and very old men can manage, with a notepad propped up on one bony knee. This cop was droopy eyed, spoke slowly and moved even slower, but Matt had a feeling his brain zipped around like greased lightning. He'd have to be careful around this old man. There was something almost *Southern* about Reid, even though he didn't have an accent. Or maybe *gentlemanly* was a better way to describe him.

"Situation?" Matt had repeated wearily.

"Yessir," Reid said, nodding sleepily. "Early yesterday morning we got a call about a house fire over on Maple Avenue—8220 Maple. That's where you live, isn't it? Or *lived*? White house with green shutters?"

"Yes."

"I wouldn't call our fire department the fastest around, but they're pretty damn quick, and by the time they got to that house with their hoses and what-not it was too late. I'm exaggerating a bit here, but just about all that was left of that nice little place you're renting was ashes." Reid cleared his throat and hacked into a handkerchief he'd pulled from his pocket, then wiped his lips impatiently. "Ashes, and your wife. Well, what was left of her, anyway."

Matt closed his eyes. The spots behind his eyes throbbed. Morphine, that's what he needed. An IV threaded into his arm and a handy little button he could push to shoot some dope into his system, so he'd be nice and buzzed. But maybe that was why the nurses wouldn't give him anything—they wanted him sober to talk to this cop.

"That fire sprung up quick, burned hot and fast," Reid said. "But that's what happens when there's a couple gallons of gasoline dumped on everything. The first spark of a match and everything's gone." Reid held up a gnarled hand and snapped so loudly, Matt twitched in surprise and opened his eyes. "Like that. You ever light your own farts, Mr. Evans?"

"What?"

Reid's liver-spotted lips spread in a smile.

"You know the old rhyme? Beans, beans, the musical fruit, the more you eat, the more you toot? Did your mama ever cook beans or chili and the next day your rear end wouldn't keep quiet?"

"I guess so," Matt said.

"I can imagine you as a little boy stealing his father's lighter out of his pants pocket and sneaking outside to see if your farts would catch fire," Reid said. He snorted in amusement. "I can imagine that, clear as day."

"My father is dead," Matt said.

"I'm sorry. How'd he go?"

"Heart attack," Matt said, balling up a fistful of bedding. "It was a long time ago. When I was a teenager."

"So your mother raised you alone?"

"Yes. She's dead now, too."

Reid made a mark on his notepad.

"So you never lit your farts?"

"Is this question part of your investigation?"

Reid shrugged and smiled again.

"Just curiosity."

Matt sighed, turned his head on the pillow.

"Of course I did," he said. "I was a kid once."

Reid laughed, a throaty, whistling sound that came from deep in his skinny chest, and gleefully slapped a hand against his thigh.

"I knew it," he said. "Then I don't have to tell you how quickly a fart lights up. Surprises you, doesn't it? You don't expect it to catch, even if you've done it before. It's like a miracle every time. A smelly, god-awful miracle, but a miracle just the same."

Reid laughed again, and Matt did, too. He couldn't help it—the old man's laugh was funny enough on its own. It was a good one, loud and clear as a bell, chortling and contagious. A man with a laugh like that could get an entire crowd laughing on his very own. He was a comedian's dream.

"Was it like that with Janice?" Reid asked, still smiling, and for the first time Matt noticed the smile didn't reach all the way to Reid's eyes. His gaze was watery and red rimmed but also coldly calculating, watching for Matt's reaction. "Were you surprised at how fast the fire lit once you poured that gasoline all over her? I saw her remains, you know. She looks like a charcoal briquette more than a person."

The laughter dried up so fast it might have been a figment of his imagination, and his throat clenched unpleasantly. *A charcoal briquette.* Reid was spot-on, Matt *had* been surprised by how quickly the flames moved, how fast they ate up everything in their path. He'd seen how her skin had broken and peeled back like old, dry paper, and how the flesh underneath had blackened from the heat. The sight of this had been bad enough, but it was the smell that'd finally driven him out of the house and down the street, the scent of cooking human flesh that even overpowered the stench of the gasoline. It hadn't been a bad smell, that was the worst of it. The cooking flesh had made him think of barbecues on long summer nights, of beef roasting on a grill, of the gristly bits of meat that would get caught between his teeth whenever he took a bite. Those were good times and memories, and he'd run from the house and those smells then, even as the walls were collapsing around him and the hot bile was bubbling up in his throat.

"I didn't kill my wife."

"Then what happened, Mr. Evans?"

"We were asleep. I woke up because Janice was moving around, and it took me a minute to realize that there was someone in the house with us. A man."

"What did he look like?"

"I don't know. It was dark, and I never got a chance to get a good look at him."

"That's fair. Go on."

"He had a gun, put it in my face and told me to turn over. He already had Janice tied up, and then he did the same to me."

"He used rope?"

"Yeah."

"He must not have tied you up too tightly."

"Why do you say that?"

"No rope burns on you," Reid said. One of his red, veiny

eyelids trembled in what might have been the start of a wink, then stilled. "Keep going, Mr. Evans."

"This guy, he was hurting Janice. I didn't know what was going on, my back was to them, but I could hear she was in pain. While he was busy with her, I managed to get free of the ropes."

"And you ran?"

"Yeah."

"How chivalrous of you," Reid said drily. "And when, exactly, did you get shot?"

"I was trying to get out of the house," Matt said. "He shot me from behind, but I still managed to get out."

Reid nodded, made another note on his pad.

"You got out of the house and went looking for help," the cop said.

"Yes."

Reid leaned over, put his pen and pad down on the bed-side table. Rubbed his eyes for a minute, the way a kid would, with both hands balled into fists and jammed right into the sockets.

"You know, I made a few calls before I came in here," Reid said once he was done. "Found out that in the event of your wife's death, you cash in a life insurance policy worth about thirty thousand dollars. It's not a *huge* amount, but it's quite a pretty penny for a jobless college student such as yourself. Especially a young man with no parents to help him with the bills. And no wife, either. Because Janice was supporting you, wasn't she? Mr. Evans?"

Matt's throat was clenching and loosening, over and over again. He took a careful sip of water from the plastic cup the nurse had left him. There was a straw sticking out of the top, and his hand was shaking badly enough that it took several tries before he managed to steer it into his mouth. Reid watched with interest. The old codger didn't miss much, that was for sure.

"What're you getting at?"

"Tell me what happened to your wife."

"I just did."

"No, what you told me was a very sweet, practiced lie," Reid said. "Quite a few things wrong with it. Inconsistencies, that's what cops call them. That's shop talk. Pieces that don't quite line up right."

"What do you mean?" There was panic rising in Matt's throat, thick and choking. Bitter, as if he'd let an aspirin dissolve on his tongue.

"You don't have any rope burns, even though you say you were tied up and had to struggle free," Reid said. "And that bullet wound—you say you were shot from behind, while you were trying to get out?"

"Yes," Matt said softly. Fuck. *Fuckity-fuck.*

"No, sir, *that* bullet came from your front side," Reid said, picking up his notes again and squinting at them. "Docs told me the bullet pierced your front right shoulder and exited cleanly through the back. And whoever pulled that trigger was standing awfully close to you, too. I asked if you might've shot yourself, and they didn't rule it out."

God.

"That's not what happened."

"Then tell me what happened."

"I did."

"Well, tell it again," Reid said. He grimaced, baring all his teeth like a dog. They were fake, Matt thought. Too perfect and white to be real. Dentures. Roe-buckers, he'd heard them called before. "And this time, try a little harder."

"What do you mean?"

"Well, you could just tell me the truth. Or, if you want to keep lying, at least try to make it believable. And if that's not possible, at least make it entertaining," Reid said, uncrossing his legs and crossing them again the other way. Really mashing his bony ass down into his seat, settling in for a good bit. "Let it rip, Mr. Evans. Tell me what happened to your wife that night."

CHAPTER FIFTEEN

2018

Did you push your wife off that cliff, Mr. Evans? Did you want to get rid of her, cash out her big life insurance claim, trade her in for a young hottie? Has your wife gotten flabby over the years, has she gotten ugly and nags until you're ready to either punch her or drink yourself into a stupor? And you've done well over the years, haven't you, Mr. Evans? You've made a bit of money, socked away a good-sized nest egg, but it would've been gone in a second if you filed for divorce because she would've gotten half of everything, so did you decide the better thing to do was give her a hard shove when she was standing on the edge of that cliff, send her tumbling out into the air, ass over kettle, until you heard her hit the water below?

He keeps waiting for someone to ask, but no one has. They're treating it as an accidental fall, and that's exactly what he'd hoped for, isn't it? It's the best possible outcome, going just to plan, but he's still worrying. Because you can't control anything, even if you plan for everything—he'd learned that lesson a long time before, with Janice. So he keeps on waiting for someone to suggest that he pushed Marie, that he'd murdered his wife, but no one has.

Not yet.

"Chances are she'll still be in the general vicinity of where she fell," one of the cops said. He unconsciously reached up for his chest pocket, briefly touching the pack of cigarettes there before letting his hand drop. "The river's swollen, but the current wouldn't have moved her too far."

"We'll have boats out once the sun comes up, dragging the water," the park ranger said, gazing up into the night sky. The sky was clear, but there still weren't any stars. "We'll be doing a ground search around the river as well, see if we can get a visual from the shore, but none of that's any good in the dark. We'll just have to wait."

Matt wasn't sure how to act. Exactly how devastated should a man be after his wife has taken a dive off a cliff? You had to play situations like this just right or end up looking too rehearsed, phony. Fainting would definitely be too dramatic, but what about tears? And if he did cry, how far could he push it before it started to look fake? Was he over-thinking the whole thing? This situation—like every situation in life, maybe—was a careful balancing act. Too little grief, acting like a dead fish—that would make him look guilty. Too much, and he'd look guilty. He had to be Goldilocks and get it just right. He tried to remember how he'd acted at Janice's funeral, but that time was mostly a haze of pain and confusion in his memory and didn't help now. He'd just have to try his best. Like a kid on Christmas morning who'd already snuck a look at the gifts but still had to act surprised.

He didn't cry. Didn't scream or shout or throw himself around—instead, he stayed quiet. He overheard someone say he must be in shock, which was exactly what he'd hoped they'd think. He answered the questions from the local police as simply as he could and listened, kept his eyes open. Watched. He'd learned to watch over the years, especially because he'd worked in sales—you can learn a helluva lot about a person by just watching them. It's what he'd always told his sales guys—you look for the nonverbal cues. Posture, eye movement, what they do with their hands—those alone will tell if a person is a buyer. These are the tools you need to get a person to close a deal, this is what he would tell his team when they came in for their monthly meetings, when everyone would fly in from all over the country and they'd sit around in a room together and call through the lists of potential leads—dialing for dollars, that's what they called it. But those calls were really more like spinning a roulette wheel, luck rather than skill that early in the game, more about willing someone to pick up the line and listen, getting them to agree to a face-to-face meeting because once you got a buyer to meet you in person you'd won half the battle. And once you're sitting across from that person, he'd tell his team, you'll be able to tell if they're really a buyer, or if they're just sucking your time.

You could watch a person, know how they felt, if they were buying your bullshit or not, but you had to play your part, too. You could have the best sales pitch in the world, but if your eyes were too shifty, if you were nervous, if you breathed too quickly or looked too eager, you might screw it all up.

"We're all actors on a stage," he'd tell his sales team. "That's directly from *William F. Shakespeare,* so you can take it to the bank."

"What's the 'F' stand for, boss?"

"It stands for William *Fucking* Shakespeare, numb-nuts. And I'm saying, if you screw it up with a client, you might as well throw in the towel and move on to the next one. I paid cash for that BMW sitting in the parking garage because I've learned how to read people," Matt told his team during one of their last meetings. "I watch them. I see where they look, how they respond to the things I say. If they scratch their face or rub their nose or stay quiet, you need to take a different tack. Try something else. You've gotta sniff out a person's trigger words, see what'll catch their attention. Profit, entrepreneur, flexibility. Those are good hooks. If they're maintaining eye contact, breathing fast, smiling and laughing a lot—reel 'em in."

So he'd sat in the rangers' station and answered all the questions the cops leveled at him, and he'd watched. He didn't get the impression that they suspected him of anything, only that they were going through the motions. Two cops and a park ranger, writing down his responses. Standard procedure. "Accidents happen," the ranger said, handing him a cup of coffee. "People fall out in the park, more than you'd think. And we've had a few people take a topple right off that same cliff. Even had a lady out here last year, a woman writing a piece for a magazine on accidental deaths out here in the park. If that's not a perfect example of irony, I don't know what is. It's a fact of life out here. Dangerous hikes and inexperienced hikers are a bad combo."

These people didn't have a clue about how to be sympathetic.

Luckily, he didn't need any sympathy.

"One of my units will take you back to your cabin tonight," one of the two cops said. Tweedle Dum and Tweedle Dee, that pretty much summed these guys up. "I know it'll be tough, but you should try to get some sleep. We'll be in touch, keep you updated about what we find."

"I'd like to go out with you in the morning, if that's all right," Matt said, and he saw the cops exchange a look. At least neither of them was like ol' Detective Reid, who'd smelled the guilt on him right away, who'd sat and stared while a cough drop rolled around in his mouth, knocking it against his dentures so it sounded like a stone in a rock tumbler. Matt still had nightmares of that sound, of the *clink-clink* that had almost driven him crazy. At least these cops weren't like Reid.

"I don't think you coming along is the best idea," one of them said. "You need time to process what's happened. And if we find something unpleasant—"

If they found Marie's body, that's what they meant. If she'd fallen from the cliff and splattered against the rocks instead of washing away in the river and her skull had cracked open like an egg, it would be unpleasant. But it wasn't as if he hadn't dealt with unpleasant before.

"I want to be there," Matt said. "I need to be part of the search for my wife."

"Why?"

Matt stared at the ranger.

"I've been married to Marie for over twenty years," he said. Swallowed hard, so they could see it. So they'd think he was choking back tears. "I think I should be involved in looking for her."

And I need to make sure she's dead.

The cops looked at each other again, but there still wasn't suspicion in their eyes. That was fine with him.

"Okay," one finally said. "We'll pick you up early to start the hike down to the base of the cliff."

CHAPTER SIXTEEN

Matt barely slept at all that night, just tossed and turned in the thin cotton sheets of the rental cabin, and when the cops came to pick him up they mentioned how tired he looked. How the bags under his eyes were so dark and the lines in his face were so deep. It hadn't been grief for Marie that'd kept him up all night, although that's what the cops thought, or even guilt. No, it was the anticipation. He'd felt the same way he did before a big presentation at work, or just before heading into a dentist's appointment. It wasn't exactly an unpleasant feeling, this buildup to the big moment, but a person could live without it.

The car ride into the park was a silent one. Too early for conversation, Matt supposed, or the cops were just being kind. Leaving him alone with his grief. Or maybe he was reading them wrong, and they were suspicious of him. They were letting the quiet drag out so his guilty conscience would catch up to him and he'd start babbling like an idiot.

His hand twitched at that idea, sloshing coffee over the side of the paper cup one of the cops had given him when he'd climbed inside. It splashed onto the leather seat and he mopped it up with his sleeve. The cop in the passenger seat looked around to see what was happening, then turned away when Matt gave him a nod. Did the cop turn just to *look*, because that was a normal thing to do, or because he thought Matt had shoved his wife off that cliff? Stupid, paranoid thoughts. You could see guilt anywhere if you looked hard enough, and Matt had thought he'd be fine this time, that this would be easier to deal with since he'd been through it before. Same shit, different day. But that wasn't the case, not at all. It turns out guilt has a way of feeling fresh every damn time.

He hadn't actually seen Marie fall—he'd closed his eyes when it happened, but it wasn't as if he could close his ears. She'd screamed, *shrieked*, and then the sound had stopped so suddenly it might've been cut with a knife, and he'd guessed that's when she'd hit the river. Or a rock. He could imagine her plunging under the surface, her mouth still wide open in a scream, sucking in the water and choking, unable to claw her way to the surface, her blood smoking up the water. Or maybe she was already dead before she went in, her skull fractured or her neck broken. But he had to be sure. He'd crept to the edge of the cliff after her scream, dropping to his hands and knees and crawling for the last foot or so because he didn't like heights, never had. One good gust of wind could send him right off the edge himself, and where would that leave him? Nowhere except a hundred feet down, drowning in the churning river, as good as dead.

Like Marie?

He didn't know. He hadn't been able to see anything once he managed to poke his head over the edge, except for the black river rushing underneath. He'd told the cops that, and it was true. It was too dark by then to see much, especially from so high up, although it was easy to hear the rushing water, the lapping wet sounds it made as it roared underneath. Matt even thought he could feel the spray of it on his cheeks, but once he sat up and passed a hand over his face he realized it was sweat, cold and sickening. He was scared, sitting at the spot where his wife had gone over—the fear he felt then wasn't caused by the height of the cliff; or the way the sky had gone the murky bluish-black of dusk except for the orange-red splash of color at the horizon; or even the thought of living the rest of his life without Marie. No, this fear was something he'd felt before, it was familiar in a way he didn't like. It was a fear that crept up his throat, thick and choking, that made him short of breath and dizzy. He'd last felt this fear when he'd stumbled away from the house where he'd lived with Janice, the baking heat of the fire on his back.

What am I going to do now? That'd been his thought back then, and it was the same thing that came into his head as he sat on the cliff. He'd planned this, he'd prepared, and he'd put so much thought into it, but it didn't matter. What the fuck am I going to do now? He'd lived his whole life that way, it seemed. Always looking over his shoulder, worrying that his stupid decisions would come back to bite him in the ass, and here he was again. Full circle, back to where he'd started.

"We're here," one of the cops said as they pulled over, the nose of the car crowding into a copse of trees. They were at the parking lot at the bottom of the trail, the same spot they'd left the night before. Around and around, his life was full of circles. His stepfather used to say that all the time, and it'd stuck with him. *Same shit, different day.* His car was still there, locked up tight near the back of the lot, one of the rear tires dipping into a rut in the packed dirt. "We'll start here and hike down to the cliff base."

There were others already waiting for them. Another cop, and a few park rangers. Each of them looked at Matt and gave him a tight, quick smile or a nod and then walked on, starting the hike down to the bottom of the cliff. They kept Matt in the center of them as they walked.

CHAPTER SEVENTEEN

He hadn't brought enough water, but the others were more prepared. One of the rangers fished a bottle out of her backpack and handed it to him when she noticed he was struggling.

"I didn't think it'd take this long to get there," he said. "It only took us about an hour and a half to get to the top."

They'd been hiking for almost an hour by then, struggling through scraggly undergrowth and over piles of loose gravel and rock, and they didn't seem any closer to the bottom than where they'd started. The trees were thick enough that the sky only peeked through over their heads occasionally, but it was still warm, even in the shade, even though it was just barely midmorning.

"It usually is faster to hike downhill, but there's no defined trail that comes down here, so we're forced to break our own path. Plus, the way the mountain is formed forces us to take a more extended route. There's really only one way to come down off a cliff faster," the ranger said. She paused, looking embarrassed. "Sorry. Talk about putting my foot in my mouth."

At first he was confused by her apology, then he understood. Because it had been *much* faster the way Marie had come down, *straight down,* she'd hit the bottom in a matter of seconds.

They hiked on. The river encroached upon the trail in the last thirty minutes, not so much becoming a part of the landscape but *taking it over* completely, as if the water were a living thing. And it was—it chuckled and burbled in some parts, roared furiously in others, but even in the calmest spots none of them approached the shore to cup water in their hands to splash on their foreheads, or to soak a bandanna in to press against the backs of their necks. Matt knew why. Because Marie was in the water. A dead woman was floating in there.

"Here we are," the ranger said, unloading his pack from his shoulders and dropping it on the rocks with a sigh, and it took Matt a moment to process, to take his brain off autopilot and blink the sunshine out of his eyes. Barely mid-morning, but it felt like a week had passed since he'd climbed out of bed. He was stuck in a daze brought on by the sun and the heat and his aching muscles, but mostly it was the fear. He could understand how deer froze in the sight of oncoming headlights, because that's how he felt now. Like an animal waiting to be run down in the road. "What a hike. I guess I can skip the gym today."

Matt looked up, shading his eyes with the flat of his hand, and there was the cliff far above their heads, the spot where Marie had stood less than twenty-four hours before. The edge where he'd crawled and peered over. It looked so much different from down here—the cliff seemed almost close, as if it wasn't that high at all, but when he'd hunched over the edge the night before it'd seemed like he was looking down into a dizzying eternity. They were standing in the shadow of the cliff now, the rock on their right and the river on their left, the cliff forming a ceiling above their heads as it sloped out, and it felt more like a shelter than a terrifying drop-off. Comforting instead of scary, but it was all perspective.

"Spread out along the shore," the cop said. "From any point off that cliff she would've fallen directly into the river, so we're going to start our search in this area. Everyone will take ten-yard segments along the shore and look. Water level's running higher than usual and visibility is low, but there'll be some boats heading down this way soon to help, and they'll be able to get out toward the middle where it's deep. Bodies sink like rocks, so chances are that she's somewhere in this immediate area and hasn't moved far. You got that, Mr. Evans? Evans, you got me?"

The cop came over and clapped a hand on Matt's shoulder, making him jump.

"Yeah, I got it," Matt said. The cop nodded and walked the few yards back to the river's shore, but Matt didn't move from his spot beside the sheer wall of rock. He was still looking straight up, at the spot from which Marie would've fallen. Tried to picture her tumbling from that faraway edge, nothing but a shadow hurtling through the dusky sky. He almost laughed then, but turned it into a cough, smothered into his hand.

"Evans?" the cop said. He sounded impatient. "You okay to join us?"

Matt nodded slowly. There was the river behind him, churning furiously, and the cliff over his head.

"Do you think it's possible my wife might have survived?"

he asked, looking from the cliff to the water and then back again. He'd heard someone call it a precipice. Marie would've liked the word, he thought. "Maybe she managed to get to the shore and wandered off into the woods?"

The cop stared.

"It's a possibility," he said. "But highly unlikely based on how fast the water's moving. If she survived the fall it would've swept her along pretty quick, and most likely drowned her. I'm sorry, but even the strongest swimmer would have a tough time making it out of there."

Matt slowly went to the river's edge and pretended to peer into the water, but he really wasn't seeing anything. He *couldn't* see anything, not with the silvery glint off the ripples blinding him.

Marie had always been strong, he thought, but he would never have called her a strong swimmer. She never would've made it out of the frothing, hungry pull of the river. The cop was right. He had to be. Marie was dead. His wife was dead.

But if that were the case, why did Matt taste blood in his mouth, metallic and strong, the same taste he remembered having when Janice died, and all those days Detective Reid had come to the hospital and questioned him for hours? He hadn't had that bitterness on his tongue once in the years since then, until now, but he found it was like riding a bicycle—you never forget what fear tastes like.

CHAPTER EIGHTEEN

1995

Every time Detective Reid showed up at the hospital—and he'd come by every day for a week, stopping in for hours at a time to ask questions—the nurses brought him three containers of apple juice, the kind that come in the clear plastic cups with the peel-off foil lids. Matt wondered how anyone could stand to drink yellow liquid from a plastic cup in the hospital—it looked so much like a urine sample that his throat seized up tight every time he saw one—but Reid liked it. He worried off the foil lid with bent, arthritic fingers and then slurped noisily at the opening, his purple, livery lips flapping.

My throat's so dry it's burning, he said as he finished each juice, then burped wetly into the back of his hand. Not used to all this yapping anymore.

It had been a week since Matt was checked into the hospital, had the gunshot wound in his shoulder stitched up, and was treated for the minor burns and smoke inhalation he'd suffered from the fire. Anyone else would've already been released and sent home, but they thought Matt was a killer, that he'd put a bullet in his wife's head and burned her body to nothing, and they were going to keep him in here until they proved it. Better to be shut up in a hospital than in jail, Matt thought. Better appreciate it while it lasted, because one day Reid would come in and read him his rights, officially place him under arrest.

"Don't waste any of that juice on me today," Reid said to the nurse as he dropped down into his chair with a sigh and pulled off his hat. "I won't be here long enough to get thirsty."

"You've got somewhere more important to be?" Matt asked jokingly. The old man was a cop and Matt was a suspected killer, but that hadn't kept a sort of friendship from springing up between the two of them.

"Actually, I do," Reid said. "And so do you."

So it was happening, Matt thought. Reid had finally found something that tied Matt to the murder, or Matt had slipped up somewhere during the hours of questions and now it was over. Any minute now the cop who'd been stationed outside his door day and night would come in and slap handcuffs on his wrists, and Matt would spend the rest of his life in prison. A wife killer, that's what he'd be called. He'd never survive. He wasn't strong or tough enough. He'd be dead in a week.

"Where am I going?" Matt asked, his voice catching. Reid heard it and his head ticked slightly to one side. He was still watching, Matt realized. Waiting for something, like a cat sitting outside a mouse hole. You might think the cat was sleeping, but all you had to do was take a look at that tail, twitching and alive, and you'd know different. A cat was alert and patient. So was Reid. One of Matt's hands was tucked under the blankets and he dug his nails into his thigh, trying to keep himself calm. Reid's gaze flickered down—he'd caught the movement under the bedding—and then back up to Matt's face.

"You're going home," Reid said. "Well, not *home,* since there's nothing left of it. But to a motel nearby, at least until you find a more permanent situation."

"I'm not under arrest?" Matt said before he could control himself.

Reid was amused.

"No, not today," he said. "An arrest was made last night. Looks like we found the man who killed your wife."

"A man?" Matt said blankly.

"Yes," Reid said. "You said a man broke into your home and attacked the two of you, shot you as you escaped. Or is that not the way you remember it now?"

"Yeah, that's what happened," Matt said quickly. Too quickly, maybe—he saw a frown flicker across Reid's face and then disappear. "Do you know who he is?"

Reid reached into his jacket and pulled out a notepad without looking away from Matt.

"Jesse O'Neil," he said.

"Janice's boss? Is that who you mean?"

"Yeah, that's him," Reid said. "He's been in this same hospital for the last week—east wing, though, other side of the place—recovering from what seems to be a self-inflicted bullet wound."

"What?"

"Mr. O'Neil was found on the side of the road a mile north of your place, about six-thirty on the same morning you were attacked," Reid said. "He would've died, but the woman who found him had medical training in the military and managed to help him. And he's made it through, even though he'd shot himself in the head. The gun was found nearby. Our ballistics department took a look for me, said the bullet that went through your shoulder almost definitely came from that same gun."

Matt's fingers sunk deeper into his thigh. He'd never broken a bone as a kid, never fell out of tree or even had the wind knocked out of him, so when that bullet tore into his flesh it was like nothing he'd ever felt before. His shoulder burned now with the memory.

"O'Neil made it through surgery and is awake," Reid said. He dug around in his pocket and brought out a cough drop. "Confused and groggy, but awake. And as soon as he was conscious he was placed under arrest for murder. But I'd like to hear it from you. Was it Mr. O'Neil who attacked you that night?"

"I—" Matt paused. His heart was pounding so fast and hard, it was all he could seem to hear, roaring through his head like a storm, and he was sure Reid must hear it, too, because the old man was staring at him strangely. "I don't know. I never saw his face. It's a blur."

Reid nodded and sighed, bit down hard enough on the cough drop so it shattered in his mouth. A shard of it went flying from between his lips and skittered across the floor, landing somewhere beneath the bed.

"O'Neil was found covered in blood—his own, and what we're assuming is your wife's. And some of their coworkers have come forward and said O'Neil had a crush on Janice. You might even call it obsession. Nothing good ever comes from obsession. Look what came out of it this time."

"Obsession," Matt muttered.

"The evidence against O'Neil is damning," Reid said, standing. His knees popped as he rose. "So you're free to go, Mr. Evans. I'm very sorry about what you've been through, and the loss of your wife."

"Thank you."

Reid made it to the door before he hesitated and turned back.

"So by all accounts, Jesse O'Neil is obsessed with your wife," he said. "And he gets it into his head that he has to have her. I've seen it plenty of times before. So O'Neil breaks in and attacks the two of you, and kills Janice. But you get away, so he sets the house on fire and runs. Finds himself alone in a field and puts the murder weapon up to his head and pulls the trigger. It's a story we've all seen on the news before. Easy to follow, easy to swallow, like I say. Like something straight out of a storybook. Like it'd been written and then performed perfectly."

"Performed," Matt repeated softly.

"You've been to some shows, right? Your wife did some work with the university's theater, didn't she?" Reid asked.

"Yes."

"I thought I saw that in the file."

Reid went to the door, wrapped his fingers around the handle but didn't turn it. Instead, he looked back at Matt.

"If someone wants to kill themselves with a gun, do you know how they typically do it?"

"No."

"They'll put it here," Reid stuck out his pointer finger, miming a gun, and pushed it against his chest, right where his heart would be. "I've seen that. Or they'll put the barrel against their temple, or stick the damn thing in their mouth. But O'Neil didn't shoot himself in any of those places. He stuck the gun *here*."

Reid pushed his finger against a spot just behind his left ear, pointing up toward the ceiling.

"It's an awkward spot to shoot yourself," he said, shaking his head. "It's even more awkward because O'Neil is right-handed, so he most likely would shoot with that hand. But he was shot behind his left ear. It's almost like someone came up behind him and was trying to catch him off guard, ended up getting in a sloppy shot but still tried to make it look like a suicide."

"Oh."

"My boss is up to his usual shit and wants this case closed," Reid said. "Easy to follow, easy to swallow, that's practically that fool's motto. He's convinced O'Neil did it, tried to kill himself, and botched it. But do you know what I think?"

"What's that?" Matt asked weakly.

Reid sighed and pulled a handkerchief out of his pocket, mopped his nose with it, then tucked it away. Brought out another cough drop and took his sweet time unwrapping it. Maybe Reid didn't know what to say and he needed the time to think. Or maybe he just wanted to let the sweat build up under Matt's balls.

"I think you're a goddamn liar," Reid said.

Then he pulled open the door and left.

LIKE A RECORD BABY

RIGHT

ROUND

ROUND

ROUND

CHAPTER NINETEEN

August 30, 2018

The men stood on either side of the river, gazing into the water. Some of them had long sticks and poked them down into the rocks and sand, prodding at the bottom. They'd tried to use a boat, but the water was running too high and strong to make it worthwhile. There'd been enough rainfall over the state in the last three weeks, there wasn't a single body of water not over capacity, and the risk of losing a member of the team was too great.

"No one seems in much of a hurry," Detective Marion Spengler commented. She'd forgotten her sunglasses, and the light glinting off the surface of the water was playing hell on her eyes. "Does every one usually move this slow?"

Jackson, the man in charge of the search team, looked at her in surprise.

"I didn't think we had a deadline," he said. "She's not gonna get any *more* dead, you know."

Spengler sighed. It was true, the dead stay dead, but she still didn't understand the leisurely way the men moved as they searched for the body of Marie Evans. She had several photos of Marie saved on her phone, mostly scrounged off her online social media accounts. She was a striking woman, but you wouldn't call her beautiful. Brown hair cut to frame her heart-shaped face, perfect smile. Bright, intelligent eyes. She wouldn't look so nice once they hooked her out of the river.

The search team was laughing and joking with each other, taking frequent breaks to grab sweating bottles of water from the cooler that'd been dragged down to the shore. The whole thing seemed more like a summer party than a search for a dead woman. If there were a few inner tubes floating in the water and a barbecue grill going, that's exactly what it'd be. But maybe this was how things always were and she just didn't know it. She'd worked so long in Sex Crimes that she might've become insulated from the process in every other department.

"Can I ask you a question?" Jackson said. He was wearing a fluorescent orange vest and a baseball cap. He took off his sunglasses as they spoke and perched them on the cap's bill, and she saw his eyes dart up and down her body. She was wearing nice linen slacks and a blouse that'd already been splattered with mud, but in her defense she hadn't planned on driving up to Rocky Mountain National Park when she got dressed that morning. And she certainly hadn't thought she'd be forced to walk down the side of a mountain, following the orange ribbons someone had tied intermittently around tree trunks so no one would get lost on their way down to the river. It was the only way to reach the cliff base unless you hopped in a canoe and floated down the river or piloted a helicopter. Oh, there was *one* more way to reach the spot, and that would be headfirst from the top. You'd ride the wings of gravity all the way to the bottom, 120 or so feet to the roiling waters of the Three Forks River. That's how Marie Evans had come down. Headfirst. The short, fast way.

"Go for it."

"Why'd you wear those shoes? Didn't anyone warn you about the terrain out here?"

It'd taken Spengler about two hours from the parking lot to get down to this spot, and she had marched every step of it in her brown leather ballet flats, despite the dubious looks the park rangers had given her feet when she first climbed out of her car. There was hardly any traction on the soles and she'd slipped more times than she could count. And she'd fallen, mostly backward, onto her ass, but once she'd actually gone forward and had caught herself on her hands, then sat for five minutes to pick the gravel out of her palms.

Still, she had every intention of hiking all the way back up without complaint. It wouldn't matter if her shoes were filled with blood by the time she got to her car, she'd grit her teeth and wouldn't say a word.

"No one mentioned I'd be hiking this far."

"You think they forgot?"

"I'm sure that's exactly what happened." She smiled thinly. "They forgot."

She imagined someone *could* forget to mention she'd be hiking to get to the crime scene, but she was pretty sure Detective Loren hadn't forgotten, and he'd been the one to hand out assignments that morning. He hadn't told her to go change shoes because that was the kind of man he was. Mean as a snake, crooked as a picture hanging on a slanted wall. She had the distinct feeling he wanted to see her fail, although she couldn't figure out why. He didn't know her, they'd never even met before she'd joined the department. Unless Loren was one of those men who hated women solely because they were women, and it wasn't as if she hadn't run across plenty of those before. Law enforcement was rife with them.

Detective Loren was testing her. They all were. They were trying to see how far she could be pushed before snapping. She'd overheard two of the detectives calling her the new girl the week before, then making a crude sexual comment about her. It wasn't the joke that bothered her so much as being described as a girl. But that's how they treated her—like a girl. Even though she'd been a detective longer than many of them and had made more arrests. And from what she'd seen she had bigger balls than most of the men in the department.

But unfair as it was, that was the way things worked. She'd been through this same thing every time she'd been promoted or changed departments, not that it made it any easier. There was always a period of weeks or months of hazing, but things always calmed down and she was accepted as a member of the team, or at least a part of the scenery. The same thing would happen here, but only when Loren let it. He was the ringmaster of the whole production, directed the traffic, made sure everyone danced to his piping—even if it was unofficial. He was technically a lieutenant detective, a title that put him higher than anyone else in Homicide, but even without it he'd still crack the whip and the other guys would come running. There's always one person in a group who stands out as the leader, the one who becomes the linchpin that holds it all together—and that was Loren. She had to win him over to assure her spot in the department, and a part of her wondered if that would ever happen.

"To tell you the truth, I don't understand why you were sent out here at all," Jackson said. "Aren't you from Denver Homicide?"

"Yes."

"The husband didn't come out to search this morning."

"I know. I'm just here to check things out."

"When did this turn into a murder investigation? It seems pretty cut-and-dried to me. That couple went on a hike and the gal slipped and fell off the cliff. Accidents like that happen all the time out here."

Spengler sighed again. Shaded her eyes from the sun with the flat of her hand and looked up at the cliff. It was impossible to see the top from down here—it was nothing but a solid wall of rock that shot straight up into the sky. The cliff itself jutted out like a finger, coming away from the rock so there was no support beneath. If life were a cartoon, Wile E. Coyote would've set a trap for the Road Runner up there, but when his bomb went off he'd be the one to plummet all the way down as he stood on that thin rock platform.

Spengler had watched a lot of TV when she was a kid.

"Husband and wife go on hike and the wife falls off the edge to her death," Spengler said. "No witnesses around, no one to back his story. Seems awfully convenient, doesn't it?"

"Like I said, these things happen all the time. Sounds like you folks have extra payroll to burn if you're being sent out here for this."

"I've been a cop a long time, and there's one thing that's

the same in every case," she said, turning away from the river. The whistling sound of it and the reflections playing off the water were giving her a headache. "Things are never exactly what they seem."

CHAPTER TWENTY

Things might never be what they seem, but this was how they were: This might not be a murder investigation at all. Jackson might be right. This might be a simple case of an accident. These things happen all the time, especially in Colorado's backcountry. Fall off a cliff, get caught in an avalanche, get lost in the forest and die of exposure.

But like the saying goes: your accident can be another's good luck. And some people don't wait for good luck, they make their own.

Had Matthew Evans taken luck into his own hands?

"You leaving already?" Jackson asked when he spotted Spengler walking toward the trail. He jogged over, his arms tucked close against his sides.

"Already?" She laughed. "I've been out here a while."

"It's slow work. We'll be wrapping up soon. If you want to stick around we could hike up together, maybe have a drink in town?"

She gave him a small smile.

"Thank you, but I have to get back to the station. But I'll give you my number—could you call if you find anything I should know about?"

She didn't want the drink, but she wouldn't have minded

company on the hike back to the top, except she was forced to sit and rest every few minutes because of the excruciating pain in her feet and she didn't want anyone along to see that. The shoes had rubbed the skin on the backsides of both her ankles away, leaving behind juicy red slashes of meat on the pinch of tendon, and the top of her right foot had a similar spot, just above her second toe. She paused any time she spotted a good place to sit—usually a rock or a fallen tree. Once she ended up sitting in the dirt, her knees giving out and dropping her on her ass. She'd peel off her shoes for a few minutes and wiggle her toes in the air, carefully rub the joints to try and work out the pain. She'd slipped these shoes on this morning because they were comfortable for sitting behind a desk or walking around the office in, not going on a full-blown hike. Now her feet and ankles were swollen and bruised, and she thought the shoes would most likely end up in the trash the minute she got home. Even after her feet were completely better she wouldn't want to wear them again—just looking at them would be enough to bring back some phantom pain.

By the time she got back to the parking lot the sun was much closer to the western rim of the sky, turning the blue the bright red of fresh blood. Another hour or two and it would be twenty-four hours since Marie Evans had taken a tumble off the cliff and slipped into the river's waves. Her husband had told the park rangers it'd happened at dusk, when the shadows thrown down by the trees were long and the summer heat had cooled. This part of the park was supposed to be closed well before sundown, but there were always people who ignored the rules.

Maybe that's why she fell, Matt Evans had said to the park rangers. *It was getting dark. She couldn't see the edge and miscalculated.*

Miscalculated. She thought it was an odd word for a man to use to describe his wife's fall off a cliff.

Spengler went to her car and sat on the passenger seat with the door open, turned so her legs stuck out. The parking lot was packed—Estes Park patrol units and mud-spattered jeeps from the park's rangers—and a BMW sedan. It was black and sleek and new, with windows tinted as dark as a hearse. It belonged to Matt Evans. Somehow, maybe in the panic of his wife slipping and falling over the cliff side, he'd lost his car key. He'd left his car here for the time being, until he could get back with a spare or have someone pick it up.

She rummaged through her glove box and found alcohol wipes and bandages, then tended to her wounds. She had a pair of flip-flops tossed on the floor behind the driver's seat. Cheap plastic things, but better than her flats or nothing at all. She jammed the rubber thongs well in between her toes, made sure her purse was still hidden out of sight beneath the seat, and locked up the car again. It was about a mile hike to the cliff's edge, according to what the park rangers had said. Most of the way was along a well-used trail of packed earth, with an easy incline. Easy going, but even so her feet hurt so badly she almost turned around, but by the time she'd decided to turn back she was practically there.

The rangers had roped off this section of the park to visitors while they searched for Marie Evans, closing the trail with strings of official yellow tape, so she was alone. It sometimes felt like the only place she was ever alone these days was when she was in the car, and that didn't feel like being alone at all, not when she was surrounded by thousands of other people sitting alone in their own cars, everyone creeping along the interstate together. She'd sometimes find herself desperately wanting solitude and silence, and when she got it she'd be hit with a strange loneliness. But out here wasn't so bad. The quiet out here was waiting, it seemed, listening for something to happen.

If a tree falls in the forest and no one is around to hear it, does it make a sound? Or, she thought bemusedly, if a woman slips off a cliff to her death and no one but her husband is there as a witness, was it actually an accident?

Matt and Marie Evans had come this way that day, the rangers said. The main trail headed deeper under the canopy of big pines and aspens and evergreens and was a good place to spot deer rummaging through the undergrowth for a tasty morsel. Most tourists went in that direction. There was a waterfall about a mile farther on, and it made for a charming spot to rest and eat lunch. But the Evanses hadn't gone that way. They'd instead stepped off the main trail onto an unmarked arm. It wasn't on any of the park maps. You'd have to be looking for it to know it was there, or else stumble across it by happy accident.

Spengler only found it because one of the rangers had given her a good description of where to go, and even though she was walking slow and looking, she still passed by it and had to double back. But when she finally spotted it, the path was unmistakable. The foliage had been pushed back and the wild grasses trampled flat. She pushed aside a branch and veered off onto this makeshift trail. It was steeper this way, and rocky. More than once her feet slid right out of the flip-flops and scraped across sharp rocks, and she had to reach out and grab branches to hold her balance as she gathered herself. And then, just when she thought it might have been a terrible idea to try to find her way to the top of the cliff, she pushed through a patch of tall weeds and ducked under a low tree branch and she was there.

The sheer height of the cliff was the first thing she noticed. It was one thing to be told it was over a hundred feet from where she'd been standing not too long before, because that was just a number. It was a very different thing to actually be that high up.

When Spengler had caught her breath, she stood up and walked slowly toward the rim of the cliff. She wasn't afraid of heights, never had been, but she'd also never been on an edge like this before. The sun had momentarily slipped behind a few clouds before coming back out, golden and bright, reminding her of a woman parting a set of lace curtains in a window and peering through the opening. They'd had curtains like that when she was a kid, and her mother would check on her when she was riding her bike outside, her tired, beaming face appearing in the apartment's smeary window. Like a ghost. Like the sun.

Spengler had grown up in Kansas—most of her life she'd lived in Dodge City, a town most famous for Wyatt Earp and Doc Holliday. It was a flat place, where the wind was always blowing hard, carrying the smell of manure and farmland with every gust, and the eighteen-foot-high slide at Doc's Yee-Haw Water Fun Zone was the tallest thing around, so she'd never experienced anything like this. From this spot she could see for miles. Over most of the park, she thought, acres and acres of trees and rock and land, all the way to the little town of Estes Park, where there were already small lights twinkling. Beyond that would be Denver and home, but that was lost in a mist that blurred the horizon. It reminded her of the first time she'd seen the ocean, sitting in the passenger seat during a road trip to San Diego: the Pacific had been on her right as they headed south on the freeway, but it hadn't looked real. It couldn't be real, she'd thought. It looked like a painting or some strange special effect on TV. But there were ships out there, seemingly motionless on the water, and it stretched on forever. She found it terrifying. Her mother, an immigrant from South Korea, had laughed at this.

I spent hours and hours in a plane going over the ocean to get to America, she always said. *It's just water.*

This view from the cliff gave Spengler that same creeping fear she'd gotten from the ocean. As she left the safety of the tree cover, still fifteen feet away from the edge, she was doused with an unnerving wave of nausea. Her palms and the soles of her feet were slick with sweat. She went a few steps closer before her feet refused to take another step. She leaned, feet planted wide and firm, and tried to peek over the side. From where she was she could see part of the river below, and some of the men who were still searching. From this far up they looked like ants. Earlier, there'd been plenty of chitchat and laughter between the men as they worked, but from up here she couldn't hear any of it. If they screamed she'd probably hear it, but all that came to her now was the roaring of the water, and she felt a fine spray of moisture on her cheeks. The wind had picked up and she didn't dare go any nearer to the rock's lip. She didn't think it could blow her right off, but she didn't want to take any chances.

She tried to imagine going out to the very edge to look over and couldn't. Matt Evans said that was what Marie had done. She'd wanted to look straight down, and Evans had retreated into the brush to relieve himself. He hadn't seen her fall, he said. He'd heard her scream, and when he'd come running out with his zipper open and his pants loose around his hips his wife was gone, swallowed up by the dark waters below.

CHAPTER TWENTY-ONE

Spengler took the interstate to work and back home again every day, a straight shot up and down I-25, and every evening she was sure to look at the big electronic billboard hanging over the southbound lanes. This was the message it flashed, only a few words at a time, so it read like some strange poetry:

> *Be Careful*
> *Drive Safe*
> *Number of Car Deaths This Year*
> *In State Is*
> *137*
> *Buckle Up*
> *Pay Attention*

She'd first started paying attention to the sign a few weeks before, although she'd been driving the same way to work every day for almost a year and it had probably been up that whole time only she'd overlooked it. Now she looked for it every day to see if the number had changed, if more people had died. There were days when it didn't change at all, sometimes a week when that number didn't move, and then suddenly it would, jumping up, ten or fifteen at a time, and she'd think that life is often that way. One day there's nothing, and the next day it's everything.

Tony was still awake when she got home. She saw his silhouette in the open door as she pulled up to the house, the outline of his nose and the curl of his hair where it'd grown too long on his neck. They'd met five years before at a bar downtown, close to the police station. Tony had been working behind the bar, she was a customer. It was a Tuesday night—slowest night of the week—and she'd ordered water and a Cobb salad.

"Nothing to drink?" he'd asked, gesturing at the rows of glittering bottles on the mirrored shelves behind him. He leaned over the counter on his elbows and grinned. "I can mix you anything you'd like."

"Anything?" she asked, raising an eyebrow. It was the familiar ebb and flow of flirting, comforting as the back and forth sway of a rocking chair. She'd never known how to flirt until she'd gone undercover, casing a sex trafficking ring operating out of Denver, and then she'd only gotten good out of necessity. "What if I ask for something you don't know how to make?"

"Then your dinner is on the house."

"And what if I can't stump you?"

"Then you have to buy me dinner. But not in this place."

"Deal."

"What'll you have?"

She considered.

"I once went out with some coworkers and they ordered a Corpse Reviver. I'd like one of those, please."

Three minutes later he was carefully sliding the drink onto a cocktail napkin in front of her. She tweezed out the sword toothpick that'd been stuck through a cherry and took a deep drink, then sighed in satisfaction.

"How did you know how to make it?" she asked.

He crossed his arms over his chest and smiled. Winked.

"Looks like you owe me dinner. Tomorrow night work for you?"

Years later, after they were married, Spengler thought of that drink and asked again. Tony grinned and ducked his head.

"I had fast internet on my phone," he said. "I had to look up recipes that way all the time. But I must've mixed it right. It got me that dinner."

"I have no idea if it was right," she said, grinning back. "I'd never had one before that night, but it was pretty damn tasty."

Now Tony came out the door and down the driveway to meet her. He took the travel coffee mug and the small stack of mail she'd collected from the lockbox around the corner, then held out his hand to help her from the car. She took it gratefully.

"Long day?" he asked. Tony was the only man she'd ever dated who hadn't had a problem with her job. Most men were either afraid of cops or they had weird sexual fantasies about being handcuffed and beaten.

"Yeah."

"You're limping," he said. He looked down and frowned. "You didn't wear flip-flops to work this morning, did you?"

"No. It's a long story."

"Dinner's ready. I waited to eat with you."

"Is he still awake?"'"

"Nope, been asleep for hours. He wouldn't take a nap earlier, so he crashed hard."

She went upstairs. Their bedroom was on the right, two others on the left. One was open—Tony's office. It was where he worked on the freelance writing jobs he got, although she'd noticed those had been coming less and less over the last few months. She hadn't asked about it; she didn't want him to think she was worried. They'd both agreed that she would go back to work after Elliott was born and he would stay at home. He couldn't make as much money as she did, and it just made sense. It'd been Tony's idea to begin with, and he handled the whole thing with good grace, but she could sometimes feel him bristling at the idea of being stuck at home with a toddler, cooking dinner and cleaning.

You're such a progressive family. That's what one of the mothers at the park had said to Tony not long before. *And you're comfortable with your wife being the main breadwinner? That's so neat.*

They were a progressive family, Denver was a progressive city, but the long shadows of the past were still around, hiding, waiting to trip you up if you didn't keep an eye out. Tony's mother liked to make sly comments during her weekly phone call with her son, sighing and asking when he was planning on finding a job, that real men worked while the wife stayed at home, as if they were all starving. And then there was the struggle Spengler had at work, trying to find her place in a field where men dominated. Yes, they were progressive, exhaustingly so. *Neat-o.*

The second door had been pulled halfway shut to block out the light from the hallway and she slipped inside, moving sideways to get by without disturbing anything. Elliott was on his back, his long eyelashes fluttering against his cheeks as he dreamt, his dark hair curling and damp with sweat. He'd turned two the week before, and they'd celebrated by moving him out of his crib and into a big-kid bed. She leaned over and kissed him on the forehead. She sometimes wondered if she was missing the best part of her son's life by working, but then felt guilty because she so rarely thought about either Elliott or Tony when she was on the clock.

"He still sawing twigs in there?" Tony asked when she came out again.

"Yeah."

"You want to get changed and I'll meet you downstairs?"

"Okay."

She hadn't yet kicked off the flip-flops when her cell phone rang. She dug it out of her purse. It was Jackson.

"Did you find her?" she asked, perching on the edge of the bed and looking at her feet. There was a flap of skin hanging off her ankle, and she gave it a delicate tug to see if it would peel away. It didn't, but only made her hiss in pain.

"Nope. But a group came by right after you left. They'd been out farther for the last few nights, camping."

"I thought camping was prohibited out there."

Jackson snorted.

"Some of these people think the rules don't apply to them.

Anyway, they came by and asked what we were doing, and said they'd heard a woman screaming that night. They'd thought it was a joke. Someone fooling around."

"Okay. Marie Evans screamed when she fell, her husband said that."

"Yeah, but these guys said this woman didn't just scream. She said, *Please, stop. Don't.* Shouted it, and then screamed."

"'Please, stop, don't'?"

"Yeah."

"If you accidentally fell off a cliff is that what you would scream?"

Jackson laughed half-heartedly. He sounded tired.

"I guess it may've been right to send you out here to poke around. Looks like this Evans guy might've killed his wife, after all."

CHAPTER TWENTY-TWO

August 31, 2018

Oh, he's fucked, now. Hard. No lube, either. Ralphie Loren, this is your lucky day. Bend over and grab your ankles, take a deep breath. This one's gonna hurt.

"It never occurred to you this might be something you'd want to share?" Chief Black demanded. "I sure as hell could've used a warning before getting a visit from that detective."

"I didn't think it would get this far."

"It wouldn't have gotten this far at all if you'd clued me in."

"I'm sorry. You're right, I should've told you about this."

Black paused. In surprise, maybe, but Loren wasn't sure. The chief had been working on his poker face for years and the damn thing was nearly perfect. It was most likely surprise, though, because when had anyone ever heard Ralph Loren apologize for anything? And admitting he was wrong was even more of a shock. You could say the sky was blue and Loren would harass and threaten and tease and bully until you admitted it was green—and not because he actually thought the sky was green, but because he liked to know he could force you to agree with him.

Loren was spooked, Black thought. He'd worked with Loren for years and he'd never seen him like this. It was as if the man had seen a ghost. And that's exactly what it was. The ghosts of the past had been chasing Loren for a long time, and they'd finally found his home address and come calling.

"Okay, then why don't you tell me now?" Black said, sitting back and folding his hands on top of his considerable gut.

Loren hesitated.

"I can't."

"Why not?"

"Because it would open all sorts of other questions I can't answer."

"Can't or won't?"

"Both, I guess."

"I wish I knew what you're talking about."

"I wish I could explain better."

"Then goddammit, Loren, *try*!" Black shouted. He slammed a fist on the desk. The cup of pencils wobbled and then stilled without tipping. Barely. "I get an unannounced visit from a detective based in your hometown, claiming you murdered your partner thirty years ago and they just found his body in an unmarked grave, and that's not something you can explain?"

"No, boss."

"It's a simple question, Loren. Did you murder this guy? Lucas Gallo, that was his name, right?"

Loren started to say something, then thought better of it and sat back silently.

"You're not even going to defend yourself? This detective seems pretty certain you're the one behind this. Your partner went missing, and you transferred out six weeks later. Sounds like he's got one helluva good case against you."

"I don't have anything to say."

Black wearily rubbed his hand down his face. Every conversation with Loren tended to be frustrating, but this was worse than usual. He'd never seen Loren clam up, and he wasn't sure how to handle it.

"This detective—" Black glanced down at a paper on his desk. "—Pete Ortiz, you know him?"

"Yeah."

"He said when your partner went missing, his wife and kid vanished, too. They're thinking they'll find them next, buried a little farther on. Is that what's going to happen, Loren?"

Again, silence.

"You know what this Ortiz asked me to do? He wants me to put you on an unpaid suspension while he's investigating."

"Is that what you're gonna do?"

"Hell, no. I asked if you were officially a suspect in the case, and he said no. He doesn't have anything on you except some gossip from thirty years ago. So I let him know I don't have the backup manpower available to just cut one of my guys loose. He wasn't too pleased with my response, but it isn't his decision. So I need to know, Loren. Are they going to be able to connect you to this body?"

Loren let out a deep breath, setting his lips flapping.

"I don't think so, boss."

"You sure you don't want to tell me what happened?"

"Trust me, you don't want to know."

"I do want to know, but it sounds like I'm not gonna get the story out of you."

Loren shrugged. Black seemed ready to blow up again, then thought better of it and sat back with a disgusted sigh.

"All right. You need to keep yourself busy, then. What's going on with the Simmons case?"

Dana Simmons and her three kids had been reported missing by her husband two weeks before. Two days later her car was found on the top level of a parking garage downtown, and she was dead behind the wheel. Her kids were in the back, also deceased.

"Coroner's report came through yesterday. Murder-suicide," Loren said. "She overdosed the kids on sleeping pills and then put a gun in her mouth."

"What else you working?"

"I'm waiting on ballistics for the shooting out in Curtis Park, and the DNA results for the Adoba case." Loren shrugged. "Treading water at this point, can't do anything else until the other departments get off their asses and actually do their jobs."

"Go back through the files, then. Talk to some witnesses. Tag along as help on another case," Black said impatiently. "I don't give a flying fuck what you do as long as Ortiz doesn't show up here again and find you asleep behind your desk. Try to look like a man doing his job. Act normal for once in your goddamn life. Keep yourself occupied until all this blows over."

Black's eyes narrowed as he watched Loren stand up. If Loren left without a smart-ass remark, it would be a first. The door began to snick shut, but then opened again. Loren poked his head around.

"Forgot to tell you what a nice shirt that is, boss," he said.

"Thank you."

"The way it clings to those man titties of yours is sure to get some of the boys to at least half mast, if you know what I mean. You might not want to sashay around the bullpen looking like that."

It was a typical Loren remark, but without the usual zest in the delivery. Even when he was sick as a dog Loren enjoyed giving every one shit, but this was a pale imitation.

Spooked, Black thought as he watched Loren walk away through his wall of windows. And for the first time in Loren's twenty years with the DPD, he had the slow walk and shoulder slump of an old man.

CHAPTER TWENTY-THREE

"Where you heading, Spengler?" Loren asked. She was the first detective he saw, so she'd won without even knowing she was playing. That was the bitch of things in Homicide—it was either feast or famine. There were times when it seemed like the entire city was busy killing each other, usually around the holidays or during high summer, but then there were times when everything was quiet. Those between-times felt like waiting. Waiting for the other shoe to drop, or maybe it was the ax, and this was just another one of those times.

Spengler's desk was out in the center of the bullpen, where it was the loudest. That's where the newbies started, and after a while you got to move farther out, maybe even end up in a private office. She looked up in surprise at his question. She'd just slipped her purse over her shoulder and had her car keys jingling in her hand.

She was the new kid on the block, the latest addition to Denver's Homicide department. Loren had heard some of the guys moaning over the way her ass looked in the pantsuits she wore, clutching their chests and rolling their eyes into the back of their heads when they thought she wasn't looking, although Loren had an idea she knew exactly what was going on. She wasn't an idiot, like so many others who'd ended up promoted to detective. She'd been in charge of a major sex trafficking case that stretched across several states but was based in Denver, had spent months undercover until it culminated in a bust at the Western Stock Show. She was a big deal, and when Chief Black had offered her a choice of assignments she'd asked for Homicide. She'd been with the department a few weeks now but still hadn't managed to make any friends. There was something standoffish about her that put people off.

"I'm driving out to Estes Park again."

"For what?"

"To get statements from some campers."

"Why wouldn't you have them come down here?"

"I'm going up there anyway to watch the search, I figured this would be easier for everyone. They're waiting for me at the Estes police station."

"I've never seen you dressed like that before."

She was wearing blue jeans and a T-shirt with a flannel layered over the top. On her feet were hiking boots, brown with red laces. They looked brand-new.

"I would've dressed like this yesterday if I'd known what I was in for." She smiled at him. Her lips were stretched as thin and sharp as a razor.

His cell phone buzzed inside in his pocket.

"I'm gonna tag along with you today."

Spengler frowned.

"Why? You've got cases of your own."

"Yeah, I do," Loren said. "But if I had a choice between waiting on these dipshits to deliver lab results or chew off my own fingers, I'd be nothing but palms. And then how would I wipe my ass?"

Spengler blinked.

"What're you talking about?"

Loren sighed.

"I'm tagging along," he said. "You've got a partner. Congrats, Spengler. It's a boy!"

Spengler gave him a strange look.

"Okay," she said. "Let's go. I'm already running late as it is."

His phone buzzed again.

"I've gotta take this call. Give me five minutes and I'll meet you out in the parking lot."

"All right," Spengler said. She didn't look thrilled to have him coming, and that made him smile for the first time that morning. And it wasn't one of those smarmy, polite smiles most people wear all the time, their lips pursed so tight they look like puckered little buttholes, but a real big grin.

"Preach, you there?" Loren said, pressing the phone against his ear and watching Spengler march down the hall toward the elevator. She pushed the button and then disappeared down the stairwell, too impatient to wait. But she didn't walk—no, Spengler slammed the door open hard enough that the wall shook and several heads turned curiously, and he could hear the angry stamp of her feet as she went down. Loren's grin widened.

"It's Captain Preach to you now, dipshit."

"Captain? Big mistake, putting you in charge of anything."

Captain Robert Preach had been Detective Robbie Preach

thirty years before, when Loren had first been hired on with the Springfield Police Department. Back then Loren had thought he'd live the rest of his life in Ohio—there were plenty who did, lived and died within the city limits—but now he thought of Springfield *not* as the armpit of America, but the perineum, the tender spot between the balls and asshole where the dingleberries grow thickest. He'd been lucky to escape—not that he'd gloat about it to guys like Preach, who were still there.

"You still pissing on electric fences?" Loren asked. Back in the day they'd called Preach Cocksmoke, after the night he'd drunkenly urinated on a fence surrounding a cattle ranch, and the current had zapped him and thrown him back ten feet. Loren swore he'd seen tendrils of smoke curling up from Preach's balls and disappearing into the night sky, and while the nickname didn't stick, the story had become legend.

"Fuck off," Preach said loftily. "You know I'd love to listen to your dumb ass chatter on like a schoolgirl, but I've got a meeting with the city commissioner in a few so I've gotta be quick. And you're the one who called me, I'm just getting back to you. What's up?"

This was also the Preach Loren remembered. He was a guy who'd fall asleep at his desk and fart so loud it'd wake him up and he'd tip right out of his chair, but he wasn't full of shit like so many other cops were. Straight down to business when he had to be.

"Ortiz showed up out here, paid my boss-man a visit about Gallo."

There was a pause so long, Loren thought they might've been disconnected until Preach finally sighed.

"Oh, shit, Loren. I had no idea. That cocksucker said he was going on vacation, out to California. I told him to leave you outta this whole thing, but he couldn't let it go. I'm gonna rip that idiot's asshole a mile wide when he gets back here."

Loren closed his eyes and listened to the sound of Preach's fury. It was almost soothing. Took him back to his roots. He'd come onto the Springfield PD and cut his teeth on guys who all talked the same way, and he was a perfect product of his environment—he was loud and full of curses and threats and anger. They'd all been that way. *Raucous*, that was the word for them. And they had plenty of good times. They'd spend their entire lives together—at work, then later at each other's homes, drinking and playing poker and telling dirty jokes and watching the Bengals get destroyed on the field yet again, and they fought like they were brothers. Their lives were hard, crusty outsides disguising the soft parts beneath. People around here thought Loren was a head case, always screaming and throwing around insults, but if they could only see the Springfield station when all the boys were there, present and accounted for. No one knew how easy they had it with only Loren to deal with.

"Did they really find Gallo?" Loren asked when Preach's fury had burned out some.

"Yeah. A developer was out by the Mad River, doing some digging to pour foundations, and they found the remains."

"Shit. And it's definitely Gallo?"

"Yeah. Coroner said he was nothing but bones wrapped in one of those tracksuits he always wore. You remember how loud he'd be walking around in those with his thighs rubbing together?"

"He was so pissed when I said he sounded like a giant zipper being pulled up and down."

"And then you turned on that Madonna CD he kept in his desk."

"Gallo in a tracksuit dancing to *Like a Virgin*. That's my entire recollection of the eighties."

There was a pause, and Loren again thought the connection had been dropped or that Preach had simply hung up, but then he heard a wheeze and realized Preach was laughing. He'd forgotten how he always did it silently, his belly and shoulders shaking, the tears running freely down his pock-scarred face.

"Same, Ralphie. Same. Man, fuck the eighties. It was bad."

Ralphie, another blast from the past. They all had nicknames, called each other Shitbrick and Jack-Off and Cocksmoke, the usual boys' club idiocy, but the only thing anyone had ever called Loren was Ralphie. Gallo had been a part of the good times, too, although there'd always been something a little off about him. *Skewed*, that was the best word for it. Like a figure in a picture that's just barely out of focus, and if you squint hard enough, tilt your head to one side, you just might be able to make out their face. But no one had ever complained about Gallo. Because they hadn't all just worked together, they were brothers, they were family, and you don't snitch on family.

"Should I be worried about Ortiz?"

"I—I don't know, man. He's still nursing old grudges, and he wants to make you pay."

"Yeah."

"He's been waiting for something like this to happen for a

long time. If he gets the chance he'll try to stomp you out like a bug."

Thirty years ago Pete Ortiz had been a skinny piece of shit with a zitty face and big, pouty lips that were like two pieces of raw tuna sliding against each other. He'd been promoted to detective before he was ready, but Ortiz had known important people—or he'd known *information* about important people and had gotten exactly what he wanted. He'd been made a detective, and the other guys would've accepted him except he was a know-it-all shit for brains. He'd walk around the station with his fingers hooked into the belt loops of the Wranglers he wore so tight you could see the outline of his cock under the denim and tell men who'd been on the force longer than he'd been alive how to do their jobs. And if anyone told him to go screw himself, he'd pout and whine and moan and probably add their name to a secret list of people who deserved payback, kept safe in his own head. Ortiz was the worst weasel Loren had ever met, but he was mostly beneath Loren's notice until two things happened.

First, Loren and Gallo, who'd been partners for going on five years, had a falling-out. *Falling-out* was not an explosive enough word for what happened, but it was what the paperwork put in each of their employee files stated. They were both reassigned and given new partners.

Gallo took Ortiz on as his. And Ortiz, young kid that he was, a dipstick still wet behind the ears, worshipped the ground Gallo walked on.

And then Gallo disappeared. His whole family did. And while most people decided Gallo had picked up and left town, bailed on everything, Ortiz was sure it was a case of foul play, and he'd narrowed his focus and the blame on Loren.

And man, he was right.

"This'll blow over. Ortiz isn't a bad apple, not like he used to be. He's grown up."

"Yeah," Loren said, although his question was still hanging out there—do I have to worry about Ortiz? It didn't matter to him if he was a bad apple or a good guy or a dancer in the motherfucking Lollipop Guild, he was only concerned if Ortiz was poking too deep into corners, if he was stirring up old ghosts that'd cause trouble.

"Don't worry, it's not a big deal," Preach said. "Ortiz'll get tired of Denver soon enough and come home, and I'll take care of him. You're fine."

Act normal, Chief Black had said. Keep yourself occupied until this blows over.

Do you think I did it? Loren wanted to ask, the urge so strong he had to close his fist and sink his fingernails down into his palm to keep his mouth shut. *Because it sure as hell sounds like you do, old friend. Like all you motherfuckers are sure I did it. Like you think I'm guilty and you're keeping a secret for me.*

Good times and good ol' boys like Preach, pulling together to protect their own.

CHAPTER TWENTY-FOUR

"I don't understand why you're still in this same area," Spengler said to the head of the search team. "You spent all day in this spot yesterday."

"Oh, we've moved down about a hundred yards," the man said comfortably. Loren liked the calm way he was handling Spengler. Most men saw a gun on a woman's hip strapped beside the badge and crumbled, or got defensive. "Just trying to be thorough."

"But if the victim was caught in the current, wouldn't she be farther on?"

"That's what everybody thinks," Jackson said. "But a body sinks in fresh water, you see—"

Loren wandered away, no interest in a science lesson. He already knew what the man was going to say; he'd learned it years before, no need to hear it again:

A human body sinks in fresh water, and in a river ends up down at the bottom where there's no current moving anything. So the body stays there until something physically moves it, or it begins to decompose and starts to float, rising up to the surface. But before that, when the body is fresh and the water is cold and hasn't become swollen yet, it most likely hasn't moved far from where it went under. A few hundred yards at the very most. Marie Evans had fallen off that cliff two days before, so she was just about as fresh as it got. If she was still in the water, she was somewhere close.

If she was in the water? Loren snorted. Where else would she be? A fall from 120 or 130 feet straight down to the rocks and water below, the chance she'd survived was zilch. And if the campers Spengler had spoken with were telling the truth, Marie Evans hadn't just fallen. She'd been pushed.

What made you think a woman begging for mercy was a joke? Spengler had asked. There were three of them, young men with unkempt beards and beanie caps pulled low over their foreheads. Used to be that men with beards like that were thought to be either homeless or sexual predators, but times had changed. Loren had watched Spengler interview the men at the Estes Park station while he stood off to one side, his back pressed against the side of a humming vending machine. The three men were seated around a table and kept eyeballing him nervously. Spengler shot him a single glare and then didn't deign to look at him again.

It didn't sound like she was serious, one of them said. He spoke for all of them, like they were sharing one mouth. *I swear, I thought I heard her laugh before the last scream.*

She laughed?

I don't know for sure. I might've just been hearing things.

That's why you didn't bother coming to see if anything was wrong?

Yeah. And it was getting dark out, and it's no joke getting hurt out there. No cell phone reception and it gets cold at night. We listened and didn't hear anything else.

No other screams for help?

Nope. It was quiet after that.

Were you gentlemen drinking that night?

They'd looked at each other and then back at Spengler.

Yeah, we were pretty sauced.

Smoking anything?

Yeah, maybe a little.

They'd gotten the statement and then they'd hiked down to this spot by the river, where a team had been working since first light, poking and prodding and dragging the river. It was only midmorning and the sky was still blue and clear, but the dark clouds building in the western horizon promised a storm. That was how it'd been for most of August, which was unusual. Fucking El Niño, causing all sorts of problems.

Loren walked away from the river and went toward the cliff base. It was sheer-faced rock for most of the way, smooth as if it'd been chiseled by a giant, and then, very near the top, was the rock platform. It looked like a person could jump on it hard and cause it to break and separate from the rest, and that was where Marie Evans had been standing when she went over the edge. It was like a diving board from hell.

He stood directly beneath the platform and stared straight up. It was hard to see anything from so far away and it was dark on the underside, especially with the sun almost directly overhead. Nothing but a sheet of unrelenting darkness.

Chief Black was right. Act normal, work a case. If Matt Evans really had pushed his wife, this was now a homicide investigation—Spengler's first. And she'd need help. It would keep his mind off things. Ortiz would go back to Springfield and they'd find someone else to pin Gallo's murder on, or it would stay open forever. Ortiz wouldn't find anything to connect Gallo back to him.

Would he?

No. Loren had been careful. Maybe not as careful as he was these days, but still careful. He hadn't left anything behind when he'd planted Gallo's ass in the mud beside the river, and thirty years is a long time. Time was the best way to get rid of evidence, any cop could tell you—

"Loren?"

He jumped at Spengler's voice and looked over his shoulder.

She was smiling, bemused. "You see anything interesting up there?"

"Give me a warning before you try to scare me into a heart attack, Spengler," he said. His heart was thumping unpleasantly hard against his chest and he tried to keep from seeming like he was out of breath. She gave him a strange look and turned back to the water. He didn't look up at the underside of the platform again. He'd startled and had twisted his neck at a strange angle, and in that sudden move-ment he saw something on the underside of the cliff. He looked down, rubbing and kneading the muscle in his neck, then turned his face up again.

"You see something?" Spengler asked, her eyes sweeping the rock.

"I . . . don't know," he said. "I thought I did. But maybe it was nothing."

Spengler nodded and wandered away, and Loren dropped his head, rolled it around on his shoulders to try to work out the kink. He thought he'd seen a flash of silver up there, a glint of metal, but it was a nothing. The pain jolting through his neck and up to his brain, making him see that flash of lightning.

But at his feet—what was this? Slowly, Loren kneeled to get a closer look.

It was a single dot of what looked like blood. If it was blood it had to be fresh, within the last few days. Any longer than that and the blood would have oxidized and turned black. He looked up at the rock ledge again. It was directly over his head like a roof. He pulled an evidence bag out of his pocket and scooped up the rocks flecked with the blood. It immediately crumbled into a thousand pieces at his touch, but the lab geeks would be able to find something even in that mess. They always did.

CHAPTER TWENTY-FIVE

"You plan on sticking around for this investigation?" Spengler asked Loren as they headed away from the river, back up the trail. She didn't look directly at him, but quickly glanced his way from the corner of her eye.

"Is it a problem if I do?"

"No, just asking. I wouldn't mind learning a few things from you."

"You definitely will."

She shot him a withering glare then.

"I was going to say, I've heard you're the best, although I haven't seen any indication of it so far."

"If you were a man I'd punch you in the head for that comment."

"Please don't let my lack of testicles keep you from trying it," she said. "I have a good feeling I'd kick your ass all over the side of this mountain."

Loren stopped in his tracks, shocked. Spengler ignored him and kept going up the trail. He laughed. He couldn't remember the last time anyone had dared to smart off to him like that, unless it was Gallo—

That squashed the amusement faster than anything else could have.

They passed a tree with a trunk turned completely black and dead, bare of leaves. It looked like it'd been torched in a fire, leaving it twisted and warped while everything else around was left untouched. A hangman's tree, Loren thought. With the one thick branch sticking off to one side like an arm, it was perfect.

"I've been thinking about what those campers said in their statement," Spengler said slowly.

"What's that?"

"They said they heard a woman beg, and then scream. And that was it."

"I'm not following."

"In his initial statement, Matt Evans said his wife screamed and fell. Then he said he'd gone to the edge himself and screamed her name. Said he shouted for help. He said he lost his voice because of how much he was yelling."

"So if he'd been screaming, those guys would've heard him."

"Right. Unless they were too drunk and stoned to hear anything. And that alone makes them unreliable witnesses."

Loren shot her a look.

"I understand in cases like this the spouse is almost always the killer," Spengler said.

"Yeah. I know," Loren said. "How about less talk and more walk, eh? I'd like to get outta here. Nature gives me the creeps."

Spengler drove fast, wove in and out of traffic like she had a demon on her ass, chasing her down the interstate. Loren liked that. He leaned the passenger seat back and stared out the window. A little red sports car shot by, going faster than Spengler's little import could ever hope to go, and a minivan pulled up beside them. There was a girl in the backseat, no more than six or seven years old, with her hair cut so short she looked more than a little like Peter Pan. When she saw Loren looking she flipped him the bird. It made him smile.

Spengler thought he hated her, he knew. But he didn't. He actually didn't feel one way or another about her, and he treated her with the same indifference and derision he gave everyone, she just hadn't realized it yet. She stayed silent as they drove, kept the radio set at a politely low volume. The bounce of the car as they sped along the road and the warmth of the muted afternoon light pouring through the windshield made him sleepy, and he didn't fight the heavy lowering of his eyelids. He didn't sleep much these days. *Couldn't* sleep, that was a better way to put it. The insane were often insomniacs—or was it the other way around? Insomniacs were often insane?

He couldn't remember.

His eyes shut and he didn't quite fall asleep, but instead landed somewhere in between. He heard the soft notes coming from the car's radio and the ticking noise of Spengler chewing her fingernails, but his mind was drifting like an empty raft on a calm sea. He thought of Chief Black telling him to keep busy. He'd gotten the same advice from the doctor he'd been seeing for more than fifteen years. Dr. Patel, a man with liquid brown eyes and discolored skin at his knuckles. He always had flecks of white spittle dried at the corners of his mouth, like he'd just had a glass of milk.

You have to keep busy, Ralph, Patel had said to him. His voice was soothing and melodic. A trace of a British accent around the vowels. *An idle mind is the best way to fall into old habits.*

CHAPTER TWENTY-SIX

Matt Evans had always had an appreciation for fine things, and that was probably because he'd never had any fine things of his own as a kid. He'd grown up poor. Not poor enough that he went hungry or wore rags to school, but poor enough to get the government-subsidized free lunch offering at his public school. Poor enough that his mother had bought most of his clothes at the Salvation Army thrift shop and he didn't have his own car until he was well into his twenties and he didn't have a checking account until after *that*—because if you don't have the cash to put into the bank, what was the point? He'd gone to college for a business degree (just like every other bozo who had no idea what to major in) but had never finished, and then moved to Denver after Janice's death and took the only job he could find—selling cars. He hated it, but here's the thing: it's almost always the case that a person is good at the thing he hates the most. And Matt was good. He sold a car on his first day—*beginner's luck*, the other guys scoffed. *You gotta let them get that first one so they'll feel good about themselves*. But then Matt kept selling cars, more every day, and the atmosphere at the dealership became like that of a shark tank, the water teeming with blood. Matt could sell any car on the lot, he'd attach every service plan available, every extended warranty. He sold heated leather seats and sunroofs and remote starts and car bras to keep those pesky bugs from smooshing against the hood and ruining the paint jobs.

No one could say no to Matt Evans.

That he was too talented for car sales was quickly apparent. And someone noticed—specifically, a gentleman who'd come in to simply browse the newest year's models and drove away in a car he hadn't intended to buy, one fixed up with every possible upgrade, as well as vouchers for three years' worth of oil changes, prepaid and rolled into the monthly installment. He also came away with a new salesman for his team. He was head of a growing nationwide sandwich restaurant that'd started selling franchises, and they needed good men to sell them. For the mere price of $250,000, a person could sell artisan meats slapped between slices of freshly baked bread (a proprietary recipe!) to the hungry masses—but it wasn't only about feeding people, although food is life, and *good food* is a godsend, it was also about the dream every person had of owning their own business. Being their own boss. It was the AMERICAN DREAM. (Matt's sales pitches were a thing of wonder. He was as precise as a surgeon with a scalpel, passionate as a pianist performing at their career-making concert. The underlying message was always the same, but each pitch changed, even if just a little. Every meeting he took, every person he spoke with, he came prepared, and everyone needs something different. But in every pitch he used those words—AMERICAN DREAM—and in a way that the person on the other side of the table understood it was being said in all capitals, and bolded. Times change, and people change, but the ideal of the AMERICAN DREAM was forever, and it always worked. Hooked the target like a fish, and he reeled them right to shore.)

So Matt went from selling cars to selling businesses—or rather, the AMERICAN DREAM—and his paychecks went from no big deal to heavy hitters. He was suddenly able to afford things he'd never had before—a big house and designer clothes and fancy cars—and he found he took comfort in them. More comfort than he'd ever gotten out of Marie or their two daughters.

Love is fleeting, after all. But *stuff*—stuff lasts forever.

Like now, sitting in his kitchen with the two detectives from the Denver Police Department and answering their questions about what'd happened to Marie, he was aware of the dim gleam of the stainless steel front of the Viking fridge and the E. Dehillerin copper pots and pans hanging above the island and the minute movements of the hands of the twenty-thousand-dollar watch on his wrist. In fact, he kept swiping the pad of his thumb over the face of his watch. It was a tic, one that Loren picked up on right away. It took Spengler a little longer to catch it, but not much longer. It might mean he was lying, or that he was nervous. Both, or neither.

He'd finished telling these cops what'd happened to Marie—he'd told the park rangers, he'd told the cops in Estes Park, and now these two, third time's the charm, he could only hope—and then they'd asked him to write it out and sign that it was complete and true, and that he was aware they'd also recorded an audio of his official statement.

"You said you took a picture of Marie before she fell,"

Spengler said as she folded up the signed statement and tucked it into her pocket.

"Yes."

"Do you still have it?"

"Yeah, hang on."

He picked up his phone and swiped through a few screens before handing it over. It was a good picture. The wind had gusted just before he'd taken it, and Marie's hair had flown into her face, covering most of it, making her laugh. Spengler smiled as she looked at it.

"If you'll forward that to me, I'd appreciate it," she said. She held the phone to Loren, but he only gave his head the tiniest shake. He hadn't said one word the entire time, not even to introduce himself. He just *looked,* his eyes ticking back and forth as Spengler asked questions and Matt answered, and his silence was worse than anything. Matt was a man who'd built his entire fortune on words, using them like a prod and a sword and a gentle touch, and the only people he'd never been able to sell to were the silent ones. Silence wasn't just golden—it was the best defense there was.

After a moment Spengler handed the phone back to Matt.

"Of course," he said.

"There is something we should tell you," Spengler said. "Three men have come forward, claiming they heard your wife begging before she fell." She flipped open her small notepad and glanced at the words there. " 'Please. Don't. No.' That's what they claim they heard her scream."

"I didn't hear any of that."

"In your statement you said you shouted your wife's name several times after she fell, then screamed for help?"

"Yes."

"These men never mentioned hearing you at all."

"I don't see how they couldn't have heard me. I shouted several times."

"Three men are claiming they heard your wife beg for mercy, then fall. Then silence. Three men against you."

"They're lying, then."

"Why would they lie?" Spengler was watching him curiously. Her eyes were light brown, slanted down at the corners. They made her look sad. Loren abruptly stood up and began wandering around the kitchen.

"I don't know. People do strange things for no reason at all."

"Like murder their wives?" Loren asked absently, running a finger along the edge of the granite countertop. Matt flinched at his voice. He'd learned to be prepared when heading into a sales pitch, to have all his ducks in a row, to know more than the other side. But this was a different situation, one he hadn't been able to prepare for, and it threw him off, made him nervous. It was a feeling he didn't like much.

"Are you accusing me of something, detective?"

"I'd never accuse anyone of anything," Loren said, grinning. In the light shining down from the can lights overhead his teeth looked gruesomely yellow. So did the whites of his eyes. Matt had never noticed it before, but the lights threw a sickly cast down on everything. Asylum lighting. He'd have to replace the bulbs when he had the chance. "But I do have a question. Did you push your wife off that cliff?"

"No."

"Okay." Loren started wandering again, opening up the

cabinets as he passed by and peering inside. Spengler was watching him, frowning hard, a deep line appearing between her brows.

"Okay?" Matt asked. "I'm confused."

"What don't you understand?" Loren asked. He opened the silverware drawer and pulled out a fork. Examined his reflection in the backside and then dropped it back in with the others. He tried to slam the drawer, but it was a soft close and gently drifted shut. "I asked a question, you answered it. What's confusing about it?"

"Uh, nothing, I guess."

"Good. But I do have another question for you."

"Okay."

"What's a place like this set you back?" Loren asked. "Big house in a historic neighborhood close to downtown, fully renovated, all the bells and whistles. It had to have been a pretty penny."

Matt looked from Loren to Spengler and then back again.

"Do I have to answer that?"

Loren pursed his lips and shrugged.

"Just curious," he said. "Real estate in Denver is so outrageous these days. What'd you nab this place for? A million?"

Matt coughed lightly.

"A million three."

Loren whistled through his teeth.

"That's quite a mortgage."

"It's not too bad."

Matt looked at Spengler again. She was watching him thoughtfully. If he were selling to these cops, Loren would be the impossible close. There were plenty like him, guys who'd come to sales seminars and take meetings claiming they were curious about the possible business opportunity, and they'd partake of plenty of the free refreshments and they'd flip through the literature, but when push came to shove, they'd walk. Pack it up and leave. Those guys had all sorts of questions and would try to lead you in circles by the nose, try to confuse things and cause problems just for the sheer fun of it. You had to learn to avoid guys like Loren, who took a certain cruel glee in making people squirm, because they didn't want to be closed. They couldn't be brought over the finish line, even if you held their hand and tried to lead them across the damn thing.

But Spengler—he'd be able to close Spengler. Don't pitch the bitch, a line from a movie that everyone in sales repeated, and it was mostly true. But there were those women who could be worked, and he had a feeling Spengler was one of those. It was the way she was looking at him, the way she'd sat back from the table and crossed her legs so he'd get a good look at her long stretch of thigh encased in tight denim. The feeling was nothing but the lightest tickle, but it was there, and if he'd learned one thing over all his years in sales, it was to trust those feelings.

"I do have a few more questions, if you don't mind," Spengler said.

"Not at all."

"How long have you and your wife been married?"

"Twenty-two years. We were in Estes to celebrate."

"Romantic getaway?"

"That's how it was meant to be."

"And you have two kids, don't you?"

"Two girls, yes."

"You have pictures? I'd love to see."

He opened up his phone again and clicked to a photo of the girls, then slid the phone across the table so Spengler could see.

"Hannah's on the left," he said. "The other one's Maddie."

"They look like good girls."

"They are."

"They didn't come home when they heard about their mother?"

"They did."

"They're here?" Spengler glanced toward the staircase that spiraled up to the second floor.

"No," Matt said slowly. "They rented a hotel room together."

"You have a big house here. Why wouldn't they just come home, save the money?"

"I don't know. They tend to do whatever they want. You'd have to ask them."

Spengler made a small noise he didn't know how to decipher and tapped the end of her ballpoint pen against her teeth.

"You're a lucky man." Spengler looked at the picture on the phone again, then smiled and slid the phone back across the table. "Beautiful girls. The older one looks a lot like your wife."

"Yes," he said. "Thank you."

"Okay, just a few more things, standard stuff, and we'll be out of your hair."

"Yeah, of course. I'm more than happy to answer whatever."

Spengler asked her questions. It was more than a few, and every new one made his insides shrivel. He'd expected questions, but not this many, and not thrown out so casually, one after the other, so fast. It was like being peppered with bullets from a machine gun.

When had they arrived in Estes Park for their vacation?

How long had they hiked that day?

Was Marie on any sort of medication, had there been any marital discord recently?

We'll need your daughters' cell phone numbers so we can contact them.

They were simple questions, and Evans had all the answers. Finally, Spengler flipped her notepad shut with a small sigh.

"It's been a long day for us, Mr. Evans," she said. "We've taken up enough of your time."

She stood, her chair squealing as it slid against the wood floor. He stood, too. It was over, thank god. They'd leave and he could be alone.

"If there's anything else I can do, please let me know," he said.

"Actually, there is something you could do," Spengler said. Matt saw then he'd made a mistake. He'd thought Spengler would be easy to close, she'd be the one to fool, she was eating his story right out of his hand, but he'd underestimated her. He saw it in the way she was gazing at him now, still smiling, but she might've been looking at a pile of dog shit she'd stepped in. "Could you come into the station tomorrow to take a polygraph? It's up to you, but it'll certainly help move our investigation along."

"But it's Labor Day weekend."

A vertical crease had appeared between her brows. Faint, but it was definitely there. That was her entire reaction, that single wrinkle. And then it smoothed out and was gone.

"Oh, I'm sorry," she said. "Did you have plans tomorrow? More important than helping us investigate your wife's death?"

"No," Matt said. "I just thought you might be off for the holiday."

"Oh, no. We'll be at the station there, first thing. So we'll see you tomorrow?"

"I didn't push my wife off that cliff, you know."

The words came before he could stop them. It was the wrong thing to say, he realized immediately. Too defensive. Spengler had been putting away her notes and paused with her hand still in her pocket, her gaze on him thoughtful.

"No one said you did," she said. "But we do have to cross every possible scenario off our list. Just going down the checklist, crossing off what's done."

"Then I'd be more than happy to take a lie detector," he said. No hesitation.

"Then I'll have one of the detectives call you and set up a time to come in," Spengler said pleasantly. She held eye contact for a beat too long. "Thank you for your time."

He walked them out, through the kitchen and the formal living room and into the foyer. It'd been sunny that morning but was now raining, a fine mist that seemed to blur everything. It was late enough that the streetlights had turned on, and the rain gave the impression of glowing halos around the bulbs. Loren flipped up his collar and went barreling right into the rain, but Spengler took a travel-size umbrella from the pocket of her jacket and unfurled it above her head. She hesitated, seeming ready to say something else, but instead walked down the steps to her car without another word.

CHAPTER TWENTY-SEVEN

The Evans house was an old brick place set close to the street, the kind of place everyone calls *historic,* a house that's been renovated on the outside to look *less* new and more like the way it was when it was first built. It had ropes of ivy creeping up one side, stained-glass windows that had to be original, and a wrought-iron fence surrounding the property. Inside was a steep staircase with nothing but a spindly railing to hold on to. Spengler knew there were people who liked this sort of old-timey architecture, but she was not one of them. She'd grown up in a place like this, an old house that'd been split into several separate apartments, and she still remembered the drafty winters and the high, cathedral ceilings, and the washer and dryer in the cold, dank basement that all the tenants shared.

But the Evans house wasn't that way inside, because they had money to sink into it, the funds to turn a crappy old place into something nice. The kitchen was brand-new, every surface sparkling, and the hardwood floors gleamed warmly. The house was casually decorated but still tasteful, so she knew a professional had done it, telling the Evanses just where that burgundy throw pillow should sit, or how the tapered candles on the mantel had to be cut to different heights to give the room *dimension*. And there were plenty of books. You could tell a lot about a person from what they read, Spengler knew. There was old stuff—Twain and Chandler and Christie—and there was newer stuff, too. Shelves and shelves of everything you could imagine, propped up with marble bookends made to look like classical Greek sculpture.

It was like living inside a Pottery Barn catalog. Except you didn't see police scrambling around the pages of a catalog, asking questions and taking notes and smiling grimly. And you'd certainly never see the detective in charge of the case walking slowly through the house toward the door, her hands behind her back, stopping every few steps to look at things, saving the images like snapshots in her brain. There was a statue sitting on an end table near the front door, a piece that didn't seem to fit in with the rest of the house but was there anyway. It was a sculpture of a fox, its tail curled around its delicate legs and its sleek, handsome snout pointed right at her. Her mother used to tell stories about a fox, but that story was about an evil spirit, a woman transformed into a fox with nine tails, a demon that would seduce men and then kill them. Children's stories from Korea, but that had been her mother, hadn't it? Always telling stories, so you could never quite tell the truth from the make-believe.

"Do I look like Dad?" she used to ask her mother. "Do I have his smile?"

She used to ask this, and her mother told her something different each time. That her father was an American spy and she'd never actually seen his face; that her father was famous and rich, an *American prince,* and you could see his face everywhere if you just looked; that her father was a ghost who'd come to her at night and put a baby in her belly—a sort of Virgin Mary origin story, Spengler had always thought. But finally, tired of her daughter's never-ending questions, she dug a Polaroid from deep in the zippered pocket of a suitcase Spengler had always thought was empty.

"He didn't talk a lot," her mother said. "He would just smoke. Sit at the table and smoke one cig after another."

That didn't tell Spengler a lot about her father, and the photograph, the only one they had, didn't say much more. The man in that photo was leaning against the side of a Buick, dressed in military fatigues, a cap pulled low over his forehead and mirrored aviator sunglasses covering his eyes. He had a mustache, a dark line against his upper lip, cut short and straight. There was nothing in that photo that gave her a clue about the man her father had been before deciding domestic life was for the birds and hightailing it out of there. She'd tried looking for him after her mother died, spent hours on the internet and combed public records, but her father didn't seem to exist. Or he didn't want to be found. Maybe there wasn't much of a difference.

"You drive," Spengler said, tossing Loren her keys as they walked away from the Evans house. "I need to check something."

She paused to look back at the house. One corner was rounded and rose up to a turret, the kind you'd expect a princess to live in. It was a beautiful house. But there was something old and knowing and sinister about it, too, like a house from a fairy tale where an old witch lives, busily spinning her sugar and spells and inviting children to lean into a hot oven. But maybe it wasn't the house itself that gave her the creeps, but the owners. Dogs and their owners started to look alike after a while, and maybe houses and the people who lived in them did, too.

"You plan on standing there with your thumb up your ass all night, or can we get going?" Loren demanded.

She climbed in and buckled up, then brought out her phone. Like most people, she spent too much time on it. Calling and texting and fooling around on news sites—it was all such a pointless time suck. But there were times like now when it came in handy.

"That prick is lying his ass off," Loren said.

"Oh, I'm sure," Spengler said, quickly typing a few words into the search engine bar. "But all we've got so far is statements from three men who were drunk that night, saying they *might* have heard Marie Evans begging for help. That's not enough to stand up in court."

"It's not enough to stand up anywhere. You should've given him more shit in there."

"Oh, the way you did? 'Did push your wife off that cliff? How much did you pay for this place?'"

"Why'd you pitch your voice so high to mimic me?"

"Because that's how you sound."

Loren snorted as he flipped on the blinker and turned onto Colorado Boulevard. Someone honked, and he waved dismissively.

"And what exactly did you get? Because as far I can tell you got just about diddly squat."

"Are you ever *not* an asshole?" she asked frankly. "Because it doesn't seem you know how to function otherwise."

"Oh, you know, anything worth doing is worth doing right."

"Here it is," she said excitedly, holding up her phone. "I *knew* it."

"Knew what?"

"I knew there was something weird about that guy."

"What'd you find?"

"When I was working Sex Crimes, I'd run names through our system at the station and come up with nothing. But you plug them into Google, you get back all sorts of stuff you weren't expecting. It's amazing. You can't have a mysterious background these days, not with everyone watching."

"Jesus-pleezus, Spengler. Spare me the lesson on the wonders of the internet and just do your fucking job. Did you find anything on him?"

She cleared her throat and quickly scrolled through the results on her phone.

"Okay, here's what we get with a quick search. Matthew Evans, age forty-seven. Lives in Denver. Executive vice president of sales for the Sandwich Company, LLC. And then the latest stuff in the news about the search for his wife."

"We already know all that."

"Okay, but how about this: He never said he was married previously, but he was. Her name was . . . Janice Roscoe. Oh, man."

She stopped.

"What is it?" Loren asked.

"Here, I'll just read it to you, it's from a newspaper article. Public records show Matthew T. Evans married Janice M. Roscoe on May 16, 1995, in Madison, Wisconsin. On

September 3, 1995, an unknown assailant broke into their home and attacked Evans, tied him up. Evans freed himself and got away, but Janice was killed and the house burned down." Spengler began to read faster, her voice rising with excitement. "An arrest was made, but it seems there were doubts about the suspect."

"You're sure it's *our* Matt Evans?"

"There's a photo. It's definitely him."

"So did Evans kill his first wife?"

"It looks like he was never officially charged, but the good people of Madison felt differently than the investigators. Seems people made him pretty uncomfortable, and he ended up leaving town after a while and moving to Denver."

Loren drummed his fingers on the steering wheel and nodded.

"We'll have to put in a call to the Madison PD and see if they'll send over the file," Spengler said. "Maybe it was a coincidence. Bad luck. Still not enough to arrest him."

"Two dead wives?" Loren said. For some reason he sounded happy, but when Spengler glanced at him sharply he was looking away, over his shoulder as he changed lanes. "Women have a funny way of dying around this guy. That's not bad luck. That's murder."

CHAPTER TWENTY-EIGHT

September 2, 2018

At fifteen, Spengler was walking dynamite, big in all the places men like best—breasts, ass, lips. Not that she was beautiful, just built like a woman, and there were times she'd walk down the street and cars would slow and voices would float out the open windows, men's voices speaking with the steady tones of chanting monks, floating up to the clouds like prayers. *Hey baby baby I got what you want exactly what you need yo*u'd *like everything I have to give you.* And there were other times, like when the kids found out she was only half white and that her mother was Korean, and they asked her if she always took off her shoes at home or if she only had sushi and rice at dinner, and once, a boy told her that Asian chicks had pussies that turned sideways instead of up and down, but since she was only half was hers set at an angle? He offered to check for her, leering, and his friends had been laughing and elbowing each other. She was cornered in a hallway at the high school by a half-dozen teenage boys, pressed up against a row of lockers during the seven-minute passing period, and the teachers that walked by acted like they didn't see anything at all. Safer that way, maybe. Because groups of men were like rabid dogs in heat, she'd learned it at a young age, and nothing had ever made her change her mind about *that*.

That boy, he'd been waiting for an answer, so she'd smiled and stepped close, reached between his legs, and he'd thought he was ready to get lucky, he'd grinned when he felt her hand slip down the front of his pants and her fingers tickle the underside of his balls, that stupid grin hadn't left his face until he felt her grip close down on him, pinching and painful, tight enough that he'd screamed like a pig. She hadn't let go, even when the boy started hitting her over the head and trying to get away and the rest of the boys were shouting and calling her names, and later there would be bruises on her back, scratches on her face, but none of that mattered, except for the soreness in her forearm from keeping her fist closed so tightly for so long.

"He won't talk to a girl like that again," her mother had said that night, while she was dabbing at her cuts with a cotton ball dipped in alcohol. Spengler had been suspended for what she'd done, a week at home for punishment, but the group of boys had gotten away with nothing more than a lecture. If something like that happened these days it would be all over the news and all the families would've ended up in court, but that had gone down twenty years before. It might as well have been the Stone Age. *Boys will be boys*, the principal had said, and the case was closed. That was Spengler's first real lesson in unfairness, but not her last. If you were a man you could do anything. If you had a dick and balls dangling between your legs, that gave you a free pass to do whatever you wanted, and people would shrug and look the other way. Make excuses. Boys will be boys.

The only other time her mother had ever mentioned that time was after Spengler had graduated from the police academy, when they were standing together for a picture, and her mother had wrapped an arm around her shoulders and whispered into her ear before turning and smiling for the camera.

"You squeeze all their balls now," she'd said.

Less than a year later her mother was dead from breast cancer. She had kept the lumps and the pain to herself. Spengler was never sure if that closemouthed tendency was a Korean thing, or if it was particular to her mother, because she'd never known any other Koreans. I'm too busy for friends, her mother had always said, and that was probably true, between all the double shifts she'd worked housekeeping at the Ramada Inn to support them and the ESL classes she occasionally took at night. Constantly busy, and the only time Spengler usually saw her mother was when she'd fallen asleep on the sofa after a long shift, when she'd gently ease her mother's tattered white sneakers off her feet and toss a blanket over her. That's most of what she remembered about her mother now—the soft sound of her exhausted snores from the couch, and what she'd said to her at graduation.

You squeeze all their balls now.

CHAPTER TWENTY-NINE

"Detective Spengler?"

She turned, the heel of her shoe slipping clumsily on the wet sidewalk. It'd rained steadily in the night and through the morning, and the sky was steel gray. Coffee weather. They'd spent most of the morning on the phone with the Madison PD, who'd immediately emailed them the case file on Janice Evans. It looked fairly straightforward. Janice's boss had been obsessed with her and had broken into their home one night, then murdered her before turning the gun on himself, although he'd lived. It looked like nothing more than bad luck, for Evans to have had his first wife murdered and his second fall off a cliff.

When Loren asked to speak with the detective who'd run the investigation, there was a snag. Detective Abe Reid had retired five years before and was spending his remaining years in the dry heat of the Arizona desert. No one had heard from him in a while, but they'd try to track him down, have him give them a call. Spengler had managed to pin down Evans's daughters and would be speaking to them that afternoon, but first was the polygraph test. Evans had shown up about fifteen minutes before and was in the process of being hooked up to the machine and prepped, and she had just enough time to duck out and grab a latte. Loren had turned down her offer to pick him up one, saying he only drank coffee if he was backed up and needed to take a dump. Crude, but she'd heard much worse come out of Loren's mouth, even in the last twenty-four hours.

"Yes?" she responded. "Can I help you?"

This man, whoever he was, had been waiting for her on the front steps of the police station, and for a while, by the looks of it. His hands were jammed deep in his pockets and the rain had beaded up on the fabric of his coat, and his lips had gone purplish-blue from the cold. He wasn't from around Denver, she could tell by how violently he was shivering. It wasn't that it was exactly cold outside—she was only in a thin sweater and there were plenty of pedestrians walking by in less—but he was still stomping his feet and rubbing his hands together like he was standing in a blizzard. It was the altitude and the thin air in Colorado that caught people by surprise, gave the chill in the air a sharp edge, made the cold seem worse. If you lived here you adjusted, but it took time.

"Detective Peter Ortiz," he said. He gave her his badge. There were two trees printed on the leather case, their branches entwined while a sun hovered in the sky behind. He wasn't smiling in his ID photo. "I'm visiting from Springfield, Ohio."

She handed him his badge. One quick movement and it disappeared into the folds of his coat.

Of course he'd be a cop. It was the way he dressed—nice wool peacoat, because a coat was what most people noticed first, and hopefully all they'd notice, and cheap leather shoes from a discount department store, the kind that pinched around the toes and had crappy arch support but were easy to replace. And it was the way his eyes moved back and forth over the people walking by on the sidewalk. It was his smile, too. Someone once told her you can tell a cop by their smile. This was before she went on her stint undercover. A cop's smile has a hard edge, like a rusted razor blade. A jaded smile, maybe that was the right word for it. Or bitter. Either way, a cop had to learn to hide that smile or it would give them away in a heartbeat. But this man hadn't yet learned that lesson, or he just didn't care. He was giving off his copness like a radio signal, the justice wafting off him in cartoon stink lines.

"Enjoy your vacation," she said, and turned to walk away, but he scooted around fast so he was again blocking her path.

"I'm actually here on business," Ortiz said. "I'm investigating an open homicide case, and I'd like to ask you a few questions."

"I don't know anyone in Ohio."

"It's where your partner is from, actually."

She frowned.

"Ralph Loren?" Ortiz volunteered.

"We're not partners."

"But you're working together?"

"Yes. What exactly is this about?"

Ortiz opened up one side of his coat and for a moment Spengler had the idea he might be naked beneath, this was a joke, and he'd flash her and run and she'd be able to get coffee. But instead he groped around in his coat's inner pocket and brought out two things. The first was a manila folder that'd been creased in half vertically and the other was a tin box with a hinged lid. He handed her the file, and then flipped open the tin, fished out a hand-rolled cigarette, and jammed it into the corner of his mouth.

"That's your copy," he said, reaching back into his pocket and pulling out a lighter. He cupped his free hand around the tip of the cigarette to protect it from the wind and rain, and his face was lit up briefly as it caught. He never looked away from her as he did this. His eyes were dark, nearly black, and the pores on his nose and cheeks were like the craters on the moon—deep and perfectly rounded, as if someone had scooped the skin off his face with a tiny melon baller. "I don't need it back."

"What is it?"

"I think you'll find it to be an interesting read. Thirty years ago, Ralph Loren murdered a family of three and buried them in shallow graves," Ortiz said. He took a long inhale and then blew out the dense smoke, and for a moment it hid his entire face except for the cigarette's glowing tip, like a beacon of light in the center of a thick cloud of fog.

CHAPTER THIRTY

It made suspects nervous to have cops in the room with them while taking a polygraph, so they watched the test from another room down the hall, on a TV that'd been hooked up with a video feed. The technician, an unassuming older woman, had taken her time clipping the nodules to Evans's fingers and chest and temples, where they'd best measure his body's reactions to the questions asked. Evans was polite and pleasant.

"Mr. Evans, have you ever taken a polygraph test before?"

"Yes."

"Do you recall when?"

"About twenty years ago."

"Do you recall the circumstances surrounding that polygraph?"

"Yes." That was all. Evans wasn't the type to volunteer anything. The tech made a small noise through her nose, or maybe it was only an exhalation and not meant as a judgment.

"Just to review, I'll first be asking you yes or no questions, and I'll then have you give me the details of the night your wife died. You are aware this session is being video-recorded?"

Evans's eyes flickered up to the camera above his head. "Yes."

"Do you have any questions before we begin?"

"No."

"I've never seen someone look so damn comfortable," Spengler said.

On the TV, the female technician nodded.

"Great. Let's begin, then."

Loren grunted and kept watching the screen. Spengler had the file Ortiz had given her rolled up and tucked under her arm.

"Why are you giving this to me?" she'd asked Ortiz out on the street when he'd first shoved it in her hand. "What do you want from me?"

"I need your help. Men open up to their partners and share things."

"I told you before, I'm not his partner."

"Close enough. Look, I don't want much. Just read the file, maybe ask Loren a few questions. See if you can find out anything that might help my case."

"Have you spoken to Loren yet?"

Ortiz had a grin like a shark.

"Oh, that's coming. I'm trying to build my case first."

"Have you ever met Loren? He's not exactly an open book."

Ortiz had smiled in a way she didn't much like.

"But surely a pretty young woman like yourself could get him to open up."

And then she understood. She'd heard plenty of this sort of bullshit before. Use your feminine wiles, Spengler. Charm a confession out of him. Flutter those eyelashes, reach out and touch his hand. Bend over more often than you need to. As if she was nothing more than tits and ass with a badge. A pretty young woman like you. How many times had she heard some variation of that over the years? Too many to count. Every time it happened she'd tried to tell Tony about it, turn it into a joke, but it always upset him. Not that trying to make it funny did much for her, either. Whoever said laughter was the best medicine had obviously never been told to tighten their bra straps and thrust out their chest while interviewing suspects.

Ortiz had found out who she was but hadn't dared to come into the station to talk to her—Loren would've seen him and known what was up. So he'd waited for her outside, watching for her so he could spring his trap. Like one of those spiders that hides under a rock until the unsuspecting prey wanders by to be snatched up.

She wasn't going to be snatched up by anyone.

"Mr. Evans, were you born in 1971?"

"Yes."

"Do you have two daughters?"

"Yes."

"Is there a particular reason you never told the detectives you'd been married before?"

Evans blinked rapidly. He might've been surprised, or maybe he had something caught in his eye.

"I didn't think it was pertinent," he said slowly.

"Did you murder your wife?"

Evans turned to look at the tech.

"Pardon?" he asked politely. "Marie wasn't murdered."

The tech glanced down at her notes.

"Not Marie, Mr. Evans. Your first wife. Janice Roscoe Evans. Do you have any idea who was behind her murder?"

"What does this have to do with Janice?"

"If you could just answer the question, Mr. Evans."

"I added a few questions to the list," Loren said. He was excited. There was nothing that'd perk Ralph Loren up faster than throwing a shock into someone. "Just to shake things up a bit."

"Janice's boss was arrested for her murder," Evans said. "Jesse O'Neil."

"And you do believe Jesse O'Neil was responsible for the death of your first wife?"

Evans stared straight ahead again. He didn't move, but there was something about his posture that said he was thinking, hard. The wheels were turning so fast there was smoke coming off them. He looked like a stray Spengler had once watched get chased down by the dogcatcher, his eyes bright and shining with fear and intelligence. He was cornered, that was what the look on his face said, and he was desperately trying to think of a way out but was coming up empty.

The polygraph machine would capture all the info about his pulse and heart rate and even how much he was sweating, but Spengler wished she was in there, too. When a person spins a lie there's a change in the air a machine can't measure. It made her think of the old console TVs. When she was a kid she could tell when someone turned one on in her apartment building—not because of anything she heard, but because of the low buzz in the back of her head, like a whine that came to her brain instead of her ears. She wondered if she'd hear that buzz coming off Evans if she was in there now.

"Mr. Evans?"

There's an old saying: life turns on a dime. It can go one way or the other, or lose its balance and topple over completely, and Spengler had interviewed suspects before and seen that moment of decision, when things could go one way or the other. This way or that. It's those moments that lead to confessions—or not. The truth or a lie. You'd never be able to guess which way the dime would spin, gleaming dizzily as the light bounced off the silver face.

This time, the dime spun away from them, out of reach.

"I don't know," Evans said. "I don't know anything about Janice's murder. The police handled all of that."

"Did you murder your first wife?"

"No."

"On Tuesday, August twenty-eighth, did your second wife, Marie Evans, fall off a cliff in Rocky Mountain National Forest?"

"Yes."

"Did you see her fall?"

"No."

"Did you push her off that cliff?"

"No."

"Have you ever killed anyone?"

There was a long pause. Through the TV's speakers, Spengler thought she could hear the wet, smacking sound of Evans's lips separating as he finally spoke.

"Didn't you just ask me that same question?" he asked.

The tech shrugged, noncommittal.

Evans's eyes flicked up to the camera, and Spengler didn't have to be in the room with him to feel the old buzz in her head.

"No," he said. He dropped his eyes again. "I've never killed anyone."

He was lying.

And the questions went on.

"You know these questions you gave me are highly unorthodox and will never hold up in a court of law," Judy, the tech who'd run the polygraph, said. Evans had already left.

"I don't need any of it to stand up in a court, you sweet thang," Loren said. Judy, who had to be at least seventy years old, glared at him. "What'd the test tell you?"

"The same thing every one of these tests tells me. He was nervous in there. Heart rate was up, respiration too. Blood pressure was fairly high, but he's the right age for hypertension—"

"Am I crazy or are you a doctor conducting a physical exam in there, Judy?" Loren demanded. "Did you grab the guy by the balls, ask him to turn his head and cough? Maybe you slipped a finger up his ass while we weren't watching to check his prostate, too? Christ on a cross, lady. I don't need to know all that other garbage. I just want to know if he was lying or not."

"Are you new here, Loren?" Judy asked waspishly. "You know how this works. Polygraph testing is an imperfect science. All I can tell you is when I see spikes in his heart rate or an elevated level of perspiration. Those jumps might mean he's lying, or they might mean nothing at all."

"Were there certain questions that caused a spike?" Spengler asked, holding up a hand and speaking before Loren could begin another fresh rant.

"There were definitely moments," Judy said. She turned her laptop so Spengler could see the screen. "See how the measurements stay mostly level until *here*? Then everything jumps up. Then it all lowers again, and there's a second spike."

"What did you ask to cause that first one?" Spengler said.

"That was when we were discussing the man who killed his first wife. Jesse O'Neil? It's when I asked Mr. Evans if he thought O'Neil was the one behind her murder. He said he didn't know, but based on his body's reactions I'd say that was a lie."

Spengler put her hand on the back of Judy's chair and leaned closer to the laptop's screen.

"What about this second spike?"

"That was when I asked if he'd ever killed anyone," Judy said. "He said no, but again, looking at these results I'd say that was a lie."

"But when you asked if he'd pushed Marie off the cliff—" Spengler began.

"His vitals all stayed flat. No reaction. He's telling the truth. He didn't push his wife off the cliff. But he seems to be lying about whether he's killed anyone before."

"You called the polygraph an imperfect science," Spengler said. "How accurate have you found it to be?"

Judy hesitated. Shrugged.

"It's controversial," she said.

"How long have you been administering polygraphs?" Spengler asked. Behind her, Loren was silent, but she could feel him listening.

"Almost thirty years."

"And in those thirty years, how accurate have you found it to be?"

The old woman started to shrug again, but stopped when Spengler gently touched her shoulder.

"Off the record," Spengler said. "I'm just looking for your personal opinion. No harm, no foul."

Judy sighed and pinched her leg, yanked on the skin. Amusedly, Spengler realized it wasn't skin but panty hose, the same kind her mother always wore under her waitress uniform. Sheer, with the seam running across the toes and a control top.

"Oh, a polygraph is accurate enough," Judy said. "I've been running these tests a long time, I've done hundreds of them. Lots of people are good liars on a day-to-day basis, but when I'm measuring a person's physiological response to questions, it tells a completely different story. Most people couldn't do it. When you lie, your body gives you away. It wants to tell the truth, even if your mouth doesn't."

CHAPTER THIRTY-ONE

Loren had to take a minute to catch his breath after the polygraph was over, so he went to his office and shut the door. When you lie, your body gives you away. That's what Judy said. Your body wants to tell the truth, even if your mouth doesn't. Loren already knew that, you can't be a detective without learning how to pick up on those things—but for the first time, he wondered what he'd been giving away without even realizing it.

He tented his hands over his nose and sucked down a deep breath. It could make a man crazy, trying to remember everything he'd said and done, and then second-guess every look and gesture he'd gotten. He took another breath. His palms smelled sour and tangy. Maybe that was the smell of sweat, or maybe he was already nuts and that was what the scent was. Everything has a smell, he knew that from experience. Arousal and fear, even sadness. And crazy had a particular smell, too.

The last time he'd caught a whiff of that was when Paul Hoskins went nuts, after he'd attacked a woman who'd murdered her own daughter. That freak-out had gotten Hoskins tossed out of Homicide, almost cost him everything. Loren had gone to the hospital to check on his partner after the ambulance had hauled him away, and he'd been surprised when they told him Paulie was in the psych ward. Seventh floor, eighth room on the left.

"She had a roast in the oven, did you smell it?" Paulie asked after Loren had come in and sat down. He was lying back in the hospital bed, blankets pulled up to his chest so you couldn't really tell that he was strapped down unless you really looked. "And there was a pot on the stove. Mashed potatoes, I think."

"Yeah, I saw," Loren had said. He remembered being uncomfortable, and shifting back and forth in that hard chair. Oh, he'd visited plenty of crazies over the course of his career, but he'd never expected to be doing it with Paulie Hoskins, who'd always seemed like one of the most stable guys out there.

"And there were those dinner rolls. Fresh, it smelled like. Just baked."

"Yeah."

"She was busy cooking," Hoskins had said, turning his head on the pillow. There was a long scratch running down the side of his face, from the corner of his eye all the way to his jaw. Not deep enough to need stitches, but it'd probably scar. "Cooking while her daughter was dead in the closet."

A doctor had walked by then, paused and peered in through the door's little window, then moved on. Hoskins had an IV dripping into his arm, a constant stream of medicine to keep him calm. He'd be asleep soon, a nurse had told Loren. He wouldn't be able to keep his eyes open after too long, not with the dose they'd been pumping into him.

They'd been called out to a crime scene, a nice house

down on the south end of town, not too far from the high school where that shooting had gone down over a decade before, and there was a little girl in the closet, curled up beside her Barbie Dream House, she could've been napping but she wasn't, the examiner said death had come from blunt force trauma, specifically to the skull. The girl's mother had killed her, she immediately confessed and then went back to the kitchen to check on the meal she was putting together, to baste the roast and make sure the silver was polished, and Loren had seen the change come across Paulie's face. The anger, and the disgust. A person could only witness so many horrible things before they reached their breaking point, and this suburban homemaker with her perfectly coiffed hair and pressed slacks had pushed Hoskins there. Loren had been walking that same road himself for a long time and he'd managed to keep himself under control, but Hoskins had ended up at the endgame so fast it made Loren's head spin.

Warp factor nine, Mr. Sulu. Engage.

"There were bruises all up and down her back, from being kicked. Did you see that?" Paulie whispered from his bed. "That woman kicked her. Her own mother. That woman probably heard the bones breaking. Can you imagine? Hitting a kid so hard you'd hear her bones snapping?"

Paulie and his questions. Loren didn't think he expected any answers, but just wanted to get the words out there. Wanted to hear his own voice, because it might be the only thing that was real to him now. Hoskins had spent the few years before this stint in the hospital doing a slow crumble, ever since they'd arrested Jacky Seever back in 2008. Hoskins had spent a lot of time alone with Seever in the interview room, trying to get every bit of information about the murders, it was the only way Seever would agree to talk. Only to Hoskins. But spending all those hours and days and weeks alone with a guy who'd killed thirty-some people and buried them under his house had a price, it'd filled Hoskins's head with poison he'd never be able to be free from. It'd taken time to work through his system, four years, but then it'd come to a head, like a zit, a great big one on your forehead, dead center, the kind that throbs painfully with its own life, its own heartbeat, until it erupts and spews its pus and blood.

Aftershocks, that's what they call it. Like an earthquake, but the little ones that come later, when you think it's all over, the main event has been tied up neatly and tucked away, to be forgotten. Loren could understand, he'd been through the aftershocks himself—hell, he thought he was *still* going through them, and he knew that sometimes you just have to wait for the explosion, stand there and chill, hold onto your tits, the water's getting choppy.

"How bad was it?" Paulie had asked. His hands were squirming on top of the blankets, full of their own life, even though the rest of his body was still. The nurse hadn't yet bandaged his bleeding knuckles.

"What?"

Paulie sighed, and the blankets rose and fell like an ocean wave.

"How bad did I hurt her?"

That woman had screamed when Hoskins had grabbed a handful of her hair, more out of surprise than pain. At least at first. Loren had turned away, he'd let it happen, because a part of him felt that this woman needed to be punished for what she'd done—oh, she'd go to prison, but it'd probably be one of those glorified correctional facilities for overprivileged women where she'd serve ten to twenty-five years playing tennis and gardening, and she'd never end up getting what she really deserved. She'd tortured her daughter, she'd starved her and beat her and murdered her, and she deserved to feel a bit of that, to know what it was like. If a kid is a biter you bite him back, make him feel how much it hurts, that's how they learn. That was part of why Loren had let Hoskins do it, but some of it was because it was bound to happen sometime, Hoskins had been riding the train toward Crazytown for years now, it was either now or later, so why not now?

"It was pretty bad," Loren said. Worse than pretty bad. Hoskins had ripped a big chunk of the woman's hair right off her scalp, gave her a black eye. Cracked one of her teeth and snapped a few ribs. Loren had finally stepped in and broken it up. The woman was unconscious by then, and Hoskins was weeping. "It's turning into a real clusterfuck. I guarantee that woman's got money and a good lawyer, and she's gonna scream police brutality."

Hoskins shrugged, flapped his hand. *I don't give a shit.*

"She cooked dinner, Loren. Murdered her own kid and then *cooked dinner.*"

"Yeah, I know."

Hoskins sighed, turned his head on the pillow. It made a rough, scratchy sound. Pillowcases at hospitals were always that way, like they wanted you to be as uncomfortable as possible so you'd go home sooner. The right side of his face was slack, and his eye on that side kept slipping shut.

They sat in silence for a few minutes. A thoughtful silence, you might call it. Loren had been able to hear the shuffling noises of people walking by in the hallway, and the muffled sound of laughter farther on. A machine beeped once, and then again.

"I fucking hate people," Hoskins said, his voice thick and slurred, startling Loren out of his daze. He'd been sure Paulie was out for the count. "I don't understand why they have to be so goddamn cruel."

And then Hoskins really *had* fallen asleep, his head drooping down toward his shoulder and his mouth slack. A single tear had oozed out from under one closed eyelid and got caught in his lashes. Loren hadn't wiped that tear away, but he sometimes wished to sweet Jesus that he had done Paulie that single kindness, to make up for the things he'd done before, to other partners.

CHAPTER THIRTY-TWO

Spengler left the station and drove out to the Holiday Inn near downtown. The case file Ortiz had given her was on the passenger seat, unopened. She'd been afraid to see what she'd find inside, so she'd left it there and tried to stay focused on work, although her gaze kept wandering back to it as she drove. But even when she couldn't see the damn thing it was on her mind.

The Evans girls were waiting for her in one of the hotel's conference rooms, sitting so they were both looking out the windows. The view wasn't great. A hedge gone partly brittle and brown, and then the parking lot. The sisters were sedate as they answered Spengler's questions, although Spengler suspected the calm came out of a prescription bottle of Xanax.

The oldest, Hannah, was twenty-two years old. Maddie was nineteen. Both girls wore jeans and sweaters. Typical college student attire. They both looked like Marie—brunettes with hair that swept their shoulders and pert noses, although Hannah could've passed for a younger Marie, based on the pictures Spengler had seen. But Hannah was extremely thin, nearly painfully so. It didn't suit her well. The bones in her wrists were sharp and pointed, and the razor edge of her collarbone was obvious through the fabric of her top. She was either suffering from a health problem or an eating disorder.

"Do you think Dad killed her?" Hannah asked dully. "Is that why you're here?"

Spengler had a good poker face, but she wasn't sure how well it was holding up.

"I just need to ask a few questions," she said. "That's all."

"If I was in your shoes and there was a couple who'd gone hiking alone and the wife fell off a cliff, I'd assume he killed her."

"Hannah, why don't you shut up?" Maddie said sharply.

"I'm just saying," Hannah said. Her eyes moved slowly between her sister and Spengler. Definitely drugged. Stoned out of her damn mind. "Mom and Dad have been fighting so much lately it makes me wonder."

Spengler made a note on her paper. "What've they been arguing about?"

"I don't know," Hannah said, shrugging. "Neither one of us were around much this summer."

"If you don't mind my asking, why did you decide to stay here instead of with your father?" There was a pitcher of ice water in the center of the table. Spengler poured herself a glass, then motioned at the sisters. *Any for you?* They both shook their heads.

"Dad's pretty upset right now, and he doesn't like to be seen that way. He told us it would be best if we didn't stay at home."

"Your father told me he wasn't sure why the two of you decided to stay here," Spengler said, flipping back through her notes. "Actually, he made it sound like neither one of you wanted to stay with him."

Maddie's eyes dropped down to the table. Hannah shrugged.

"I really don't remember what happened," Hannah said. She started to say something else, then fell silent.

Spengler watched the girls for a moment, hoping one of them might keep talking, but neither did.

"You said he doesn't like to be seen that way," Spengler said. "What exactly does that mean? He doesn't like to be seen what way?"

"He's devastated that Mom's gone," Maddie said. "They've been together for so long I don't think he knows how to live without her."

"A few years ago they were fighting all the time, and I asked Mom if they were getting a divorce," Hannah said. She had three or four bangle bracelets around her wrist, and she kept pushing them up her arm, then down again. "She just laughed, said it wasn't worth the effort. I asked her what that meant, and she told me her and Dad had separated before, but they couldn't stay away from each other. They were like magnets, she said. She was always saying things like that."

"Do you remember when Scottie Union dumped me on Valentine's Day?" Maddie asked her sister. "Mom told me men are like drugs. A great high, fun to use for short periods of time, but after a while they'd probably kill you. I don't know how she thought that was supposed to make me feel better, or why she thought it was appropriate to let me know about her experience with drugs."

Both the girls laughed a little, then sighed.

"What would your parents argue about?" Spengler asked.

"I don't know," Hannah said. "They'd usually shut themselves in their bedroom while they fought, so we couldn't hear much. Sometimes I'd go over to a friend's place just to get out of there."

"I'd put in my earbuds and listen to music," Maddie said. "I just didn't want to hear it."

"Did your parents have any problems that you're aware of? Marital? Financial?" Spengler asked both girls the questions, but looked at Hannah. It seemed as though the meds had loosened her tongue, or she was just the loose-lipped sister.

"Well, there was that time Dad kept hiding his phone and Mom was convinced he was cheating. She swore she could smell perfume on him when he came home from work, but I never smelled it."

"Hannah, shut up."

"What? Mom's dead, and this cop is just trying to help. Aren't you a little curious about what happened? But even if you're not, why don't *you* just shut up and let me talk?"

Maddie sat back, mollified by her sister's burst of sudden fury.

"Mom made me sniff a pile of his dirty clothes one time," Hannah said. "Gross, you know. But I didn't smell anything except sweat. She was so pissed when I told her that."

"Do you think your father has had an affair?"

"God, no," Maddie said quickly. "If anything, Dad was too scared to do anything like that. Mom would've destroyed his life and taken everything. And I wouldn't have blamed her one bit."

"Did they ever argue about money?"

"No," Hannah said, smiling a little. "That's one thing I never heard them fight about. Dad's really good at making money, that's what Mom would say. It was his special talent. I don't know if she meant that as a compliment, though."

"Do you either of you know if your mother had any interests outside of the house?" Spengler asked. "Clubs or activities, friends she might've confided in?"

"She was part of a running club," Hannah said after a moment of thought. "And a book club."

"She was president of the PTA where we went to high school," Maddie said. "She always spent a lot of time outside. Hiking and camping. She liked to take classes. Art and pottery and yoga."

"And she volunteered at the hospital and the library."

"Okay," Spengler said, scribbling into her notepad. "Anything else you can think of?"

"I don't know," Maddie said, shrugging and picking a dot of lint off her thigh. "Sometimes she tried new things to surprise Dad. She's done stuff like that before. Like the time she took those cooking classes. Do you remember, Han?"

Hannah smiled, tears standing in her eyes.

"Yeah. She took those classes for three months, specialized in French cuisine. She wanted to surprise Dad on their twentieth anniversary with a big meal and then he got so sick, so she didn't. He was in the hospital and kept joking that Mom had poisoned him. That she was trying to kill him."

"Yeah, I remember that."

Both girls laughed half-heartedly. Hannah sniffed and wiped her nose on her sleeve.

"After you've been married to someone for so long, I bet it's hard to be alone," Hannah said. "Maybe we should be with Dad."

"Yeah, maybe," Maddie said. She sounded unconvinced. Kids aren't stupid, Spengler knew. They picked up on everything, and she thought the girls knew more about Matt and Marie than they were letting on. Parents kept secrets from their kids all the time, to protect them, or to save them from embarrassment, but it hardly ever worked.

CHAPTER THIRTY-THREE

Loren didn't go straight home after leaving the station, although he should have. It was going to be a long day tomorrow, it would be a good idea to go home and get some sleep. Spengler had agreed they should split up the work—she'd left an hour before to visit Hannah and Maddie Evans, and he'd spent time scouring the records on Matt Evans himself, seeing what he could dig up. Nothing had jumped out at him so far, but Loren hadn't been at it long before calling it quits. The man might be telling the truth, but you could never be sure. It's the reason Loren had arranged for a squad car to park outside Evans's house and keep watch through the night. He didn't want him up and disappearing. If Evans felt like he was getting the squeeze, he might try to do a quick fade. It was another feeling Loren could understand.

Loren left the station but didn't go straight home because there was always a possibility someone might be following him. It had happened before and it was the last thing he wanted, for some weirdo to know where he slept at night. So he left the station and drove in circles for a bit, up Federal Boulevard and back down Kipling, *fast*, until he was pretty sure no one was tailing him. There was a billboard he always slowed down to look at, an advertisement for a child abuse hotline. It was a blown-up photo of a little boy, his eyes full of wavering, tearful hope. It would've been a good ad except some asshole had taken a can of red spray paint and given the kid a set of devil's horns and a forked tongue, then blotted out his face with four words written in straggling letters:

GOD ISN'T HERE ANYMORE.

Just words, but it still gave him bad vibes every time he saw it. God's not here anymore, but the devil is. In all the details.

His apartment was on the second floor, which also happened to be the top. He'd chosen it because he liked to sleep with the windows open at night, even in the winter, and he knew better than to do that on the ground floor. He'd seen too much bad shit go down over the years because some crazy saw an open window and took it as an invitation, and he didn't want to wake up one night with a knife against his throat and something hard and throbbing against his bunghole.

He lived on the second floor, always had, always would, and he'd stayed here so long because he was comfortable, he knew the girls working the front office and the guys who did the landscaping and cleaned the pool, he recognized the neighbors and the sounds of the traffic flying by on highway 285, he even knew the sounds of the squawking PA system and revving engines out at Bandimere Speedway on a race night. He stayed on living in this place because he was used to it—it was the little things, like having a designated parking spot and knowing exactly which way to face in the bathroom so the neighbors couldn't see you beating your meat through the window above the toilet—but it was mostly that he liked coming home to the same place every night, maybe all cops need that sort of predictability, that *routine*, it's the only way they can keep sane after a day of police work, where anything can happen and usually does.

But the problem with wanting predictability is that you hardly ever get it. Like this: Loren wanted to go home, take a hot shower, microwave a cheap frozen burrito, and go to bed, but as soon as he parked he saw that wasn't going to happen. You can spend your whole life driving in circles and trying to stay hidden, but the past has a way of finding you anyway. It's only a matter of time before it happens. Life is one big circle jerk, you'll end up at the beginning again sooner or later. It had taken some time to catch up with him, thirty years, but Loren's past had finally come back for him. It was ugly and carrying a gun.

"Peter Ortiz, you old sonavabitch," Loren said, ignoring the nervous flutter in his sternum as he climbed out of his car. "What an unpleasant surprise, to see your fat ass waiting for me."

"I'd say this isn't any fun for me, but that'd be a lie," Ortiz said, grinning and coming forward to meet him.

CHAPTER THIRTY-FOUR

Loren had once arrested an old man who'd kept women chained up in his house, to use as his personal sex toys and punching bags. That was years before, out in Ohio, when he'd first become a detective and started working with Gallo. Springfield was a town that'd once been named one of the best places to live in America but had since gone to shit, and it was the place where he'd seen firsthand how desperately bad humanity could be. Oh, but it was bad everywhere, he came to understand that over time, and sometimes he'd run across a pocket of something *really* bad, something so putrid and terrible that it didn't seem like it could possibly be real. *Surreal,* that was supposed to be the word for it, but it wasn't enough to explain it, not by a long shot. *Surreal* wasn't awful enough, but there wasn't anything else, so it would have to do.

That particular killer had been a real piece of work, Loren remembered. Lazy eyed and gray haired, he told Loren he'd been keeping the women locked up to further the population. *Breeders,* that's what he called them, because after the soon-to-come apocalypse went down there'd need to be people to rebuild. His children would do it, he said. A whole new world order would come about because of the splooge shooting from his balls.

But the old man seemed to have forgotten he'd had a vasectomy a few years before and there was no way he was getting *any* woman in the family way. He just liked women and sex and hurting people, the sick look a person gets on their face when they're in pain, and he couldn't get it unless the women were always with him, unless he got to do whatever he wanted to them without any sort of consequence. He had two women when the police came knocking on his door—it'd been three, but one had managed to escape and had gone straight to the cops and brought them back—but by the time Loren busted his way into the place and found the women, they were dead. Well, one was dead, her head split in half like a melon with a tire iron, the skull peeling back from her brain, and the other was just about there. She'd started squirming when she saw Loren come into the room, trying to scoot away because she thought he was the old man, come back to hurt her some more, to finish the job he'd started when the cops had shown up on his doorstep, and Loren had screamed that he had a "breather," *not* a "breeder" like the guy had been calling her, that he needed a paramedic right away.

Please, she'd said, gurgling the words through the blood running down her throat. *Please don't.*

A young Ralph Loren, who had a normal childhood, who had parents who loved him and who ate a home-cooked dinner with his family every night as a kid, who'd graduated the police academy before he had hair on his chest, when his voice still sometimes cracked and turned high pitched—he'd never known how really fucked up the world could be until that moment. The past, it makes a person who they are, and if Loren was asked what the watershed moment in his life was, the experience that defined him, he would say there were a few of those moments in his life, and finding that woman on the floor of that attic room was the first of them. Of course, if anyone ever asked Ralph Loren a dumb-ass question like that, it was much more likely he'd tell them to go fuck themselves than answer.

But if Loren decided to open his mouth and spill the beans, this is what he would say: Breaking the lock on the thick oak door to that attic room, kicking at the knob so hard he wouldn't be able to put any weight on that foot the next day, barely able to hear the screams of the old man as he was arrested downstairs, and then walking into the room, into the smell of shit and blood and death and sex, and being hit by an overwhelming wave of dizziness, because this couldn't be real, could it? This room was something you'd see in the movies, you'd see it on the big screen and then you'd go home to your nice, clean home, where there wasn't a dead woman curled up in one corner like a shrimp, her arms thrown up over her face to protect herself. This couldn't be real. Could it? Could it?

But it was.

It was an attic room the women had been kept in, the small windows boarded up with thick planks of wood, and big O-hooks had been screwed into the walls with the chains binding the women's ankles threaded through them. In one corner was a plastic paint bucket with a lid, the kind anyone could get at the hardware store, and even though the lid had been snapped into place the thick smell of shit still hung around it in a cloud. It was their toilet, Loren realized sickly. And written on the wall above this makeshift toilet were five words, scrawled up there with a red marker, or maybe it was blood, he never knew. There were other things, too, little sketches and tick marks, maybe the women drew them to count the days or just pass the time, but none of it caught his eye, except those five words. And those words might as well have been burned into his brain because Loren carried them with him for the rest of his life, like a mean, grinning monkey on his back who'd decided to hitch a ride. Words can be the most powerful thing in the world, sometimes they were the best things but they could also be the worst, and he could never hear any of those words alone without it bringing the entire phrase to mind.

ALL TOGETHER
NOW
WITH FEELING

"It doesn't matter what it means, Ralphie," Gallo said when he mentioned it. "We caught the sonavabitch. He won't spend another day out at King's Island trolling for sluts to lock up in his attic."

"They weren't sluts."

"All women are sluts, Ralphie," Gallo said. "Even your mama was one once, I don't care if you think otherwise. It's true."

If anyone made a comment like that to Loren these days

they'd most likely be swallowing their own teeth, but back then Loren ignored those sorts of things. Let them pass. Like water off a duck's back, his mother had taught him. The days of turning his cheek were long behind him though, and a lot of that was because of Gallo. He learned a lot during their time as partners. Gallo showed him the ropes, taught him everything about working Homicide, about analyzing the scene and becoming the suspect, going on the hunt. Loren learned a metric shit-ton from Gallo, maybe too much. And then it soured. A partnership is like a marriage, like Hoskins always said; a good one is hard to find. And it was good with Gallo, until it wasn't.

All together now, with feeling.

What did it mean? No one cared, but Loren couldn't stop thinking about those words, about that phrase, and it was the girl who'd escaped who finally told him that one of the dead women had taught choir at some high school and she used to say it when the old man wasn't home and they'd all scream in unison, in the hopes that a neighbor would hear and come help.

"'All together now, with feeling,' that was kind of our mantra, know what I mean?" the girl had told Loren with a wry smile. That girl had been tough, but she'd spent months chained up in that attic, living through things no one could even imagine, things no one would *want* to imagine, and less than a year after she'd escaped she was dead. Her sister found her hanging in her own closet, the cords from the window blinds looped around her neck. "She'd yell that, and then we'd all start screaming. Harmonizing, she called it, and sometimes we'd laugh about it. But it never worked, no matter how loud we were. No one ever came to see what all the racket was about."

Many years later, many miles away from Springfield, a *lifetime* away, Loren would walk into another crime scene that looked like one of Jacky Seever's but wasn't, and there would be words written on a wall, a different phrase, but it wouldn't matter because it would still bring him back to that attic room, to the woman on the floor, her eyes bright with terror as she tried to scoot away before making one final, choking gurgling noise on the blood in her throat and then dying. Two different crime scenes, with nothing in common except Ralph Loren, one man bridging the gap between them, because everything is connected, everything is a circle, it's all the same even when it isn't, and it'll never be over.

Second verse, same as the first.

And right now the past was coming back with a roaring vengeance. There was Pete Ortiz, his hands folded across his chest, waiting for him to come home. Just like he'd done thirty years before, except now Ortiz wasn't so skinny or zitty, and he was dressed nice, good shoes and a wool coat with his hair slicked back from his face, but the ghost of the kid he used to be was still there, lurking behind the mask of his adult face, peeking around the edges.

"This has happened before, right?" Loren wanted to ask Ortiz once he'd thrown his car in park and climbed out. "We've done this before, this same exact thing? You waited for me outside my house after Gallo disappeared because you wanted answers. You were angry and I hit you, and here you are again. I'm not crazy, am I? That's what happened? Am I remembering it right?"

But Loren didn't ask, mostly because he was afraid of the answer. He was sure it did happen, Ortiz had been waiting for him, angry and frightened, and then slunk away after Loren broke his nose, but he'd been sure about memories before and been wrong. And if he was wrong, if he asked the question and Ortiz looked at him like he was crazy, he wasn't sure what he'd do.

So instead, he asked Ortiz if he wanted to go out and grab some dinner, maybe try to make some peace.

CHAPTER THIRTY-FIVE

Loren didn't sleep much these days. It might be because he was getting old—he could remember his old man getting around three hours of snooze a night and functioning just fine, although Marvin Loren always said that any damn fool could turn wrenches and unclog drains on *no* sleep, especially a fool who'd been working as a plumber for most of his life.

"I don't need eight hours to yank the nest of hairs out of the Sanborns' bathtub drain once a month," he'd said once over dinner, when he'd had one too many beers. "That whole family has black hair, but when I unclog that tub there are always blond ones mixed in there. White-blond *long* ones, and there's only one person in town with hair like that, son, and she rings groceries down at the Big Bear Supermarket, and has lately been seen in the company of Gary Sanborn." He snickered and kicked back another mouthful of beer, swished it around in his mouth before swallowing. "Sanborn, that sly ol' dog. He thinks he's fooling everyone, but let me tell you something, Ralphie. You might flush your shit down the toilet, you might think it's gone for good, but your plumber could still find it. There'll always be people like that, who can sniff out the bad shit everyone does, and they'll ruin your entire life if they can. You've gotta be careful of those men. Remember that and it'll save you a helluva mess of trouble in the long run."

Loren did try to remember those words, and all the things Marv Loren used to say, stupid or not, especially lately. The old man had been dead for a long time now, but Loren could still hear his voice clear as day and sometimes even smelled the cologne Marv always wore—English Leather, that's what men wear, English Leather or nothing at all—and today was one of those days when his father was muttering nonstop, the same way he would when he'd fall asleep in front of the ol' boob tube, kicked back while *The Dick Van Dyke Show* was on. Those mutterings didn't usually make sense, they weren't much more than half conversations transmitted from dreamland, and little Ralphie Loren had learned to tune them out like background noise as he sat Indian style on the shag rug in the warm radioactive glow of the TV, but sometimes his father would say something that'd make the hairs on the back of his neck stand straight up. You paid attention when a person said something in their sleep, you made *note* of it, especially when it was your father, and that rule still held true. He heard Marv Loren in his head pretty often these days, although Dr. Patel said it wasn't actually his father but his own *inner monologue* or some baloney like that.

"You're not crazy, Ralph," Patel had said. "It's your own thoughts you hear, only your mind is telling you these things in your father's voice. There's nothing wrong with you. Believe me, it's perfectly normal. I find this is typically brought on by stress or anxiety, but nothing to worry about."

Loren wasn't so sure he bought into Patel's explanation completely, but then he never did trust doctors. Of course, he never thought much about his father's voice at all, although it was like radio static more often than not, non-sensical and irritating, but then there were the days when the station suddenly came in, usually only for a moment, like he'd been twisting the tuning dial and finally hit on a local channel, and Marv Loren's voice was shouting in his skull, *screaming* to be heard.

And today just so happened to be one of those days when his old man's voice was coming in loud and clear. And when his father was talking Loren made sure to listen. The old man had helped him before, whispering advice only he could hear. Marv should've skipped the shitty plumbing career—har, har—and become a cop.

There'll always be people who can sniff out the bad shit you've done. Be careful of them.

Ortiz was one of those people, Loren thought. Always had been. Loren remembered his old man's words and still hadn't been careful enough, and now it might be ready to bite him in the ass.

"The lo mein here is pretty good," Loren said. "Thick noodles, nice and greasy."

Ortiz pushed aside the menu without giving it a single glance.

"I don't get it, but maybe you can help me understand. No one likes you, Loren. No one has ever liked you. In fact, people seem to actively *hate* your ugly face. But they still won't tell me anything. It's like they feel some kind of loyalty to you."

Loren laughed. He caught sight of his reflection in the glass wall behind the bar, moving behind the long row of white plastic cats with one paw up in the air, waving back and forth in unison.

"You're still the same hateful, petty prick you were thirty years ago, aren't you?" Loren said. The waitress came by and slid a bowl of egg drop soup in front of him and walked away. Ortiz had refused to order anything, but Loren wouldn't let that affect his appetite. "I bet the only time anyone is nice to you is when you're in the backseat of your car with a hooker, isn't it? And then they're done with your sorry ass once you open your wallet and pay."

"I keep asking questions about you and what happened to Gallo, and no one will give an inch," Ortiz said. He reached into his pocket and pulled out a lighter. "I can't figure it out. Why would anyone care about protecting your ass?"

"What if they're not protecting me?" Loren asked. He slurped loudly at the soup, making Ortiz turn away in disgust. "Have you ever considered the fact that I'm innocent?"

Ortiz flicked the lighter a few times before a flame appeared. It was a cheap plastic one a person could buy at any gas station. It reminded Loren of his father, who'd smoked like a chimney for as far back as he could remember. Even in Marv's last few years alive, when he was toting around a can of oxygen, he'd still smoke, left lit butts all over the house, balanced on the edges of ashtrays and propped up on saucers, forgotten, and the old man had constantly been misplacing his lighter. He kept a drawer of those cheap ones in the kitchen so he'd never be without, right alongside the silverware.

"You still smoke?" Loren asked.

"Yep."

"Cigarettes are for assholes," Loren said. Loren had smoked a few times before, but he didn't like it much and the habit never stuck. Most men looked like complete idiots when they smoked anyway, pinching the filter between their fingers and then sucking so hard their cheeks looked hollow and pinched, like they were sucking down a big ol' cock. Effeminate, that was the word for a man smoking. Cigarettes would kill you, they'd turn your lungs black and your teeth yellow, but they'd also make you look like a jackass while they did their work.

"Putting a bullet in your partner's skull is for assholes, too."

"I didn't put a bullet in anyone's head, jackass. Blast the wax outta your ears and listen for a change. You might surprise yourself."

"You're still going to keep up this charade?" Ortiz asked. He said *charade* all fancy, pronounced in a way that made Loren want to hit him, and Ortiz already had a punchable face. *Sha-rod.* "We both know it's only a matter of time before this whole house of cards comes tumbling down around your head."

"Did you love sucking Gallo's dick this much? Enough to follow me across the country after thirty years? Get over it."

"I'm not doing this for Gallo. I'm doing this because you're a killer and I'm the police. It's my job to arrest the bad guys."

"That's why you're here now?" Loren snorted. "Because you think I'm a bad guy?"

"You've spent your entire career chasing down criminals," Ortiz said. "Killers. The worst people out there. The irony doesn't get to you? The guilt?"

"Guilt?"

"Yeah. The guilt of knowing that it's your job to protect people from the scum of the earth, and you're just another one of them. You're a killer, Loren—you know it. And I do, too. And once I prove it, none of the guys back in Springfield will be able to protect your ass anymore. They all keep saying how nice you are, what a great cop you were. But Gallo told me all about you. How you were porking Connie, trying to take over his family. Ready-made wife and kid, all you would've had to do is step in."

"None of that's true."

"That's not what Gallo told me. You were his favorite topic."

"Gallo was off his fucking rocker," Loren said. The waitress had come by again with his plate of Kung Pao chicken, and he saw her raise her eyebrows at his language. He winked at her and she smiled. All the staff here knew Loren, they had gotten used to him. Plus, he was a good tipper. "He was always making up stories."

"It's funny you say that, because I've heard the same thing about you," Ortiz said.

"Oh, yeah?" Loren asked. He turned the full brilliance of his grin on Ortiz. Loren wasn't a smiler, never had been—a look of joy on his face had a predatory quality about it, something hard and glittering and dangerous. It was the smile of a shark, of a skull bleached white by the sun. In primary school Sister Mary Agnes had prayed over that grin, and his mother had wept over it. Later, the men Loren arrested felt their balls tighten up at the sight of it. There were only two people who'd never shuddered at his smile—his father was one. Connie Gallo was the other. "What kind of things have you heard?"

"I've heard about the crazy shit you do," Ortiz said. "The way you act and talk to people. The way you make up bullshit and remember things all wrong. Twist it all up in your head. I heard you go hunting your suspects, start acting like them. Doesn't that remind you of someone else?"

"I don't have a clue, but I'm sure you'll tell me."

"Gallo used to do that same shit," Ortiz said. "You learned from the best, didn't you? Then you killed him, and did you start turning into Gallo? I've heard of that happening. The murderer takes on his victim's quirks."

Loren's fork paused halfway up to his mouth, the tines loaded up with chicken. The corners of Ortiz's mouth were twitching with amusement.

"I bet people out here either think you're a genius or some sort of freak for acting like that, but I'd also bet you never tell anyone you learned how to troll victims from the man you killed in cold blood," Ortiz said. He leaned over, so the edge of the table cut into his chest. "Does anyone else know, Loren? Do any of them know you're a killer? Has it been hard living with that secret for so long?"

Loren put the fork down slowly. He tried to keep his hand from shaking, but Ortiz saw, and it made him smile.

"I remember you swaggering around back in Springfield, all puffed up, a real Billy Badass. Just the same way Gallo always did. Did you think acting like that would help you win Connie over—and then she still didn't want you?" Ortiz said.

"You don't know shit," Loren said roughly. "Do you know

why cops like you get stuck working cases thirty years cold? Because you don't have any imagination."

Ortiz laughed.

"Imagination? That's what you think I need?"

"Yeah. You know how much creative juice I think you got? None. Zero. Zilch. And without that you can't even begin to understand what happened thirty years ago. You're never going to find anything to pin Gallo's death on me. You might as well be trying to catch a whiff of a fart that left my ass six months ago."

Ortiz's smile actually widened.

"Oh, we'll find something," he said. "It'll take some time, but my team back home is thorough, and testing is much different than it was back when we were young pups. If you left one hair on Gallo's body, *one fucking hair,* your ass is grass. So it looks like you're wrong. I don't need imagination, all I need is a little patience."

He doesn't have anything, Ralphie, his old man whispered. *He came out here to poke at you.*

"It sounds to me like you got a whole lotta nothing, Ortiz," Loren said, as confident and mocking as he ever was, but the Kung Pao had turned to tasteless ash in his mouth. "Did you come all the way out to Colorado just to talk shit? That's what it seems like. You should've saved those airline miles for a trip to Hawaii. What a waste."

"I do have one more question, Loren," he said. "Were you in love with Constance Gallo? Did you love her, and killed her because you couldn't have her for yourself?"

CHAPTER THIRTY-SIX

September 4, 2018

She was standing on the edge of a cliff, the rock rough on the bottoms of her bare feet as she stared at the rushing waters below, mesmerized by the shining peaks and ripples, until she heard a twig snap behind her. She turned, slowly, but before she could see what was coming she was flying through the open air, weightless, her arms pinwheeling uselessly—

And then she was awake.

One thirteen in the morning, according to her cell phone. Elliott was crying in his room. By the sounds of it he'd just started and was gearing up to start screaming if one of them didn't go in. Tony jerked up and started to swing his legs out of the bed, but she shushed him, gently pushed him back down. He never woke up and wouldn't remember it in the morning.

She shrugged into a robe and hurried across the hall, scooped Elliott out of his bed, and held him cradled against her chest. He woke up often during the night, wanting to be soothed. Tony's mother always said they should let the boy cry it out, they were raising a needy wimp by responding to his every need, but Spengler found that she couldn't do it.

She'd been woken up by enough nightmares herself over the years, her heart pounding and her throat squeezed down to nothing, and she wasn't going to let her son wake that way with no one to comfort him.

She paced the room, patting his back and murmuring the nonsense all mothers do, and in less than five minutes he was asleep again. She put him back in bed and went downstairs. She wouldn't be able to fall asleep again, not for a while, if at all. She padded into the kitchen and poured herself a glass of water from the sink and reached into her soft leather briefcase, pulled out the file Ortiz had given her. She still hadn't looked at it, but the thought of it had burned in the back of her brain all night. Like an itch she couldn't quite reach. She'd have to read it sometime, so why not now?

She let herself out on the balcony and sat in one of the patio chairs. The back of the house faced west toward the mountains, that was part of the reason they'd bought this place to begin with, but there was nothing to see now, not at this time of night. Just a few dark shadows against the sky that you could only see from the corner of your eye, which disappeared when you tried to look straight at them.

It was chilly and damp outside. The sun had finally broken through that afternoon and warmed things up, but the temperature in Denver had a way of dropping like a rock when the sun went down. The bare skin of her arms prickled and tightened with goose bumps, her nipples twisted and hardened. She cupped her hands over her breasts and hunched over, like she was curling in on herself. She'd seen plenty of people sitting that way before, she realized, but not necessarily because of the cold. It was a natural reaction to try to protect yourself, to bend over and cover your most sensitive parts. During her years working sex trafficking cases she'd seen lots of women sitting like that, even when there was no one else around, because it became a habit to be wary of getting a punch in the stomach, of having a hand creep around your breast and pinch down. It was the worst thing in the world when violence became typical, when a person flinched away if you put your hand up because they were used to being smacked around. A person got used to expecting things, to being on constant watch for pain, and she wondered if Matt Evans was the type of guy who inspired that sort of reaction from the women around him.

Women have a funny way of ending up dead around that guy, Loren had said.

She took a sip of water. The inside of the glass had a flat, fishy smell that reminded her of the Three Forks River. The team was still searching for Marie Evans; they'd be back at it again once the sun came up. Two or three more days of searching and they'd call it quits. They had a budget to consider, and other cases the men should be working, and it might be that they'd never find Marie at all. Rivers all over the state were swollen enough that several people had drowned and their bodies remained unrecovered, and this might be another one of those cases. But even if they found her body, it might not give them any more information than what they already had.

Do you think Dad killed her? Hannah had asked.

"Yeah, I think he probably did," Spengler muttered. A cricket chirped nearby, as if in response. She'd spent the night before putting out all sorts of feelers—requesting records from Evans's banks and credit cards, his insurance companies. Money was one of the big reasons people killed, and Matt Evans had a lot of it, a lot of access to it. And it had always seemed to Spengler that the more money a person had, the more debt they had, and the more desperate things got when it all went south. *Mo' money, mo' problems,* Loren had said when they'd first pulled up in front of the Evanses' home for the first time. If Evans was in some sort of money trouble, that might be his motive. Kill his wife, collect the life insurance, move on.

But it might not be about money, so they'd do their due diligence. On paper, Evans didn't raise any red flags. Good job in sales, nice house. A seemingly stable marriage, two daughters in college. A handsome man. The kind of guy who took care of himself, who worked out and used sunscreen and knew that a person's appearance was important. He was college educated, paid his bills on time, hadn't gotten so much as a traffic ticket since 1998, when he'd been pulled over for going ten over the speed limit.

Oh, from all outside appearances, Matt Evans was a normal guy.

But Ted Bundy had seemed normal, too, even nice, and he'd killed more women than anyone had ever thought possible.

But it was almost always the person you least suspected who was the most horrible—Spengler had learned that from her time in sex trafficking. It was the men who looked the most pulled together who liked the worst things, the guys who wore good suits and carried Italian leather briefcases and used proper grammar who requested the youngest girls and boys for their vile needs. These were the guys who kept the most disgusting things on their computer history, who liked to use people as their own personal slaves, who did things to other human beings that Spengler would never say out loud.

And then there was Ralph Loren. The minute Loren opened his big mouth you knew he was a man capable of anything, but it didn't mean he'd done anything. Sure, he'd done things—Loren liked to mouth off and fight and enjoyed nothing more than to light a keg of gunpowder under your ass and sit back to watch the sparks fly—but part of that might be his own insecurities, or his strange sense of humor. Guys who blew the most smoke were almost always full of hot air, and that might be the case with Loren. Or not. She didn't know. That was the awful thing. Even if you knew a person well, even if you considered their life to be an open book and you knew their family and their middle name and how they liked to take their coffee, it didn't matter. You still couldn't know what was inside them, in the deepest hidey-holes of their heart.

Maybe Loren was a killer. Maybe Evans was a killer. Maybe Marie hadn't even known that her husband had been married before. It was a possibility. His own daughters hadn't known, either. And maybe Marie hadn't known that her husband's first wife had died gruesomely, so she'd been unprepared when she felt his hands against her back, shoving her over the edge of the cliff and into open air, hurtling her to her death below. But even if Marie had known, would it have mattered? Maybe not, because you never knew until you *really* knew, and by the time that happened someone was almost always hurt.

Or dead.

Spengler opened up the case file Ortiz had given her and started reading.

CHAPTER THIRTY-SEVEN

Matt Evans's office didn't look toward the mountains. Loren was surprised by that, because that seemed like the only thing people in this neck of the woods wanted: open concept homes, stainless steel appliances and granite countertops, and a view of the Rockies. Instead, Evans's office looked toward downtown—he could see the ugly white façade of Republic Plaza from the windows, and the odd curving outline of the Wells Fargo Center. Not a great view, but interesting enough.

"That's Writer Square," Jill said. This woman worked as Evans's assistant, and had been more than happy to show Loren around since Evans was still out of the office. She'd let Loren into the office but wouldn't leave him alone, and now came up to the big window and gestured at the plaza seven stories below them. There was a lot of action going on down there—little boutiques with racks of clothes pushed into the sunshine to lure in customers, and a coffee shop with bistro tables set up on the cobblestones outside, shaded with big striped umbrellas. "It's pretty this time of year with all the flowers blooming."

"Yeah, I guess," Loren said, turning away from the view and looking over Evans's desk. It was the biggest one he'd ever seen—it had cost over thirty thousand dollars, Jill had told him in an awed half whisper. Handcrafted by an artisan in Santa Fe. Please don't touch it. "This thing is big enough, you could have an orgy on top and still have room for chips and dip. Not exactly the most sanitary setup, but useful."

"Pardon?" Jill said, frowning. He knew she'd heard him right but was just too polite to let on otherwise.

"Never mind," he said. "Could I ask you a few questions about your boss?"

"Sure," Jill said, smiling brightly. "Anything I can do to help. I know this is a tough time for him."

"I'm sure it is," Loren said, dropping down in one of the plush chairs in front of the desk. If he'd sat behind the desk instead, he thought Jill here might throw a fit. "I know Mr.— ah, Mr. *E* would appreciate you helping me out."

Jill nodded and sat down in the chair beside him, her back straight and her knees pressed primly together. Eager-beaver Jill: there was one like her in every office. Jill, who had huge tits but still wasn't sexy, because you could tell by the way she moved that she treated them like a hassle because they were sure to catch spills and lint and everything else, like they had their own gravitational pull. It was impossible to tell her exact age—she was somewhere between twenty-five and forty, but where exactly did she fall on that scale? You couldn't know. Jill, who'd be sure to bring her boss a slice of cake on a paper plate when someone in the office had a birthday; Jill, who'd start dating a man and then be left in tears when he ghosted her. Sure, Loren had known plenty of women like Jill, who were all smart and hardworking and great assistants, and they were always so damn *eager*, but they were also easy to overlook. They were background noise. Static. Always there, but you wouldn't notice them until you needed them. Or needed to get rid of them. Loren had *known* Evans wasn't here, that he was at home away from prying eyes, but Loren had come anyway, because there was always someone in the office who knew more than anyone thought, who brought coffee and carried away secrets. And that person, Loren thought, might just be the woman sitting beside him, chewing nervously on a hank of her hair.

"Okay," Jill said, nodding so hard her hair bounced around her shoulders. She looked like a kid ready to start a test and hoping they had all the right answers. "Fire away."

"How long have you worked here?"

"Three years."

"And you like it?"

"Definitely," Jill said.

"Your boss is a good guy?"

"Yes. He's the best."

"And you know his wife?"

"Not very well," Jill said, her tone turning stiff and awkward. Ah, Marie was a sensitive subject with this one. She stood up and went back to the window, looked down over the view again. "I was horrified when I heard what happened. I'm sure he's devastated. I had a fruit basket couriered to him from the office with a card we all signed. We feel terrible about it."

"Did Mrs. Evans stop by the office a lot?"

"Uh, sometimes. She was just here last week. Stopped in while Mr. E was out at lunch to pick up his golf clubs. She wanted to get them engraved for his birthday next month." Jill pursed her lips. "She asked where he was, but Mr. E wasn't picking up his cell phone and I didn't know where he had gone or when he'd be back, and she wasn't very happy about it."

"What did she do?"

"She was upset. Came in here without me—Mr. E doesn't like anyone in here alone because there's sensitive paperwork and financial documents, but she insisted. Said she was going to make a few calls, and then she left. Didn't even say good-bye."

"Do you know where he was?"

Jill licked her lips.

"Like I *said*, I had no idea," she said.

She tugged her collar again. Most people aren't good liars; they give themselves away. Little things, usually. Gritting their teeth or looking away or touching their noses—signs of a liar.

Jill was lying.

"Your boss-man, is he porking anyone in the office?" Loren asked, a grin slowly blooming on his face.

"Pardon?"

"Oh, you heard me, Jilly. Is there some hot little piece of ass in the mailroom that might be riding his baloney pony during lunch hours?"

"Oh my," Jill said, sitting back suddenly, practically wilting into the arms of the chair. The color had drained from her face.

"Don't have a fainting spell, Jill!" Loren said. "I didn't

bring my smelling salts today. It's a simple question. Is your boss having an affair with someone in the office?"

She stared, gap-mouthed. Loren barely noticed, it'd happened so frequently before. The shock of having a cop—a detective, no less—speak like that was always a kick in the teeth.

"Well, Jill? Was he getting himself some *strange*? Was Mr. E dipping his wick in some other inkpot?"

"I—I don't think so," Jill stammered.

"Then *where* was he when his wife came looking for him? I think you know, Jill. Did you book him some fleabag room down on Colfax so he could spend his lunch hour bending a lady over the side of the bed?"

There were tears standing in her eyes, and one blink sent them rolling down her cheeks.

"Why're you crying?" Loren asked. "What's making you so upset?"

"I don't know," she said, turning to look at the ceiling and gently patting the delicate skin under her eyes. "I've never had to talk to the police before, and I guess I didn't expect you to be so—so *crude*."

Loren laughed. He'd been called plenty of things before, but he didn't think *crude* was ever one of them.

"Well, since this is your first time, let me give you some tips. When a cop asks you a question, you don't just sit there and boo-hoo. The proper response is to *answer the damn question*."

She was weeping now. Loren sighed. Time to change tactics. Sympathy came in handy during these times.

"Jill, I know you care about your boss. Maybe you even

love him. No judgment, it happens. But I'm the *police,* and I'm asking you a question. Has your boss been having an affair?"

He let her cry for a moment, then grabbed the box of tissues off the desk and thrust it into her hands. She dabbed at her eyes, then noisily blew her nose.

"I don't want to get Mr. E into any trouble," she said.

"Oh, he doesn't need your help with that. Between you and me, Jilly, Mr. E is doing well enough getting himself into a whole heap of trouble."

"What did he do?"

"You're forgetting how this works, aren't you? You're not supposed to be asking the questions here, I am. Now, I'm only going to ask one more time before I start to get pissed, and I promise I am not pleasant to be around when I'm pissed. Was Matt Evans romantically or physically involved with a woman who works in this office?"

"Okay," she said, her lower lip trembling as she watched him warily. "I don't know for sure, but I've heard a rumor that Mr. Evans has been friendly with a girl down in real estate."

"A rumor? You see this man every damn day and that's all you got? Can't do any better than a rumor?"

"All right!" she cried. "He's been meeting up with a woman during his lunch hour. Sometimes after work. And they've spent a lot of time alone in here with the door locked even though she doesn't directly report to him."

"What's her name?"

She gave him a sour look.

"Riley Tipton."

"See, was it really that hard to just open up and tell the police the truth?" Loren asked. "Do you know if this Riley Tipton is here today?"

"She's on vacation," Jill said. "She left last week for a trip to South America."

"When will she be back?"

"Not for another week at least. September twelfth at the earliest."

"How convenient," Loren muttered.

"Pardon?"

"Did you book the trip?" Loren asked, winking. "That's how you know all this? Mr. E is footing the bill for his lady love's time abroad?"

Jill wouldn't look up from the tissue crumpled in her hands.

"Yes. If Mr. E is traveling, I do all the legwork for him. Booking flights and hotels, renting cars. All of it."

"All right," he said easily. "Now, I just have one more question. If you're the one booking all these trips for your boss, you probably planned this one out to Estes Park, too?"

"No," Jill said. "All he asked me to do was request some literature about the area for him, but I didn't actually plan any of it."

"Do you happen to have any of those things lying around? I'd love to take a look if you do."

"Give me a second, let me see." She stood and leaned over the desk, grabbed a tissue, and noisily blew her nose, glaring at Loren as she did. Then she opened one of the drawers. Slid the first one shut and opened another. "Yes, it's right here. It's stuff about the town and things to do. Restaurants and shops, that kind of thing. And there's a map of the national park."

Loren smiled and took the thin sheaf of papers she held out, shuffled through them. Flipped open the map.

"Thank you," he said. "You've been a big—"

He paused. His heart had taken a small skip and was now thundering away in his chest, loud enough that he was sure this woman could clearly hear it.

"Detective?" Jill said. "Is everything okay?"

"Yeah, everything's fucking dandy," he said, pushing past Jill and out of the office, past the cubicles fluttering with activity and the front reception desk and into an elevator. The whole place smelled like fresh-baked bread—Jill had explained that the corporate kitchens were upstairs and they'd been testing a new recipe that morning, one that'd hopefully end up being rolled out to serve in the restaurants. When he was alone in the elevator, heading back down to the ground floor, he pushed a button and waited until the movement shuddered to a stop, then kneeled and opened up the map again. It was a map of Rocky Mountain National Park, just like Jill had said. All the landmarks and trails and lakes and restrooms and campgrounds had been drawn out so curious tourists could plan their days, but someone had put an extra mark on this map. It was an X, written in red, and the pen had pushed down so hard on the paper it'd nearly ripped through to the other side. And that X had been put right where Marie Evans had fallen to her death.

X marks the spot.

CHAPTER THIRTY-EIGHT

There are two types of people in this world. The first are the people who'd love to go back to high school if they could, those were their glory days, that's when they peaked.

The other type is made up of people who'd like to forget those four years completely.

Spengler had always fallen firmly into the second category. She'd grown up poor, raised by a single parent who constantly struggled to make ends meet. She looked different than everyone else, had a mother who didn't speak English well, couldn't afford the little things all teenagers want to have. Marion Spengler was doomed to be a high school loser from the moment she was born, and once she graduated she'd never expected to set foot inside one again.

But here she was.

"We've all been friends with Marie so long, the news of what happened was such a shock," one of the women said. "Detective, could you hand me that seashell? No, not that one. The curvy one. Yes. Thank you so much."

Book club, running club, volunteer work at the hospital and library—all of those things in Marie's life led back to a particular group of women: the PTA at Taft High School. They'd be happy to assist any way they could, Spengler was told when she reached the school's front desk—they were spending all day at the high school decorating the gym for the upcoming dance, but she was welcome to join them. The theme was Under the Sea, and when Spengler came in it looked like an ocean reef had thrown up. It was corny, but she'd seen worse.

"Isn't it beautiful?" one of the women asked, sighing as she gazed around. "I wish I'd been so lucky to go to dances like this in high school."

Personally, Spengler thought the kids wouldn't give a damn about the decorations, but she kept that opinion to herself. Ten years from now, this event would be nothing but a vague blip on the high school memory time line. She had a feeling it meant more to the PTA than it did the students.

"Who's running the PTA?" she asked the woman.

"No one is, now that Marie's gone. We're planning another election, and I'd guess Alice Schottelman will win. Alice and Marie always had a kind of rivalry."

"Which one is Alice?"

"The one over there. In the yoga pants."

"Everyone in here is wearing yoga pants."

"Oh, right. She's the one with the short blond hair. It's a good salon job, but you can see her roots if you look close enough."

Catty, Spengler thought. The women in the gym—about twenty of them, maybe more—were a tight-knit group, but they played with their claws unsheathed. Their kids had grown up together, they all lived in the same neighborhood and played Bunco and shared cocktail recipes. They were a group of women drawn together because their husbands had money; they had big houses, they had big diamond rings on their fingers that were definitely the real deal. These women were the modern-day Stepford Wives, but as it usually happens, they didn't see it for themselves.

Walking through the gym in her blue jeans and boots, Spengler was reminded of a video she'd found online not too long before. It was eight minutes long, and there were no actual people in it, only a single female mannequin wearing a sleek blond wig and dressed in exercise gear, posed in different positions for each changing shot, sometimes moving with arms and legs hooked up to wires and pulleys. A robotic voice had been dubbed over the whole thing, distorted and harsh, chanting the same words again and again.

I am good and fine.

Eight minutes of this, 480 seconds of shaky camcorder footage of a pale plastic figure and that chanting robot voice, it was one of the creepiest things she'd ever seen, and she wasn't exactly sure why these women reminded her of that video and that creepy, weird mannequin—maybe it was their perfect, unlined skin or their rail-thin bodies, or maybe it was because these women had taken themselves and slapped a thick coat of shellac on top and called it good.

And by all accounts, Marie had been the leader of them all.

"Alice?" Spengler asked, tapping the shoulder of the blond woman who'd been pointed out to her. "Alice Schottelman?"

"Yes?"

"I'm Detective Marion Spengler." She flashed her badge. "I'm here asking questions about Marie Evans."

"Oh, god," Alice said, putting a hand to her chest. "I was

torn to pieces when I heard what happened. Marie and I were best friends."

"Then you're exactly the person I need to speak with," Spengler said. "Is there somewhere private we can go?"

"Of course," Alice said. Her glossy lips parted in a glittering smile. "And I'll grab a few of the other girls. They wouldn't want to miss this."

CHAPTER THIRTY-NINE

Spengler had once heard Loren say a man had a punchable face, and she hadn't understood what he meant. Now she did, because she'd have liked nothing more than to knock every one of Alice Schottelman's perfectly capped teeth down her lousy throat.

"Marie's been the PTA president for the last five years," Alice said. "Even though Maddie graduated last year, she was elected for another term. She still runs the place. Or *ran,* I guess. There'll be another election soon to fill her position. I might just throw myself into the race, see what I can do."

She winked.

"Make Taft High School great again," one of the other two women said.

All three of them tittered, their sharp, high-pitched laughs bouncing off the walls of the teachers' lounge and piercing Spengler's ear like a knife. She cleared her throat.

"Did you all know the Evans family well?"

"We were best friends," Alice said. "I knew about the trip to Estes. Marie was excited. She said it was Matt's idea. A nice romantic getaway. But for it to end like this—it's so awful."

"Terrible."

"Horrifying."

"I think the worst part of it is that Marie fell off a cliff. I literally can't imagine her falling off anything. She didn't like the unexpected. She'd plan her days down to the minute, wrote it all down in this thick planner she'd carry around. She put what time she'd be going to sleep at night, can you imagine? Sometimes I wondered what would happen if she'd suffered from insomnia and couldn't fall asleep according to schedule. It would've driven her crazy." Alice sighed. "I can't think she'd put her foot down in the wrong spot. But you're here investigating Matt, right? Because I'm sure Marie didn't fall. Matt had to have pushed her. It's the only thing that makes sense."

Spengler had discovered that Alice only stopped talking when she needed the oxygen, and then she'd only pause for the briefest moment. Spengler started to respond but didn't have time to form a single word before Alice started talking again.

"Yes, when I heard it was Marie who'd fallen, I was sure it was a mistake. The media screwing things up, reporting errors. But when it turned out to be true—well, every couple has problems, I guess. But if you'd asked me who'd murder who in that marriage, I would've put my bet on Marie. She was great at planning things."

"Do you remember the time Marie planned that surprise party for Holly?" the third woman asked.

"Or the winter carnival two years ago?"

"Or what about—"

This was one of the most bizarre conversations Spengler had ever heard. These three women were enacting a strange sort of memorial service for Marie, remembering all the things she'd done. She let them go on, trading stories and laughing, although she had her own questions she'd ask when there was a break in the conversation. Was Marie afraid of her husband? Had she ever complained about money problems? Did she ever mention feeling in danger in her own home?

No, everything was no. Nothing like that had ever happened. None of them had ever noticed anything was wrong in the Evanses' marriage. In fact, they all agreed, Marie and Matt never really seemed to have problems—at least, they didn't air their dirty laundry for everyone to see. Instead, the three women were more interested in rehashing every memory they had of Marie.

"—that time Marie dealt with Kara Mason?"

"God, that was awful."

"Yeah, I never thought Marie would take it that far."

"What happened with Kara Mason?" Spengler asked curiously. The three women exchanged looks, but she didn't think she'd have to push them to talk about this. They *wanted* to tell her what'd happened, that's why it'd come up in the first place. The juicier the gossip, the more satisfying it was to pass along.

"Last year, Marie suggested a change to the school's lunch menu," Alice said. "Kara Mason opposed it and things got pretty nasty between them."

"I'm sure you've realized our school is named after former president Taft, who was *severely overweight,* and obesity is a huge issue facing our children," the woman to the right said, her eyes lit up with a fervor approaching something holy. "At the beginning of the school year, Marie implemented a program to offer much healthier options to the students. Low-fat, gluten-free, responsibly grown food from local farmers. Artisanal breads, meats, and cheese that comes from free-range, grass-fed cows. Do you know what I mean?"

I had a Pop-Tart for breakfast, Spengler thought, smothering a smile. She nodded, because she recognized the look in the woman's eyes. It was obsession, plain and simple. For some people their obsession was drugs and alcohol, for others it was plastic surgery or biting their fingernails or gambling. But for women like these the obsession was food, in monitoring every bite they ate, in making careful lists for the grocery store. *Organic, gluten-free, grass-fed, seasonal*— those were their buzzwords. These were women who had the leisure time to spend hours poring over their meals, who didn't have to budget their grocery bill. These women drank black coffee blended with coconut oil and a pat of butter, who drank water only if it was full of electrolytes.

"Kara was extremely vocal against the changes," Alice said, leaning forward and lowering her voice. It'd started to feel like she was telling a ghost story around a campfire. "She started spreading all sorts of lies about Marie. Said she'd seen her eating cheese puffs while she was waiting in the carpool lane and that she'd caught her sticking her finger down her throat after a PTA dinner to purge. And then Kara started going around with a petition to have Marie removed from her post as president."

"And people were actually signing it," woman number three said, holding up her fingers and counting off the complaints. "They said Marie's plans weren't budget friendly.

That she was running the school like she owned the place. That she didn't actually care about the students, just herself."

"So Marie decided to call a truce. She rented out a banquet hall and had the whole thing catered, made Kara the guest of honor. She told everyone she was waving her white flag, that she wasn't up for the fight anymore. They needed to put their differences aside and do what was best for the students."

"I was at the same table as Marie and Kara that night," Alice said. "You'd think those two were best friends, the way they were laughing and toasting champagne."

"It was a good party," number three said.

"Oh, it was a wonderful party," Alice said. "But I think Kara must've had a bit too much to drink, and she started throwing up all over the table and herself. It was disgusting. And the next day, the nudes started showing up on Instagram."

"Nudes?" Spengler asked.

"Kara claimed her phone had been stolen that night at the party, and her personal photos were starting to pop up on her Instagram feed," Alice said. "Sexually explicit photos, if you get my drift. They were so obviously Kara, she didn't even try to deny it. And sometimes they'd be up online for *hours* before she'd figure out how to remove them."

"And there was a man in some of the photos. Not her husband."

Spengler looked back and forth between the three women. They might've been rehashing the drama of their favorite soap opera, that's how involved they were. It was almost scary.

"So Kara's husband left her, and all she had were her kids and the PTA. But everyone was so disgusted with her at that point, no one would really even speak to her, and her petition died," number two said. "Then she baked a tray of brownies and brought them over to Marie's house as a peace offering. Figured the best way to get back in everyone's good graces was to make nice with Marie."

"Oh, I was there when she dropped them off. Poor thing looked like a wet, dirty rag, that's how bad things had gotten for her," Alice said. "And Marie was so gracious, accepted the brownies and said the family would eat them for dessert that night. But they never did. I was with Marie in her kitchen and that stupid cat of hers jumped up on the counter and started eating them. I saw it with my own eyes. And then that thing started howling and choking, and then it fell over and died."

"What happened?" Spengler asked.

"Marie took it to the vet and had tests run. They all came back inconclusive, but you know what I think?" Alice leaned closer. Her eyes glittered meanly and her lips had gone razor thin, smearing lipstick on her teeth. "Kara had tried to poison Marie and her whole family because she thought Marie had stolen her phone and published those nudes. And once everyone found out about those brownies and Marie threatened to press charges, Kara was done. She had to pull her kids out of the school and move. None of us have seen her since."

Alice sat back, satisfied with herself.

"Did Marie steal Kara's phone and put the photos online?" Spengler asked. She'd thought all three might be shocked and offended at the question, that they'd shut her down and ask her to leave, but that wasn't the case.

"Of course she did," Alice said. "I'm sure Marie has done all sorts of crazy things, but she's smart about it. Doesn't tell anyone and never gets caught."

"Like the time Maddie was the understudy in *Romeo and Juliet*, and Juliet just happened to slip in the locker room and break her leg, so Maddie took the role." Woman two shrugged. "I could never figure out how she did it, but it had to be Marie. She was *furious* when Maddie didn't get the part."

"Or that time Principal Lee denied Marie's request for a larger PTA budget, and Lee's tires were slashed the next week? Officially it was blamed on a student, but—*c'mon*. Totally Marie."

"You all knew what she was doing and never said anything?"

"Well, we *knew* what she was doing, but it's not like we *knew*, if you get my drift," woman number three said. "And it's not like she ever killed anyone. Well, I always wondered about the cat. I know how it looked, but I couldn't really see Kara trying to poison anyone. But I guess you don't have to kill a person to destroy them."

"So you think Marie—"

"Oh, I don't *think* anything. But Marie doted on that cat. Fancy canned food. Always letting it up in her lap, letting it sleep in their bed. When it died she was devastated." The third woman paused, running the sharp point of her tongue over her lips. "All I'm saying is that I wonder. The cat turning up dead in front of everybody was the best way to get rid of Kara, once and for all."

"If you stayed on Marie's good side, she was the most generous, loving friend a person could have," woman two said. She looked down at her hands while she spoke, spinning the wedding ring on her third finger. "She was always a lot of fun. But she could be crazy."

CHAPTER FORTY

Spengler was driving back to the station when her phone rang. She pulled over to answer. It was the Evanses' insurance agent. The woman hadn't bothered returning any of her calls or emails, so Spengler had stopped by the office that morning before heading to the high school to meet with the PTA ladies. People moved faster when they saw a badge and a gun.

"Sorry it took so long," the woman said. "With the holiday weekend and tech issues, I've been swamped."

"Of course," Spengler said graciously. That was the standard excuse when anything went wrong these days. Tech issues. "What do you have for me? Any changes to their policies recently?"

"Marie Evans came in at the end of January and upped her life insurance policy," the insurance agent said. Spengler unrolled her window as she held the phone to her ear, hoping for a breath of fresh air, but the street smelled faintly of wet garbage. "Mr. Evans's policy stayed at three million dollars, while Mrs. Evans's went from a half a million up to three."

"That's a lot of money," Spengler had said. A homeless man strolled past on the sidewalk and saw her sitting there. He grabbed his crotch and shook his hips in her direction, stuck out his tongue in a leer. It was like some men were conditioned to be disgusting and disrespectful to women. She wasn't in the mood. Not that she was ever in the mood for it. Without putting the phone down, Spengler pulled her gun from the holster at her waist and pointed it at him, mimed pulling the trigger. *Bang.* He ran in the opposite direction, giving her a terrified look over his shoulder. He wouldn't be shaking his dick at anyone again in the near future. It was unfortunate, but sometimes a woman had to take extreme measures to teach a man a lesson.

"It *is* a large policy but not unheard of, especially for a couple with the net worth they have," the agent said. "What is unusual is to have that amount of coverage when Mrs. Evans wasn't generating any income. It was ultimately approved after she'd gone through a physical and had blood work—all standard procedure on a policy that high—but it did seem odd."

"Did both the Evanses come in to your office to update the policy?"

"Oh, no. Just Mrs. Evans. Such a nice woman. As she was signing the papers, she did say one thing—I really didn't think about it until I reread the notes I'd put in the system after she left."

"What's that?"

"She mentioned it was her husband's idea that she up her policy. She said he'd been pushing her to come in and take care of it. She thought it was funny, I remember. She laughed."

Of course Evans had pushed his wife into it. But here was the question: Why? Spengler had received most of the Evanses' financial records and one thing had become clear after one look: if Matt had killed his wife, it hadn't been for the insurance. They had a big house—the mortgage balance almost paid—lots of money in savings, fat retirement accounts. They had virtually no debt and plenty of capital. They were comfortable. So why would Evans want his wife to have such a high insurance policy on her head?

"I did tell Mrs. Evans she could certainly come back anytime and we could lower the amount of the policy if she was having second thoughts, but she never did. And I'd completely forgotten about the whole thing until I got your call. Are you thinking Mr. Evans pushed his wife off a cliff so he could collect her life insurance?"

Another call came through before Spengler could answer, not that she intended to give any sort of response to the woman's question.

It was Loren.

"Spengler, Evans had a fucking map in his desk," he said. "It's got the point where she fell marked, like he'd planned the whole thing ahead of time."

"Hang on," she said. Her phone had started buzzing as she held it against her ear. Another call was coming through. It was Jackson, head of the search team.

When it rains it pours, she thought.

"Hikers spotted a body about ten miles farther south," he said. "I'm here now, we got her out of the water. Looks like your gal."

CHAPTER FORTY-ONE

September 5, 2018

"You all right?" Spengler asked, concerned. "You look dead on your feet today."

"I'm fine," Loren said. He took both hands off the wheel and rubbed the ridges of his brows. Alarmed, Spengler saw he was steering the car with his left knee. "I didn't sleep well, that's all."

"Maybe you should let me drive—"

"Yeah, right," Loren said. He put a hand back on the wheel and Spengler's heart rate dropped again. "As if I'd let *you* behind the wheel of my pride and joy."

"You call *this* your pride and joy?" she asked, astonished.

"What would *you* call it?"

Loren waited for her answer, but Spengler kept her mouth shut. Probably the best decision. He snorted and reached over, twisted the volume dial on the radio. His car was an early-nineties brown Chrysler LeBaron—*This is the height of luxury,* Loren told her when she first got in, thumping his fist on the steering wheel, and she hadn't been able to tell if he was trying to be funny. Probably not. The car was old, but it ran nicely and the interior was in perfect condition. She'd been surprised at how comfortable it was inside. *Good lumbar support,* Loren had said as she settled into the passenger seat, not the merest flicker of a joke in his eyes.

Loren was an old white man driving an old white man's car, all kinds of stereotypes there, and she'd assumed that he'd listen to news radio when he drove, or to country music. But Loren liked rap music and R&B, would only listen to a local Denver station, and he always played it loud.

"One-oh-seven-five," Loren said when she asked. "It's the only thing worth turning on around here."

Maybe she still hadn't worked with Loren long enough to realize that you couldn't put him in a box, that if you tried to guess what he was going to say or do you'd almost always be wrong.

"Watch yourself!" Loren shouted, jerking the car to the next lane to avoid being hit, causing her shoulder to ram against the door. He might have been yelling at the other driver, or it might've been directed at her. It was impossible to tell.

She'd gotten back to the station before Loren and run upstairs, ducked into Chief Black's office without knocking first. He'd been typing when she came in, his fingers moving surprisingly fast over the keyboard. She'd expected him to be a hunter-pecker sort of typist. She'd dropped the file Ortiz had given her on his desk and waited as he flipped through. Then he'd turned his rheumy eyes up to her, unimpressed.

"This Ortiz guy sure is getting around," he said.

"You already know about this?"

"Not much goes on around here I don't know about."

"So what do you want me to do?"

"I don't want you to do anything. Give it to Loren if you don't want it anymore. Or shred it. That might be even better."

She didn't understand what was going on. It was like watching shapes move under a blanket. Were those bumps just feet sliding around, or were they monsters? Someone else might know the truth, but she didn't.

"Here," she said, not looking away from the road as she jammed the rolled file at Loren, poking him in the side until he took it from her. "I think this belongs to you."

"What's this?"

"Look at it."

"In case you haven't realized this, Spengler, I'm driving," Loren said drily. "So unless you'd like Jesus to take the wheel, maybe you'd better just tell me what it is."

"Detective Ortiz gave it to me."

Loren gave her a measured look from the corner of his eye, then accepted the folder, laid it across his thighs.

"You read it?"

"Yeah, last night."

"Okay."

"Did you kill your partner?"

He didn't answer.

"Ortiz thinks you did," she said. "And from what's in that file, it sure looks like you might've murdered him."

She'd joined Homicide fully aware of all the gossip surrounding Loren: he was mean as a rabid dog, and sometimes stupid. There were stories about his hot temper and the way he liked to use his fists, and the crazy things he'd do to close a case. She'd heard he'd once assaulted a suspect, kicked the guy between the legs so hard it'd actually ruptured his balls. He dressed up like the criminals he was hunting, took on their personas, ate what he thought they ate, picked up their bad habits. Hunting, that's what he called it, like he was dressed in camouflage with a shotgun slung over his shoulder, pushing aside the undergrowth to track prey.

She'd heard all of this about Loren and laughed. How could all that be true about one man? But when she met Loren, when she spoke to him and saw the slow, pendulating way his eyes would constantly swing back and forth and how he'd clench his fists, open and closed, over and over again, she thought the stories might be true.

"Loren, did you hear me?"

Loren was mean and ugly—so ugly he didn't just fall outta the ugly tree, he planted the damn thing, put it in the dirt, and pissed on it to make it grow—but he was also smart and quick and funny—she'd heard him call Chief Black Rumpleforeskin and Queef Biscuit—but he also seemed . . . *lost*? She couldn't put her finger on what was wrong with him, because it wasn't just one thing. It was everything. It was the way he'd always hum under his breath without seeming to notice, or the way he'd start speaking out of nowhere, as if he was restarting a conversation that'd already ended, or the way he'd hold his phone up to his ear and listen, even when the screen was black. And it was his office, the walls covered in crime scene photos and typed reports, and the clown paintings. There was an evidence bag tacked up beside his office window, holding a single child's shoe. Toddler sized, with several drops of blood dried on the toe and laces.

Loren scared her, but she pitied him, too, although she didn't know why.

"What if I told you I didn't want to talk about it?" he asked slowly.

"I guess I'd have to accept it. For now, at least," she said. "But everyone talks, sooner or later."

Loren sighed.

"You're a fool if you believe that, Spengler."

He didn't speak again for the rest of the drive.

CHAPTER FORTY-TWO

Loren's father was singing and he wouldn't shut up.

Bad boys, bad boys, he crooned. *Whatcha gonna do, whatcha gonna do when the law comes for you?*

"Inner monologue, my fucking ass," he muttered.

"Loren, you alright?" Spengler asked. She couldn't hear the singing, of course, that was his own special gift, a little welcoming gift for his descent into Crazy Town.

Loren closed his eyes, didn't respond. Nothing, that's what he figured he'd do, until he didn't have a choice. He didn't have the time to worry about Ortiz and Gallo and all the other ghosts from his past. He was supposed to be thinking of other things at the moment. Like the dead woman on the ground in front of him. She was bloated and pale, her dark hair still wet and stringy from the water. Her skull was shattered in the back. It looked like an egg that'd been cracked once against a counter and then the yolk had done a slow exit.

The body would be taken to the coroner's office and Evans would have to identify her in the next day or so. Loren had already made some calls, requested a warrant so they could search Evans's house. It'll be interesting, Loren thought, to see the man looking down at his dead wife. Most times bodies are identified through a photo or a video feed, set up in the least traumatic way possible. It was rarely done in person, but Loren wanted to get a good look in Evans's eyes when he lifted the sheet and saw what he'd done. And at that exact moment, Loren planned on asking Evans about his first wife, Janice.

Did you love both these women and you still killed them? That was what he'd ask. It was almost the same thing Ortiz had asked him.

Did you kill Constance, even when you loved her? Because you couldn't have her?

Loren knew you could love a person, be in love with them, and still want to hurt them. To kill them. He knew it from experience.

Constance Gallo. That's what Gallo had always called her, *Constance.* But Loren had called her Connie, like Connie Francis, that singer from *wayback,* and the two women had even looked a little alike, with the same curling dark hair and big Spanish eyes. She'd begged him with those eyes. Please don't do this. One of those eyes had been swollen completely shut and one side of her mouth pulled down in a grotesque frown. There'd been so much blood and tears, that's what he remembered most. All the blood, and Gallo on the floor, the back of his skull blown away to nothing and the grayish-yellow fluid leaking from the smoking hole in the bone, and Connie's weeping. Her begging, down on her knees, bunching handfuls of his shirt into her fists. He burned that shirt in his fireplace that night, watched as the flames ate away the bloody handprints she'd left on the fabric.

Please, Ralph, she'd cried. *Please don't do this.*

CHAPTER FORTY-THREE

"Could the river have really swept her ten miles downstream in a week?" Spengler asked. "You said bodies sink."

They were standing on the river's rocky shore, in an area where the water made a sharp twist and things that'd been floating along without any problem suddenly got stuck on the edges of rocks and caught on the broken branches. There was plenty of garbage out there, too. Hamburger wrappers and clumps of paper and plastic milk jugs and lots of dead leaves. The bend didn't only catch trash, though. It was where the nude body of Marie Evans was spotted, a branch stuck through the meatiest part of her thigh, sticking her in place the same way you'd pin a butterfly to a board.

Jackson shrugged. He was chewing gum; she could see the flash of bright green between his jaws every time he spoke, stuck to the ridge of his teeth.

"Anything's possible, I suppose," he said. His hands were jammed deep into the pockets of his fluorescent orange vest. "I never would've thought so, but stranger things have happened."

Spengler was standing on top of a flat rock, but the moisture had still managed to seep in through the soles of her shoes even though they were supposed to be waterproof.

Loren was closer, looking over the body, but she stayed back. The smell was awful, and she was afraid if she came any closer she'd vomit. Besides, she could see enough from back here. Marie Evans had bloated in the water; her face had taken on both the grayish-green color and swollen shape of a winter melon, except the backside of the skull, where the bone had been crushed in, broken and shattered like a walnut shell. Otherwise, there was little recognizably human left. Her eyeballs were long gone, her nose was a sunken mess, her mouth a gaping, empty maw. And strangely, all that made it easier to look at, because then it wasn't like looking at a person at all but just a *thing*, maybe something slapped together out of papier-mâché by a toddler.

"She's bloated up pretty bad for not being in the water so long," Jackson said, watching the body bag slowly zip up over her face. "Almost looks like she's been dead a lot longer than she has."

CHAPTER FORTY-FOUR

September 7, 2018

"It's right through here," Detective Spengler said. "We'll just need you to take a look and make a positive ID. It might be a little disturbing—"

"I'll be fine," Matt said, and Spengler didn't say anything, just blinked. That was the extent of her surprise, the lowering of her eyelids. But he guessed she'd seen just about everything during her time as a detective. Grief made people crazy, it made them act out of character, and he imagined she'd been trained to handle just about anything.

Loren, standing off to one side, grunted.

"Okay, then," Spengler said. "Follow me back."

She led the two men through the swinging metal doors, into a smaller room. They were in the basement of the Denver County Coroner's Office, in the morgue. It was cold and airless down here, all cement and metal, the unforgiving white lights not allowing for any shadows. He hadn't had to identify Janice, he'd never even seen what was left of the body that'd been pulled from the house. *A briquette,* that's what Reid had said. *She burned fast and bright, until there was barely anything left. Just a handful of bones.*

He'd gotten the call from the PD the night before, sitting at home with a book open on his lap, trying to watch TV and not really seeing what was on the screen. They'd been searching for Marie for more than a week now and had found nothing. It was hard in the mountains, picking their way through the trees and scrubs and rock as they searched the water and along the shore, but at least now it was over.

There was a polished steel table in the center of the room with a woman laid out on it, a white sheet pulled up over the swells of her breasts, all the way up to the base of her throat. He could only see the top of her head from this angle, her dark hair and the messy wound where her skull had caved in. Marie had grown her hair out over the last year and dyed it to hide the gray, darker each time until it was nearly black. Whoever had laid her out on the table had smoothed it back from her face, and the length of it was coiled on the metal table beside her head. Like a snake.

"Are you okay, Mr. Evans?" Spengler asked. She sounded concerned, but Loren was smiling. Enjoying Evans's discomfort. Getting off on it.

"Yeah, I think so," Matt said. He stumbled to a stop a few feet away from the body. The smell of chemicals became stronger as he got closer, bitter and sharp and tangy all at once, scents that reminded him of the days his mother would get it into her head to clean the entire house, when she'd wrap her hair up in a bandanna and go through with her bucket of hot, soapy water and pile of rags and unending arsenal of sprays and scrubs and bottles and turn everything inside out and upside down. Those were days Matt knew to make himself scarce, to head to a friend's house or at least lock himself in his room, and he sucked down a deep breath as the door closed behind him, remembering those days before his mother had passed, before his father had remarried and became one of *those* guys. Everybody knows them—the guys who fuck their secretaries, who leave their wives and families behind when they get a taste of something new, men who let their dicks lead the way, and that's exactly what his father had become, and they'd grown distant over time, until the old man had died when he was a teenager and it'd been too late to mend things by then. And maybe that kind of behavior was embedded in a person's DNA, could be passed down through the generations, because Matt had been heading down that same path himself, hadn't he? Why, yes. Yes, he had. He'd been fucking a girl from the office, and his relationship with his daughters had become strained and awkward—enough so that when the two of them came home the week before to help in their mother's search they'd both checked into a hotel instead of staying at the house where they'd been raised. East, west, home's best—but not in this case. His own daughters treated him like a stranger, and it was easier when they weren't around, but Marie had done the same thing over the last few years, hadn't she? He'd sometimes come home from work to find her reading a book or bent over one of her never-ending quilting projects and she'd look up with surprise, like she hadn't expected him to come home again. Like she *hoped* he wouldn't come home again. Like he was some random man she just happened to sleep beside at night.

They'd been together for a long time; they had two daughters, two imported cars sitting in the driveway of their renovated house; they had a lifetime of memories together. They had everything, that's what people said, but there were times it felt like nothing. Less than nothing. Matt would sometimes be on his way to work, driving his nice car and drinking the pricey latte he'd picked up at the coffee shop, and he'd think, This is it? This is the life I get to live, on and on, the same routine every day until I die? Maybe he was having the midlife crisis people were always talking about. He'd turned forty-seven on his last birthday, closer than ever to fifty and an AARP membership, and he'd started to get man-tits and the roll of lard around his middle that made it so he had trouble seeing his own cock when he looked down; his hips sometimes ached for no reason and there were nights he'd go to sleep and then wake up again for no reason at all, awake for the day. All because he was getting *fucking old*.

They'd gone to marriage counseling a few years back, and the therapist had suggested they keep the lines of communication open. Find time to talk to each other every day, she'd said. Tell each other how you're feeling, what you're worried about. Express your emotions. You have to feel connected to each other.

It was good, pithy advice, but like all advice, it was easier said than done.

A perfect example: when he'd mentioned his fear of getting old to Marie not long before, this fear that this was *it*, there was nothing else to look forward to, that it wasn't enough, even though he had a big house with a man cave and a car with fine leather interior and thick hand stitching on the steering wheel, real *craftsmanship*, even though he had money in the bank and there was plenty of food in the fridge and the girls were well behaved and smart and polite. Maybe he *was* having a midlife crisis. But it still wasn't enough, and Marie had been offended, as if he'd said *she* wasn't enough. That was Marie for you—always making herself the victim, twisting a simple conversation so it'd turn into an argument. The therapist had said they should talk, communication would bring them closer, but those times instead turned into battlefields, strewn with land mines and trip wires, where a single misstep could blow up in his face.

He'd told Marie it wasn't enough, but he hadn't meant to make it about *her*, at least he hadn't thought it was, but maybe it was about her after all, because he'd started sleeping with Riley while Marie was still angry about his comment and wouldn't speak to him, during that stretch of days when she'd gone stalking around the house slamming cabinet doors and going to bed with her back turned. He'd been fantasizing about going to bed with Riley Tipton, who worked down in real estate at his office and wore those high-waisted skirts that clung to her thighs and had a wiggly way of walking when she pushed the cart that made men turn and stare, but he'd never thought it would happen, he'd never thought it was even a *possibility*. Oh, he'd slept with plenty of women over the years of his marriage, but Riley was so young and *tight*. Out of his league. An idle fantasy, that was all, the same way he'd imagined sleeping with the teller at the bank or the young women pushing strollers through downtown as they window-shopped. Completely harmless fantasies, but never going to happen. Not in the cards.

And then he stayed late at the office one night, trying to

catch up on paperwork but really just avoiding going home since Marie was still pissed, and Riley came into his office after everyone else had left and he hadn't been able to help himself. He'd had a few indiscretions over the years, usually when he was traveling away from home and alone in a hotel room, but he'd never done anything with any of the women in his office.

You don't shit where you eat, George, the man who'd first brought him on with the company, hired him straight off the dealership lot, had always said. *You need a woman, don't look inside this building for her. That'll cause nothing but trouble in the long run.*

And Matt had managed to live by that rule until Riley showed up with her blouse unbuttoned low enough he could see the lace of her bra and her skirt hiked high up on her thighs and sat right on his lap. He didn't put up much of a protest. Part of that was because he and Marie didn't have sex very often anymore, she said her libido was down, probably hormonal, she'd promise to go to the doctor to check it out and would never make an appointment, but some of it was just *because.* There are no reasons, sometimes.

So Matt gave in, he pushed Riley up against the big window behind his desk and had her. Afterward, he'd spat in a tissue and wiped away the handprints she'd left behind on the glass, as well as the two smeary circles left by her breasts. It could've been a onetime thing, a foolish decision made on the spur of the moment, he *knew* that, but he hadn't been able to stop, because Matt *did* need something more than Marie, although he'd never say that to her, not in a million years. He loved Marie, but he needed something more, and there was no way he would've been able to get out of his marriage in a normal way, not with the history he had with Marie, not with everything they'd been through together.

Now she was dead. And he was free.

Or was he?

"I know you're not happy," Marie had said. She'd come into the bathroom as he was brushing his teeth and perched on the counter beside the sink, folded her legs beneath herself. They were bare and toned, the golden hairs on her thighs barely visible in the fluorescent lights above the sink. They'd spent tens of thousands of dollars renovating this house, shipping pendant lights in from France and having them installed in the bathroom, and their light was soft and comforting. It didn't strike him as bad until later that he knew more about those lights than he did about the thoughts going through his wife's head. "And I think I understand why."

"You do?" he'd asked, shifting the toothbrush from one side of his mouth to the other.

"Of course I do. I know you so well I can practically *hear* what you're thinking." His heart gave an uneasy thump at those words, because what he'd been thinking about was Riley coming into his office and kneeling between his legs while he sat at his desk and sucking him off like she had just a few hours before, but Marie was smiling, she couldn't have known. Could she? "You need some excitement in your life, and I know just how to give it to you."

Years before, that smile and those words would've made his heart race and given him a raging tent in his pants, but he was older now. Maybe not any wiser, but wise enough to know that when Marie wanted to do something exciting it couldn't be good. Like the time she'd said she wanted to do something different in bed and asked him to put his hands around her throat as their bodies ground into each other, to squeeze until her face had gone purple and swollen and full of blood. And he had, he'd put both hands around the delicate stalk of her neck and clamped down until her eyes had bulged from her head and she was clawing at his hands, trying to signal at him to let go, and he'd come so hard he'd nearly passed out. It was the control that made it so good, he figured. If he'd held down on her neck for a minute longer— *thirty seconds longer* would've done it—things would've been different. But there was a time and place for everything, and he'd held off.

"You could've killed me," Marie had said, rubbing the rising circlet of bruises around her throat. Her voice was hoarse for days after that, like she was coming down with a chest cold.

"Maybe I should kill you," Matt said, and she'd laughed.

"I'd haunt you from beyond the grave," Marie said. "You'd never get rid of me."

No big deal, that's how they'd always talked to each other, they'd joked about those things, wink-wink nudge-nudge, but in the past week Matt had tried to remember if they'd ever talked like that in front of anyone, or had they only done it when they were alone?

He wasn't sure.

"I don't need any excitement," he'd told his wife, holding his toothbrush out in front of him like a weapon, the bubbles from the toothpaste filling his mouth and squirting out the corners, but he didn't spit, he didn't want to take his eyes off Marie, even for a moment.

"Yeah, you do," she'd said, and he'd felt his balls shrinking up into his body. Did he love his wife? Yes, he did. He sometimes thought he'd come to love her more over all the years they'd been together, he even admired her, but he was also a little scared of her because once Marie got an idea in her head it was as good as done. He was supposed to be the brilliant salesman but he sometimes thought it was the other way around, because Marie had always been able to talk him into anything.

Spengler and Loren stayed where they were, near the examination room's door, and Matt crept around the side of the table until he could see the woman's face. It was swollen and bruised—she looked more like an inflated ball of uncooked bread dough than a human. She was unrecognizable.

"Is it Marie?" Spengler asked. Her arms were folded across her chest.

"Just curious, but was it like this when you identified your first wife after she was murdered?" Loren asked. He was grinning. Matt's hand jerked involuntarily, and Loren's grin widened.

"No," he said. "They never asked me to look at Janice."

Matt came to the table and grabbed a corner of the plain white sheet and lifted so he could see the rest of her body. When they'd first married, Marie had always slept naked, and he used to lift the bedding in this same way to get a look at her in the middle of the night, ripe and rounded, and more often than not he'd wake her up for a little roll in the sack. She'd never complain about being woken up, she never said anything at all, just let him do what he wanted. The bedroom was the only place she ever gave in, sat back and let him take control. Encouraged it. *I don't mind taking one for the team,* Marie used to say, and he always hated that, because it didn't feel like they were part of a team in bed, but like he was by himself, using her for what he needed. What he wanted.

The woman's body wasn't in much better shape than the face. Swollen and broken, cuts and sores dotting the rubbery flesh. Her nipples had gone a grayish color, her fingernails were black and crumbling away at the tips, there was a long slash across the bottom of one foot.

Loren's cell phone rang, and he left the room. Spengler stayed. Matt kept looking. It seemed to him that his vision had begun to swim in and out of focus, like a camera lens trying to readjust.

There was a mole at the base of her left breast, the kind that's raised and dark brown with the texture of a raisin, sitting right where a bra would nuzzle up against the skin. Matt had kissed that mole the week before, nibbled on it, and she'd laughed and pushed him away. He'd been at her place, saying their good-byes because Riley was going on a trip to South America. She'd always wanted to go, so he'd had Jill book the trip. She'd screamed when he told her, jumped into his arms and nearly bowled him over. Riley was supposed to be in Machu Picchu now, out of cell phone range as she explored the ancient ruins, but she wasn't. She was *here*. Here. Dead. Her face beaten and swollen, her hair a thick rope on the cold metal table.

His vision swam in and out of focus, and it felt like the volume on everything had been turned down, too. Spengler said something, but it was muffled, as if he had pillows pressed against his ears. Maybe *this* was shock.

He dropped the sheet. It caught the air for a moment, billowed out like a cloud before it settled again, slowly, as if by magic. The door opened and Loren stuck his head in, said something to his partner. Spengler nodded and left, shot a long look at Matt before closing the door behind her.

Matt's cell phone was vibrating in his pocket. He slowly pulled it out, looked at the screen. He was getting a call from an unknown number. He considered declining the call, letting it go to voice mail, but then answered it anyway. Because he knew who it was. She'd always had impeccable timing.

"Hello?" he said. Cautiously, because he thought it might be a hallucination, his own mind playing tricks on him. It wasn't all that far-fetched, not after everything that'd happened in the last few days. He might be imagining the phone was ringing—hell, he might be imagining the phone altogether, and if he pulled it away from his head and looked, he might be holding a banana up to his ear. That thought made him giggle hysterically, and he clamped a hand down over his mouth, because how would it look, for the cops to hear him laughing like that? "Hello, is anyone there?"

There was a crackle of static from the phone, and a hiss, as if the call was being beamed to him from a great distance. Outer space, maybe, directly to his ear. Incoming call for Matt Evans; Denver, Colorado; Denver County; State of Colorado; United States of America; the Earth; the solar system, the universe.

The eye of Marie.

"Matt?" a voice said.

There was a buzz of feedback, and an echo, so it sounded like someone had shouted his name down a long tunnel. "Matt? Matt? Matt?"

"Who is this?" he said, clutching the phone so hard his knuckles had gone white and numb. "What do you want?"

There was another blip of static and then it was suddenly gone, and the voice in his ear came through crystal clear.

"Matt?" she said, using that breathy, high-pitched voice he hated so much, the one that sounded a little like Marilyn Monroe. He heard that voice in his dreams, sometimes. He'd recognize the voice of his wife anywhere. "Didn't I say you needed some excitement in your life?"

CHAPTER FORTY-FIVE

Shawna Goodall had been working at the coroner's office for nearly fifteen years, and she'd seen a lot in that time. Plenty of bodies coming in and out through the swinging doors, sliding in and out of the cold boxes on the wall, getting cut open and stitched back up again. There were some murder victims—not as many as a bigger city might see, but maybe that was something to be thankful for. And although Shawna had been around long enough that death had become a normal part of her day, just more of the usual between the time that she punched in and punched out again, there were times when it got interesting.

Like now.

Shawna was standing outside Prep Room 2, wanting to open the door and head in to grab the reports she'd typed up the day before and then forgotten—she'd been in attendance for the initial examination of the victim they'd brought in, *riding bitch* is what they called it, which meant she hadn't done anything herself, only witnessed it and took notes. She thought it was a waste of time, having to double up like that, but there'd been funny . . . *things* happening to some of the bodies coming in, and the new rule had sprung up. So she'd perched on a stool while Mo had worked, typing in everything she heard. It wasn't a full autopsy—that would come later, after the body had been properly identified. Some of it was boring—like the color of the victim's eyes, the texture of her skin, the placement of different moles and birthmarks. But other things were more interesting. Like this: the woman's teeth had been mostly broken and shattered from being tossed around in the river, but two of them had made it, molars near the back of the mouth, and Mo had taken X-rays and a mold to include in the record, to be used for comparison against dental records for identification purposes. Standard procedure.

"Two or three hard hits in this same spot would've done it," Mo said. She was bent over the head wound, poking around with her gloved hands and forceps. "She was hit from behind with—" Mo paused, and straightened up. Dropped something she'd snagged out of the wound onto a metal pie pan. It clinked as it landed. Shawna leaned forward, looking. It was a small chunk of metal, gleaming dully in the bright overhead lights.

"Chrome?"

"Looks like it," Mo had said. "Plating that came off the— the head of a golf club, maybe? The wound is about the right size for a nine iron. We'll have to run some tests, see what we can find."

It was all in the report, and Shawna had meant to file it the night before but had forgotten. She'd been in a hurry to get home—she had a new recipe in the Crock-Pot and she didn't want it to burn, and her shows were on. So she'd meant to sneak back in first thing and snag the report, hoping no one would realize it was a little late, but there were people in there already. Shawna quickly retreated around a corner when the door started to open, just out of sight but able to hear everything that was happening.

A man came out first, talking into his phone. A cop, she realized. There were always plenty of them around here, too; she'd gotten used to the way they spoke and moved, the way they were always watching, their eyes shifting back and forth. But mostly she'd gotten used to how scary they were, how these cops sometimes seemed dead themselves, nothing but a shell with a badge, especially when they worked murder cases.

The door opened again, and closed, and now there were two cops in the hall, the man and a woman.

"Judge Ramirez issued a search warrant for his house," the male detective said. "It's about damn time. I told him to either shit or get off the pot, looks like he took my advice. I'll meet a team over at his house and get them started, then come back."

"All right. I'll take Evans back to the station and get him to answer a few questions."

The two of them walked away from the room, talking about things that didn't make a lot of sense to Shawna— someone named Janice and an old case file and a map and Wisconsin, of all places. When they finally turned a corner Shawna came out, thinking that the room was empty and it was safe to go in, but then she heard a muffled voice and paused with her fingers wrapped around the doorknob. There was a man still inside, she thought, and he was weeping. Shawna had seen and heard plenty of tears in this place over the years, it was nothing new, but maybe this wasn't crying at all, maybe it was—laughter? She leaned closer. Yes, the man was definitely laughing, hysterical and giddy, a loud donkey bray that turned into a high-pitched pig squeal at the tail end. That sound made her think of women in old black-and-white movies, when they were so frightened they crammed most of a fist into their mouth, when their eyes were rolling around in their skulls like loose marbles. It was a laugh, but it was also *frightened,* the sound a person makes when there is no other option, when the choices are to cry or scream or laugh, and the latter seems like the safest bet, although it's ultimately the worst.

"Can I help you?" Shawna jumped and screamed at the voice behind her—the female cop had come back and was looking at her with an unreadable expression. "Hear any-thing interesting?"

"He's—he's laughing," Shawna stuttered, stepping away from the door. First chance she got, she planned on high-tailing it away from this room, out from under this cop's dark frown. A deep vertical line had appeared between her eyebrows, and Shawna didn't think that was a good sign. Not for anyone, but especially not for the guy in Prep Room 2.

The cop didn't tell Shawna to leave, or to stay put. She didn't say anything at all, just walked right back into the room without warning and left the door open behind her. Shawna could see partway into the room—the cop's back and a slice of the clean white tile floor and the woman on the table and the man. His shoulders were slumped and he looked defeated.

"You see something funny in here, Mr. Evans?" the cop

said. She folded her hands across her chest and glared—if this woman had pulled her over on the road, Shawna probably would've wet her drawers. But she had a good view of the laughing guy's face through the open door, and he seemed unimpressed. Like he'd come up against far scarier women than this one.

"Yeah, I do," he said. "You brought me all the way down here and this isn't even my wife."

"Who is it, then?" the cop asked.

He laughed again, a scoffing sound that reminded her of a rubber-soled shoe against linoleum.

"Her name's Riley Tipton," he said. "She worked for me. I was going to—" His voice caught thickly. "I was going to leave my wife for her."

There was a pause. The cop seemed to be considering what to say next, and the guy stood still beside the dead woman on the table, his hands down by his side. He swallowed thickly, his throat convulsing. All of them, all *three* of them, were waiting to see what would happen next, Shawna thought. See who would speak first. Like it was a game.

"I didn't kill Riley," he finally said. "I didn't kill her, if that's what you think."

"Then who did?" the cop asked.

"It was Marie," the man said. He laughed again, sharp and painful, and Shawna thought she saw the flat gleam of moisture in his eyes. "Marie must've found out about me and Riley, and she killed her."

The cop paused.

"Your wife?" she said doubtfully. "You're saying Marie did this?"

"Yes."

"How would she have done that? Your wife fell off a cliff." The man laughed again, and this time he didn't stop.

CHAPTER FORTY-SIX

They could keep Evans in custody for forty-eight hours before they'd have to either formally charge him with murder or let him go home. It wasn't long—two days was a small window, and they'd have to work fast. They'd requested his cell phone records and credit card statements, even the surveillance footage from the parking garage under his office. The map and the insurance agent's statement were enough to get a search warrant, but they needed more. The wheels of the world turn achingly slowly at times, Spengler realized. Hurry up and wait.

"You thirsty?" Loren asked. They were keeping Evans in one of the interview rooms, which amounted to nothing more than a cell with a door instead of bars, a table and chairs instead of a cot and toilet. "Coffee? Coke? Water?"

"Water, please," Evans said.

"Sparkling or tap?"

"Sparkling would be fine."

Loren laughed nastily.

"I'll make sure you get your top hat and pocket watch, too. What do think this is, the Four Seasons?" he said. "You'll be lucky if I don't serve you toilet water, fuck boy."

They'd spent the last hour in the interview room with

Evans, questioning him on everything they could think of, but he hadn't said much of anything. He hadn't even requested to see his lawyer yet, but only sat silently, his hands folded sedately on his lap, staring blankly. It had to be difficult with Loren breathing fire right into his face, taunting and teasing, shouting angrily. The only reaction Evans had was when the vein running up one side of his forehead began pulsing with the beat of his heart and the blood began creeping up his neck, but he kept his mouth shut.

"Let's start again. You said Marie killed Riley," Spengler said. "But if we believe your story, your wife is dead. How do you know she had anything to do with your girlfriend's murder?"

Nothing but silence.

"Let me explain this to you, one more time, just so you understand where we're coming from," Spengler said slowly. "We know your first wife was killed under questionable circumstances. We've received the case file from Madison PD—you were ultimately cleared, but the whole thing sounds funny. A little over twenty years later your second wife falls off a cliff, you're the only witness to her death, and now you're saying the woman in the morgue is your girlfriend and you're completely innocent of any wrongdoing. Do you really expect us to believe this?"

"I guess I'll call it a night," Loren said. "Jump on my unicorn and head home to the gingerbread house I live in. I mean, since we're living in a land of legend and fairy tales."

"Loren," Spengler said warningly. "Mr. Evans, maybe it isn't clear, but it's in your best interest to be completely honest with us."

"I'm telling you the truth."

"We're attempting to contact Ms. Tipton's family to verify her whereabouts," Loren said, ticking off his fingers. "The coroner is running dental and DNA records to nail down the woman's identity. So we'll know soon enough who that woman is, but what I still don't understand is how you know Marie killed your girlfriend, especially since she took a dive headfirst from a hundred feet up. But maybe that's not what happened? Maybe you know more than you're letting on and can clear up these muddy waters for us?"

"Here's my question: How do you know my wife's dead?" Evans asked suddenly. "How can you be sure? What if she's still alive?"

Spengler glanced at Loren. He'd sat back, was staring hard at Evans. The only thing that moved was the one hand he had resting on the table, the pointer finger and the thumb moving apart and then coming together again in a pinching motion.

"According to you, she fell off a cliff," Spengler said, frowning. "Down into a river that's been running hard. Even the best swimmers couldn't swim across it in its current conditions, and it's been over a week and her body hasn't been found, so we're going with the assumption that she's dead. Unless there's something you want to share with us."

There was a moment of silence. Then two. Evans sighed and muttered something under his breath, passed his hand over his face so his features stretched like putty before snapping back into place.

"Pardon me?" Spengler asked.

Evans sat up.

"Marie's not dead," he said. "She faked the whole thing. I don't know how she did it, but she's trying to set me up for murder. For her murder, and Riley's."

There was another beat of silence. Then Loren laughed. Threw back his head and laughed so hard tears sprung out of his eyes. Spengler didn't react at all.

"That's the biggest load of horseshit anyone has ever tried to feed me, and I've been a cop a long time," he said. "How about we'll leave for thirty minutes, give you time to come up with something else? I could use another good laugh."

Spengler held up her hand to silence Loren.

"What would make you come to that conclusion?" she asked. "And if what you're saying is true, why didn't you tell us this before? Right at the beginning?"

"I suspected what she'd done but I wasn't sure. I was taking a leak when she fell, and she screamed for help—"

"So those campers *did* hear her?"

"Yeah, Marie screamed. Made it sound like she'd been pushed. And when I came out of the trees she was gone. It made me wonder if she was trying to set me up. But I wasn't positive until I saw Riley's body. And then I knew."

Spengler made a small dissatisfied noise and sat back, glanced at Loren.

"I know how this looks," Evans said. "But I didn't kill Riley, and I didn't kill my wife. She's behind all of this."

"What makes you even say that?"

"She's been acting—*funny* the last few months."

"I'm afraid acting funny isn't a good enough explanation," Spengler said. "You'll have to do better than that."

"It started about a year ago. She stopped sleeping through the night. I'd get up and she'd be downstairs, watching TV or reading. She was angry and anxious all the time. She started taking meds. Antidepressants. But none of it seemed to help. She kept accusing me of cheating on her. Of spending all our money. Of hiding things from her."

"Was she right?"

"I . . . was seeing Riley," Evans said. He looked down at his hands. "But that's it."

"What else?" Spengler asked. "That can't be it."

"I started noticing she was watching a lot of true crime on TV. And there was that book that came out a few years ago, when the wife fakes her death and sets her husband up for murder? You know the one? She read that thing over and over. Kept it on her nightstand. I finally went out and picked up my own copy and read it myself."

"So your wife watches crime TV and reads some books, and that's how we know she's faking her death?" Loren looked incredulous. "Dude, I've been around the block more than a few times, and I've never heard anything quite as stupid as this."

"Don't you think I know how it sounds?" Matt said. "That's why I didn't say anything from the beginning. It's all so unbelievable, I can't expect you to buy it. But it's all the little things. The jokes she'd make about disappearing, the things she'd say."

"So let's say Marie did fake her fall off that cliff," Spengler said, leaning forward and cupping her chin in her palm. "How would she have done it? I've been up there. There're only two ways to get down—either back down the trail or straight off the side and into the river. If she didn't pass by you on the trail, she would've had to go over the side. How could she have survived it?"

"I don't know."

"That's not good enough, Mr. Evans," Spengler said. "If you're expecting us to believe that your wife is alive out there, you've got to try a little harder than that. I'm going to ask again. How would Marie have gotten down off that cliff without you knowing?"

Evans hesitated. The briefest of pauses, nothing more. But Spengler caught it, and so did Loren.

"I don't know. But I didn't kill my wife."

"Your *wives*, you mean?" Loren asked. He was smiling again. "You've had two of them, remember?"

"Yeah," Evans said. "That's exactly what I meant. You can't kill Marie. She's like a goddamn cockroach."

"What is that supposed to mean?"

Evans's mouth opened, then closed again.

"Have you seen Marie?" Spengler asked slowly. "Talked to her? How are we supposed to verify any of this?"

Evans thought. Then he closed his eyes and sighed.

"There's something you should know about my first wife," he said. "She—"

The room's door opened and another officer stepped in, followed by a man in a suit, carrying a nice briefcase. He brought a cloud of heavy cologne in with him.

"As your legal counsel, I'm going to advise you to stop talking right now," the man said. Evans fell into silence and the man spread his lips over perfectly capped teeth.

"Detectives, I'm sure you don't mind if I have some time alone with my client."

"Fucking shyster lawyer," Loren spat.

"Idiot meathead cop," the man said pleasantly. "Now, if you'll excuse us, I believe your time with Mr. Evans is up."

CHAPTER FORTY-SEVEN

"Fuck this guy," Loren said once they were in the hallway.

"He's not telling us everything, that's for sure," Spengler said thoughtfully. "But I think we should consider the possibility that part of it might be the truth."

"What are you even talking about?" Loren barked laughter. "You actually believe the bullshit coming out of his mouth?"

"I said *some* of it *might* be true," she said. She started walking, heading back to the bullpen and her desk, and Loren had to hurry to keep up. Pissed him off, his legs moving fast like he's a toddler trying to keep up with mommy. "Blast the wax out of your ears and pay attention for once in your life, Loren."

"No way he's being honest about any of it," Loren scoffed. "This guy's a piece of work. He killed his girlfriend and gave his wife a shove off that cliff. And as soon as he realized that was his girlfriend in the morgue and felt the heat under his ass he came up with this story. Desperate times create desperate men, Spengler. Happens all the time."

"But let's just say maybe Marie Evans is alive," Spengler said. "Oh, good. The Evans file was put together like I asked."

She snagged a folder off her desk and flipped it open,

pulled out a photograph of Marie. It was the one Evans had taken on the cliff before she fell, the wind blowing her hair in her face as she laughed. "She was in great shape. Look at her legs. She ran and did yoga, kept herself healthy."

"It wouldn't matter if she was goddamn Spidergirl," Loren said. "That cliff is a hundred feet high, straight up. No way she climbed down, if that's what you're thinking."

"But she *did* get down somehow," Spengler mused.

"Yeah, straight into the water."

"You're probably right," she said. "But Evans says she's alive. He *believes* he's telling the truth. I don't need a polygraph to tell me that. I saw it in his eyes. He says he didn't see his wife fall off that cliff, he doesn't know how she got down and won't tell us why he thinks she's alive—"

"So he knows more than he's letting on."

Spengler sighed impatiently.

"Yes, I already said that, Loren," she said, flipping through the file again. "He's not just saying she's alive because he thinks so. He *knows* she's alive somehow."

"You think he's seen her? Talked to her?"

"I don't know. But I talked to all of Marie's friends and her daughters, and there's something—*weird* about the whole thing. People were afraid of the things Marie would do. And if she'd found out Evans was cheating and getting ready to leave her for another woman, she might've gotten mad enough to plot revenge. Faking her death sounds like it might be right in her wheelhouse. And think how easy it'd be to set him up—she married a guy who'd been suspected of murdering his first wife and was cleared, so he already seems guilty. All she had to do was disappear, and out in the mountains that'd be easy enough. Then she could start over. Their daughters are grown, she doesn't have a job or any other family, nothing holding her down here. Except her marriage."

Loren stared at her, frowning. But Spengler saw something in his eyes, deep down. The beginnings of belief, or maybe it was a memory rising to the surface.

"This still sounds like ten pounds of bullshit to me," he said, troubled. "Why go to all the trouble? Just file for divorce and be done with it."

"That's a good question," Spengler said, still flipping through the case file. "But maybe she wanted it to hurt."

Spengler handed him another sheet of paper. It was the coroner's initial report on the body that'd been pulled from the river. The woman who Evans claimed was Riley Tipton.

"Cause of death appears to be blunt force trauma to the skull," Spengler said. "Traces of chrome were found in the head wound, possibly from a golf club. Maybe a baseball bat."

Loren looked at her.

"Evans's secretary said Marie had stopped by to pick up his clubs. She was getting them engraved."

"Okay, so we might have the weapon and we have the motive," Spengler said. "Where's the suspect? If she did manage to get down off that cliff, I'd think she'd be long gone by now. Halfway across the country and never looking back. We might never be able to find her."

"So let's pull her cell phone records, take a close look at their bank statements. See what purchases she's made in the last six months, or if she's done a lot of cash withdrawals. Not that I think this shit is likely. And we'll have to go back out to the cliff ourselves and take a closer . . ."

Loren trailed off, his eyes jumping back and forth in their sockets. He looked like a man desperately trying to think of a word that was on the tip of his tongue and very quickly slipping out of reach.

"Loren?"

"Shut your cakehole for two seconds, Spengler," he said. "I'm trying—oh, man."

He pushed past her, practically running for his office. She was right behind him. Every person in the bullpen turned to watch, but neither of them noticed.

"Where is it?" Loren said, pushing the papers around on his desk. A stack went flying, scattering in every direction. "I don't think I took it home—"

"What are you looking for?"

"Ah, here it is," Loren said, pulling a small plastic evidence baggie out from under a stack of books. It had about an inch of dirt and gravel along the bottom.

"What is this?"

"There was blood under that cliff," Loren said. "One drop of it under the ledge, away from the river," Loren said. "I collected it when we were there but forgot to turn it in. But if Marie did fake her death, I have an idea how she might've done it."

"How?"

Loren shook his head. His eyes were glittering with excitement. It was the hunt, Spengler thought. It was on.

"I'm not exactly sure, but I have some ideas. Let's head out there first thing in the morning. Tonight let's have all the phone records pulled, all the financials. For both of them. Location pings on their cell phones for the last few weeks and credit card transactions. There's gonna be something there, I'm sure of it."

"What about Evans?"

Loren waved his hand dismissively.

"Let that asshole cool his jets in holding. We can keep him here for forty-eight hours, and that's exactly what we're going to do."

AS I WATCHED
HIM ON THE
STAGE MY HANDS
WERE CLENCHED
IN FISTS OF RAGE

If you try to fake your own death without a plan, you will fail. And even if you have a plan, even if you think you have every possible problem and outcome accounted for, even if you write a plan that reads like a Choose Your Own Adventure book and seems waterproof, soundproof, *bulletproof*, you'll probably fail anyway. Because even if everything goes perfectly, even if it all lines up like the contrived plot coincidences in an old Gothic romance novel, you still have to account for human nature. And if there's one thing for sure about people, it's that you can never be sure about people. Most humans are as unpredictable as a stick of old, sweating dynamite—you just never know when they might blow your ass to the moon.

Take Corey Wendt, for example. Back in 2005, Wendt decided he wanted out of the United States Army, after enlisting only a year before. Some of it was because the military is *tough,* and Wendt had always been something of a wimp. A *poontang in the balls department,* Loren might've said. Wendt had always been lazy, early mornings and hard work had never agreed with him, and besides, he'd only enlisted because his parents were pressuring him to do *something* with his life. So he'd joined up, then immediately regretted it, and he'd spent that first year trying to come up with ways to get free. He didn't want to eat meals at the dining hall with all the other grunts anymore, he didn't want to be deployed out to the Middle East like his commanding officer kept threatening, and he didn't want to have to live in those shitty barracks down at Fort Carson. Wendt didn't know exactly what he wanted, but he was pretty sure what he *didn't* want—to be a soldier.

He could've made them believe he was crazy—that wouldn't have been too hard, his aunt was a certifiable loony-tune, thought she was married to Jesus, the *actual* Jesus Christ—or he could've pretended to be injured, but both those would've taken *work,* he'd really have to be dedicated, make himself seem nuts or hurt every hour of every day for as long as it took. A long time, probably, because once Uncle Sam got his hooks in a man it was nearly impossible to get free.

So Wendt decided, after not all that much thought, to fake his own death. He and a friend drove a few hours north of Colorado Springs one August morning, telling everyone they were going for a hike on Longs Peak, but Wendt never came back. His friend did, though, and made a frantic call to the police department once he could get cell phone service and said Wendt had slipped when they were scrambling over a particularly narrow pass and had fallen, his arms pinwheeling in the open air, seeming to be moving in slow motion.

How far did he fall? Maybe twenty-five, thirty feet, the friend said. Straight down, onto a bed of rock, and he'd screamed and cried, his leg bent at a strange angle, and there was so much blood. So the friend had gone for help, and he'd told the police that he couldn't remember exactly where Wendt had fallen, that in his panic he'd gotten confused. This friend wasn't much help at all, in fact, and the rescue teams had been forced to sweep the entire park; over three hundred people were involved in the effort that lasted an entire weekend, not counting the helicopters that flew overhead for hours, kicking up all sorts of dirt and gravel. The searchers did find one interesting thing—a bone that was later identified as a human femur, picked clean by animals, although it was quickly established that the bone belonged to either a child or small woman, not Corey Wendt. It was never discovered who that femur belonged to, and Wendt's body couldn't be found, either, and the authorities suspected he was dead. Lots of people die out in the Colorado backcountry, and some of those remains are never found. Animals drag the remains away, or the snow and rain sweep them to other parts, or searchers simply look in the wrong areas.

And everyone assumed that was the end of Wendt, until his friend came down with a debilitating case of guilty conscience and told the police what had actually happened, and less than an hour later officers found Wendt, napping in a queen-size bed in the Lyons Holiday Inn Express, no broken leg, no sign that he'd even been out to Longs Peak at all, and the news coverage of his own disappearance playing on the TV.

Corey Wendt might've gotten away with faking his own death, but he hadn't accounted for one thing—human nature. Wendt's friend was the unknown factor in the equation, he was X, and that's the way it almost always plays out. You can never know what a person might do, and if you try to guess, you'll almost always get it wrong. A person's actions can't be choreographed; life isn't a ballet recital, after all, it's a *rave*, and you have to keep your feet moving to the beat, keep your eyes open so you don't get knocked to the floor.

Loren told Spengler the story of Corey Wendt before they each left to head home for the night. Because if they were going to believe that Marie Evans had faked her own death, he said, they'd have to take human nature into account. One is the safest number for keeping a secret, but it's also the loneliest. Two's better, if you find the right person, but how often does that happen? Once in a million years. Just about everyone is the wrong person, but everybody is looking to unload their secret onto someone else. A secret's not really a secret until you share.

"And once two people are in on a secret, it's that much more likely to get out," Loren said. He was looking out his office window to the parking lot below, but didn't seem to actually see anything. Spengler shuddered away from the look in his eyes. "It's like that old saying: two can keep a secret if one of them is dead."

He still had the file Ortiz had given Spengler in his hands, was smacking the rolled-up length of it against the flat of his palm. He was staring off into the distance and grinning, and Spengler wondered what he was seeing. What memories he was reliving.

"So here's the question," Loren said. "If Evans is right and his wife did fake her death, she told someone. It's just a matter of finding that person."

THINK ABOUT
IT EVERY NIGHT
AND DAY

CHAPTER FORTY-EIGHT

September 7, 2018

"So you're the new hotshot addition to Homicide everyone's talking about," the man sitting behind the desk said. He was leaning back in his chair, his feet kicked up. The tarnished gold plate nailed up on his office door said DETECTIVE PAUL HOSKINS, COLD CASES, but she'd already known who he was when she took the long elevator ride down to the basement. She'd walked out with Loren—*get some sleep,* he'd said, *we have an early morning*—but had doubled back and gone downstairs.

If it takes two to keep a secret, was someone holding one for Loren? And she figured there was only one possibility: Paul Hoskins.

"Yeah, I guess," she said, reaching out her hand to shake. He put down the tennis ball he'd been tossing back and forth and took her hand. His hand was dry and hot, smooth. "Marion Spengler."

"Good to meetchya."

"I'm glad I caught you before you went home."

Hoskins made a noise that might've been a laugh.

"Oh, this is it for me," he said, throwing out his arms.

"Nice and cozy down here, don't you think? I just need to hang one of those needlepoints above the door. 'Home sweet home.'"

She smiled thinly but didn't respond. She wasn't sure what to say. This man had spent a long time as Loren's partner but now worked down in the basement, going over the old cases no one really cared about anymore. Chief Black had been trying to get him back upstairs, but he'd refused every offer. Rumor was that Hoskins preferred the dark. The chill of the cement walls.

"You and Loren must have the same decorator," she said, looking around the little office, at all the papers and photos posted on the walls. It was a tiny space, claustrophobic. No windows, no sunlight. Nothing to keep the air moving. If anything it was even worse than Loren's office: smaller, more cramped. More gory crime scene photos on the walls. It was a room that could drive a person crazy. Or maybe it was the other way around: a crazy person had made the room. "No extra chair I can use while we chat?"

He started tossing the tennis ball again.

"You're here visiting me unannounced," he said. "If you wanted to sit, you should've brought a chair with you."

"Sounds like you learned your manners from Loren, too," she said.

"That's what I hear," he said wryly. "Now, what can I do for you? I have an idea you didn't come all the way down here this evening for my fine company."

"I was approached by a detective from Loren's hometown—"

"Ah, Ortiz got to you, too? That guy is a total shithead."

"What did he say to you?"

"I imagine it was the same thing he said to you. Gave me a copy of the file, asked if I'd try to get Loren to admit he'd killed his partner. I told him to pound sand or I'd put my foot so far up his ass he'd taste leather."

"But what do you think?"

"About what?"

"Did Loren do it?"

"That's why you came down here?" Hoskins looked bemused. "You should've just asked Loren himself."

"I tried that. He ignores me."

"Sounds about right."

"So do you know?"

"Do I know what?"

Spengler sighed. She'd slung her briefcase over her shoulder and gotten in the elevator to head down to the parking lot to go home to her family and dinner and the warmth of her house, but had ended up riding all the way to the bottom. B2. Not even the basement, but the sub-basement. She hadn't been able to stop thinking about what Loren had said, about unloading secrets, and it'd made her wonder about his old partner.

"Do you know if Loren killed his partner and the guy's family?"

Hoskins stood up and wheeled the chair around the desk, pushing it at her so she could sit. Then he started pacing behind his desk, alternating between tossing the tennis ball in the air and bouncing it off the cement floor. His movements reminded her of a caged animal, desperate to break free of its bonds.

"Spengler, let me tell you a story. When I first joined the force I was assigned the bullshit job of checking up on guys out on house arrest, do a surprise visit and make sure they were minding their manners, you know what I mean?"

"Okay," she said, mystified at the turn the conversation was taking.

"One day I end at this guy's place, a total dump out in Aurora. And not in the good part—this is the shittiest area you can imagine. And this guy, he'd been locked up for attempted murder, tried to knife a bunch of holes in some other guy over some dumb-ass turf war, that's what these gangbangers are about. Turf, like any of it really belongs to them. But this guy was small time with no priors, so he got one of those anklets popped on and was sent home to live with his parents. And this guy, he was nothing but a kid. A baby gangbanger." Hoskins grinned at the memory. "Pants sagging halfway down his ass, wearing a wifebeater, all tattooed up. Mean look permanently on his face, like he's got something to prove. A *cholo*, that's what they call guys like him."

"Is there a point to all this?" she asked. "If you don't know—"

He shushed her.

"So I walk into the house, and his parents tell me he's downstairs in his room, that he's refusing to come out. That he's been hiding something in his closet and won't let anyone see. And I'm assuming there's going to be trouble, because what else could it be? He's got guns in his closet, I figure. Or maybe he's harboring drugs. You always think the worst with these types, that's where your mind goes. So I head downstairs and knock on the bedroom door, ready to pull my gun out if I need to, but he opens the door right away when he knows it's me, lets me in. And when I ask to see what's in his closet, what he's been hiding in there, he doesn't want to show me. House arrest and having a cop find something bad on your property—that would land his ass in a cell for sure, with no chance of seeing freedom for a long time, and he knew it. But I insisted, and finally he rolled back his closet door. Let me take a good look."

"What was he hiding?"

Hoskins grinned again.

"It was mama cat in a cardboard box, her kittens all snuggled up next to her, nursing. This kid, he'd found them in the backyard and knew they wouldn't survive on their own, so he'd made them a little nest and snuck them in, had been taking care of them. But his old man was allergic, he said, and would make him get rid of the cats if he found out. So he'd been hiding them. Sneaking milk out of the kitchen for the mother, making sure they were warm enough."

Spengler shifted her weight from one hip to another.

"I don't understand what your story has to do with anything."

"I'm trying to make a point about Loren," Hoskins said. "He's not a bad guy, but that's what most people think when they meet him. Don't get me wrong, he's a mean motherfucker, he's stubborn and rude and doesn't take shit from anybody, but that doesn't mean he's bad. You shouldn't take anyone at face value. I've seen Loren do plenty of kind things, although he wouldn't admit to a single one."

"So you don't think Loren killed his partner?"

"I don't know," Hoskins said, slowly. "Maybe he did. And if he did, maybe he had a good reason. Who the fuck knows? Or maybe it doesn't matter. It happened a long time ago. Maybe it's better to let dead dogs lie."

"Don't you mean sleeping dogs?"

"Whatever."

"You really think a murder doesn't matter? And Ortiz said the partner's wife had disappeared, too. And their baby."

"I don't know," he said. "All I'm saying is, the world isn't black and white." He propped his foot up on the lip of his desk and yanked on his shoelace, untying it, then got to work retying it again. "And it's not just shades of gray. There's every color of the rainbow out there, you just have to open your eyes."

"I don't know what you're talking about."

"Yeah, join the club."

CHAPTER FORTY-NINE

September 8, 2018

The next morning the park rangers in Estes were more than happy to let Spengler and Loren into the lot they still had roped off—this investigation was the most excitement they'd seen in some time. There'd been that bear sighting a few weeks back, and the rabid pack of raccoons that'd been attacking hikers, but otherwise it'd been a slow summer and the constant presence of Denver police was a welcome distraction. Like today. It was the cops, same two who'd been around already, but they also had a couple in the backseat with them, a man and woman both tan and ropy with muscle, who were carrying big bags of equipment with them as they headed up the trail to the cliff's edge. It was a nice hike, the trail dotted with purple and yellow flowers, the last of the season before the cold would move in. Spengler saw an old newspaper in the undergrowth and tried to snag at it with a stick, complaining about people littering, but it was actually the corpse of a squirrel, and she only managed to burst the swollen skin so they could hear the munching sounds of the maggots on the flesh beneath. They all fell into silence during the last part of the hike, when the climb was steep and hard, and they were each occupied trying to keep their balance.

"Here we are," Spengler said to Loren and the couple when they pushed out of the trees. The man went to the edge and peered over and down without any fear. The woman joined him. These two—Jenny and Mark—were rock climbers. Not professional, but close enough. Loren knew them somehow, mumbled a quick explanation to Spengler and then wouldn't say more. "So if you were up here and wanting to get down fast, how would you do it?"

"I think the quickest way down is pretty obvious," Mark said. He wasn't trying to be funny. "But we're not necessarily looking for the quickest way. Just a *different* way."

Spengler and Loren stood back and let them work. They'd brought up a lot of equipment in their packs—ropes and pulleys and clips, plus all sorts of things Spengler didn't have names for. She'd never realized there was so much gear involved in climbing, or all the terms she overheard Mark and Jenny use that she didn't understand. *Choss* and *jug* and *dihedral*. They sounded like nonsense words to her ear, or a completely different language. Mark and Jenny stood together, looking over the side and discussing options in quiet, calm tones.

Spengler sat down in the shade of a pine tree. Her phone was sitting on her thigh, but out here it was completely useless. It was amazing to think that there were still places a person could go and be completely out of touch. These days you could get ahold of anyone, anytime; you were always plugged in. Connected. The small metal and plastic rectangle sitting on her leg was completely useless out here. She'd known they were heading into a dead zone before they'd arrived, of course, so she'd listened to her voice mails on the drive up.

The first was from the coroner's office—it was definitely Riley Tipton that'd been dragged out of the river, based on dental comparisons. Her parents had been notified and were flying out from Tampa Beach to take her remains home. Her mostly packed suitcase was found on her bed, pools of dried blood and bone shards on the living room carpet. She'd been getting ready for her trip to South America but had never made it out of her own apartment alive. The last time anyone could confirm seeing Riley alive was Wednesday. Matt and Marie had arrived in Estes Park on Sunday. Marie disappeared on Tuesday. Long periods of time in which anything could've happened.

It was the last voice mail that Spengler replayed for Loren, who wanted to listen to it twice. It was from the techs who'd been going over every inch of Evans's home and cars. They hadn't found anything in the house, but the trunk of Marie's car had recently been bleached and steam cleaned. Despite the effort, traces of blood still remained.

"That would explain the advanced decomposition in Tipton's body," Loren said. "Marie could've dumped her in the river before leaving for their trip."

"Hey guys, it looks like someone tied a rope around this tree," Jenny said, waving them over. Spengler stood and dusted off her backside. Jenny and Mark were standing beside a tall pine that'd rooted closer to the cliff edge than the others, like a cheater starting a race before the gun sounds. "See here, where it's worn around the trunk? This was made recently. If I was going to lower myself, this would be as good a place as any to anchor. It's sturdy, not too far from the edge. This is where we'll anchor, too."

Down near the trunk's bottom, where the roots disappeared into the ground, was a spot where the bark had been rubbed away. An almost perfect half circle of smooth white wood. If someone had tied a rope around the trunk it might've made that mark, Spengler thought, rubbing her fingertips against the line. The friction would've worn the bark right off. And if you had a long enough rope, you could tie onto this tree and lower yourself right over the edge.

"But if Marie Evans had tied a rope around this tree and lowered herself over the edge, how would she have unattached the rope without her husband knowing?"

Jenny tapped the side of her nose.

"It's the only way she would've been able to get over the side. This isn't a great spot for climbing," Mark said. He was stepping into a harness and cinching it down around his waist as he spoke. "The river's right below the cliff edge and dry ground is under the platform. Unless she was able to hook into a spot under the cliff, it wouldn't be worth it. She'd be lowering herself right into the water."

"But could she have done it?" Spengler asked.

Mark winked.

"Anything's possible with enough determination," he said.

Jenny laughed and tugged on the harness she'd put on herself.

"Determination and zero-gravity climbing skills," she snorted.

Mark looped a rope around the same tree and threaded it

through his harness. His fingers moved confidently, then he helped Jenny do the same, so they were anchored securely to the same tree. "I've seen climbers do some crazy things. Having no fear will get a person just about anywhere."

What had Marie been afraid of?

Mark lowered himself over the edge slowly, with Jenny keeping an eye on the ropes to make sure they were secure. They were both tied to the tree with the worn-away circle. They stayed silent and serious. Loren kept back, well away from what was happening, but Spengler strayed closer.

"Is it okay if I go out to the edge?" Spengler asked.

"Yeah, just don't bump the ropes," Jenny said. She kept her eyes on her partner.

Spengler walked as near to the edge as she dared, keeping well clear of the rope Mark was hanging from, then dropped to her knees. Went forward a bit more, then dropped again, to her belly, and army-crawled to the edge, like a snake. She peered over. It was a long way to the water below, and the wind seemed to blow harder out here. She couldn't hear a thing. A wave of vertigo hit her as she looked down, and she started to scoot back to safety.

When she was far enough away she sat up and started to dust off her hands. There were hard grains of sand stuck to her palms, and a single nylon thread. It was bright blue, much like the rope Jenny had threaded through her harness. Spengler tweezed the piece up in her fingers and held it up to the sky, rolled it between her pointer finger and thumb. It was a small clipping, frayed on one end and cut straight across on the other, and it would've been easy to overlook. Carefully, she tucked the piece into her pocket.

A hawk glided lazily above their heads, wings outstretched as it circled, looking for prey below, and the river roared beneath them, hard enough that Spengler could feel the vibrations through the rock and all the way up into her legs. A woman falling into that water would be sucked right under and lost forever, maybe never found.

Unless she never fell into the water.

There was a shout from over the side of the cliff, and Jenny started to pull on Mark's rope to help haul him back up while staying far enough back to keep safe. He unclipped something metal and shiny from his belt and tossed it at Loren, grinning. Loren held it up so Spengler could see. It was a strange piece of metal, two grooved half circles on one end that tapered out to a loop.

"It's called a camming device," Jenny said. "A climber can jam one of those into a crack in the rock and pull the trigger so those metal bits expand."

"That's exactly what she did," Mark said, grinning. "And it wouldn't have been as hard as we first thought. That cam was sticking out of the cliff underside and would've been an easy grab once she got herself lowered over the edge. The hardest part would've been getting over the lip of the cliff, but it'd be smooth sailing from there. As long as she wasn't afraid of heights. But there is one problem."

"What's that?"

"There's no way she could've done this without anyone knowing. I don't care how long of a piss her husband claims he was taking, it wouldn't have been long enough. He knows exactly what happened, and if I had to guess, I'd say he helped her every step of the way."

CHAPTER FIFTY

This isn't over, Loren thought. Another phrase from the past. *His* past. He was in the shower at home, letting the hot water beat against the back of his neck, rinsing away the sun and sweat that'd built up on his skin from their hike to the top of the cliff. He didn't usually stay in so long on account of how bone dry Colorado always was, but all the rain they'd been getting must be good for something. He was lathering himself up and thinking, circling around again, back around to the same old garbage. *This isn't over.* Those had been Jacky Seever's words, the freak show who'd dressed up like a clown and killed dozens before his arrest. That was a real blast from the past, thinking about Seever and the toxic shit that poured out of his mouth, but maybe there was something to it after all, because it wasn't over. It sure as fuck wasn't over for Loren, because Ortiz wasn't going to let any of it die. Could the past ever die?

Nope.

There was this new investigation on Matt and Marie Evans, and there was Ortiz and Gallo and Connie, and that first case, the women in the attic room, the breeders, and those words *All Together Now,* and the smell of shit rising lazily from their homemade toilet in the corner. That moment, the woman dying, and Gallo saying those words didn't matter—it hadn't been the beginning of the end for him, but more like the beginning of the *beginning*, when things had become clear.

This is when you started hearing your father's voice? Dr. Patel had asked years before, when he first became a patient. Patel had gazed at him over the rims of his tortoise-shell glasses, and if Loren had sensed any judgment in his look, any skepticism, he would've left then, left and never looked back. But he didn't sense anything like that from Patel, only a gentle curiosity. *After seeing this crime scene, your father began to speak to you? Perhaps as a coping mechanism?*

No, Loren had said. The wind was blowing hard that day, and the brittle branches of a pine tree were scraping across the window like fingernails. *No, it wasn't to cope so much as to help me see things. The truth about people.*

Like what?

"You're not going to shoot your partner in the back," Gallo had said. He'd been smiling, gritting his teeth at the feel of the gun pressed against the back of his head, the circlet of cold steel up at the point where his skull sloped into his neck, but there was sweat standing on his upper lip, beaded up on his nose. "That's not you, Ralphie. We're *partners*, for chrissake. And friends, right? You're not going to shoot me."

A partnership is like a marriage, and sometimes they're good, but sometimes they're bad. And sometimes you have to cut yourself free. Shoot yourself free.

Loren twisted the bar of soap through his wet hands and mashed the lather into his hair. No extra bottles in his shower—bar soap was good enough for everything. Keep it simple, stupid, as they said. He'd used a bar of soap on his hands after he'd buried Gallo out in the hole by the Mad River, and it'd been good enough to work out the grime. And after it was done, after all the blood and dirt had washed down the drain, Loren had washed the soap itself, holding it under the tap and massaging it the way he'd seen raccoons do to their food in running water, until he thought there couldn't be any trace left of what he'd done. And then he'd flushed that bar of soap down the crapper. Sometimes the thought of that white brick of soap swirling through the sewers drove him batshit, kept him up at night, even this many years later.

A bar of soap made him think of his father and made him think of Gallo and then of Connie, and then brought him back around to Marie and Matt Evans. Round and round. Connie even looked a bit like Marie, with those dark eyes framed by smudges of delicate purple skin and the lips that came together like a puckered little heart. Women who looked so innocent it made you want to teach them a few lessons—in love, or in life. Maybe both. But Connie hadn't been nearly as innocent as she looked, Loren had found that out quick enough.

Round and round. Life was a circle; they were all drawn in. It had the force of a hurricane, pulling things toward the eye. He was being flung around, caught in a never-ending loop. But that's how life was. History repeats itself. Everything that's happened will happen again. It was cliché but it was also true, Loren had experienced it himself. Most people had. That was déjà vu. Evans was feeling it now; Loren had seen the look on his face. He'd been through it before with his first wife, although that'd been different, hadn't it?

Was that how Evans remembered both his wives, together like a chorus, the lines between them blurred until they became one? Like the guy Loren had once known who'd married three different women named Pam. He'd divorce one and marry the next. *Easier that way,* he'd said. *One Pam gets old, I trade her in for a younger Pam.* He'd been elbowing Loren in the side as he said it, like it was a joke. It took everything Loren had to keep from twisting that stupid fuck's arm up behind his back until he squealed.

All together now, with feeling.

Loren's chest was tight, and he was having trouble breathing. Maybe it was the steam building up in the bathroom; a stupid old man like him should know better than to stay so long under hot water. Or maybe it wasn't the heat at all, maybe it was the fact that he was riding that carousel back around again, that Ortiz was still in town asking questions, that he was back to what happened almost thirty years ago. Had he loved Connie? Yes. Hell, yes. He loved her still, even after all these years. She was the only woman he'd ever really loved.

Did you love her, and killed her anyway?

He'd been in love with her from nearly the moment they'd met. But he was just a stupid kid back then—young and dumb and full of come—and not used to being around women, and she was so friendly and kind to him, and beautiful. He'd spent a lot of time with her that first six months after he'd been partnered with Gallo, ate dinner at their house and sometimes crashed on their sofa, and he'd spent a lot of time alone with Connie, because Gallo had a tendency to get so drunk he'd break things, he'd scream and get violent and angry, he'd threaten to kill his wife, to gut their dog, to rip the baby right out of Connie's belly and throw it into the street. It was a good night when Gallo blacked out from the booze, when he'd fall where he stood and sleep it off and wake up better in the morning, grinning sheepishly and asking for a glass of water and two aspirin. Loren stuck around as much as he could, to protect Connie from her husband, because he loved her, and she must've known. She must've known how he felt, although she never mentioned it. And Loren had never said anything to Connie for two reasons—it would've been a real pansy thing to do, to declare his love for this woman like he was Romeo swooning around beneath a balcony in the middle of the night; and the second reason, maybe the most important one: she was married to his partner.

And then they'd gotten into an argument one day at work, because Gallo stuck it to hookers during his lunch hour and Loren didn't like it, he'd kept his mouth shut long enough but then piped up one day. But that wasn't the only thing he was pissed about, was it? No, Loren had a laundry list of complaints against Gallo. He'd respected the guy at first, even *admired* him, but that'd soured over their time as partners. When a man comes home he takes off the mask he's worn all day for the outside world, and if he's a monster underneath—well, it's his family who suffers. And boy, did Connie suffer at the hands of her husband.

Have some respect for your wife, Loren had said, and Gallo swung. That punch was the beginning of the end for a lot of things: their partnership, their friendship, and ultimately, Gallo's life. The two men ended up rolling on the ground, throwing punches and knocking over desks and chairs in the bullpen, and Loren had come out on top without any big problems—he was young and quick and strong back then, and he was angry. He'd jammed his knee right up between Gallo's shoulder blades, pinning him to the ground, and he'd had his gun out, had the cold metal barrel pushed up against the soft spot of flesh where the stalk of the neck meets the skull. There was snot running out of Gallo's nose and a gash above his brow was dripping blood down into his eye, he'd lost the fight but not the *war,* and they both knew it. Their fight had been over Connie, and she was at home, waiting for Gallo, making his dinner and scrubbing the trail marks out of his underwear, and that was always where she'd be. Gallo had been pressed against the filthy linoleum, laughing as the other guys circled them, trying to talk Loren out of pulling that trigger, and Gallo had laughed, his mouth was full of blood, his teeth were swimming in pools of red, but he'd still laughed.

You're not gonna shoot your partner, Ralphie. You don't have big enough balls.

Loren didn't shoot him, just stood up and walked away, disgusted with the whole thing, and they'd both ended up suspended, sent home for a week without pay. And Connie must've found out what went down somehow, and that was why she'd shown up at his home one evening, when he'd still been nursing a bruised rib cage and had decided to stay in, he'd answered the knock without a second thought, never thinking it might be her. He'd been in the middle of eating dinner, a ham sandwich he'd slapped together and brought to the door with him, although he dropped it when he saw Connie. He ended up scraping the American cheese and mayonnaise out of the carpet, but that was much later, when he had time to consider such things.

"Oh my fucking Christ," he said, his voice rising in pitch, until it was more like the warbling tone of a frightened old man. He never heard that particular sound come from his own throat again. "What happened?"

Connie was in a bad way. He'd see worse in the coming years—women with teeth knocked right from their mouths and cigarettes put out on their breasts and on one memorable occasion a woman who had been hit so hard her eyeball had come free of the socket and was dangling from the stalk of veins and stringy muscle in a meaty red bag—but he'd only been with the force two years by then, and he hadn't seen much yet. But it was bad enough, maybe worse for him because he was in love with her. Connie had been beat to shit, and that was putting it lightly. Gallo had used her face as a punching bag, and the skin around one of her eyes had already begun to swell and pinch shut, the way black eyes tend to do. There was a wide gash across the bridge of her nose, and by its mushy, smashed shape, Loren knew it was broken, and by the way she was swaying in the doorway he was shocked she'd been able to keep a grip on the baby wrapped in a blanket and tucked under her arm.

If Loren had been around it wouldn't have happened, but it wasn't like he could be around all the time, especially not after the knockdown he'd had with Gallo.

"*Ralph*," Connie said, her puffy, bloody lips barely able to form the words. The one eye she could still see from was unfocused and dull; it reminded him of a blind woman's, not really seeing anything at all. She reached out, groping for him, until he took her hand. "*Hel' me.*"

Her one staring eye, hopeless and vague, it'd filled him with a rage he'd never known before, and he knew then that he was capable of murder. A man in love will do just about anything, after all. He will kill if he has to.

The memory of that moment, of Connie standing in the doorway of his home with her one blank eye and the way his palm itched for his gun so he could point it right at Gallo's smarmy face, made the gooseflesh rise all up and down his arms, despite the fact that the water pouring from the shower was scalding hot. Aftershocks, even after so many years. Like the aftereffects of a huge earthquake, moving him to the very core. It'd been a long time, but he still felt them, and there are some things that never leave you, no matter how much you wish they would.

You might as well just admit to Ortiz you did it, his father whispered. *You plugged Gallo full of lead and then planted him like a goddamn sunflower out by the Mad River.*

"But I didn't kill him," Loren said. He stuck his head under the shower-head and came back out sputtering.

There're pills for people who hear voices, you know, ol' Marv rasped in his ear. *Happy little pills that'll make everything A-OK. Make me go away.*

"But then I wouldn't have the pleasure of hearing your voice every five god-damn minutes," Loren said. "And then what would I do? Probably die of loneliness."

Oh, he'd given plenty of things a try to make the voices go

away, to make the *anger* go, the anxiety, but none of it had worked. Pills and therapy and even those stupid-ass coloring books they marketed to adults. Nothing had worked.

Or just keep pretending like everything's fine, Marv said. *You're gravy, right? Good on everything. How's that working out for you so far?*

"Shut up."

You're one fucked up hominid, you know? his father said, laughed. It was wild, rollicking laughter that bordered on hysterical. Loren had never heard his old man sound like that when he was alive, not once. He put his hands over his ears, but it was only a reflex and it didn't help. Not when his father was camping out in his brain.

He got out and grabbed the towel off the rack, dried himself. He'd go to sleep, but the thought of sleep made him think of Gallo, too. That's how Gallo had looked after that bullet went through his skull—like he was sleeping. If you could ignore the shards of bone and the blood and the grayish-yellow brain matter that had gone everywhere, exploding like a fucking grenade, you might've thought Gallo was conked out for the night, counting sheep and floating on a cloud. That's how Gallo had looked in the grave, like he was snoozing, as if the man had decided to crawl into a hole beside the Mad River and doze. The only thing that had broken the illusion was when Loren had started dropping shovelfuls of the moist, nearly black soil over Gallo, when it rolled into the dead man's open mouth and got caught in his hair. The shovel's wood handle cut into his hands, made them slick with blood from his own palms, but he kept at it, dumping more dirt into the hole until it was full. But not too full. A mound of dirt heaped over the grave might attract attention, so he scattered some of the extra soil around, tried to make it all seem natural. And then it was done. Loren had sat down for some time beside the loose dirt where he'd buried his partner, exhausted, thinking about what had to be done next. He hadn't wanted to get up. The Mad River had been beautiful back in those days, clean and free of trash and overgrown, wild, and he'd enjoyed sitting there, the shovel propped up across his thighs, but he'd still been aware of Gallo under him, the process of decomposition already started. It wouldn't be long before his old partner was a meal for the worms. A bird started to sing, deep and throaty, and then stopped abruptly, and Loren knew it was time to go; this area didn't see many people, but sometimes there were kids out this way, throwing rocks in the rushing water and sailing wax-lined paper boats, and he didn't want anyone to spot him. Especially carrying a shovel and filthy with dirt, that would've been bad news.

Besides, he'd had more work to do. There was still Connie and the baby. He had to get rid of them.

He'd missed a phone call while he was in the shower. It was Spengler.

"Shouldn't you be getting your beauty rest?" he asked when he called her back.

"You're the one who needs it, not me," she snapped. She was getting quick. "The station's been trying to reach one of us, but I was putting my kid to bed."

"You have a kid?"

"And you call yourself a detective? Jesus."

"What's going on?"

"We have a visitor waiting to see us," Spengler said. "It's Detective Abe Reid. Retired from the Madison PD. He was in charge of the investigation on Janice Evans's murder. Drove all the way out from Phoenix to talk to us."

"Tell him to check in at a hotel, we'll see him tomorrow."

"Oh, I think you'll change out of your Underoos and drive back to work for *this*," Spengler said. "Reid is saying Janice Evans isn't dead."

CHAPTER FIFTY-ONE

Detective Abraham Reid, now retired, stood up in the interview room to greet them, but it was slow. He rested his weight on his hands, palms flat on papers on the table in front of him, his knuckles red and swollen. Those hands might've been quick with a gun at one time, but those days were long past. If he held anything these days, it was a golf club on a course in Phoenix, or a glass of iced tea. And this old man, Spengler thought in wonder, his face deeply lined and what was left of his hair nothing but delicate baby wisps clinging to his spotted scalp, had driven the twelve hours from Arizona alone.

"I'm eighty-nine years old," he said, recognizing the look on Spengler's face. "But I've still got a few brain cells rattling around in my upstairs. Enough to steer a car, anyway."

"I hope the drive up wasn't too bad," she said, sitting. Loren stayed by the door, his arms folded across his chest.

"Nah. Nothing but interstate, and the Caddy just about drives itself."

"If it's okay, I'd like to skip the small talk and get straight to the point," Spengler said. "I'd like to get back home to my son."

"Of course," Reid said. "And I'd like to head back myself.

I love Colorado, but I can feel the humidity in the air right now and it's not agreeing much with my joints."

He held up a hand to show her. He had a candy pinched between his fingers and he fumbled it, sent it tumbling to the floor. Spengler leaned over and picked it up. It wasn't a candy at all, she saw, but a cough drop. She handed it back to Reid and he held it in both hands, bent fingers worrying the wrapper until it came loose. The process took long enough that she considered asking if he needed help, but kept her mouth shut in the end. No need to offend the old man.

"I still call my squad out in Madison once in a while to catch up," Reid said. "About once a week. The newbies like to pick my brain if they have a head-scratcher come through. Old-timer like me has plenty of advice to give, I guess. And when I called yesterday, they mentioned some detectives out in Denver had asked to take a peek at the Janice Evans case."

"They sent it right over," Spengler said. "It looked pretty clear-cut."

"Did they send any photos?"

"No, just copied and pasted the text of it into an email."

"Of course they did."

Reid chuckled, which turned into a harsh, grating cough. Alarmed, Spengler stood to get water but Reid waved her down.

"I'm fine," he gasped. "I'll be better when I get home."

"Okay."

"You're right," Reid said once he could speak again. "It does seem pretty clear-cut. Husband and wife get attacked in the middle of the night. Wife is killed, husband escapes. The woman's boss is arrested for the murder, case closed."

Reid grinned. His teeth were too big and perfect to be real. "Easy to follow, easy to swallow, am I right?"

Loren laughed and came to sit down at the table.

"I like that," he said.

Reid winked.

"I thought you might. So it was case closed, my boss makes me move on. But there were things that didn't quite add up. Evans's story, and the bullet wounds. It was almost perfect, and I wanted to keep going, see what I could come up with, but the chief wanted to move on."

"I've heard that plenty of times before," Loren said.

"We all have. For the head honchos it's less about justice and more about controlling costs. So we moved on. Jesse O'Neil couldn't remember anything of that night on account of the bullet that plowed through his head, and it was easier to put the blame on him. Use him as a scapegoat. But it still bothered me. And then, about six months after Janice's murder, when the case had been closed and Matt Evans had already moved out to Denver, I saw her."

"What do you mean, saw her?" Spengler asked.

"I saw Janice Evans, in the flesh," Reid said. "I'd stopped by the A&P on my way home to pick up a quart of ice cream for dessert—my wife had a weakness for mint chocolate chip, god bless her—and I saw Janice there. Standing in the frozen foods, right in front of me. I'd spent the last half year staring at her photo and there she was, ten feet in front of me, belly all full of baby. It took me about ten seconds to get over my shock and then I marched right up to her, called her Janice."

"And what did she say?"

"Oh, she just looked at me real innocent and said she didn't know anyone named Janice. *Her* name was Marie, she said, and she had to get home because her ankles were so swollen."

"Marie? Is that what you said?"

"That's right," Reid said. "She said it like it was the honest-to-god truth, but I got a good look in her eyes when I called her Janice. Fear is the most honest emotion there is, nothing else sticks to it, and that's what I saw. That woman, that was Janice Evans. But if Janice was alive, whose bones had been pulled out of that house? We'd assumed it was Janice, because who else would it be? We had no reason *not* to think it was her."

"Who was it?"

"I don't know," Reid said. "We might not ever know. No local girls were reported missing, but that doesn't mean much. Girls disappear, and half the time no one gives a damn. And as soon as the remains were released they were cremated. So I went to see Janice's mother. She was living west of Madison, out alone in the middle of nowhere, and I asked what'd really happened. If her daughter had actually been killed. And I asked why there was a cute little red sport coupe in the driveway parked next to her truck. *Why*, I asked, *does a woman who lives alone need two cars?* She asked me to leave, but I saw the fear in her eyes, too. She was nervous. Already had a cocktail in her hand even though it wasn't even the lunch hour. And I heard someone moving around upstairs. A person trying to be quiet, but back then these satellites picked up everything. When I asked who was up there, her mother looked over my shoulder, wouldn't even meet my eyes, and said it was my imagination. *You must be hearing things.* But these ears had never steered me wrong before." Reid yanked on one of his lobes. "Janice was up there hiding out, waiting for me to leave. And you know what I think? As soon as I did leave, I think she got in that car and disappeared. Out to Denver, I presume."

"Matt Evans told us today that his wife faked her death and is trying to set him up for murder," Spengler said.

"And I believe it," Reid said. "But I'd guess it's not just her—it's both of them in on it. They've been careful enough for the last twenty years, but I've found that if a person gets away with something once, they'll most likely try it again."

Reid flipped over the paper in front of him and slid it across the table. It was a photograph, blown up to eight-by-ten, a nice glossy of a woman standing in front of a tree, her hair blowing lightly in the wind. A posed photo taken by a professional.

Spengler took her phone out and pulled up one of the pictures of Marie Evans she had saved and looked back and forth between the two. Marie's hair was darker than the other woman's, and she was much thinner and had more lines in her face, but both of them were smiling, both had their heads tilted a little to the right as they gazed into the camera. And both women had a small scar on their chins, almost perfectly in the center. Small things, but that's life. That's police work.

"The devil's in the details," Loren said. He sounded like he was going to be sick.

"That's right," Reid said. "This picture was taken a little over twenty years ago." He tapped a bent pointer finger against the photo he'd laid on the table. "That's a young Janice Roscoe, about a year before she married Matt Evans, and about a year before she faked her own death and started going by another name. And it seems to me that she's back to her old shenanigans."

CHAPTER FIFTY-TWO

"We believe you, Mr. Evans," Spengler said. They'd had Evans brought out of holding and back into an interview room once Abe Reid had departed for the warmth of Arizona. "Your wife is still alive and is attempting to set you up for murder."

Evans looked sullenly at Spengler. He'd stayed mostly silent since talking to his lawyer.

"I think you're saying it wrong, Spengler," Loren said. He grabbed a chair and dragged it around the table until he could sit right beside Evans. Uncomfortably close, their knees practically touching.

"What should I be saying, then?"

"He hasn't had only *one* wife," Loren said. "Evans here's been married twice. Two different women. Both dead. Supposedly. Unless . . ." he trailed off, watching Evans closely. He stared back with no reaction. One of the best poker faces Loren had ever seen, except for Gallo. Gallo had been the best, by far. A master.

"Unless what?" Spengler asked.

Loren waited to see if Evans would fill in the silence. Nothing.

"You remember Detective Abe Reid, don't you?" Loren

asked. "Old guy who handled the investigation on your first wife's murder?"

Evans nodded slightly.

"He was a smart ol' dude," Loren said. "Noticed everything, took a lot of notes. People thought he was nuts, but he had some good ideas. He wasn't completely bought in on the idea that O'Neil had killed your wife—did you know that?" Loren waited for a response, didn't get one. "He didn't think you were being completely honest about what happened. You'd left out important bits. Reid had a dead woman, your story about a guy breaking in, and O'Neil shot through the head. All wrapped up neatly with a bow. Easy to just close up the case and move on."

"Easy to follow, easy to swallow," Evans murmured.

"Hey, that's how your friend Reid put it," Loren said, leaning back in his chair and slapping a hand against his thigh with delight. "That's exactly the idea. The best joke is the one easiest to tell, you know what I mean? Simple enough that even a drunk deaf-mute could follow it."

"Loren?" Spengler said, frowning. "Maybe you could get to the point?"

"You got an appointment to get to, Spengler?"

"No. But your constant yapping is giving me a headache."

Loren smiled and turned back to Evans, leaned close.

"So Marie is still alive, like you said," Loren said softly. "You told us 'I didn't kill my wife' and that was the truth, because you've only ever had one wife. And she's alive. Marie is alive, and so is Janice. Because Marie and Janice are the same person, isn't that right? Twenty years ago Janice faked her death, and she decided to do it again."

Evans blinked, surprised. It was the first real reaction they'd gotten from him.

"I know your lawyer said to not tell us anything else, so let's play a little game," Loren said. "If I'm right, if Marie and Janice are the same person and she's still alive out there, don't say anything."

Evans didn't say a word.

CHAPTER FIFTY-THREE

September 10, 2018

The press conference the police pulled together was set up outside the station, on the concrete steps that led up to the wide double doors. There was a lectern on the landing, a cheap wood thing kept in the utility closet for occasions like this, weighed down at the base with a sandbag to keep it from tumbling down the steps and blowing away. On the front was a cutout of the city's emblem, and standing behind it was Detective Marion Spengler.

She looked terrified, the people on the steps said. Reporters and journalists and cameramen were gathered there, waiting for a snippet to publish about the woman pulled out of the river. And about Matt Evans, because the entire city knew he had been arrested, that he had been taken into custody for the murder of his wife. No one knew the entire story—most reports had come from a woman working at the coroner's office, who dished to a reporter from the *Post,* who then quickly spread the word—but that's how life is, isn't it? You never know the whole story.

But the police were going to comment now, which meant that there'd been some new development, and the crowd waited anxiously. None of them had ever gotten a statement from Detective Spengler, who was new to Homicide. Ralph Loren was a familiar face, although Loren had been banned from speaking to the media after an unfortunate incident years before, when a sixteen-year-old girl had been found in a ditch, raped and strangled. The victim's mother had agreed to speak to the media, which had been a mistake—the questions had somehow become about the girl's sexual activities before her death, and what she'd been wearing on the night of her murder. And Detective Loren, who'd been standing beside the mother as she began weeping and the questions kept coming, finally intervened.

Are you saying this girl deserved this? he'd shouted into the crowd of reporters. Without waiting for an answer, he'd kicked over the lectern and dug a handful of change from his pockets, then started flinging the coins into the crowd. A single video of the incident existed, and in it Loren looks like a man trying to skip rocks over water, only he's throwing coins with deadly accuracy. There were reports of broken cameras and eyeglasses, and one woman claimed to have gotten a black eye from a quarter. The Denver PD paid out on any claims, removed Loren from that particular case, and agreed to never let him speak at a press conference again.

But Spengler was fresh blood, and no one was quite sure what to expect.

"I hope she doesn't throw up," someone said. There was a smattering of laughter.

It had rained that morning but had let up just before lunch, leaving the sidewalks and streets dark with moisture. It was cool out, but Spengler was warm. She'd never liked crowds, didn't like public speaking. She'd barely passed that class in college and now here she was, dozens of eyes—both real and digital—trained on her.

Keep it simple, stupid. That's what Loren had told her. *Just like we practiced.* Easy for him to say from his spot standing behind her.

Afterward, she could never remember her walk up to the lectern that'd been set up on the steps, a slim wooden thing with a microphone on top, like a cherry balancing at the peak of an ice cream sundae, or even the long moments she spent standing in front of the reporters. She wasn't thinking about Matt and Marie Evans in those moments, or even Riley Tipton. Instead, she was thinking about men. She'd seen men do terrible things, arrested and testified against them, but no one ever realized a woman could be just as terrible, and when they *were* everyone was surprised. But times were a-changing, weren't they? After consulting with his lawyer, Evans had told them his wife was a killer, cold and calculating, she'd roped him into faking her death and then kept him hostage to it for twenty-plus years. She'd killed that first woman and made it look like it was her, and she'd plugged a bullet into his shoulder to make it look like they'd been attacked. She'd tried to kill her boss, she'd killed Riley, and now she was setting him up for murder.

I know she's alive because she called, Evans said. *When I was in the morgue with Riley. Called my cell just to gloat. She always has to get the last word.*

Spengler had checked and it was true—Evans had received a call from an unknown number during the short time he'd been alone with Riley Tipton's remains. The call lasted two minutes. Had it been Marie, watching her husband from somewhere nearby, wanting to poke him?

Women were called the fairer sex, sometimes the lesser sex. They were called delicate and weak and frail. If you wanted to insult someone, you'd tell them not to act like a girl. Don't run like a girl, throw like a girl, cry like a girl. But when something awful happened it was easy to blame a woman. Women were seductresses, temptresses, witches. They lured men in and turned them into pigs, or their vaginas were lined with teeth and they'd chomp men alive. These women were drowned, they were burned at the stake, they were called hysterical and given lobotomies and shock treatment. A woman could be an easy scapegoat. Or they were ignored, and that might even be worse. Looked over, told to quiet down, to keep their mouths and their legs shut. It started young, and it never stopped, did it?

But it wasn't that Spengler thought Janice Marie Evans was an innocent. No, quite the opposite. There was a ring of truth around Evans's story, but there were areas that seemed gray and blurred. Spots where the puzzle pieces didn't quite line up to make a clear picture.

Was Marie Evans innocent?

Nope.

But Spengler didn't think she was the only guilty one.

Matt Evans declined to have his lawyer present in the interview room while he told them everything. The whole truth, nothing but the truth. His own words. It was, perhaps, the biggest sales pitch of his life, and he had to give it his all. But it's one thing to say you'll do something and another to actually go through with it, and Spengler thought he might've been struck with a few flights of fancy as he recounted the last twenty or so years he'd spent with his wife. He made himself out to be a saint and Marie the villain—good me, bad her—but one side of the story wouldn't cut it. Every cop knows there's three sides of every story. His side, her side.

And then there's the truth.

Spengler didn't remember later how the crowd shifted uncomfortably as they waited for her to speak, wondering if there was something wrong. She snaked her hands around the top of the lectern and dug her nails into the wood. There was her own husband and there was Matt Evans and there was her father and there was every other man on the planet, and some of them were bad and some were good but most were just okay. Nothing special. *Be a man,* that's what people said when they wanted you to be tough and get control of your life, but that was bullshit. She was tougher than most men she knew, and she had a feeling Marie Evans was, too.

You squeeze all their balls now.

She cleared her throat.

"It was widely reported that Matthew Evans had been placed under arrest for suspicion of murdering his wife," Spengler said suddenly, the words bursting out of her like water through a broken dam. "We did take Mr. Evans into custody several days ago, but we'll be releasing him today."

A murmur swept through the crowd, then stilled. Spengler had read about cases where press conferences were used to a certain advantage—most killers were ego whores and loved to follow the news about themselves—and the media had been used to communicate a message. Send a message, or draw the killer out.

"We don't believe Mr. Evans has committed any sort of crime," Spengler said. "We apologize to Mr. Evans for any inconvenience. Our investigation will continue in a different direction."

Send a message, that's how some cops used press conferences. Appeal to a person's humanity. But Spengler didn't give a damn about anyone's humanity. She wanted to catch a killer. Draw them out into the open.

Both of them.

I told you I didn't do anything wrong, Evans had said that morning when they'd gone in to tell him he'd be released soon. But Spengler had seen the flash of surprise in his eyes. He hadn't been sure they'd believe him. *This is all Marie's doing.*

She'd been there when Riley Tipton was pulled from the water. Floater, that's what they called those victims. The body had been swollen up like an inner tube. *More cushion for the pushin',* she'd heard a tech on the scene say, but his laughter dried up when he saw her staring at him. She'd been watching, so he'd behaved himself. But that was people for you. They acted right when they knew they were being watched. The only guy she'd ever met who acted the same under any circumstance was Loren, and that was because he didn't give a damn what anyone thought.

There was nothing worse than a man laughing behind his hand at a woman, she thought. A man thinking he's getting away with whatever he wants, that he's so smart, that he's pulling the wool right over everyone's eyes.

That's what Evans was doing. Laughing.

"Mr. Evans will be immediately returned to his home and has said he will cooperate fully with our investigation," she said.

This whole thing was less about sending a message and more about setting out the bait.

"What about the woman found in the Three Forks River?" one of the reporters shouted. "Has she been identified as Marie Evans?"

Spengler paused and smiled. She'd been practicing it in the mirror. She'd practiced that same smile before telling Evans they believed him and he'd be released. Kept her lips relaxed, lots of teeth. Practice makes perfect, after all, and if things were going to play out the way they wanted, Evans had to think they'd swallowed his story.

Swallowed it and licked the bowl clean.

"We will release more information as it comes to light," she said. "Thank you."

Marie's not going to just turn herself in, if that's what you think, Evans had said. He was different once he thought they were on the same side. Confident and opinionated. She liked him better when he was quiet and scared. *She's not stupid. She's out there, watching. Probably laughing at me. And what are you fucking cops doing about it?*

That was what Spengler was counting on—that Marie was watching all this unfold, that she'd see her husband had been seemingly cleared of wrongdoing in her death. She'd think they were all laughing at her, that her husband had gotten away scot-free, and she'd be infuriated. Female black widows eat their mates once they're done with them, and that was what Spengler was hoping for—that the spider would learn her mate was still alive and well and come out of her hidey-hole, that she'd show up in her web again, hunting for her man.

CHAPTER FIFTY-FOUR

September 11, 2018

Matt slept through the night like a baby, hard but fine, even though he was sure he'd be up all night trying to figure out what was going on. But he hadn't gotten much sleep over the last few days and was exhausted. It was nearly impossible to sleep on the hard cot in the cell where they'd kept him for two days—there were the noises from the other prisoners and the footsteps of the guards that echoed up and down the bare hallway, and there was his own brain, not wanting to shut up, yammering on, asking if he'd made the right choice in talking to the cops. His lawyer had advised against it, but he'd done it anyway. A cop dropped him off at home and he'd gone inside and made himself a turkey sandwich and then went to bed, was asleep before he could even manage to climb under the covers. Back in his own bed, in his own home, it was difficult not to be comfortable.

The bed was a king—California king—and he'd never before realized how much room there was without Marie in it, but that was how life with her had always been. She'd come into a room and suck all the air from it, all the life, like a black hole. It was part of the reason he'd fallen for her to begin with. She'd sucked him right in.

He might've even slept better than usual since Marie wasn't there to press her cold feet up against his legs, or keep him up with the light of her phone when she woke up at three in the morning and couldn't go back to sleep. She'd been doing that a lot over the last year—he'd tried to get her to take sleeping pills to help her make it all the way through the night without waking, but she'd refused. Typical Marie. She didn't even like to take aspirin.

I'm not trying to poison you, he'd say.

How can I be sure about that?

He was confused when he first woke up, because the sun was out and the birds were chirping, and he'd gotten used to the dry dark of his windowless cell. Two days, that was how long it took for him to get used to something, and now he was startled to wake up in the brightness of his own house. It smelled clean in here, like coffee and laundry detergent and *home,* and he was glad to be back but also confused. The cops had let him go, just like that. Asked him to hang around the house for a few more days, cooperate with the investigation, and he didn't know what the detectives had done or where they'd gone because neither of them had come back, and then a cop he'd never seen was unlocking his cell and handing him his clothes and offering him a ride home. He was free to go, any charges had been dropped.

Just like that.

But what about my wife? he'd asked the officer.

They're taking the investigation in another direction, the cop had said, shrugging. *Loren said your story checks out.*

Easy to swallow, easy to follow, something like that. They said to let you go.

So he'd come home, the cops said it was all good, he just needed to keep his mouth shut, but that seemed wrong. There was something about the silence that was deafening. The calm before the storm. Or maybe he was just paranoid. Maybe he shouldn't look a gift horse in the mouth, he should be happy they'd actually believed him. He could remember feeling this same way twenty years before and it'd all turned out fine that time, hadn't it?

And it wasn't as if he'd lied—well, most of it was true. Part of being a good salesman was being ready for any eventuality, any question or problem that came up, and he was the best. Always had been. But he hadn't accounted for this particular situation, had he? He hadn't even seen it coming. *Blindsided* was a good word for it. He'd been blindsided by his wife. Or you could say he'd been completely strung up by the balls and left to dangle helplessly.

Either one worked.

He swung his feet over the side of the bed and sat up. His back hurt from lying down all night, so the walk down the stairs was slow. One stiff step after another, gripping the banister all the way down so he wouldn't slip and fall. Once he was in the kitchen he grabbed a mug from the cabinet and poured a cup of coffee. It tasted burnt, even though it was a thousand-dollar machine. Matt dumped in a dollop of cream to cut the taste, and a half a teaspoon of sugar, and when he was done he went to put the spoon in the sink. There was nothing that bothered him more than a dirty spoon lying on the counter, something that Marie had always done, it didn't matter that the goddamn sink was right—

He hadn't started the coffee maker, he hadn't been home for days, and this coffee was fresh. Hot. It was a process he hated—rinsing out the carafe, pouring fresh water into the reservoir, tipping grounds into the new filter. Too much work, and if he had to get it all ready himself he'd end up at Starbucks. It was Marie who didn't mind getting the coffee ready, and there was almost always a fresh pot when he woke up or got home from the gym.

But if he hadn't started the coffee maker, who had?

What about my wife? he'd asked the cop, who'd shrugged again. *She's still out there.*

There was a creak above his head, like someone was walking the second floor. It's an old house, it could just be the sound of settling, but he doesn't think so. He's lived here long enough.

"Hello?" he called. His voice sounded too loud in the empty house, and for the first time he wished they had a dog. They'd had the cat for a while, Mr. Mittens, and that'd turned out badly. Something furry and warm and alive pushed up against his leg would've been a comfort. "Is someone there?"

Another footstep, rasping its way across the floor above.

"Hello?" he shouted, coming out of the kitchen and taking a small step toward the staircase. Half a dozen would get him close enough to see up the steep slope to the landing. "Is there someone there?"

There was a long pause. The ice maker on the fridge groaned and spit out another cube, and a car drove past on the street. The sounds of life. A dog outside barked and he jerked in surprise, dropped his coffee. The mug hit the ground and shattered like a bomb, showering his bare legs with hot liquid and shards of porcelain, but he barely felt any of it. He was scared, more so than he'd ever been in his entire life.

What about my wife? he'd asked, but the cops hadn't seemed worried. He'd called Detective Spengler's cell phone when he got home, asked the same thing. But first he'd made sure all the windows were shut, the doors locked. *What about Marie? Have you found her yet?*

We're working on it, Spengler had said. *But she's probably in Mexico by now, don't you think? Relaxing on a beach and drinking a margarita. Stop being paranoid, get some rest.*

Paranoid, that's what he was. But what if he wasn't? Marie had planned all of this and he hadn't had a clue—what else did she have up her sleeve? Being married to Marie had been a little like turning the handle on a jack-in-the-box and waiting for the clown to pop out. You knew it was going to happen and scare you, but you never knew when.

There, again. A creak above his head.

It was like those horror stories kids told each other about a babysitter getting a call from a man—but *the man was in the house.* They'd lived in this same house for going on fifteen years, and it was suddenly full of sounds and creaks and groans he didn't recognize, but maybe they'd always been there and he had never noticed. He grabbed a knife from the butcher block in the kitchen and went through the entire house, looked in every room, every closet and cabinet. Behind every shower curtain and under every bed. Because you never knew. It was only when he was sure he was alone in the house, positive that Marie wasn't waiting to creep up behind him, that he went back to the kitchen and carefully started picking up the shattered remains of his mug, piling the pieces up in a kitchen towel so he wouldn't cut himself. He must've set the coffee maker himself before falling asleep, he thought. And then he'd forgotten he'd done it.

He told himself that same thing all day, but still didn't quite believe it.

CHAPTER FIFTY-FIVE

September 12, 2018

"What if she doesn't show up?" Spengler asked. "Then what'll we do?" Loren snorted, fiddled with the binoculars in his lap.

"She'll be here," he said. "Women like Marie Evans—you heard her husband. They always want the last word. That's how just about all women are. Always wanting to be right."

Spengler turned to stare at him mutely. They were in his car, the ol' Le-Baron, parked across the street from the Evans home, hidden deep in the shadows thrown by the homes and trees, far from the circles thrown down by the lampposts standing at intervals. They waited, and watched and watched some more. Evans had been released the day before and there'd been someone outside the whole time, keeping an eye on the place. In case Marie decided to come home, in case Evans decided to run. And now Loren and Spengler were there, taking the next shift. Five A.M. until dinnertime.

"No offense," Loren said. "But you know what I mean. With those kind of women."

"No, I don't know what you mean," Spengler said. She blinked, wide eyed. "Why don't you explain it to me?"

He rolled his eyes and looked toward the house. It was all quiet, no movement. Not that they could tell all that much from here—the house's blinds were pulled, the drapes shut. The entire neighborhood was silent. It was still early enough that the only movement had been the station wagon creeping down the street thirty minutes before, its driver tossing newspapers onto front stoops.

"I haven't seen Ortiz hanging around lately," Spengler said, looking out the window instead of at Loren. "You heard from him?"

"Last I heard he'd gone back to Springfield."

"Oh? How do you know that?"

"He left a nasty note on my door."

"How mature."

"Yeah. I guess I'm off the hook."

Spengler made a small noise of disbelief through her nose.

"Just like that?" she asked. "That easy?"

"Sometimes that's how things go," Loren said. "Easy as pie. Easy-peasy-lemon-squeezy. Easy as a whore looking to turn a trick to pay her rent."

"You had me until the last one," she said drily. "I'm not so sure you're capable of having a normal conversation without dropping in something offensive."

"Gallo's wife used to say the same thing," Loren said. "Constance, that was her name."

"I saw that in the file."

"But I always called her Connie. Did Ortiz tell you that?"

Spengler shook her head.

"Yep," he said. He was looking at the house but running his fingers along the underside of the steering wheel, round and round. "She was Connie to me, Constance to everyone else. Even her own husband. But sometimes I used to wonder what he called her when he was pounding her face into a bloody pulp. I never knew, I was never around when he did it. I just saw it afterward. The black eyes and the broken noses and the bruised ribs. He almost killed her once."

His voice caught. He took a tissue from the box sitting on the dashboard and coughed into it, then blew his nose. Spengler kept her eyes on the Evans house. He knew she was being kind by not looking at him, giving him a bit of privacy even as she was listening, and he liked her for it.

"He almost killed her once, and she showed up at my place with her baby, begged me to take her in. To help her. She didn't want to go to the hospital, so I patched her up. Put her and the baby to sleep in my bed and went to the store to get her medicine. Stood in the drugstore and stared at the shelves, wondering what could possibly help a woman who had a face beaten bad enough it looked like an old, spoiled apple." He laughed, but there was no pleasure in it. "The only thing I could get my hands on was aspirin, can you believe that? Nowadays you can get a prescription for just about anything, anytime, if you know the right doctor, and if you can't get it at the drugstore you can buy it off any crackhead walking the street. But back then all I could get was a lousy bottle of aspirin."

Shut yer yap, his father said. *You really gonna tell her all this shit, just unloose it on her? What if she decides she can't keep it to herself? Then what?*

Loren laughed, because he didn't give two shits if Spengler knew the truth anymore. He could remember walking into the house, the aspirin in the plastic bag from the store dangling from his fingers, and hearing the baby's scream. It was the kind of cry that sounds weary and put out, as if the baby had been crying for a while and was confused about why it'd been left alone for so long. For one terrible minute, Loren had thought that Connie might've died, that maybe she'd been bleeding internally and had passed in her sleep, that it'd been a mistake not to take her to the ER despite her protests. But when he hustled into the bedroom the baby was alone in the middle of the bed, its tiny red fists waving angrily in the air. And Connie was gone. On her way out she hadn't forgotten to surround the baby with pillows so it couldn't roll off the bed, she'd still wanted to protect her kid even when she'd left it behind.

But she'd made sure to take one thing: the gun Loren used for work. He always left it on top of his dresser when he was off duty, and it was gone.

"I knew where she'd gone," Loren said. "Home, to Gallo. So I wrapped the baby up in a bathroom towel and laid it on the front seat of my car and drove over to their place. One hand on the wheel, one hand on the baby to keep it from rolling onto the floor. Moving in a hurry, because I thought I might be able to get there in time to stop anything bad from happening." He took a quick sip from the water bottle nestled between his thighs. His mouth was dry, his voice cracking. "But when I got there it was already done. Connie had shot Gallo right through the head, and when I walked in she begged me to help her cover it up. Got right down on her hands and knees and *begged*, crying, snot dripping outta her nose, mixed in with all that blood. She didn't want to go to jail and have the baby put in a home. It wasn't fair, she said. He deserved what he got, she said."

"So what did you do?" Spengler asked. For the first time since he'd started talking she'd turned to look at him, but there wasn't any judgment in her gaze. Only curiosity.

"What was I supposed to do?" Loren demanded angrily. He slammed his fist down on his thigh. Later there'll be a bruise there, purplish-black and tender. "Of course I helped her. Because I was in love with her and she knew it. And he did deserve it. It was the best ending for a piece of shit like him. I loaded Gallo's body up in my car and drove out to the Mad River and buried him. Then I came back and cleaned up that place as best I knew how. Wiped away all the blood and bone and brains and shit that'd splattered everywhere, and then I helped Connie pack up all her stuff and drove her eighty miles south, down to Cincinnati. Put her and the baby up in a motel and came back. Acted like I had no idea what was going on."

"What happened?" Spengler asked. She was so calm they might've been discussing the weather.

"Nothing," Loren said. "People figured Gallo had skipped town. No one missed that bastard except Ortiz, who'd just about crawled up my ass and wanted to live there. But I still managed to sneak away every so often and drive down to see Connie and the baby, bring money and buy them food, make sure they were fine. But Connie, she started acting funny."

"What do you mean?"

"She started saying things like if anyone ever found Gallo's body, they'd be able to tell that the bullet had come from my gun. She'd seen something like that on TV, and I ignored it. But the next visit, she said the same thing. And said that if someone found out about Gallo, they'd assume I'd killed him. No one would ever think she'd done it. And she was right, of course. If you saw her back then, so small and sweet, face like an angel, you would've thought the same thing. There's no way this woman was capable of murder."

"What did she want from you?"

"I don't know," Loren said, shrugging. He drank off the last of the water in the bottle and put the bottle in the bag in the backseat. "But I was spooked. There was something about her eyes. Trouble brewing. There's nothing scarier than a woman with a plan, and I figured it'd be best to get gone. I never went back to see Connie. I transferred to Florida, didn't leave a forwarding address. Disappeared. Maybe she didn't want anything at all. Maybe she said those things because she was scared and didn't know how else to act. But my wind was up. I was in love with her, but I knew that if I stayed, if we were together, she'd always have that hanging over my head. And if she got mad enough one day, she might turn me in. Or kill me, just like she had Gallo. It reminds me of this whole mess." Loren waved his hand at the Evans house. As they watched, the burning lights flanking either side of the front door turned off. A new day had started. "How often did these two idiots talk about what they'd done?"

"It takes two to tango."

"A truer thing was never said." Loren ran a hand down his face wearily. "I made the decision to bury Gallo out there, went along with it of my own free will and made myself an accessory to murder. Connie didn't hold a gun to my head, she didn't threaten me. If I hadn't wanted to do it, I could've turned and walked. Turned her over to the feds and let her take the heat and never looked back. But I didn't. I was a willing participant until the water got too hot, and then I bailed. But what if I would've stayed? What if I'd stayed and married Connie? How would that have been, to spend the rest of my life with a woman reminding me of how she could destroy me?"

"Do you think Marie was doing that to Evans?"

"Or it was the other way around." He paused. Considered. "Or maybe they're both just fucked-up people."

"Yeah, maybe."

"I left the state to get away from Connie, to keep the secret we had safe," Loren said. He shifted in his seat, the leather squealing under his weight. "But these two had a secret and then stayed together. Twenty years is a long time to hang on to resentment and hold shit over your partner's head. They both might've been held hostage by that."

"Evans does like to play the victim card," Spengler said thoughtfully. "It's easy enough to make anyone seem like a villain when they're not around to defend themselves. You know, those PTA women who told me about Marie made her out to be ruthless and crazy."

Loren laughed a little.

"You know, I've noticed that men can be ruthless and power hungry and people will up and applaud them. But women—boy oh boy, you come across a woman who acts like that, she's automatically a bitch. I've heard you called that a few times, actually."

"Fuck off," Spengler said, but she laughed, too. Shook her head. "So you told Ortiz all this about Connie?"

Loren's father laughed in his head. Loud.

He didn't hesitate with the lie. Forty years as a cop, more time spent undercover than he'd like to admit, and one good thing had come from it: he could fib his sweet ass off. He could make a person believe he was a goddamn penguin if he needed to, he could sell ice to an Eskimo.

"Yeah," he said. "I told Ortiz everything, and he was satisfied. Went home to Springfield, is gonna check it all out. I'm sure I'll have to go back and give a statement sometime, I might still be in some hot water, but at least they know the truth of it."

Oh, the lies. Why had Ortiz gone back to Springfield? Loren didn't know, only that he was gone as suddenly as he'd appeared. People said no news was good news, but Loren knew from experience that was mostly bullshit. Quiet time was prep time. No news usually meant things were gearing up to explode right in your face, splat shit all over the walls and cover you in it. He didn't know when it would happen, or where, but it felt like there was a storm coming.

They kept watching. Two days passed, then three. They were watching the Evanses' bank accounts, their credit cards. They sat outside the house and drank gallons of coffee, ate old ham sandwiches from the refrigerator case at the gas station—made with the kind of ham that always has a gristly, chewy part right in the center that squeaks in your teeth when you take a bite. They were monitoring phone lines and emails and everything they could think of, but there'd been nothing. Evans had hardly set foot outside his house and hadn't attempted to contact anyone for a week. He was crouching low, keeping his head down, hoping to let the storm pass. Just like he had twenty years before, when he'd waited for the storm of his first wife's murder to pass him by. They'd coddled and soothed him, made him believe they'd bought his entire story of innocence.

Still, nothing. Silence is called golden, but that's another crock of shit for you. Silence is damning, silence is awkward, silence is anything but gold. Loren and Spengler waited, Evans waited. The people of Denver waited. Most everyone thought Marie Evans was dead from an accidental fall off a cliff, and the police didn't issue a statement to correct those assumptions.

They were all seated in the great waiting room of life, impatiently flipping through the old *Reader's Digest* Condensed Editions, twiddling their thumbs and picking at their teeth, waiting for something to happen.

Waiting for Marie.

"She could be in Mexico by now," Spengler said.

"I doubt it."

"What makes you say that?"

"Listen, I know you're a gung ho feminist and I'm just an old fart, but if I've learned anything about women over the years, it's that a woman like her isn't going to let anything go," Loren said. He reached over and popped the glove compartment, grabbed the dental floss he had stashed inside. "You want some? These cheap-ass sandwiches get all caught up in my teeth every time."

She shook her head.

"She's out there, waiting," he said, cutting off a good-sized length of floss and wrapping each end around a pointer finger. "She went to a helluva lot of trouble to set this whole thing up, trying to get him arrested for murder. She's not going to like it much that he's at home, sitting on his ass in front of the TV instead of crying his poor eyes out in jail."

"I don't know."

"We just have to wait," Loren said. "Be patient, Spengler. It's a fucking virtue, you know."

During the hours they sat outside, Spengler reviewed the case until her eyes swam from looking at the words so long. She hadn't slept much in days—she'd always been that way when she was deep in a case, her brain wouldn't shut up long enough to let her relax—and that might've been some of the problem, but it was also that this whole thing was so damn muddled.

Easy to follow, easy to swallow. She'd heard both Reid and Evans say that, and now Loren had picked it up. But there was nothing easy about any of this. Nothing simple.

Once Evans admitted that Marie and Janice were the same person, they couldn't get him to stop talking. He said his wife had forced his hand. That she'd done everything, planned it all out. She was a killer, she was ruthless, she was guilty. At one time it would've seemed crazy, a woman doing something like that. No one would've believed it. Women were soft, they were delicate. Oh, there were the freaks that popped up occasionally, those women who poisoned and plotted and got their revenge, but they were outliers. But times, they had changed. There were women who killed, who hurt children and their spouses and sold drugs and committed all sorts of crimes. Those women were run of the mill these days.

Spengler had once arrested a woman who'd been pimping out her daughters since they were babies, who'd accept ten dollars for a few minutes with one of her own children. Awful women, but was it even more awful because they weren't men? Maybe—but why should it be? Over the years more people had come to accept that women could be just as bad. And maybe Evans was being honest about his wife, maybe Marie really was one of those women who'd stop at nothing to get her way. She'd even murder and kill and fake her own death.

Or maybe it was just easy to make Marie seem like that. She was a jealous woman, she was ruthless and didn't let people stand in her way. She was a bitch.

And she wasn't there to defend herself.

They watched and waited. They'd trade off with the next team of detectives and go home, but Spengler didn't sleep. She'd lie in bed and wonder what Evans was thinking. What Marie was thinking. If either of them thought they were safe.

She called me, Evans had said. *To tease me. Taunt me. She always wanted the last word.*

Spengler pulled all his phone records. He'd said Marie had called from an unknown number, but when you're the police there's nothing unknown. One of the geeks in IT was able to get the phone number easily enough and figure out it'd been assigned to a throwaway burner phone, the kind you can buy at any grocery store for cash. The kind of phone you'd have if you didn't want anyone to trace you.

Evans had gotten a single call from that number, and the call had lasted two minutes. Two minutes is a long time when you think about it, 120 seconds you can fill with all kinds of words. What had been said during that conversation?

You could say nothing in two minutes, or you could say it all.

Spengler called the number once from her own cell phone. It rang five times, then went to voice mail. She wondered if Marie was holding the phone when she called, if she'd considered answering but resisted the temptation. It was a general voice mail box, nothing personal, the greeting a smooth robotic voice. It could belong to anyone, or it could be Marie's. And that was the question. If Spengler left a voice mail, would it be Marie who listened?

She thought about that voice mail box for an entire day; then, that night, sitting on her deck once Tony and Elliott were both in bed, under a sooty black sky that held no stars, she called it again. At first she didn't know what to say, but then the words came and it was easy. She left her message and then called back, left another. And again.

Sometimes she thought it was like screaming into a bottomless pit, but sometimes she was sure she could feel the ear at the other end, listening to every word.

GONNA LOVE YOU UNTIL YOU HATE ME

CHAPTER FIFTY-SIX

If you want to kill your husband, it should be easy. Because you're tougher than he is, and you're stronger and faster. Giving birth to two big-headed daughters without medication and all those early-morning runs and Pilates classes haven't just been for fun, right? But most of all you're smarter than he is, even though he thinks he's got all the brains, he thinks he's the smart one because he has a job and a private office and makes all the money and goes out to nice restaurants for lunch and *networks* while you're at home, cooking and cleaning and wiping runny noses and changing poopy diapers. He thinks that just because he puts on slacks and a tie and has an agenda and you're going to spend the whole day baking cookies for the school sale and you probably won't manage to take a shower until after lunch—if at all— that he's better. But what your husband has managed to conveniently forget is that *you* are the one who helped him get through college, *you* are the one who wrote the résumé that got him that fancy job, *you* are the one who took the online personality test his job required before they'd hire him, and his boss thinks he's an *empathetic* leader, that he's *strategic*, but those are actually *your* results. Not that they'd ever hire *you* to lead a team of men selling businesses to other men. You're missing one vital part, and it doesn't matter the slightest that you'd be better at the job than your husband, because if you don't have this one particular piece you don't have anything.

You don't have a dick, so you don't *get* dick.

But you *could* get over all that if your husband would behave right, but that's something out of his realm. He thinks he's smart, that he's sneaky, but he doesn't realize you're at home, waiting, while he's at *her* place, balls deep between her thighs, groaning about how things would be so much better if *you* weren't around. And when he's done with this woman— and you've seen her, she's younger and better looking than you, but probably an idiot—he comes home, smelling like sex and sweat and not even trying to hide what he's done, and he says he's too tired to eat dinner with the family and to spend time with the girls, he has a headache and a backache and he had a long day and needs some alone time, unless, that is, you're down to give him a blow job.

So honestly, your husband has had it coming for a good long while now, and needs to be taught a lesson. He has to die.

BUT.

Maybe divorce is a better option. Maybe it's a little overkill to plan your husband's death, and you might be right. But here's the thing: if you got a divorce you'd get alimony payments, but it probably wouldn't be enough to live on, and you could certainly get a job but you'd be making next to nothing because no one's going to hire a woman who's spent her entire adult life at home with kids. And you can't even put down that you've been to college, you can't even put down your real name, because you're not technically even a person anymore because you took on the identity of the woman you caught your husband in bed with, and that woman is someone you know nothing about, a woman who might not have even graduated high school, and if you ever use your real name again, or your social security number, the government will be on you like white on rice, and you'll go right to prison, do not pass go, do not collect two hundred dollars. And with no school and no work experience and no identity there's only one conclusion:

You're fucked.

BUT.

There's a third option. You could make it work. You could put up with your crappy marriage and ignore what your husband does on the side and try to be patient, because he'll probably kick the bucket before you. All that beer and the gut he's been picking up over the last few years can't be for nothing, right? So you could wait it out, hope for that heart attack to happen. Plenty of women have done it before, silently dealing with their lot in life, and you could, too, if you had to. And maybe, after a while, you'd even get used to it.

But here's the thing: you're not the kind of woman who can get used to anything. And you're not a patient woman. You never have been. And while blood and violence don't bother you, you've had enough of that to last you a lifetime. So you decide to make that motherfucker pay for what he's put you through. You were a forgiving woman once, you overlooked his flaws and moved on, but you're also not an idiot. Your mother had always warned you about men, said that once a man hurts you it's only a matter of time before he does it again, and it's better to be safe than sorry. You've always had a secret stash of cash on the side. A runaway fund, your mother called it. A safety net.

So over the years you've put some money back, a bit at a time, not enough for him to miss and ask about. It's not a fortune, it won't keep you rolling for the rest of your life, but it's enough to make a start. So maybe, deep down, you've been planning this for a long time. Or laying the ground-work, at least.

And then, one day, you realize the years have leached away your patience and you're done.

So, when it really comes down to it, you don't have much of a choice. This man is a cheater, he's weak, he's a louse. You've had to stick around in this marriage because you haven't had any other choice, and it's been fine, but things have changed and there's no damn way you're going to stand for this. It's not about the money, because you've come to realize that what people say is right—money can't buy hap-piness. You've been putting up with his bullshit for far too long, but if you put up with it just a little longer, lay your traps and set the stage just right, you can pull it off, *no problemo*.

But then you realize something that could screw the whole thing up:

Your husband isn't actually as stupid as he's led you to believe.

CHAPTER FIFTY-SEVEN

September 3, 1995

"I want a divorce," she said. The two of them had stopped laughing when they realized she was there. The girl had pulled the bedding up to her chin and was staring with wide, frightened eyes, but she hadn't screamed. Janice had to give her that. She hadn't screamed, and she didn't seem very surprised. Just wary. "I can't believe I've wasted so much of my life with you."

Matt got out of the bed and held his hands up. He was completely naked, his body smooth and gleaming in the low light, his cock swaying gently between his thighs as he came closer. He looked ridiculous, she thought. She should shoot him right now, in that stupid dangling thing he was so proud of. That would teach him a lesson.

"Janice, it doesn't have to be like this," he said softly, coming closer. Hands still up. The love line that cut across his palm was especially long, ran almost from one side of his hand to the other. "Put down the gun and we can talk. This isn't what you think."

She'd been holding the gun down at her side, the barrel pointing at the floor, and brought it up now, looked at it in astonishment. She'd practically forgotten that she'd grabbed it as she'd come in, and she couldn't believe it was still in her hand. She held it out toward Matt, meaning to give it to him, to let him take it out of her hands because she hadn't wanted the damn thing in the first place. But he must've thought she was going to shoot, that she meant to kill him, because he sprang forward and grabbed her, trapping her hand on the gun's grip, forcing her fingers tighter around it and pointing it away from himself. She tried to pull away, to get free, to let him have the damn gun so she could leave, but couldn't. Afterward, she wondered how often bad things happened because of these sorts of miscommunications. Afterward, she never knew how long they struggled over the gun, her trying to give it and Matt trying to take it away, both misunderstanding the other, but it ended when the gun fired. Janice felt the heat of the bullet streak past her face and the silver-white flash of light and gasped, stumbling back, and Matt did the same.

The gun clattered to the floor between their feet.

They looked down at themselves, then at each other, checking to see if either of them had been shot. They were both fine, but the woman in the bed was not. She'd been thrown back on the pillows, her arms flung out and her eyes open, a single drip of blood running down the center of her face. The bullet had gone cleanly through her left eye, a once-in-a-million shot, and the force of it had knocked one of her front teeth out. The bedsheet had fallen down so her breasts were bared, her areolas large and pinkish-brown. Janice went to the bed and pulled the sheet up to her neck, covering her up. A silly thing to do for a dead woman, but she did it without thinking.

"We killed her," Matt said.

"It was an accident."

"No one will believe that."

"But it was an accident. We didn't mean to do it."

Years later, they'd blame each other for the girl's death. They'd say it was on purpose, that one of them was more guilty than the other even though they'd both been holding the gun when it fired. This girl came up every time they argued for *years*, because once you have some bit of information to hold over another person's head you have to use it whenever possible. But now, standing beside the bed they'd shared for less than a year, they were in it together.

For better or worse.

"What are we going to do?" Matt asked.

"What are we going to do?" Janice echoed.

Life was spinning like a dime again—which way would it turn? They might've gone a different route, they could've called the cops and reported it, explained what had happened, and everyone might've understood and things would've turned out much differently, but they didn't.

That would've been too easy.

This is what they did in the panicked moments after the bullet had entered the girl's brain: they decided to burn the body, to burn the whole house down. They came up with the story about being attacked, and practiced it. They'd make it look like it was Janice who'd been attacked and killed. It was a good story, they said. A believable story.

Desperate times call for desperate measures, you see, and create desperate people.

But who came up with the idea for all this? Who was the brains behind the whole thing?

Does it matter?

Of course it matters, and the answer is that they *both* did. Two voices became one. *All together now, with feeling,* as Loren would say.

"Matt?" Janice said. They were in the bedroom, Matt pouring the last of the gasoline out of the canister and over the girl's body, his back to her. It was the only thing she could trust him to do. She'd told him to knock the girl's teeth out to make identification more difficult but he'd refused. Because he'd known her, Matt had said. He'd cared for the girl.

How much did you care for her? Janice had asked. *Did anyone know about the two of you? If someone realizes she's gone missing, are they going to come looking for you?*

I don't know. I don't think so.

He'd refused to help knock out the girl's teeth, so she'd done it herself. If you want something done right, she thought, don't ask your husband to do it.

Then she'd taken a pair of pliers from a kitchen drawer and pulled one of her own teeth to leave with the girl's body, for identification purposes. She'd sat on the side of the bathtub as she did it, not sure that she could go through with it, but then she remembered the breathless pain of seeing her husband with another woman earlier that night, and her heart hardened. She lost consciousness as she pulled that molar, but when she came to it was done.

"Matt, look at me."

There was one more thing to do, and she knew he wouldn't like it.

He didn't even have time to register surprise before she pulled the trigger. She'd been aiming for his arm, high up, hoping to graze the meat of his bicep, but she'd never shot a gun before and was lucky the bullet didn't end up in his heart. It ended up going into his shoulder, and years later the puckered scar tissue left behind would look a little like a starfish.

"You shot me," he screamed, falling to the floor and writhing in pain. She thought he was being a little dramatic—surely a hole that small couldn't hurt much—and tried to explain that he couldn't walk away without a wound, not if the cops were going to believe their story. He had to be hurt, and it had to be believable. "You didn't have to shoot me."

"Yes, I did," she said. She'd shot him so their story would seem believable, but she still had to admit that a part of her had taken pleasure in shooting him, at seeing Matt weak and squirming, weeping in agony. Much later, she'd wish she'd pointed the gun a little higher and put a bullet between his eyes, instead. It would've saved her so much misery in the long run.

She kneeled over her crying husband and fed him his story, gave his ear a hard tug to make sure he was listening—guy broke in, I tried to run, he shot me—and then stood up, tucking the gun into the waistband of her jeans. Rubbed her hands together and looked around for anything she should take before they lit a match and let the place flame up—and saw Jesse O'Neil's face in the window. He must've come to check on her—he'd done it before, when she and Matt had gotten into one of their screaming fights—and had come around the backside of the house when no one answered his knocks on the front door, stood in the flower beds and peered through the bedroom window. The drapes were pulled, but they were gauzy and light as air, and sheer enough that she could clearly see the shock on Jesse's face. And the window was wide open. If she'd been able to hear Matt and his little girlfriend laughing, she had no doubt Jesse had heard every word they'd said.

So it wasn't really a question of what Jesse knew—she had to assume he'd seen and heard it all, or at least enough to get them into big trouble.

So the real question was this: How was she going to fix it?

"I have to go," she said, picking up the dead girl's purse and giving it a brisk shake. There were car keys jangling around inside. "For chrissake, Matt. You're fine. Quit being a fucking baby and finish this. I'm going to my mother's house."

She nudged him, not gently, with her foot and ran outside. Her mouth was bleeding, badly, and she turned her head to spit so she wouldn't drown in it.

Jesse was still out there, stumbling away from the house with a numb look on his face. It was simple enough to convince him to get in the girl's car and to drive away with her. He wasn't scared. Jesse loved her, and he didn't think he had anything to be worried about. Even though she had a gun, even though he'd watched her shoot her husband. That pissed her off a little. Don't worry about that *woman*, she's harmless—she won't shoot you in the back of the head so the police will think you're a killer.

But she did shoot Jesse—although she screwed that whole thing up royally, didn't she?—because Jesse was only a guy she knew from work and Matt—although he was a scumball who'd probably picked up crabs from a hooker and passed them on to her—was her husband. And they'd taken vows, and those vows meant something. Till death do us part, for better or worse. As long as we both shall live.

So there really wasn't a choice at all.

CHAPTER FIFTY-EIGHT

She was at the city limits, heading toward her mother's house, when she pulled the little car over to the side of the road, clambered out, and went down a gentle slope to the shores of a pond to wash the blood off. There was a lot of it, and she had to scrub, using grass and weeds yanked out of the ground to slough away what had dried on her skin. She was finally clean, wet and cold, too, and opened up the girl's purse to look for a comb or a brush, anything to help her look less like a drowned rat, and she instead found the girl's wallet. Inside was her state ID and a bank card. A few dollars in cash. Marie, that had been the girl's name, and so now she was Marie, too.

CHAPTER FIFTY-NINE

And what exactly brought Janice and Matt back together, even though she'd thought she'd never see his face again? Janice had planned on staying with her mother and giving birth to the baby—what an awful surprise that'd been!—and maybe moving somewhere warm, close to a beach. And all that might've happened if her mother hadn't twisted her ankle and Janice hadn't been forced to go into town for food, where that old cop had recognized her. She'd gone straight home and told her mother—who'd never once asked questions and would've done anything for her only child—who jammed her hand deep into the tin flour canister she kept on the kitchen counter and dug out a handful of powdery cash. Told her to go, to stay safe.

Fear made Janice run, and there was only one other person she knew to go to.

Matt.

So she went to Denver and enjoyed the surprise on her husband's face when he opened his front door and saw her there, belly round with their daughter, and it wasn't as if he could turn her away. Not if he wanted to keep her quiet. When two people share something as intimate as murder it's sure to bring them together, like two powerful magnets, drawn violently to each other. It was their secret, and it pulled them together. The Law of Attraction is when two similar energies are inexplicably drawn toward each other— Loren would say two sick fucks will always find each other in a crowd, and that's not wrong.

It's science, folks, but it's also life.

CHAPTER SIXTY

They lived normally for a long time. They bought a house and had the girls. She'd had an easy pregnancy with Hannah, and an easy birth. Easy, everything had been easy until Hannah went to school, heading to preschool in pigtails and a navy-blue jumper, a Disney princess lunch box swinging from her hand. No one had told Marie how it might be, that Hannah might hate school, that she'd refuse to learn the alphabet and how to read, that the only thing she was interested in was recess and what they were having for snack time. Marie could remember going to the school, fat and sore and still uncomfortable from giving birth to Maddie, who wasn't an easy baby like Hannah had been. No, Maddie screamed for at least three hours a day and couldn't be calmed down, and vomited constantly, it wasn't *spit-up*, nothing as simple as that, but actual *vomit*, projectile and chunky, and Marie wouldn't have been surprised if her head had spun in a full circle as well.

Hannah's teacher was polite but condescending in that way so many women who work with the very young or the very old are—speaking extra loud and slow, their voices bright and overly cheerful. *Hannah needs help,* the teacher had said. *She's behind the other students and isn't catching up.*

We may want to consider holding her back a year. And Marie had left the school with her eyeballs pounding in their sockets, nearly *vibrating,* and when had she last been so angry?

She knew the answer to that question, didn't even have to think about it. She'd last been that angry when she'd been thinking about Matt in bed with that woman. Bad things had come from that rage. And here she was, angry again, and over what? Over nothing, that was the worst of it. Angry over nothing at all, except that Maddie wouldn't stop crying and Hannah couldn't seem to figure out her goddamn alphabet and Matt was always at work, and Marie would sometimes be sitting beside the tub, washing down the girls, and she'd catch herself fantasizing about holding them under the water, about watching them struggle through the iridescent soap bubbles, and once they went still and stiff letting them float in there, facedown. She thought about hurting them, making them scream. That's what her thoughts were full of. Shaking them until their heads whipped around on their thin necks, throwing their little bodies into corners and seeing the sick looks on their faces, taking *pleasure* in it, and she would've cut the thoughts out of herself if she could've, scooped them out and threw them away, she loved the girls more than anything, but those thoughts wouldn't stop, she'd be watching TV or taking a shower or making dinner and it would happen, and she'd cringe away from them, squinch her eyes shut and try to make them disappear, but there was still some attraction there, some horrifying lure. Like driving past a bad car accident and slowing down to get a better look. Once, she'd tried to talk to Matt about it, and he'd looked disgusted, shook free of her hand on his arm.

"Are you trying to get attention?" he'd asked. "Stop being dramatic. If someone else heard you say things like that, they'd think you were crazy."

Crazy, he called it. If she'd gone to the doctor they might've called it *post-partum depression,* but she never did go, didn't think she could bring herself to sit in an office and repeat those thoughts to some stranger in a white coat. You kept things like that to yourself, that's what she'd learned. You kept your mouth shut about the time you killed a woman and shot a man in the back of the head, and you didn't tell anyone you'd been fantasizing about hurting your kids and yourself. You couldn't tell your husband, either; even that wasn't safe, because he'd think you were faking, *trying to get attention,* that you were crazy. Her hands shook and there were occasional flashes of light in the corners of her eyes and she'd sometimes hear screams in the grinding motor of the garage door opening, but after a few months things calmed down and those bad thoughts stopped coming as often, until finally they were gone completely.

Well, maybe not *completely.*

And here's the thing: maybe she *was* crazy. After all, what woman did the things she'd done? A crazy woman, that's what she thought, a woman probably not fit to be a mother. Or a wife. That's what people would say about her if they found out what she'd done, and it was true. Motherhood was never her *thing,* not like some women, who'd breastfed and made crafts and played games with their kids all day. She'd tried hard, sometimes too hard, and she'd always ended up with a headache, the kind that started behind her eyeballs and stretched all the way down her neck. Was she automatically a bad mother because she'd rather watch TV than carve pumpkins at Halloween? Was she a bad wife because she sometimes had trouble following what Matt told her about his job, all the complicated ins and outs, and he'd end up walking away when she asked ignorant questions, disgusted and not willing to explain?

Yes, it seemed. She was a bad wife and a bad mother. *What exactly do you do all day?* he'd ask her. That question came more and more often over the years. What do you do all day? Why isn't dinner ready? What have you been doing with your time? Those kinds of questions made her feel stupid and lazy, even though she was the one holding the house together, even though she made sure the kids got to school and there was food in the fridge and there was always clean underwear in everyone's drawers. But there was no glory in that, she guessed. Matt went out every day, he worked in an office that looked out over 16th Street Mall, he *sold* things. He made money, and that was important to him, not that she'd gotten down on her knees and spent hours scrubbing all the baseboards in the house, or wiping down every window, inside and out. Matt didn't see any of that, and he didn't care. She'd once been in school, she'd been smart and useful, she was going to be someone, and then she'd married Matt. She began to understand why so many women took antidepressants. She almost started taking them herself, actually filled the prescription, but then tucked them into the back of the medicine cabinet, unopened. It was better to deal with things like she always had. A clear mind.

But what bothered her the most was that everyone wanted

something from her. If you walked down a street in downtown Denver you'd run into a panhandler on a corner sooner or later, asking for spare change or food, and at least they were honest about it. They wanted something from you, and it wasn't as if you'd get anything in return. That was the unspoken contract. But the people in her life were the same way. Her family, the neighbors, the members of the PTA. Everyone had their hand out. They wanted her time, her work, her attention. But the thanks were few, if any, and Marie supposed that being taken for granted was to be expected. But it was exhausting to be constantly giving and never getting anything back. Especially from Matt, and she started to resent him without even realizing.

Matt wanted her to keep the house clean, to cook meals, to listen to him ramble on. He'd also like his back rubbed, please, and his dressy shirts buttoned all the way to the collar before she hung them in his closet—his mother had always done that for him and it helped them keep their shape. He'd also like to sleep in on his days off and to have his coffee ready when he woke up and maybe receive a blow job in the afternoon, and while Matt had always been generous with others, he hadn't gotten her a single Christmas or anniversary or Valentine's gift in the last ten years, because, as he explained to her, isn't it better to just go out and buy what you want for yourself? Then you get what you like.

There were times she felt like she didn't even exist.

CHAPTER SIXTY-ONE

"Your mother murdered a woman once," Matt said one night over dinner. It was a Saturday night and they'd had a good day together, lingering over breakfast and reading the paper over their coffee, but then this. A surprise waiting for her like a trap hidden in tall grass. "Then she shot a man. Framed him for murder."

He was sitting at the head of the table, she was at the foot. The girls, both home from college for a long weekend, sitting between them, looking back and forth between their parents as if they were watching a tennis match.

"Yes, it's quite a story," she said, dabbing at the corner of her mouth with a napkin and standing. "But what's more interesting is when I caught your father in bed with another woman. Matt, I'm sure the girls are *dying* to hear that one."

He shot her a sour look. More than twenty years of this, baiting each other, and it was only the girls who kept them from actually killing each other. Matt was a terrible husband but a good father, and as long as the girls were around they'd managed to keep civil. But soon enough they'd be both be back at college, and then what? It wouldn't be an empty nest—the nest would explode into flames. Fire in the hole.

Marie went to the kitchen then and came back with

chocolate pudding dotted with candied violets. She went around the table and set down the bowls, ending at Matt.

"I made this one special for you," she whispered to him. "Added in a little extra something. Do you remember how much the cat enjoyed it?"

Matt's face had gone pale, and he hadn't taken a single bite. Later, Marie had laughed and eaten every bite of it in front of him.

CHAPTER SIXTY-TWO

For Christmas two years before, Matt had a Jacuzzi hot tub installed in the backyard. At first Marie had hated it—the stupid thing was an eyesore, and when the motor turned on twice a day to cycle the water it always startled her, and it was costly to maintain. But mostly she hated it because it was another one of those things Matt had done himself, without discussing it with her—like the time he'd flown in that woodworker from New Mexico, a hippie who smelled like patchouli and BO, and paid him an obscene amount of money to carve a desk from reclaimed wood.

"What does it matter to you?" Matt had said after she'd blown up about the desk. "It doesn't have anything to do with you."

"It's our money, Matt. It has everything to do with me."

"You can't keep me under your thumb for the rest of your life," he said, and then he'd shut himself in the bathroom. It was the only room in the house he could have peace, he'd say. *I'll take laxatives all day long for a few moments alone.*

Maybe she had been keeping Matt under her thumb—it was for the best, wasn't it? But over the last few years he'd been flexing his independence, doing whatever it was that came into his head. Like the damn hot tub.

"If I want to get in hot water I'll take a bath," she'd said, although Matt and the girls enjoyed it plenty. They'd usually go in at night, when the air had turned crisp and cool and the stars were out, and she'd hear the bubbles start up and the sound of her family's talking and laughter, but she still didn't join them. She was trying to make a point, and planned on sticking to it until the end.

But she woke up one morning with a kink in her neck and a sore back from sleeping in an awkward position, and Matt convinced her to get in the hot tub.

"The jets will help," he said. "You'll see."

Aspirin and a heating pad didn't help with the pain, so she gave in. Put on her swimsuit and climbed in. Matt came in with her, and rubbed her feet while she closed her eyes and put her neck and shoulders in the bubbles.

"You were right," she said after a while. She'd almost fallen asleep in the hot water, her muscles gone slack and relaxed. "This is just what I needed."

Matt let go of her feet and slid his hands under her body, one under her neck while the other looped behind her thighs, the way a person might cradle a baby, and lifted her off the seat so she was floating in his arms. She leaned against his chest, his chin resting on top of her head. She'd been wrong to complain so much about the hot tub, she thought. She'd tell him after they got out and dried off. Apologize for being such a bitch about it.

Matt's chin lifted away and his mouth dropped onto her head. A kiss, she thought at first, but she felt his lips move, and she thought he said *good-bye,* but she'd never be sure.

"What was th—" she started to say, but then she was

plunged under the water. And held there. She struggled, flailing and fighting desperately, needing to get her head clear of the hot water that'd felt so good only a moment before and now seemed like a nightmare, going up her nose and down her throat when she sucked in a breath. Matt's arms had turned to vises around her, kept her from breaking the surface, and through the water she could see the vague, blurry image of the man she'd married so many years before. He was watching her, she realized. He was drowning her, and maybe it was a trick of the water distortion or her own mind, but he seemed to be smiling.

How long did Matt hold her under the water? She didn't know, but it felt like an eternity. And when he finally let her go and she surfaced, sputtering and gasping in big whooping cries, he was already stepping out of the tub and reaching for the towel he'd brought out.

"What the fuck kind of game are you playing?" she screamed once she caught her breath.

"What're you talking about?" he asked, briskly drying his hair. "Are you okay?"

But she'd seen Matt's face. His awful, smiling face.

CHAPTER SIXTY-THREE

Twenty-plus years is a long time to be with a person you'd grown to hate, but Matt and Marie made it work. But then, they didn't *always* hate each other. There were moments when Matt would say or do something that would remind Marie why she'd fallen for him to begin with, and things would be good for a while.

And then things would do a full one-eighty. Jump right off a cliff, you might say.

It was at the start of the holidays the year before when Marie discovered Matt had started seeing another woman and realized it was serious this time because he'd started dressing differently, listening to country music, and talking about getting a tattoo. Maybe some men changed on their own, but Matt wasn't that way. When he saw a pretty face, when he fell in love, that was when he changed. His cell phone was full of calls and texts from this woman—not that she was a woman, but a girl. Marie didn't have to do much detective work to find out about Riley Tipton. A girl only a year older than Hannah, who liked to take pictures of herself to post online with her tongue sticking from the corner of her mouth and her breasts pushed together.

"It's completely innocent," Matt said when she first asked

him about all the calls and texts going back and forth between the two of them. "She's easy to talk to."

"She's young enough to be your daughter," Marie said. "What could you possibly have to talk to her about?"

Matt shrugged, uninterested in explaining himself to her, and that pissed her off more than anything. The fucking *gall* of this man, to not even bother hiding the fact that he was frolicking around with a girl half his age, and then not caring that she knew. He wasn't even going to the trouble of covering his tracks, because he didn't care. He had her, all right. He knew he could do whatever he wanted because they were stuck together. She was dependent on him, and what could she do to keep him in line? Threaten him with a divorce? That she was going to pack up and leave? No. That's exactly what he wanted, what he came to her and asked for, and she wasn't going to give in so easily, like a dog rolling right over and showing her belly in defeat.

If they divorced, Matt told her, she'd get half of everything, plus a monthly alimony check. She'd be comfortable. But it wasn't about the money anymore. It was about her pride. If Matt thought he was going to get rid of her so easily, after everything she'd done for him, everything she'd given up for him, he was wrong. She'd given up her life, her actual life—her name, her identity, everything. She'd given it all up for him, and now he wanted to get rid of her.

She told him to go to hell.

Matt was silent for a week. He didn't come home until after dinner those nights and then slept in the guest bedroom, and on the eighth day he came to her. He had a plan, he said. So they could both get what they wanted.

CHAPTER SIXTY-FOUR

2018

"Once the insurance cashes out we'll split it, sixty-forty," Matt had said. "You'll need the money to start over, and I'll still be here. I'll have the house and my job."

"Eighty-twenty," Marie said. "I'll be the one pulling the disappearing act again. It's only fair."

"Okay, deal. Eighty-twenty," Matt said. "You're right. That's fair."

"Thank you." Later, Marie would remember this conversation, when Matt so easily shrugged and agreed to give her what she wanted, but she already had an idea what he was planning. She'd known since he'd held her under in the hot tub, when she'd been able to see the smile twisting his mouth. But she'd been planning, too.

A woman should always have a safety net and a backup plan.

"We could make it look like you've been attacked," he said. "Or you could—you could fall somewhere, make it look like you got swept away in a river. You're always going hiking alone, that should be simple enough."

"We'll split the money, and then you'll be free to be with your girlfriend."

He studied her face.

"Yeah," he said, ignoring her comment. "We've done this before. We could do it again."

"I know where I could go to make it work," she said. They were just sitting down to dinner, shrimp scampi, and she wondered if any other couples had times like this. Sitting down to a nice dinner and good wine and discussing how they'd best pull off insurance fraud. The entire situation was hilarious, but also somehow deadly serious. "There's a cliff out in Estes Park I've hiked plenty of times. It'd be perfect. Plenty of people would see me going up, but I'd have to go down over the side of the cliff to the bottom, otherwise I might get spotted hiking down."

"Could it work?"

She considered. There was a particular cliff where she'd spent a lot of time. She was familiar with the terrain and knew it was a spot not frequented by tourists. But would it work for what she needed?

"Yeah, I think it could. But what about the girls?"

"We'll tell them the truth after a while. They can visit wherever you end up."

So they planned. They planned over their scampi and they sat up in bed and planned that night, and they spent their evenings over the next few weeks brainstorming and hashing out ideas and ruling out possibilities. They had all the time and privacy in the world with the girls both at school, so they didn't have to creep around and try to hide anything.

For the first time in over twenty years of marriage, they could be themselves.

And as the weeks passed, Marie realized she was having fun. For the first time in a long time she was enjoying spending time with her husband. It reminded her of why she'd fallen in love with Matt, and why she'd stayed married to him after everything. He knew how to make her laugh, and they operated on the same wavelength. And he'd been coming right home after work every night, and she thought he might've broken it off with Riley.

She was looking at him through rose-colored glasses, maybe, because she still loved him even after everything they'd been through, and maybe that's why this had all happened to begin with. It wasn't so much a plan about faking her death and collecting the life insurance—it was the plan that would save their marriage. And maybe they wouldn't go through with it at all, she thought, but it showed they could still get along. They still had a chance at a life together. They were planning a crime, but if the result was a happy one, what difference did it make? The ends justify the means, don't they?

She'd had these thoughts all through the spring, including one evening as she washed the dinner dishes—there were so few of them with the girls gone, it didn't take long—and after she'd carefully dried her hands on a towel she went to find Matt, to tell him how she felt. She'd bare her soul to him—a romantic thought—and they'd make love. They hadn't slept together in a long time, and it was overdue.

Matt wasn't in the small room near the front door that served as his home office, but in the powder room he'd had put in beside it. It'd cost an arm and a leg to put a bathroom in an old house like this, but Matt had called it a *necessity*, not a luxury. And he spent a lot of time in that bathroom, maybe more than he did in his actual office. Matt had always spent lots of time in the bathroom, she thought as she walked toward the closed pocket door, raising her fist to knock. It made her smile. He went in there to relax and be alone, and he'd even fallen asleep on the toilet before. When you were married as long as they'd been, you got to know a person's habits and quirks, the things no one else would know, and that was all a marriage was, wasn't it? The secrets two people keep from the rest of the world, that's what makes a marriage.

Matt was on his cell phone in the bathroom. She couldn't hear what he was saying, but she didn't need to—he was using a voice she knew well. It was cooing and soft, the baby voice he thought was sexy but was just silly. When they were first married he'd used that voice on her all the time, leaning over as she'd studied and whispering right into her ear, and more often than not they'd end up in bed. She couldn't remember the last time she'd heard him talk like that, but here it was.

And she'd been fool enough to think they could make it work.

She turned away from the bathroom, her face burning with embarrassment. She'd come looking for Matt in love and was walking away with hate. It was a terrible thing to be alive, she thought bitterly, especially with the wrong person. She stopped beside Matt's desk and picked up the single framed photo. It was the two of them smiling at the camera as they stood in front of the house, their arms wrapped around each other, and they certainly looked happy, but what was the truth? It was easy enough to fake happiness, to smile and make people believe. That was the entire foundation of social media—to make everyone believe your life was perfect, even if it was falling apart at the seams.

Matt's desktop computer was lit up, the search he'd done on the Three Forks River taking up the whole screen. The river was running at max capacity these days, hard and fast, and it ran right beneath the cliff where they'd been planning to fake her fall. Not that she'd ever get anywhere near the river. She'd hike to the top and set it up to look like she'd been trying to take a selfie from the cliff but slipped and fell to her death, but would instead lower herself over the edge, down a hundred or so feet, and hike to safety. Matt could come up later under the guise of looking for his wife and get rid of the rope, and all the cops would ever find of her was her phone and supplies on the cliff. A handful of people had fallen into area rivers over the spring and had been swept away, their bodies never recovered, and sooner or later people would assume it'd been the same for her, especially if the rains kept up.

It was a flawless plan.

The bathroom door slid open behind her.

"I've been thinking," Matt said. He came close and wrapped his arms around her, pulled her close. She shut her eyes. Her skin crawled where she could feel his breath and the touch of his skin. "We should plan a romantic weekend up in Estes. Rent a cabin and go out there together. Hike up that cliff, and you could lower yourself over the edge. Once you get down safe I'll go looking for help."

"If I go alone it'll keep you from being a suspect," she said. Blithely, she hoped. "We should stick with what we've planned."

"If I'm there, I'm a witness, and we need a witness to pull this off. The cops aren't going to find your body, so they'll need a story about what happened."

"But what if they find out about Janice?" she asked. About *me,* she thought. "Two dead wives will make you look suspicious."

She felt his shoulders rise and fall in a shrug.

"It was fine that time, it'll be fine this time," he said. "I'm an unlucky guy, that's all. This is the only way I can see this working. I have to be there."

Marie turned slowly. Matt was taller, and when they stood close she had to look up to see his eyes. He'd spent their entire marriage looking down on her—both literally and otherwise—but she could still clearly see his eyes. A person's mouth could say one thing but their eyes would say something else, and what were Matt's eyes saying?

"It'll be safer this way," he said. "Easier for you. I'll make sure you're good and I can get rid of the rope, too. Throw it in the river right then instead of going up after. One less thing for us to worry about later."

She stared up at him. He looked right back, unblinking. He had the flat, black gaze of a lizard, she thought. There was nothing loving in his look, nothing even human. In that moment she realized why Matt was insisting he should come along with her to the top of the cliff, why he'd agreed so easily to splitting the insurance money so unevenly. You couldn't be married to someone for so long without developing a sort of low-grade telepathy, and her antennae were vibrating.

Matt didn't want to fake her death.

He wanted to come along to make sure she really did die.

"Okay," she said slowly, as if she'd been considering, turning his suggestion over in her head. "If that's what you think is best."

He'd been excited then and kissed her, and she'd kissed him right back, even though she would've liked to bite his tongue right out of his mouth and spit it out onto the floor between them. It was so easy, she thought, to keep your hate to yourself. To let it simmer like acid in your stomach. You started to live on it after a while. It fed you, kept you going, until you started to get hungry for it, and it became an active craving. A diet of anger and hate could slim anyone's thighs.

Matt was making his secret plans, so she did, too. She paid their insurance agent a visit and upped her life insurance policy, told the nosy old bag it'd been Matt's idea. She marked spots on maps of the park and left them behind. In his office, in their home. Matt wouldn't be looking for these things, but the cops would. She didn't think she'd have to do much—he was a man who'd been suspected of murdering his first wife, and that was sure to come up sooner or later. If it didn't, she'd make sure it would. It would be enough if Matt were arrested for murder, if he spent the rest of his life in prison. It would make everything worth it, to know he was suffering.

An eye for an eye.

So she planned.

Easy to follow, easy to swallow, like Matt always said.

CHAPTER SIXTY-FIVE

August 28, 2018

"It's a long way to the bottom," Matt said as he watched her hook the rope around her waist. It was the second time he'd said it in the last few hours.

"Yeah," she said. She yanked on the rope to make sure it was secure and then looked at her husband. The sun had sunk behind the mountains and it was hard to see much in the gloaming, and the shadows on Matt's face gave him the look of a skull. "Don't forget to toss over my pack when I'm down. I'll need it."

"I won't," he said. He didn't come any closer to the edge. "Don't worry, hon. Everything will be fine. The cops'll never guess you faked your death."

She gave him a sharp look, but Matt had turned away, was fiddling with the ropes. She wished she could take one more look into his eyes, just to see what was there, but what did it matter? It didn't, that was the answer. She already knew what she'd see there.

Matt didn't try to kiss her good-bye.

It all went scarily well until Marie had started lowering herself over the edge of the cliff on the rope she'd tied around a tree trunk. It was a long coil of rope, a huge amount; she gripped it in both hands and had it looped through the safety harness on her waist, enough rope that she should've been able to lower herself all the way down to the ground beside the river with some left over. But she was no more than fifteen feet down when she felt the rope tremble and vibrate in her hands and she knew what was happening. Matt had stayed back from the edge, he was scared of heights and always had been, and he'd let her go down, watched her lower herself until she was at the point of no return—and then he'd started to cut the rope.

She'd expected this. Even prepared for it. But she hadn't thought he'd start cutting so soon. She should've known. Matt had never been a patient man.

"Matt?" she'd said, alarmed. Did she have enough time? She wasn't sure. Never trust men, she'd taught her daughters, the same lesson her mother had taught her. She could've loosened her grip on the rope then and unlatched the harness and zipped all the way down to the bottom before he cut all the way through, she would've lost most of the skin on her palms in the process, but she would've made it; she would have landed dangerously close to the river, but she would have lived. But she didn't want that. She wanted Matt to think that he'd gotten away with it, that he'd managed to kill her. She wanted him to glory in it. At least for a little while.

So she held on to the rope. She wanted it to stay taut, so he'd feel her weight on it. She had other plans. She'd come up to this cliff after she'd guessed what Matt might be planning, several times, day trips he never knew about, he never bothered to ask what she'd done while he was at work, he didn't care—and lowered herself over the edge like this alone, only she'd planted several camming devices deep in the underside of the cliff and threaded a second rope through them, long enough that it was doubled up, and left it there to dangle. If anyone hiked to the cliff base they'd spot that rope immediately, might even report it, but it was a chance she had to take.

"Matt, what's happening?" she shouted as she reached for the rope she'd planted. It swung out of reach once, squirting out of her sweaty grip, and she really started to feel the beginning threads of panic. If he managed to cut through before she could get a good hold—well, it'd be game over. All her planning was for nothing, and Matt would get exactly what he wanted. She'd be dead. "Is everything okay up there?"

For the first time, it occurred to Marie that if she fell into the river and drowned, her body would be found with the climbing gear still on, the harness still strapped around her waist and thighs. She didn't know how her idiot husband planned on explaining that to the police, unless—

Unless he was planning on telling the police that she'd been trying to fake her death and had failed. Plunged to her death. It was just enough of the truth that it just might work.

"Matt?" she screamed. "Can you hear me?"

He didn't answer, but she could clearly feel the sawing motion of his knife through her line. Marie allowed herself one terrified glance down. The river took up her entire field of vision, the violently thrashing water seeming to reach up for her. It was hungry, that was the best word for it. It wanted her to plunge under those frothy waves so it could hold her under no matter how hard she struggled and her lungs would fill, she'd drown. The sound a river makes as it flows past was usually described as roaring, or rushing, but to Marie it sounded like it was laughing. A wetly satisfying chuckle because it was waiting for her. This same river had already drowned several people, and she'd be the latest.

"Get your shit together," she muttered, tearing her eyes away from the water and reaching out again. Second time's the charm, and she finally caught hold of the second line and tried to get it latched into place on her harness, but the trembling panic in her fingers made her clumsy, her sweat made the metal slick and hard to grab. But she had it in her hands, at least.

There was a snap and she gasped when she dropped a few feet down, then jerked to a stop. He was almost all the way through the rope, then. She had ten seconds at most before it gave way completely, probably less. That wasn't enough time to get as safe as she wanted, so she'd have to make do. The best-laid plans, and all that. Time to improvise. She took the rope and wrapped it several times around her wrist and swung her legs to get a loop of it around one of her calves.

Then she waited. Not that she had to wait for long.

"Matt?" she screamed and held the rope tight against her face so the fibers scratched. Closed her eyes and took a deep breath. It was all or nothing, make it count. "No! Please, don't!"

And then the rope snapped, made a sound like a whip cracking. She'd thought the tension in her backup line was perfect, enough to send her down only a few feet before catching her, but she'd miscalculated and went plunging through the open air for a dozen feet before it went taut, catching her weight. She screamed in surprise and fear, and that was probably for the best—the scream she'd been practicing for the fall wouldn't have been quite the same—and the sudden drop didn't just send her down, it sent her swinging out in an arc, first away from the cliff and then toward it, and she rammed into the rock wall at an awful speed. It was her elbow that took the brunt of the hit, the very point of the bone against the stone, and it shattered on impact, sending a jolt of pain through her entire body. If pain had a color it was silver, like lightning behind her closed eyelids. That long flash of agony reminded her of other times—that final push when she was giving birth to each of the girls and the sense of strange emptiness once they'd left her body; the throbbing ache of a tooth that'd needed a root canal and kept her up several nights before she'd gone to the dentist; the memory of standing on the steps outside the little rental house in Madison and hearing Matt laughing with another woman. It was all the same pain in that moment, pieced together in the giant movie reel that served as memory.

She almost blacked out then, dangling from the underside of the cliff, and wouldn't *that* have been hilarious? If she'd lost consciousness she certainly would've lost her grip on the rope and gone hurtling down to the ground or into the river, dead despite all her plans. But she didn't black out, things only went grayish and mushy around the edges and she managed to hang on. Barely, but barely was all she needed. She turned her face into the crook of her shoulder and took a deep breath, tried to calm her racing heart and keep from weeping in agony. This wasn't what she'd planned, this wasn't how it was supposed to go—but when did anything *ever* go perfectly? It was the story of her life, improvising as things came up.

She'd thought that once she'd gone over the side and Matt thought she was gone, she'd be able to take her time and lower herself to the ground below. It would be hours before anyone could make it down to the cliff base, especially once the sun set, and she'd hike to the supplies she'd hidden several miles away, start a fire, and sleep well under the stars. Then she'd wake early the next morning and keep moving away from the cliff and river. It would take a few days to get to Estes on foot, but once she got there, to the car she'd bought and parked in a spot downtown, she'd be home free. She'd probably go west. California, maybe. She'd driven west to get to Denver from Madison, and maybe it was time to keep going.

But now, things had changed. The pain in her arm had dulled to a low scream, but the thought of trying to get it working to lower herself down the rope another seventy or so feet was enough to make her light-headed. And days of hiking over uneven ground as she clutched her bum arm to her chest? God, no. This whole plan was going to be tough enough with both her arms functional, and now—well, how bad was this whole thing going to be now?

But she couldn't think any further ahead than right now, otherwise she was setting herself up for failure. She concentrated on the rope looped around her good arm and the sharp wind against her cheeks and the flat, tinny smell of the water below. Deep breath. In through the nose, out through the mouth. She thought there was a good chance she might die anyway, that she wouldn't be able to lower herself with one arm and she'd end up falling to her death, smashing her head open on the rocks, and all of it would be for nothing.

Marie was still hanging there, considering her situation, when two things launched over the side of the cliff. She recognized the shapes, even in the dark. It was the rope and her pack of supplies. They both came hurtling down and went right into the river, sucked under the waves. She didn't care about the rope, but the loss of her backpack hurt. There were things in there she could've used. She moaned and closed her eyes, pressed her forehead against her own rope so hard it was surely leaving a mark. There were bottles of water in that pack, and squeeze tubes of applesauce that would've been heaven on her raw throat. No use thinking about it now, though. The bag was long gone.

Getting rid of the evidence, that's what Matt was doing. Cleaning up anything that might point to his guilt. Make it look like an accidental fall. Just as they planned.

She waited, her good arm trembling from the strain of holding herself in place and the other shrieking in pain. She wasn't sure what she was waiting for until she heard it.

His laugh. It's what had started this entire mess so many years ago, and here it was again. A pleased, low burbling sound that seemed to come right out of his gut, like a baby's laugh, and now he was laughing because he thought she was dead, that he was finally rid of her.

That laugh gave her strength, fed the hate-beast in her belly. Then she knew she wouldn't die. She wouldn't allow it. It took a long time—she never knew how long, didn't even want to know—but she managed to slide down the rope bit by bit, until the ground was only a few feet below, and then she let go. She landed on her feet, barely, but her knees gave out beneath her at the jolt of pain that shot up her arm—the pain had been silver but was now black, thick and choking—and she went facedown in the gravel. There were a few uncertain moments when Marie didn't move at all, but she finally struggled to sit up. There was blood on her face and her one arm was twisted and hanging at a strange angle, and at first glance she looked like a crazy person. But if you'd managed to get a good look at her eyes, you'd see they were calm and clear and sane. Moving slowly and carefully, Marie stood up. She'd double-looped the rope so she was able to pull it down with a hard tug, and after it fell into a coil at her feet she tossed it into the river. Get rid of the evidence. The sun had dropped low enough that she couldn't see very much, so she shuffled through the dirt where she'd landed, hoping to scatter anything she might've dropped or left behind, and then moved on. She had so much to do, and time would be tight. But it was all going to happen.

Because she didn't plan on ever letting her husband laugh like that again.

CHAPTER SIXTY-SIX

September 7, 2018

"Matt?" she'd said, using that breathy, high-pitched voice she knew he hated so much. He'd once said he'd like to choke her when she used that voice, so she used it now, meaning to get him riled up. After twenty-four years of marriage you learned what buttons to push. "Didn't I say you needed some excitement in your life?"

It'd taken her two days to hike out of the park and get to the car in Estes, and instead of driving off into the sunset like she planned she rented a cheap motel room outside of town. Once she got a full night's sleep and a meal in her stomach and bought a sling for her arm from the drugstore and started to feel somewhat normal, she drove back out to the national park and watched some of the search. It was an all-around bad idea—someone could've recognized her—but she went anyway. She couldn't stay away. So it was true what was said about criminals, she thought grimly. They always returned to the scene of the crime.

So she put on a baggy old sweatshirt and pulled a weathered ball cap low over her eyes and watched as a team floated slowly along in a boat, peering over the side, and others stood at the shore, poking and prodding the river bottom. There were plenty of others there, a crowd drawn out by the gruesome proceedings, and no one gave her a second look. They were searching for a dead woman, after all. Not a living, breathing one. Marie overheard snippets of conversation from those who'd watched the news and seen her photo and commented about how terrible it was, what a silly waste, a woman in her prime falling to her death while trying to take a selfie, but that was life these days, wasn't it?

It was a little like attending her own funeral.

She even saw Matt, standing beside the river with his hands in his pockets, not bothering to pretend to be helping. She overheard whispers that he hadn't spent much time helping with the search, but only came out to make an appearance. But that was Matt for you—he'd always been good about putting on a show.

He looked glum, as a man who has lost his wife should. He was playing his part, at least. The girls hadn't come with him—that much she regretted, although it would've put her at risk. She would've liked to see her daughters one more time, but they were grown and had their own lives, and seemed more like strangers than the babies she'd had so long ago. Matt looked away from the river and she considered pitching a rock at his face, but turned around and left instead.

She went back to the motel and got comfortable and kept an eye on the local news. For a few days everything was quiet, and then she saw the report of the woman's body pulled out of the river about ten miles downstream as soon as it broke. The cops thought it was her, and that'd made her laugh hard.

"Where the fuck are you?" Matt hissed over the phone.

"Oh, I'm sure you'd like to know," she said airily. Making that phone call she felt more like her old self than she had in days, and her confidence had returned. She knew exactly where she stood now, and the view was a good one. "But don't worry, dear husband. You'll be happy to know I'm perfectly safe."

"Where are you?" he asked again.

"That's for me to know and for you to never know," she said. "Listen, I've been keeping an eye on the news, and I saw a woman has been pulled out of the river. They're saying it's me, but since I'm talking to you right now, I'm guessing they're wrong."

"Shut up."

"I also have a guess about who that woman is," she said. "Is it your girlfriend, Matt? Is it Riley?"

Silence from the other end, but she could hear his breathing, light and quick.

"So I was right!" Marie crowed laughter. "Tell me, did you enjoy killing her? Riley didn't even see it coming, did she? She went out thinking you were actually in love with her, isn't that right? How *humane* of you. And now that I think about it, didn't you use my car right before we went to Estes? Said you'd get it detailed and have the oil changed—but you really needed it to haul her body in, didn't you? And if the cops found her blood in my trunk—well, I'd automatically look guilty."

"I wish I'd had the chance to bash *your* skull in," Matt said. His voice was thick with rage. "I wish I could've killed you instead of her. But I had to do it. Prove to everyone what a jealous, crazy wife you are. Wait till I see you again. I'm going to choke the life right out you."

"Oh, my thighs are aquiver with anticipation," she said. She shifted the sling that was holding her arm in place—it cut into her shoulder in the worst way, but it was the best available until she could see a doctor.

"You bitch."

"Is that really the worst thing you can call me?" she asked. "I hope you think of something better before we see each other again. I've been spending plenty of time out in the park, you know. Did you know I saw you there last week, with that search team?"

"You were there?"

"Of course I was. Close enough I could've spit on you. Haven't I told you not to wear those cargo pants? They make you look like a fat old grandpa, but if that's the look you're going for these days—well, you're on the right track."

And then she hung up. Because she knew there was nothing that bothered Matt more than *not* getting the last word. They were similar in that respect, at least.

CHAPTER SIXTY-SEVEN

September 24, 2018

How did she do it? How did she get away with it? That's what Matt wanted to know, how Marie managed to live. But the police had managed to cut him completely out of everything, so much that he actually found out he was no longer being considered a suspect through Twitter. The Denver PD had released a written statement to local news outlets saying any charges against him would be dropped, that he was innocent of any wrongdoing, and it was all over his feed. He read the statement and then quickly put his phone on the table, facedown, like he was scared of it. And maybe he was, a little. Scared and excited, because it was over. He'd told the detectives everything—well, *some* of it—and it'd been enough to keep him out of prison. He'd given them enough of the truth to make himself look innocent. It couldn't have gone better, he thought. Marie? *Gone*. Riley, who'd started to get so clingy and needy, who'd been talking weddings and babies every time he saw her? *Adiós*. It was over.

Or was it?

He was sitting up in bed that same night, watching one of the home renovation shows that seemed to be everywhere these days. He wasn't really watching it, but instead wondering if Marie had seen the statement from the police about his innocence. That was his only regret—he missed the opportunity to see his wife's face when she realized she'd lost. Marie was a sore loser—a sore winner, too, she'd never really learned to play nice with others—and he imagined the fit she'd throw when she saw the news. And what could she do about it?

Not a damn thing. His lawyer said he was safe. That even if Marie came forward tomorrow and told her side of things, she couldn't talk her way out of trouble. It was in her best interest to stay away. And Matt had stuck around, he'd stayed calm, he'd cooperated with the police—those things counted, the lawyer said. *Makes you look like a good guy. Makes you look innocent. A helpless man held virtually hostage for over twenty years by a controlling woman. It'll make one helluva movie of the week,* he said.

Matt chuckled to himself and flipped back the blankets, padded downstairs and got himself some dessert. Vanilla ice cream with hot caramel drizzled over the top, and he'd be able to eat it without suffering through all the dark looks and comments from Marie. He'd rediscovered all kinds of little pleasures like that over the last week: not having to hide out in the bathroom to get some alone time; sleeping in the center of the bed without having to share; being able to throw trash right into the can without getting a lecture about recycling. He came back upstairs with the bowl, humming as he climbed back into bed. Life was good. It would be better, now.

He'd left his phone on the bed when he went downstairs,

and when he got settled back down and ready to dive into his ice cream, he noticed he'd missed a call from an unknown number. And there was a new voice mail.

His hands were shaking.

It was Marie who'd called, somehow he knew it before he even looked. He'd been thinking about her and she'd known, she'd always seemed to know what he was thinking, and it didn't matter that she wasn't here with him. She could be in a different house, in a different country, on an entirely different *planet* and she'd know. A marriage connects people, for better or worse, forever. People say diamonds are forever, but marriage is, too. Forever and ever, until the bitter end.

He thought about taking his cell phone and dropping it in the toilet and flushing the damn thing down, just so he couldn't listen to that voice mail. Or opening up the window and tossing it out onto the street. But he didn't. He couldn't. Matt Evans had never been very good at denying himself, and it wasn't as if he was going to turn over a new leaf now.

So he listened to the voice mail. He didn't have any other choice. He listened to it once, and then again. And again, countless times. Then he turned off the TV and left his uneaten ice cream on the bathroom counter and went to bed. He may have gone to sleep, or he may have stayed up all night, but either way he was up early the next morning. Tumbled some sunscreen and water bottles and other things into a backpack and got in his car. He drove west, toward the mountains.

And about a half mile behind him, far enough back that Matt never noticed, was a brown Chrysler.

CHAPTER SIXTY-EIGHT

"Do you really think you've gotten away with anything?" Marie's message had said. She was using that voice again, the one he hated so much, high-pitched and mocking. "Well, I left them a little surprise at the bottom of the cliff that'll make them think twice about their decision to let you go. Just thought I'd give you a heads-up, in case you wanted to pack a bag and make a run for it. Do you think a pretty guy like you will be popular in prison, Matt?"

Marie had laughed then, a tinkling laugh that wasn't like any sound he'd ever heard her make. It wasn't the laugh that pissed him off so bad, but the confidence in her voice. The idea that this woman, *his wife,* had big enough balls to call and taunt him, to sound so goddamn sure of herself when she should be running, scared and frustrated, out of options. Instead, she was laughing. She was fucking *laughing,* and he didn't like that one bit.

She didn't have any surprise for the police, he knew. He'd covered all his bases. It was a trap, of course. She was trying to get him out there again, lure him out into the open. It was a bad idea to go, but what else was there? At least if he went, it would mean an end to things. If he didn't, he knew Marie wouldn't just shrug her shoulders, disappear, and move on.

No, he'd spend the rest of his life wondering when Marie was going to appear again to make his life hell. Marie was the terrible heart beating under the floorboard; the bloodstains that would never wash off his hands; the bad smell that just wouldn't go away.

The wife who wouldn't die.

It had to end. His wife had left his life once and had come back, and he couldn't stand to have it happen again. He had to finish it.

Or maybe he didn't have a choice. When Marie played her pipe he came dancing, he'd follow her wherever.

He had a knife in his backpack. The longest, sharpest one they had in their kitchen. It wouldn't be the easiest way to end things, but it would work.

I've been spending plenty of time out in the park, you know, she'd said.

He hiked down to the bottom of the cliff, enjoying the feel of the sun on the back of his neck and shoulders. It was good being out after being inside for so long, even if it was down to the same spot where he'd last been with cops and rangers. Almost two hours down, picking through the underbrush and along the trail that sometimes faded away to nothing. Past the withered, blackened tree he remembered from last time and along the edge of the frothing river. It'd been almost a month since he'd last been here and it was much warmer than he remembered, an Indian summer, the air warm and full of bugs, and he stopped several times and dipped his hands in the river, all the way past his wrists.

He almost missed the spot beneath the cliff, just like he had the last time, almost kept walking right on but caught himself at the last moment. He shaded his eyes with the flat of his hand and looked up, felt the gentle spray of moisture coming up off the river and misting against his arms and the backs of his calves. The cliff seemed so far from down here, and he wondered how it must've been for Marie, dangling from the edge of it. But how had she managed to make it safely down? He still didn't know. He couldn't tell anything from this point, because there was nothing to see from so far down, but it must have been terrifying. His wife was tough, he had to give her that much.

There was a crunch of gravel behind him and he whirled around. He'd been alone the whole way down, hadn't seen another soul, and he'd let his guard down. At home everything was so quiet. The girls had gone back to school without saying good-bye, and the TV was his only company, although he didn't turn it on much. It was as if everything was listening, waiting for Marie to come back, and his ears were always straining for the sound of her. Her light footsteps on the stairs, the sound of her hand trailing against the banister. But out here his ears had been filled with twittering birds and the rush of the river, and he'd stopped paying attention until now. It could've been an animal making that sound, it could've been the wind snapping a branch off a tree, but it was too *deliberate*, and he knew who was standing behind him before he'd fully turned.

"Marie," he said. He'd known who it was, but he still couldn't believe his eyes, couldn't make his brain believe she was actually there, twenty feet behind him, watching, her back to the river. "There you are. I've been looking for you."

CHAPTER SIXTY-NINE

A muscle in the side of her neck jumped, then stilled. It was the only part of her that moved, except her eyes, which were wide and glittering like gems in the bright midday sun. He'd always thought her eyes were a honey brown, but now, from where he was standing, they seemed to be devoid of any color at all. They were all pupil. Nothing but black.

"Hi," she said. That was all. She'd lost weight, enough that he could see it by the way her cheeks were hollowed out and the tendons in her neck stood out like ropes. There was a bruise under her eye, faded and yellowing, and a scratch running down the side of her face. The sweatshirt she was wearing hung down to her knees, and one of her arms had been wrapped in a sling and was held awkwardly against her chest. The blue jeans she was wearing were far too big, making her look like a little girl playing dress-up.

"You said you left the police a surprise," he said. He had the knife in his hand, had come all the way down carrying it. Just in case. "Are you the surprise?"

"Maybe," she said, shrugging. "I knew you'd come out here if I called."

"What do you want, Marie?" he demanded. Without

thinking, he lifted the knife and shook it at her. She didn't look impressed. "Why can't you just go away?"

He took a step toward her. The river was still running high and fast, and he had the knife. If he could get close enough, if he ran at her hard with the blade out and then pushed her in—

"Don't do that," Marie said sharply.

"Do what?"

"Come any closer," she said. "I know what you're thinking."

"You always do," he said.

The birds had fallen silent, he noticed.

"Did anyone follow you out here?" she asked, peering up the path he'd come down and up at the cliff. He took another step closer while she was distracted. Fifteen more steps, maybe twelve—that would get him there.

"No," he said. "The cops are busy. I told them everything. What're you going to say when they find you?"

Marie smiled and tilted her head to one side. It was her same smile, the one he could remember from last month, last year. Twenty-four years ago.

"They're not going to find me," she said. "Besides, they've already figured out everything on their own. I only helped a little."

"What are you talking about?" he asked. Another shuffling step.

"Stop right there," Marie said mildly. "I've been getting strange phone calls. From one of the cops. A woman. She knew it was my number, she must've gotten it from when I called you. I knew I shouldn't have, but I couldn't help myself."

"What did the cop say to you?"

"Oh, I never answered. But she left a voice mail. *Several* voice mails, actually, telling me what you'd said. How you'd blamed me for everything. She even played a recording of you, so I'd know she was telling the truth. Of course, I'd already figured all that out, so her calls just confirmed it."

"Why would she call you at all?"

"To taunt me. Try to piss me off and get me to come after you, I think," Marie said. "So I thought I'd do the same thing to get you out here. And it worked."

Marie reached behind her back then, and when her hand reappeared it was holding a gun. The movement was so smooth and casual that it was like a magic trick. It was a small gun, snub nosed and dull silver, very much like the gun she'd shot him with so long ago.

"I just wanted to see my husband one last time," she said. "I wanted to see what I felt when I saw the face of the man who wishes I was dead again. And I love you. Even after everything, I still do. I've tried to make myself stop. I've never understood how I could love you so much, and hate you at the same time, too."

She straightened her arm, aiming the gun at his face.

"I should've done this twenty-three years ago," she said. "Think how much trouble I could've saved the two of us."

"Put the gun down!" Spengler shouted. She stepped out of the trees and onto the gravel of the river's shore, Loren close behind her. They both had their guns drawn and pointed at Marie.

"Man, the two of you just can't stay away from each other, can you?" Loren yelled.

Marie was distracted, watching the cops come out of the trees, so Matt took the opportunity and lunged. Ran the dozen or so steps at her, the knife out. It was sharp enough that it would slide right through her skin and past flesh and bone to the innards beneath, and there wouldn't be time to call for medical assistance, and his wife would die here, on the shore of the Three Forks River. He saw all of this happening in his mind, and then Marie whipped around to face him, the gun still out, pointed at his head, right between the eyes. No way she could miss, not from this distance.

She was always one step ahead of him, it seemed.

Marie pulled the trigger.

There was the blast from the gun, and he felt the heat of the bullet entering his flesh, strangely familiar, not into his head but into his chest, and he thought that she might've shot him in the same exact spot she'd shot him before, even though she hadn't been trying to kill him that time. But history repeats itself, doesn't it?

The bullet had hit him, but it wasn't enough to keep him from barreling forward and shoving the knife into Marie's gut, and the force sent her flying back, end over end, somersaulting through the air until she came down into the river, the arms of water reaching up and seeming to embrace her, to suck her down into their depths. Matt managed to stand long enough to watch his wife get swept away in the fast current and then he collapsed, a pool of blood spreading around him.

CHAPTER SEVENTY

October 1, 2018

"Ortiz is back in town," Preach said. "Didn't I tell you, Ralphie? He just wanted to shake you up a little." There was a crackle and buzz over the speaker. Preach must've been on his cell, in an area with shit reception. "Wanted to see if you'd break down and admit to anything. There's a new suspect in the case, so you're outta the hot seat."

Loren closed his eyes, leaned back in his chair. Outside his open office door he could see the bustle of Homicide, gearing up for a busy fall. The temps had dropped and the overcast sky seemed to be threatening snow instead of rain.

"That's why I called," Loren said. "Ortiz left me a note before he skipped town, taped to my door. Said he knew what he knew, but I'd somehow managed to pull a fast one on him." Loren paused. "But I didn't do shit, Preach. Do you know what happened?"

Preach sighed.

"It's been taken care of, Ralphie. That's all you need to know."

Loren closed his eyes.

"What'd you do?"

There was a long pause.

"Turns out old evidence resurfaced connecting Gallo to a drug ring up in Philly," he said. "Looks like he was making some extra cash by working with some dealers, but he crossed the wrong guys and ended up with a bullet in his head. A guy out in Terre Haute already confessed to killing Gallo."

"Preach—"

"This particular guy didn't have a snowball's chance in hell of walking free even before this confession, so it doesn't much matter one way or the other," Preach said. He sounded almost cheerful. "Another life sentence added on top of the five he already has—a dead man walking can't get any more dead. You know what I mean, Ralphie?"

"Yeah. I guess I do." It was more of the same, Loren thought. Good ol' boys pulling together to protect their own. It wouldn't have taken much to convince a man serving life at Terre Haute to confess to one more thing. Some cold hard cash, maybe, or a little something for the family he had outside. And it took care of everything. Case closed, because that's all anyone wanted. To close a case, put it behind. Easy to follow, easy to swallow, like old Detective Reid said. "But listen, I've gotta tell you what happened—"

"Ralphie, let it go," Preach said sharply. "I don't know where this sudden spurt of honesty is coming from, but channel it in a different way. People say sharing is caring, but that's the biggest pile of donkey shit I ever heard. Why don't you pay your taxes on time, or start tipping your waiters a decent amount instead. Use that warm feeling you're suddenly having to spread some good in the world."

"Fuck you. I'm a great tipper."

"Not from what I remember."

"You don't remember shit."

"Maybe not." Preach laughed. "But I'm serious, Ralph. You coming forward and getting shit off your chest is nothing but trouble. Better to let it go, that's what I think. Keep your trap shut."

"But—"

"Listen, I go down to Cincinnati sometimes," Preach said, and Loren lapsed into silence. "There's a nice lady down there, makes a helluva pot roast. She always asks about you."

Loren had left Ohio thirty years before without a word and he'd never looked back, not even to check on Connie once. It'd bothered him for a long time, that he'd dropped and run, but it was what he did. He either got mad, or he got gone.

"She's alive?" he asked.

"And doing real well," Preach said. "She reached out about a year after you left. She was looking for you, and fed me some half-baked story about how Gallo had upped and run off with some stripper, left her with the baby. She's got a couple kids, a half-dozen grandbabies. I had a little free time after you called, so I drove down there. Told her what was going on with you. She went pale, had to sit down. I thought she might've had a heart attack, but it was just shock. Then she brewed a pot of coffee and told me everything. She confessed."

"No."

"Yeah, I think she's still carrying a flame for you, although

I don't understand how anyone could love a man with a face that resembles an ugly dog's ass end."

"Fuck you."

"I think I'll pass on that offer, Ralphie," Preach said easily. "Anyway, she asked me to help keep you outta trouble. Made me promise I'd help, and you know me. I never could say no to a pretty face. And the only reason Connie got to keep her face pretty is because of what she did."

It was easy to start over in those days, and Connie had done it. Janice Evans had done it, too.

"I don't know what to say."

"Then keep your mouth shut. Lucas Gallo was a piece of human sewage," Preach said. "We all knew it and we dealt with it because he was one of us. Maybe we shouldn't have. He'd been thumping that wife of his hard, and you were the only one who ever stepped in and said something. Maybe that makes us all shitheads. You always were the best of us, Loren. Not the best looking, but you know what I mean."

"Fuck you, Cocksmoke."

"But whatever Gallo got in the end, whoever gave it to him—he deserved it. And it really doesn't matter how he ended up in that hole. It just matters that he got there, sooner rather than later."

Loren grabbed a tissue from the box on his desk and blew his nose.

"You crying, hoss?" Preach said. "Is all my talk making your eyes well up, maybe giving you a little wood?"

"You remember that time you pissed on that electric fence? I bet that's the most action you've seen in years. Your dick's probably still smoldering."

Preach snorted.

"Same old Loren," he said. "See you soon, maybe?"

"Not unless you go to your mom's house for dinner this weekend. That's when I'm busy banging her."

"Fuck you, numbnuts," Preach said, but he was laughing. "My mom's been dead for ten years, unless you're into that necrophilia shit. One more piece of advice, Ralphie?"

"What's that?"

"Quit whining and just take what life gives you. People are nice because you're so damn ugly, and if sympathy kindness is all you're getting you should be thankful."

They hung up, and Loren blew his nose again. Would he ever go home, back to Springfield? Maybe a weekend trip to Cincinnati? Probably not. Too much bad shit had gone down out there, and he'd didn't need that in his life anymore. And he'd keep his mouth shut, like Preach had suggested.

He sat up, shoved his feet into his shoes. He took them off when he sat at his desk because they'd been swelling lately, but it was a part of getting old. The Sunday edition of the *Post* had been on his lap and wafted to the floor, fell so he could see the front page. It was a photo of Matt and Marie Evans, and a short article about the events of the last month. Not that any news outlet had the whole story—hell, he wasn't sure anyone knew exactly what had gone down between the Evanses, except that it was fucked up. But that's how marriages were—like a private room for two, where no one else could see inside. And even if you could, you might not want to.

Looking at Marie's picture on the front page, he realized she didn't remind him of Connie so much anymore. Not at all, really, and he wondered why he thought it in the first place. He'd tried to see a connection, but there hadn't been one.

Life isn't a circle, he thought. Life is a diamond, with all the facets and points and corners reflecting the light back and forth so quickly that you can't ever begin to figure out where it all actually started, or where it's going to end.

GAVE AWAY
THE THINGS
YOU LOVED
AND ONE OF
THEM WAS ME

As much as everyone would've liked, it wasn't the end.

There was a wire tree standing on the round table near the window, a foot tall and decorated with what looked like tiny eggs hung from hooks, painted in orange and black. He'd asked the nurse what the little tree was and was told it was called a celebration tree. You could keep it up all year long and just change the decorations to fit the next holiday. Halloween was next, so the branches were sagging with little pumpkins and skulls.

There was a soft knock on the door, and then it pushed open before he could respond. It was the on-duty nurse, a woman named Kimmy, although Matt wouldn't have remembered if it wasn't written on the whiteboard beside his bed, the *i* dotted with an overinflated, cheerful circle.

"The police are here to speak to you," Kimmy said. She was wearing pink scrubs with white hearts scattered across them, like she was still stuck back on Valentine's Day. Or maybe looking ahead. "If you're not feeling up to it yet, I'll make them wait."

Matt nodded. It was like it'd been before, with Reid visiting him in the hospital with all his questions. The same, even down to the bullet wound, although this time Marie had managed to hit farther from his shoulder and closer to his heart. He couldn't remember any of the time after Marie had shot him, except for a brief few moments inside a helicopter, a paramedic leaning over and snapping an oxygen mask over his face. He'd woken up in the hospital, having already made it through surgery and into recovery, feeling like an elephant was sitting on his chest. That was different than last time, at least—the pain. Worse because of where the bullet had gone this time, or because he was getting old?

He wasn't sure.

You're very lucky to have made it, one of the nurses had said to him.

He'd laughed at that, which had turned into a grimace, and then he'd clutched at his chest.

Luck wasn't the reason he was alive, he wanted to say. Marie could've shot him in the forehead, she had a clear shot, and he'd seen her eyes shift at the last minute, and the gun's muzzle drop. She could've killed him, but she'd decided to let him live.

"It's okay," he said. "I can talk to them."

"I'm serious."

"I know you are," Matt said. He thought Kimmy would be more than up to bossing around some cops, even though she was young and petite and looked naïve, but she was also what Matt's grandmother would've called a *firecracker*.

Firecracker: *noun*. Grandmother-speak. A woman who gives no shits what anyone thinks.

"I'll talk to them," Matt said again. He held up the wand with the button at the end, the one that connected to his IV and pumped morphine into his system every time he pushed it. "If I start feeling overwhelmed, I'll just hit this a few times. They won't be able to get a coherent word out of me after that."

Kimmy grimaced.

"You know that button doesn't do anything."

"Yeah, I know."

"Seriously, though. If you start to feel bad, we'll give them the boot."

"It's fine, really. I suppose they need to wrap things up before I go home."

"I should really ask Dr. Hammett—"

"Kimmy. Let them in."

In all honesty, he wanted to get it over with. The cops had come by the day before, caught him when he was in serious pain, in that long thirty minutes before the next dose of good medicine came, when he thought it might be better to be dead than to feel this way. They'd left without saying a word. And now they were back. They were going to talk to him sooner or later, better to get it over with.

"I don't have a good feeling about this," Kimmy said, but then left to get the cops anyway, the door wheezing shut as she went. The sound of muffled footsteps out in the hall came to him, and a smattering of laughter, all before the door closed. He looked at the little tree. It would be getting cold outside, the leaves would begin to change and fall. Maybe he'd be out of here by then, enjoying the change in seasons from his home.

There was a knock on the door and it pushed back open. No laughter came in this time, and no Kimmy, but just the cops. Loren and Spengler.

"So sorry to bother you again, Mr. Evans," Spengler said, pulling a chair to the left side of the bed. It made an unpleasant squealing sound as it dragged across the linoleum. She didn't sound very sorry. "We just wanted to touch base with you, let you know what's going on."

"We won't take much of your time," Loren said. He didn't bother sitting.

Matt nodded and smoothed his hands over the cheap hospital blankets. They could've been the same ones from twenty-three years before.

"How are you feeling today?" Spengler asked.

"Much better, thank you. I hope to go home soon."

Spengler's eyebrows drew together over her smile, and she glanced at Loren. Matt looked back and forth between the detectives.

"I'm afraid you're not going anywhere near home soon," Spengler said. "You'll be staying here until the doctor gives the okay for you to leave, and then we'll be placing you under arrest. A guard has been stationed outside the door to keep an eye on you."

He looked back and forth between the two, thinking it must be a joke. He cleared his throat. It was time to sell, he thought. It was all or nothing at this point. The pitch of a lifetime.

"Look, I know I'm in trouble about Janice faking her death, but my lawyer said it's not that big of a deal. It was Janice who orchestrated the whole thing, and it was twenty-three years ago. I know I'll have to pay back that insurance money, but I have the cash in the bank—"

"First of all, what you did twenty years ago *is* a big deal,"

Spengler said. "But that's not the reason we'll be arresting you."

"You're arresting me?" he asked slowly. "Let me get this right. Marie faked her death, set me up for her murder, killed Riley—and you're arresting *me*?"

"That's right," Spengler said, smiling.

"Your wife was a sneaky gal," Loren said. "Spengler here kept calling and leaving her voice mails, and then Marie responded. She didn't actually have to call her back—you can just respond to a voice mail with another voice mail, did you know that?"

Matt shook his head.

"Anyway, your wife sent Spengler a voice mail. Well, not an actual message, it's just a recording Marie made."

"I think you'll find it interesting. Here, listen." Spengler held up her phone and pushed a button on the screen. There was a moment of static and then there was Marie's voice, light and breathy, the one he hated so much.

"Tell me, did you enjoy killing her?" Marie whispered. "Riley didn't even see it coming, did she? She went out thinking you were actually in love with her, isn't that right? How *humane* of you."

"I wish I'd had the chance to bash your skull in," his own voice said. He didn't recognize himself, as was the way when a person heard a recording of their voice, but he'd know his own words anywhere. "I wish I could've killed you instead of her. But I had to do it. Prove to everyone what a jealous, crazy wife you are."

Spengler stopped the playback. Matt leaned back on the pillows and closed his eyes. It was like he'd gone back to the beginning again. Twenty years back, don't pass go, don't collect two hundred dollars.

"Have you found Marie yet?" he asked.

Loren laughed.

"The search continues," he said. "We've been sweeping the river for a mile downstream from where she went under, but there's been no sign of her yet. The team keeps saying there's no way she could've survived that current, but I've heard that malarkey before."

"And here's a funny thing," Spengler said. She looked amused. "A ranger found a life jacket abandoned on the shore a few miles downstream. There was some blood on it, and a rip that looked like it'd been done with a knife. Now, I don't remember seeing Marie wearing a life jacket, but that sweatshirt she had on was awfully big. It could've hid a lot, I suppose."

"But I'm sure she's dead," Loren said.

"Oh, yes. Definitely," Spengler said. "But we've all said that about your wife before, haven't we, Mr. Evans?"

The cops didn't stay long. They didn't have much else to say to him, now that they had what they needed. As they left and the door eased shut again, Matt saw the uniformed cop sitting right outside his door, scrolling through his phone.

He slept after a while. It was restless and full of dreams, although some of it might've been real. He saw someone come into the room and put flowers on the windowsill, and Kimmy came back in to take his blood pressure. And there was Marie, standing at the foot of his bed, her lovely face

smiling, pointing a gun right at him, and he came awake
with a start, a hand clutching at his throat, gasping for air.

He was alone.

No one had pulled the blinds, so the late-afternoon sun
slanted through hotly, and there was sweat gathered on his
upper lip. He reached out to push the call button, to ask a
nurse to come to his room and flip the blinds, but then the
phone rang. It was the phone on the table beside his bed,
jangling with such ferocity that it shook in the cradle. Once,
and then again.

Was it Marie? Would he ever hear a phone ring again
without wondering if it was her, calling to taunt him?

No, she was dead. Had to be. Drowned. Or bled out from
where he'd stabbed her.

But there was that life jacket.

He put a hand out to grab the phone and had the sudden
awful thought that even if he ripped it right out of the wall,
cord frayed and broken at one end, it would ring anyway,
that there was no escaping her, that he'd made his bed and
had to sleep in it, just like his mother used to say. *Till death
do you part, as long as you both shall live* and all that jazz. He
considered pushing the phone off the table, sending it clat-
tering to the ground, but answered it instead. He couldn't
help himself.

You could never kill Janice.

Or Marie, either.

"Matt," she said breathily, and if he'd been able to reach
through the speaker and strangle his wife he would've gladly
done it then. "Are we having fun yet?"

ACKNOWLEDGMENTS

If you've ever spent time in Rocky Mountain National Park, you'll know there is no cliff that overlooks the Three Forks River, as I've made the place up. There are other things I've changed or added here and there to suit the story, and a sharp-eyed reader will be sure to notice.

As always, I'd like to give my deepest thanks to Stephanie Cabot, Ellen Coughtrey, and all the team at the Gernert Company. Immense thanks to the entire team at Flatiron Books, especially to Amy Einhorn, Christine Kopprasch, Conor Mintzer, and Amelia Possanza. Also, thanks to the copy editor, Greg Villepique, who understood every time I used italics and gave some amazing suggestions.

I'd also like to thank Jennifer Thomas, who is one of the most thoughtful, caring women I've ever met and will definitely be killed in my next book; as well as Jess Hartlep, who made me laugh at least 250 times. But no more than 255. 300 at most. Thanks to Leigh Raper, who always knows the right card to send for every occasion; and to Sandi Reinardy, who talked me through some tough times with wise words.

And of course I'd like to thank my family. Cade, Jacob, and Lauren, who are quite simply the best kids I could ask for, and have somehow turned out to be kind, brilliant human beans despite how screwed up I am; and to my parents, who raised a writer. And to Jason, who helped piece me back together again.

Recommend *As Long as We Both Shall Live* for your next book club!

Reading group guide available at
www.readinggroupgold.com

Loved *As Long As We Both Shall Live*?

Discover JoAnn Chaney's first novel *What You Don't Know* . . .

Do you really know your neighbours?

Jacky Seever was a beloved local businessman and pillar of the Denver community. Until thirty-one bodies were discovered in the crawlspace of his house.

Detective Paul Hoskins was lauded for bringing down one of the most ruthless serial killers of the decade.

Sammie Peterson, the lead reporter on the case, finally obtained the success she craved.

And Seever's wife, Gloria? Well, she claimed to be as surprised as everyone else.

But when you get that close to a killer, can you really just move on?

OUT NOW IN PAPERBACK.

An extract follows here . . .

HOSKINS

December 19, 2008

If this were a movie, it would start with this shot: two men climbing out of an older-model brown car, dressed in cheap suits and cheaper shoes. One of them is wearing a hat, a black panama, and it makes him look a little like a time traveler from the 1920s. But this isn't Prohibition and this isn't Miami; this is Denver in the year 2008, and it's cold outside, so the man in the panama looks foolish, although you wouldn't tell him that, not if you want to keep your asshole firmly intact, because this man might look foolish but he's also one mean motherfucker, you can tell that if you manage to get a good look at his eyes. You might think it was a woman who gave him the hat, who teased him into wearing it, telling him he'd look so handsome in it, so debonair, but you'd be wrong. This man's name is Ralph Loren, a name that sounds like a bad joke but isn't, because nobody teases Detective Loren, *nobody*, even if they're pretty and young with tits out to *there*. Loren doesn't have a sense of humor—it's not that he has a weird one, or a mean one; he just doesn't have one at all. He was born missing that part of his insides, and life is a hard row to hoe without a few laughs along the way, but you don't miss what you never had. At least that's how the saying goes.

But it's the second man you should watch, the one climbing out the passenger side, the tall man with the big shoulders and the beginning shadows of a beard. This man comes around the front of the car, not bothering to avoid the dirty snow piled up at the curb but plowing right through it. He'll regret this later, when he's back at his desk, his socks wet and cold and frozen between his toes. Paul Hoskins is that kind of man who doesn't think too hard about what he does and regrets these decisions later. He's always been that kind of man and he always will be, until the end of time, amen.

"We're finally doing it, huh?" Hoskins says, looking up at the house they've come to visit. It's large and brick, a house taller than it is wide, with a big bay window over the front yard. It's traditional, not the kind of house you'd normally find in Denver, but this housing addition was built back in the '80s, thrown up quickly for the crowds rushing in from all over—California, mostly, if you listen to the locals, all those jerks and their terrible driving skills—and it doesn't look cheap, not like some of the other houses on the street. There are trees and shrubs planted in tasteful clusters around the property, although the foliage is faded and brown now, with nets of colored Christmas lights wound through the branches. There's a man-made pond out back too, with a slat-wood dock and a rowboat made for two. There are fish in that pond, and frogs, but the water's covered over with a thin sheet of ice now, and Hoskins wonders if all that has to be replaced every spring, if a delivery truck swings by with foam coolers full of wildlife. "Time to get the bad guy?"

Loren sighs, pushes back the flap of his jacket, and flips away the strap keeping the gun secured at his waist so he can get to it fast if he needs. These two are cops, detectives and partners; they've been together a long time and they'll be stuck that way awhile longer, although neither one is overly fond of the other. But they're kept together because they work well, they *click*, and that doesn't happen as often as anyone would like. A good partnership is a lot like a good marriage, and as anyone can confirm, a good marriage is hard to find.

But even in the best marriage, things can go very wrong.

"It's about damn time," Loren says. "If I never see this dipshit again, I'll die a happy man."

They walk up the long driveway, which has been neatly cleared of snow by the kid next door for ten bucks, and up to the front door. It's big and solid, oak, and the opaque sidelight is dark. It's early, not quite seven in the morning, and everything is quiet. Inside the house looks dark, lifeless, but Hoskins catches a faint whiff of brewing coffee and his stomach growls.

"Ready?" Loren asks.

"Yeah."

"Yeah?" Loren says, mocking. "When's your ball sac gonna drop? That high-pitched voice you got makes me want to punch you in the face."

Hoskins doesn't respond to this. He's been taking this kind of shit from Loren for the last ten years, and he's learned that it's best not to respond. Safer. Loren can shovel it out to anyone who'll listen, but he certainly can't take it. The last time they had it out was three years before, when Hoskins made a smartass remark about Loren's mother—that's what you do, if you want to piss a guy off, you go right for his mom, even if you don't know her, even if she's dead—and Loren broke his nose. There'd been an investigation, and a reprimand. A few visits to the department psychologist. But they'd still been forced to work together. If Hoskins had learned one thing about his partner, it was this: Keeping quiet is better. It wasn't that he was afraid of Loren, and he'd be able to hold his own in a fight, but if it came down to it, if you really got down to the brass knuckles (which is how Hoskins had thought the saying went since he was nine years old), he thought it was better not to speak if there wasn't anything to say. His father used to tell him to keep his pie hole shut more often, and the old man was right: Silence often made things easier, kept it simple.

Selected for Waterstones' Thriller of the Month

A stunning debut thriller, *The Missing Girl* by Jenny Quintana is a gripping novel full of twists and turns, and a desperate hunt to solve a decades-old mystery.

Anna Flores was just a child when her adored teenage sister disappeared.

Unable to deal with the pain, Anna took the first opportunity she had to run from her fractured family, eventually building a life for herself abroad.

Now, thirty years on, her mother has died, and Anna must return home to sort through her possessions.

In doing so, she has to confront the huge hole her sister's disappearance left in their lives, leaving just one question unanswered: what really happened to Gabriella?

Because not knowing is worse than the truth.

Isn't it?

Who can she trust if she can't trust herself?

Rachel Teller and her husband David appear happy,
prosperous and fulfilled. The big house, the successful
business . . . They have everything.

However, control, not love, fuels their relationship and David
has no idea his wife indulges in drunken indiscretions.
When Rachel kills a man in a hit and run, the meticulously
maintained veneer over their life begins to crack.

Destroying all evidence of the accident, David insists they
continue as normal. Rachel, though, is racked with guilt and
as her behaviour becomes increasingly self-destructive she
not only inflames David's darker side, but also uncovers
her own long-suppressed memories of shame. Can Rachel
confront her past and atone for her terrible crime? Not if
her husband has anything to do with it . . .

Winner of the East Anglian Book Awards for Fiction 2019

Who do you know better? Your oldest friend? Or your child?

**And who should you believe when one accuses the other
of an abhorrent crime?**

Jules and Holly have been best friends since university. They
tell each other everything, trading revelations and confessions,
and sharing both the big moments and the small details of their
lives: Holly is the only person who knows about Jules's affair;
Jules was there for Holly when her husband died. And their two
children – just four years apart – have grown up together.

So when Jules's daughter Saffie makes a rape allegation against
Holly's son Saul, neither woman is prepared for the devastating
impact this will have on their friendship or their families.

Especially as Holly, in spite of her principles, refuses
to believe her son is guilty.